The tall woman in the shimmering white gown just this side of proper could only be the Lady Louisa Darwen. Gervase was very well aware that those rose petal lips and lustrous black lashes had not been hers when he met her in Lady Mulford's morning room. She looked, in fact, quite as fast as Gervase had originally suspected her of being.

"Lady Louisa, it is a pleasure to see you showing—dare I say your true colors?—at last."

Louisa looked at him through her darkened lashes in her most provocatively innocent manner. "You do not consider, then, Cousin Coldmeece, that I have defamed my natural beauty?"

"Not at all," said Gervase truthfully, and rather to his own surprise.

TURKISH DELIGHT

or, The Earl and The Houri

By

Rosemary Edghill

FAWCETT CREST • NEW YORK

A Fawcett Crest Book
Published by Ballantine Books
Copyright © 1987 by Rosemary Edghill

Library of Congress Catalog Card Number: 86-26114

ISBN 0-449-21586-5

This edition published by arrangement with St. Martin's Press, Inc.

Manufactured in the United States of America

First Ballantine Books Edition: July 1988

To
GLORIA EDITH
EDGHILL,
THE BEST
OF
MOTHERS

Chapter
ONE

The early morning sunlight of the brilliant late March day sparkled off the sills and railings of the quiet row of town houses in this fashionable section of London. It was weeks before the start of the Season, and few of the upper ten thousand had yet stirred from hearth and home to make their annual pilgrimage to London.

But one knocker, at least, was on its door, and the house itself bore an indefinable air of habitation. The occupant of the livery coach drawing up before it was emboldened to think that the house looked welcoming, though she realized that this might be only a reflection of her own hopes, and not truth in fact.

A coachman stepped down to assist the passenger out. The lady, obviously a lady of Quality, stopped to remind the driver—once again—that he was to walk the horses; then she hurried up the steps to where the watchful butler was already swinging the door wide.

Josephine, Lady Mulford, was a short, plump lady, well past her middle years, with blue eyes that normally danced with mirth and a wealth of silvery hair kept tucked, with little success, beneath a widow's lace cap. She suffered herself to be conducted to the morning room, where the butler assured her, in sepulchral tones, that: "his lordship will be with you directly, my lady."

Left to her own devices, Lady Mulford surveyed the room. Yes indeed, the tenth earl of Coldmeece had done well by the earldom; in the seventh earl's time, the town house had fallen into wrack and ruin. It had certainly been better for the family when poor William took himself and his family off to the Continent.

Still, all had ended well. After being handed about the Darwen family for five years, the title—and concomitant debts—had settled on her godson and nephew, and he had worked hard to repair the depredations of his predecessors. Josephine had not been in England since before he had assumed the title, but she had been kept well informed and knew what a fantastic recoup was represented by the bright morning room with its French-gilt furniture and hangings of oyster brocade.

By all accounts, the whole estate was doing equally well. After William's tenure, of course, there had been nothing left but the entailed property, but the present earl had cleared a sizable portion of the burden of debt from it, and that in only three short years.

More than ever, Josephine wondered about the reason for her summons. She had written from Vienna that she and her entourage were coming home for the Season, but she had not expected to be greeted at Dover by a peremptory summons by the head of the family.

She had last seen her godson five years ago. Then a dour young man of thirty with a malicious sense of humor, he had nevertheless not been backward in any courtesy, and Lady Mulford was about to ring for the butler to see what was detaining him when the doors to the morning room swung open and the earl stepped in.

Bevan Gervase Timothy St. George Darwen, Earl of Coldmeece, Viscount St. Germain, Baron St. George of Harrow and Coldham, Baron of Ness, Lord Landsowne, and holder of other minor titles and dignities, was the tenth earl of Coldmeece, his father and elder brother both having preceded him as earl in just two short years. At thirty-five, Gervase was one of the wealthiest peers in the realm. Following the convention that any man of sufficient rank and wealth must automatically be deemed handsome, Gervase was handsome, though in a lesser mortal the gray-blue eyes with their disconcerting glint of mockery, the unruly reddish-brown hair in its unfashionable curls, the full lips, and the strong features, might have earned a less flattering epithet.

Gervase was dressed quite casually; his tall, muscular form was clad in dove-gray pantaloons, yellow weskit, and a stuff coat of dull green. His jewelry was restricted to an heirloom signet and a single fob, and his hair seemed to have escaped his attention altogether. In short, save for some new lines about the eyes and a not uninteresting reserve, Gervase Darwen was much the same as Lady Mulford remembered him.

At the sight of her, the earl smiled. "Dearest Godmama!" he said, coming forward. "I hope I have not kept you waiting long, but Salvington attacked me at my dressing this morning and would give me no peace until I had settled some small matters. But come! You must be perishing; I am abominable to have dragged you from your home at this confoundedly early hour, but I had no choice."

Lady Mulford had raised enough nieces and nephews among the prolific Darwens not to know when she was being charmed for motives having little to do with familial duty to one's elders.

"Well, Gervase," she said composedly, seating herself on a sopha, "if you had no choice but to post a messenger to await us when we landed, the matter must be urgent indeed."

"Ah," said the earl, apparently momentarily at a loss. He was saved by a footman bearing ratafia and biscuits; as he poured a glass for Lady Mulford he seized the opportunity to change the subject.

"And how does Lady Louisa find London, Godmama? It must be quite a change after—That is, it must be quite a change," he finished lamely.

Lady Mulford sipped her ratafia and considered the question. Her niece and traveling companion, Lady Louisa Darwen, had not set foot in Mother England since she was ten years old, when her father, the seventh earl, had decamped with his wife and child for European destinations. Lady Louisa's subsequent peculiar upbringing was a family scandal, but far from wishing to sink into respectable obscurity in the arms of her homeland, she had, on the docks at Dover, burrowed her militant chin into her scarf of Russian sables and announced loudly that she wished to return to Paris. Lady Mulford rather thought that put an end to plans for an English Season, and only the summons from Gervase had steeled her to endure Louisa's waspish comments and post up to London to see what he wanted. Louisa's wrath had abated somewhat once she was tucked into bed at Mulford House, but Lady Mulford did not think they would be remaining long.

However, it would hardly do to make Gervase privy to any of these interesting intelligences.

"Your cousin Louisa," said Lady Mulford blandly, "finds returning to England quite interesting—and as you were one of the loudest proponents, five years ago, of the odd idea that she should be left in Turkey, I hardly understand this sudden interest in her welfare."

The earl had the grace to blush. "Now, Godmama," he protested, "it was hardly my decision—and who knew if the chit'd turn out presentable? She is presentable, isn't she?" he asked with some anxiety.

"Quite." Lady Mulford considered her niece's dazzling career in St. Petersburg, Brussels, and Vienna, and wondered just what sort of notions Gervase had formed of his cousin. "Still, you hardly dragged me up to Town at a breakneck pace to congratulate me on Louisa." Lady Mulford pursed her lips interrogatively and waited.

The Earl of Coldmeece rose to his feet and strode about the room, finally coming to rest with his elbow on the mantel above the fireplace. He then glowered off into space, his strong features and prominent eyebrows giving his countenance a forbidding cast that, Lady Mulford knew, was quite unintentional.

"Godmama," he said at last, "I intend to marry."

For one mad moment Lady Mulford entertained the notion that Gervase meant to offer for Louisa. Only the knowledge that Gervase considered Louisa the most thoroughly unsuitable of all possible brides for any respectable man kept her from putting this notion into words.

"Well," she said at last, "it is time and to spare, certainly—but what has it to do with me?"

The earl regarded her with the blank expression of one who feels he has already made all clear. "I shall," he amplified, "be taking a wife."

Lady Mulford cast an amused eye upon her godson. Gervase was plainly unused to explaining his pronouncements. "Ah," she said, as one enlightened, "and had you any particular maiden in mind, Gervase, or did you call me to Town to beg my help?"

An answering spark of amusement tugged at the corner of the earl's mouth. "How odd you should put it that way, Godmama, for I must ask your help—throw myself on your mercy, in fact." He picked up a small chair and moved it to a comfortable position near her, then seated himself and leaned forward confidingly. "It's the most awkward tangle, Godmama. Before I knew you would be in England I had thought of asking your sister, Lady Templeton, especially as her son is my heir and she must feel herself beholden. But all of her appalling brats are down with the measles and she won't even be coming up to Town this Season. I was almost at a standstill, when your letter came and I knew I might count upon you. It's a matter of some delicacy."

Having thus prepared his audience, the earl continued. "Lady Celia Darwen-Neville—she's my great-uncle's granddaughter; perhaps you may recall that her father, the late Earl of Orleton, died two years ago, and I am one of her trustees—"

Lady Mulford tapped her foot impatiently. "Gervase, do, I beg of you, come to the point!"

"Well, in any case," the earl said hastily, "the child is now of an age to come to Town for her first Season, and of course she has no close female relatives that might take her in. And while she may be my ward, you must admit it would hardly do for her to stay under *my* roof."

"Is Caroline still in Italy, then?" Lady Mulford asked.

The earl grimaced. "The so-dear dowager countess of Coldmeece, my most esteemed sister-in-law, has returned home, having run through all her allowance for this quar-

5

ter and the next. She currently resides in Bath, where I can only hope she will continue to make her abode for an indefinite period. But surely, Godmama, you can see that it would not answer. I could not have Caro present Lady Celia—for one thing, it's only fair that the chit enjoy her first Season, and once Caro found out I intend to marry the girl, well . . .''

''Marry Orleton's daughter? That *would* put Caro's nose out of joint!'' Lady Mulford, familiar with Caro Darwen, could only agree that she was not the person to place in charge of the young lady in question. ''But—do you mean to say Caro does not *know*? Has it not yet been announced?''

''Not a soul knows of the marriage as yet,'' the earl affirmed. ''Lady Celia is living with a governess at Thornage Hall in Yorkshire. She is just seventeen, has lived buried in the country all her life, and I'm tolerably certain she would welcome a London Season before she marries.''

Lady Mulford's eyes grew misty as she thought of her own long-ago first Season. ''It would certainly be a shame if she must put off her come-out,'' she agreed. ''But I don't know, Gervase, my plans aren't certain—we may not be staying in England long.''

''But, Godmama,'' he protested, rising to his feet again, ''you haven't set foot here for—what? Five years? Six? You must stay for the Season at least. I'm sure Lady Louisa would rate you very poor-spirited indeed if you forced her to miss it. And she would like to have Lady Celia for company.''

Lady Mulford knew a mouse when she smelled it. Gervase had never shown the slightest interest in his Turkish-raised cousin before, except to urge the family to bury her safely in some out-of-the-way place. To find him now concerned with Louisa's likes and dislikes would have made even a more credulous soul than his doting godmother suspicious. ''But perhaps,'' she suggested, ''Lady Celia may not wish to know such a—a dashing young lady as your cousin Louisa. That die-away wife of Orleton's was a notorious bluestocking, wasn't she? What, then, is her daughter like?''

The earl shrugged. "Well enough, I suppose."

"You *suppose*?" Lady Mulford said. "Don't you know? Gervase, what is it that you are trying—unsuccessfully—to keep hidden from your godmama?"

"Really, Godmama! It is a common enough thing, after all. It is simply that my father and Lord Orleton were great friends, and for some reason they decided when Lady Celia was born that a marriage between the two of us would unite the families most happily."

Lady Mulford frowned perplexedly. "But the family knew nothing of this!"

The earl raised his brows with sudden humor. "My father, as you know, was not wont to explain his actions to anyone. This marriage was arranged when I was eighteen, but I knew nothing of it until this year."

Lady Mulford raised her brows in an expression of supercilious doubt, which the earl smiled to see.

"Yes," he said. "I too thought it might be an attempt to snare the earldom of Coldmeece as a marriage prize. But when I had Salvington look into the matter, it was discovered that the contract had been most properly drawn up, with dowries and settlements arranged, when Lady Celia was still in leading strings. And there the thing stood—until recently. And it's my opinion," he added as an aside, "that our respective honored papas quite forgot about the matter.

"In any case, my father never said anything about it to me. And then Edmund died too, and affairs were in the most wretched muddle I ever saw or heard of. Salvington assumed Edmund had discussed the betrothal with me, and so left it in my hands. There matters might have ended, save that the girl's other trustee wrote me a few months back asking if I intended to honor the contract, and, if not, what should be done about Lady Celia."

"And so you proposed marriage to a girl you've never seen?" said Lady Mulford. She hadn't yet decided whether Gervase's tale was romantic or heartless. His next words, however, decided her.

"Oh, there'll be time enough for that when she arrives. I must marry to secure the line, as the family has been at pains to point out to me. One female is as good as the next, and we Darwens always marry our cousins—nearly always, that is—and what difference which cousin? No doubt the chit's tolerably attractive, and with Orleton for a father, she can't be a lackwit; she's—"

"Gervase," Lady Mulford exclaimed in awful tones, "never tell me you haven't even *offered* for the girl! All this talk of marriage and a Season—with a girl you've never seen, and who will refuse you as likely as not!"

The earl gazed at his wrathful godmother with an expression of mild surprise. "But my dearest Godmama, why should she refuse me?"

Such effrontery struck Lady Mulford speechless. How could her beloved godson have grown so odiously high in the instep as to coolly suggest that any damsel would naturally marry him at his lightest request? Sputteringly, she attempted to put these feelings into words, but the earl interrupted her with a minatory gesture.

"My dearest Godmama, I am the Earl of Coldmeece. I can think of no reason that Lady Celia Darwen-Neville would consider marrying plain Gervase Darwen, but that is not what she is being asked to do. She will be the Countess of Coldmeece."

"And that must carry all?"

"Many people," drawled the earl sardonically, "seem to feel that being the Countess of Coldmeece is a pleasure worth any amount of exercise to attain."

Lady Mulford pursed her mouth in sudden understanding. So Caro was making an attempt to revive her old romance with Gervase and become countess once more. That infernal woman's meddling must be the spur to Gervase's sudden desire to marry.

"Unfortunately," said the earl, "it seems that Lady Celia will not have the felicity of making that choice—at least, not this Season—since if you will not bring her out, she must remain in Yorkshire another year. Tell me, how does Lady Louisa fare in European society?"

Bewildered by this ruthless change of subject, Lady

Mulford could only answer, "Oh, well, of course it is so very different than what she was used to. But I fancy that between us, Augustus and I have turned her out tolerably well."

"Ah," said the earl, dismissing for the moment this reference to his cousin and heir, Augustus, in view of the larger prize. "Then I trust I may have the felicity of soon seeing the announcement of her engagement in the *Gazette*? She is what? Nineteen? Twenty?"

"She is twenty-three, as you well know, Gervase, and as you must also know, has received no offers of marriage as yet."

The earl studied his fingertips with assumed indifference, which made Lady Mulford warier than all his cajoling graces had. "A pity," he said to his signet ring. "I'm sure you would be happy to see her comfortably established. I'm sure I need not tell *you* that you must make a push to do so soon, before she is too firmly on the shelf."

Since this was no more than Josephine thought herself, she contented herself with an abrupt nod. She had hoped for great things from their London Season; here in England the Darwen name might make up for a great deal in the way of eccentricity and lack of dowry. Lady Mulford was fond of her wayward niece, and feared for Louisa's lot after she, Josephine, was no longer there to take care of her.

"Perhaps," said the earl with an air of sudden discovery, "you might consider remaining for the Season after all. It would be a great opportunity for Lady Louisa, and you might consider taking Lady Celia as well."

Lady Mulford could see the trap Gervase was laying for her now but was powerless to avoid it. Desperately she temporized. "We had been planning a—a *quiet* Season, Gervase. I'm sure it would not do for Lady Celia at all."

"A quiet Season, Godmama?" said the earl with mockery. "Oh, no, that would never do, you know. Tiptoe back meekly and all the *ton* will be sure you have something to hide! No, if you are ever to get Lady Louisa off your hands, you must fire her off with flare—and what better way than by having her share Lady Celia's come-out? I will even,"

9

he added magnanimously, "give a ball for them here at Coldmeece House. Oh, and I'll pay all the expenses for both girls, of course."

"There's no need for that," snapped Lady Mulford, thoroughly irritated with her high-handed, managing godson, even while she admitted the wisdom of his plan. "I am quite capable of managing my own affairs! Never fear, I shall see to it that poor little Celia has her come-out, and Louisa too, and I hope you may not come to regret your incredible foolishness!" She rose to her feet with an angry flounce.

The earl accompanied her to the door. "Never fear, Godmama," he told her, sounding very well pleased with himself. "The earldom can carry all—even the debut of a female raised in a harem."

Chapter

TWO

It was through no fault of her own that Lady Louisa Darwen had spent most of her formative years in the harem of the Grand Seraglio at Constantinople. In 1806, when she had been just ten years of age, her improvident father, the seventh Earl of Coldmeece, had fled England and towering indebtedness with his wife and child. Since the Corsican Monster had, at that time, been terrorizing the Continent, the little party had landed in Portugal, beginning an aimless journey that took them progressively farther south and east, until at last they came to rest in Constantinople. There her feckless but charming father had happily deposited his countess and his daughter in the ladies' quarters of the Sultan's palace for safekeeping while he went off on some mysterious plan for recouping his fortunes.

Louisa had instantly adored the harem—the warmth, the bright colors, the chattering monkeys and birds, the gaily decked and painted ladies who lavished every care and attention on the pale, gawky English child. She had hardly noticed when her mother, who had never become reconciled to harem life, died some time later, and her father never reappeared to claim her. Her last link with England gone, Louisa had settled quite happily into Eastern life and her role as the indulged pet of the lovely French Sultan Valide.

The Darwens had been informed of the demises of the seventh earl and the countess; the child of his dear friend, so the Sultan wrote, was, of course, under his care in the harem, and what was to be done with her? Owing to the uncertain nature of mails and travel during Napoleon's tenure, the answer to this query was never received, and Lady Louisa Darwen—or, as she had been renamed, Amber Pearl—dwelt contentedly in the seraglio until the momentous year of 1814. During the lull that followed the Corsican Tyrant's banishment to Elba, another letter found its way to England and the head of the Darwen family, then Louisa's cousin Edmund, the ninth Earl of Coldmeece. This second letter rather tartly informed the Darwens that the child of his dear friend was now a young woman of eighteen, and inquired whether her family *ever* intended to claim her, or whether a proper marriage should be arranged for her in Turkey. It was the arrival of this missive that had resulted in Lady Mulford indignantly making all haste to Turkey to rescue her niece.

It was a moot point as to whether aunt or niece had suffered the more dreadful shock upon meeting. Lady Mulford, expecting a demure, persecuted damsel in white muslin, had nearly suffered a spasm upon being presented with a painted houri clad in brilliant silks and decked out in jewels. Amber Pearl, equally appalled, had regarded Lady Mulford with wide, kohl-rimmed eyes, tugged doubtfully at her waist-length braid of hair hennaed to the color of glowing coals, and responded dutifully, first in Turkish, then in French, and then, with some difficulty, in English so heavily accented as to be almost unintelligible to her horrified relative.

That had been five years ago; today, Lady Mulford flattered herself, her niece could pass herself off with credit in proper society—although it was a thousand pities Louisa couldn't seem to be made to see what a scandalous and dreadful place that harem had been! Lady Mulford sighed, then pushed open the door to her niece's room.

This room, one of the first to have been readied, showed no trace of the chaos afflicting other areas of Mulford House. Heavy velvet curtains were pulled snugly over the tall windows so that no ray of sunlight might intrude. In the center of the room was a massive four-poster bed, elaborately draped in rose brocade. In the center of the bed, like a dormouse in a nest, slept Louisa.

At twenty-three, Lady Louisa Darwen showed little sign of her exotic past. Her curly waist-length mane of hair had long since returned to its natural color. Most unfortunately, that natural color was sandy red, which meant, equally unfortunately, that her skin had the greenish pallor of skimmed milk, and that her lashes—virtuously free of the kohl Amber Pearl had once used so lavishly—were as pale as her skin, invisibly fringing eyes of some indeterminate color. There was no denying, Lady Mulford thought regretfully, that her darling niece was quite . . . quite—well, out of the common style of fashionable prettiness. And if only she weren't so *tall* . . .

However, Lady Mulford thought, looking resolute, prettiness was not all. No matter what the effort, Louisa would have her London Season, and would not be allowed to destroy her own chances for security and happiness. Lady Mulford turned away from the bed and threw open the curtains.

Sunlight suffused the room and the sleeper burrowed deeper beneath the covers, but Lady Mulford showed no mercy. Seating herself by Louisa's side, she pried pillows and bedclothes from her niece's grasp, until Louisa sat braced against her pillows regarding her aunt with faint interest.

"Now," said Lady Mulford brightly, "don't you wish to hear what your cousin the earl had to say to me?"

Louisa rubbed her face sleepily. She did not wish to hear about her normally adored aunt's morning. Furthermore, Aunt Josephine knew that she didn't, and they both knew she knew. Therefore, it must be that Louisa's angelic aunt had News to Impart, and was going to do so no matter what protest her woefully-tried niece might make. This being the case, Louisa rallied her forces for a concerted show of alertness.

"The earl," she suggested, "has declared war upon France, and we must go back there until it is over."

Lady Mulford made clucking noises. "Dear Louisa, are you certain you are quite awake? You cannot be forever burrowing in your bed; you will see nothing of London, and it is such a lovely day!''

Before Louisa could frame a suitable reply, the door opened again and Rigsby entered, bearing a tray.

"I thought Miss would be wanting her chocolate," the abigail said, with a baleful look at Louisa. Louisa accepted the tray with unabashed gratitude and settled it across her knees. The warmth of the delicate china cup was comforting in her hands. She had been only a week in this abominable Frankish purgatory and she doubted that she would ever be warm again. And this, so she had been assured, was spring!

"Well," her aunt began confidingly, "you remember that dear Gervase left a message at Dover that I was to call upon him at once?" She paused dramatically before adding, "Louisa, he is planning his nuptials!"

Louisa gazed attentively at her, awaiting some further revelation.

"It is high time that he was about it, too," Lady Mulford continued, "as he is quite five-and-thirty, and ought to set up his nursery before he is very much older. And his bride is to be Lady Celia Darwen-Neville—she is a cousin of yours, darling."

Louisa, plainly unimpressed, yawned and stretched. "Half England can call cousins with me, Aunt. There are Darwens so thick upon the ground there's hardly any distinction in it. But I cannot see that there is anything in that to cause my-cousin-the-Earl to drag you off the docks to listen to it!"

"Well," said Lady Mulford, "that wasn't *quite* all. He wanted to know my—our—plans. Poor little Celia has not yet made her come-out; she is an orphan with no close female relation to present her. Gervase is her trustee, and of course he must find someone to take charge of her for the Season."

"The Dowager Countess Caro being impossible," Louisa commented dryly. "Aunt Templeton?"

"Measles."

Louisa made a face. "Oh, poor Augustus! I hope he

didn't catch it when he went home—he would look dread-fully queer all over spots! Great-aunt Serena, then?''

"Serena Darwen hasn't come up to Town in ten years, and you know Gervase doesn't get on with the woman—not that anyone *does*,'' Lady Mulford added in a fair-minded fashion. "And before you ask, your Aunt So-phronia is still in America, and unlikely to return after thirty years to present Lady Celia.''

"Ah,'' said Louisa broodingly; then, "I have it! Cousin Coldmeece can marry his Lady Celia from the nursery! Then she may live under his roof in all propriety and have her Season. I hope you suggested it to him, Aunt, for I'm sure it is the very thing that will answer.'' Louisa quickly seized a roll from her breakfast tray and began to butter it, an expression of sublime forbearance playing on her face.

"In fact,'' said Lady Mulford cunningly, "I *did* suggest that very thing, but it will not do, as Gervase has never yet seen or spoken with dear little Celia—and so of course she has no idea of his feelings,'' she added hastily.

Louisa choked and began to cough, and it took several minutes' frantic pounding on the back by Lady Mulford to restore her.

"And so you see, darling, he can hardly marry her from the schoolroom,'' Lady Mulford finished.

Louisa chortled in delight. "Marrying a girl he's never seen! And doesn't know! And hasn't *asked*! What if she won't have him?''

Ruthlessly sacrificing Gervase's character, Lady Mul-ford said, "It is Gervase's opinion that no woman will turn down the opportunity to be a countess, and the truth of this can hardly be determined if Lady Celia remains in the country.''

Louisa had long ago developed a fixed dislike of her noble cousin the Earl of Coldmeece, based on nothing more than the information that he had been firmly against bringing her back to England from the seraglio. Louisa, upon discovering this, had instantly declared that he had wished to have her put in a sack and drowned in the Bos-phorus, a theme upon which she had then embroidered with every assistance from her cousin Augustus, who thought it a famous joke. Therefore Louisa now regarded with glee the discomfiture of this ogre of her own creation. "Oh, I hope she *may* refuse him! *I* most assuredly should, in the circumstances!" She clasped her hands to her bosom in a theatrical expression of maidenly sensibility. "I *must* meet her! When is my dear, sweet little cousin coming to Town, and who did Coldmeece cozen into bringing her out?"

Lady Mulford took a deep breath. "Me."

Louisa stared at her. "But that's ridiculous! Doesn't the man know we aren't staying in London? What could he have been thinking of?"

"As to that," said her aunt, "it is I who have been doing the thinking, and I have come to realize that Gervase was righter than he knew when he urged me to stay in London this season. Do you remember what we talked about in Brussels?"

"You, my love, had a notion you'd like to see some dear stolid English faces once more, and that somewhere on the Marriage Mart you might find some paragon tall enough and rich enough and stupid enough to marry me," Louisa recited obediently. "But I assure you, Aunt, you need *not* remain on my account. We can find this mythical creature in Italy as well as here. Everyone's traveling, you know, since the Beast was got rid of."

"Louisa, do try to listen to sense! It is true that part of the reason I wished to return home was to find you a husband, and now I see that we should have come back sooner, as soon as you were able. It's no good putting these things off, and you must marry."

Louisa stared mulishly down into the dregs of her chocolate. "I don't see why, Aunt Josephine—unless you wish to be rid of me."

Lady Mulford took her niece by the shoulders and shook her gently. "Don't be silly, Louisa! You have a home with me for as long as you like, but you know I shan't be here forever—now don't you laugh, child—I might be carried off at any moment!"

"By an impatient beau!"

"That's as may be. But it's no secret how Mulford left the property settled, and the trustees say there is no way for me to settle even a modest income upon you. Oh, if only my dear brother William had been more provident!"

"If Papa had been more provident, he would have married a lady of larger fortune—and he would have run through it just the same," Louisa said philosophically. "Dearest Aunt, I know I have no dowry and that your husband was most shockingly clutch-fisted. But I do *not* see what all that has to do with marriage, Cousin Coldmeece, Lady Celia, or the idiotish notion that we should stay one moment longer than we must in this cold, dark, damp, cold—"

"St. Petersburg, may I remind you, Louisa, was far colder," her aunt said.

"But St. Petersburg had closed-stove heating. Oh, may we get a stove, if we are to stay, Aunt? I should be *warm*, then! I do not see why the Frankish persons here do not adopt the idea. I shall start a reform movement: 'For the Adoption and Promulgation of Closed-Stove Heating, for the Health of all Sane Frankish Persons.' "

Lady Mulford looked penetratingly at Louisa, and when she had her niece's full attention once again, she continued. "Say what you will, Louisa; in marriage lies your only true security. How would you manage if I were gone?"

"I should become a governess, of course," Louisa responded promptly, "like all those dreary romantical heroines."

"Even if you were suited to such a life—which I doubt very much, miss—you have none of the qualifications looked for in a governess. Now, let us be *sensible*, Louisa. It is true you have a Past, but here at home I am not without influence. Our family is one of the very best in the country, and that must count for something. And *that* is why I told Gervase I will take his dear little ward Celia; nothing could be more proper than my presenting you both, and becoming the friend of the future countess of Coldmeece can only be to your advantage. You must look to your future, darling."

17

"I can't see that it's to my advantage to appear at the side of a blushing English country flower. That *will* make me look a sight! How old is Lady Celia? Twelve?"

"She is just seventeen, and from what Gervase says, well educated and quietly raised."

"Yes, but is she tall or short? Dark or fair? A chatterbox or a sphinx? And don't tell me the blushing bridegroom hasn't a clue and couldn't care less, because if you do, Aunt, I shall go off into whoops again. I never heard of anything so infamous!"

Lady Mulford could only agree with her niece, but she was relieved that the matter of remaining in London for the Season had been disposed of so quietly. She only hoped that Louisa would approach the quest for a husband with the gravity and care the matter deserved.

"I'm sure you will enjoy London, Louisa—it may not be as fashionable as Paris or Vienna, but it is far more important for you. And if you cannot like it here, I shall not tease you to stay. It is only for Lady Celia's come-out, and she may, of course, prefer spinsterhood to marrying Gervase—which is quite well for *her*, as Orleton left her possessed of a large fortune. But it will hardly do for you, darling. Oh, it will be so good to be *home* again. We shall *both* need new wardrobes—some of the Paris gowns will do, but the Russian frocks are quite ineligible, and no one has yet had a decent robe cut in Italy. I cannot think what possessed me to have the puce satin made up there . . . such lovely fabric it was, too. Well, perhaps Rigsby can find some use for it—which reminds me, Louisa, now that we are home we must see about providing you with a proper maid."

Louisa was half asleep, listening to her aunt's flow of happy chatter and vowing to herself to be very good and stick England without a murmur of complaint, when the mention of a maid aroused her attention. Louisa had very definite views on maids.

"Oh, Aunt Josephine!" she protested. "Not another! 'Yes m'lady, no m'lady,' and never anything the way *I* like it. I *had* proper maids once," she said darkly, with the air of one brooding upon past wrongs.

"Louisa," said Lady Mulford warningly.

"The sweetest black twins—"

"Louisa *Darwen*—"

"—and they were *mine*. They were a present from Nak-shidil Valide."

"Louisa, I wish you would not discuss that—that unfortunate incident!"

Louisa stopped in midcomplaint and eyed her aunt quizzically. "Unfortunate incident? Really, my love, I would hardly describe six years in the harem as an incident. 'Career,' perhaps, but . . ." She looked innocently at her aunt.

With a stifled sigh, Lady Mulford got to her feet. "That's as may be, but it is all behind you now—and I hope you will keep it there! Now, I shall send Rigsby in to you—it is time you were up and about. We have a great deal to do here." Favoring Louisa with a cheery smile, Lady Mulford trotted from the room.

Louisa pulled the bedclothes up around her ears to savor the last of the blessed warmth before Rigsby came to drag her from her bed, pour water over her, and insist that she behave like a proper young English lady of Quality. She was sorry now that she had teased Aunt Josephine; her aunt was always made acutely uncomfortable by references to Louisa's childhood, although Louisa still couldn't quite understand why.

For all that people said about the ties of home and family, Louisa wondered whether it wouldn't have been far better for all concerned if she had been let to stay in the only home she had ever really known, and all the incomprehensible English Darwens had gone about their own business. However, it was about five years too late to alter matters, so she supposed she must make the best of them. With a resigned sigh, Louisa thrust the bedclothes from her and went to select a walking dress.

Something warm.

Chapter
THREE

The freakish fair weather of early spring could not last, and so it was to no one's surprise that a string of jewel-bright days was followed by as many more that were as gray and forbidding as any pessimist could wish.

The earl of Coldmeece occupied himself with the continuing business of increasing an already large estate, and with preparations for the coming ball. It would have been a matter for his hostess, did he have one, but he was reluctant to inflict the work on Lady Mulford, and he had not yet determined to have her fill that place. It would be seen by everyone as a shocking slight to the dowager countess, and Gervase had no desire to engage Caro's volatile temper. There would be tantrums enough once Caro learned that he was marrying Lady Celia.

These musings were cut short by the arrival in Gervase's vestibule of a dripping figure in a voluminous coat of many capes, swearing and soaked. The earl appeared in the library doorway to watch the fun. From what could be seen through the still-open door to the street, the voluble incognito had arrived on horseback, and his mount, a blood bay stallion of uncertain manners, was currently trying conclusions with one of Gervase's grooms.

"Why, Augustus," said the earl mildly, recognizing both horse and coat, "how kind of you to call."

The Honorable Augustus Leslie Templeton, at twenty-five one of the most eligible of *partis* ever to grace the *ton*, turned and doffed his dripping headgear to his cousin before handing the drenched article to a footman. He brushed a careless hand through his curly black hair and smiled ruefully. "Yes, I know, It's shocking of me, ain't it? But I didn't have any idea it was going to *rain*, I assure you, and Prometheus don't like it above half."

Correctly understanding this last to apply to Augustus's mount, the earl suggested they repair to the fireside. "I don't see, Augustus, how you could expect any colt of Witchfire's to take to the wet."

"Oh, well, but you know Papa'd bred her to Torchlight at the Low Farm, and *he's* gentle as a lamb. Not that it matters; it's only a bit of temper that'll easily work out. I'll match him against your Champion any day!"

The earl raised an eyebrow noncommittally. "You might be surprised by the result," he said. "But what brings you to Town so far in advance of the Season? When I heard you'd come home with Lady Mulford, I made sure you'd be stopping in the country for another month."

Augustus accepted a glass of the earl's excellent port and stretched his hands out to the fire. "And so I should have been, recruiting nature in the bosom of my family, except that the week I arrived one of the nurserymaids came out in spots, and what should my revolting siblings do but catch it, every one, from Deborah down to the baby. You never heard such howls. This was to be Deb's Season, and now there's no hope of it, and Mama running half mad, and couldn't remember whether I'd had them or not. Not that it matters to me, but she packed me off to the Dower House!" Augustus looked outraged. Gervase's mouth twitched, but he sternly schooled his features to an expression of sympathy. " 'The house at Temple Down,' " Augustus recited, in dark pedantic tones, " 'is built on the site of ruins of Great Antiquity'—and it's a ruin of great antiquity itself, if you ask me. No chimneys, no drains—no *cook*—and the roof leaking with the everlasting rain. I tell you, it's a miracle we stood it as long as we did, but there is a limit to what mortal flesh should be asked to bear. Even Town would be better, so I rode up to see about rooms at Grillon's or some such while Sasha packs. Thought I could beat out the weather, however—"

He shrugged. "I am as you see me. When the rain lets up I shall be on my way."

The earl regarded him fondly. "Don't be a fool, Augustus. You must stay here, if you think you can bear it. Think how much more convenient. Besides, you can support me, if you will, through the rigors of what promises to be an exceptionally trying Season."

"Ah," said Augustus superciliously. "Off to France again for cattle for Coldmere? Or is it Italy? Or Ireland, for horses? No." Augustus shook his head wisely. "It will never do. You see before you the veriest stay-at-home, knocked up by the rigors of five years on the Continent."

"Liar," said Gervase without heat. "But the Season to which I was alluding is right here in Town. I am presiding, for my sins, over the come-out of Lady Celia Darwen-Neville, the daughter of the late earl of Orleton. She's a ward of mine, and it's high time she was brought out."

"Good God!" said Augustus. "You're never letting Caro get her hooks into her? It won't do, Cousin, it just won't do. Orleton lived buried in the country, didn't he? Odds on the gel's never even seen a city, and to hand her to Caroline—she'll go for a governess, you wait."

"Hardly that," said Gervase. "As a matter of fact, Lady Celia's to be the Countess of Coldmeece, though I agree with you about Caro. The betrothal's not to be made public yet, by the way."

"I say!" Augustus bounded to his feet and seized Gervase's hand. "This is a stunner! Well, let me be the first to wish you very happy, though I don't suppose the last. It's about time you were pulling in double harness—Mama said that very thing, just before Deb came out in spots. When's the day?"

"Oh," said the earl vaguely, "sometime toward the end of the Season. There's no need to rush things, and I'm sure Lady Celia will have enough on her mind at first without cluttering it with wedding preparations." Then he eyed his cousin keenly. "You don't mind, Augustus?"

"Now that you've crushed my boyish dreams of becoming an earl when I grow up, by finally knuckling down to married life and setting up your nursery?"

"The thought had crossed my mind," said the earl.

"Stuff!" said Augustus roundly. "After the hey-go-mad time I've had traveling about with our sainted Aunt Josie, I'd think it pretty tame to settle into a respectable earl-dom."

"A fate you seem perfectly ready to wish on me, how-ever."

"Ah, well. Born to it, don'tcha see? Darwen on both sides, odiously respectable, while I'm no more than a skimble-skamble Templeton."

"One of the oldest and richest families in the country," the earl commented.

"Which ain't the same thing at all," Augustus finished happily. "No, no. To you the title, cousin mine, and I shall simply scrape along on my graces and the miserable pittance I'm to get from Great-aunt Serena." He raised his glass to Gervase and looked pious.

Since the "miserable pittance" referred to was, at a conservative estimate, something over ten thousand pounds a year, Gervase doubted Augustus would suffer much pri-vation.

"So what are your plans now, Augustus, the avenue of 'respectable earldom' being closed?"

"Well," Augustus began, "after I've seen you safely married—" He broke off. "Perhaps I shall pursue the wastrel course of the younger son; with Charles in the Army and Harry minding Temple Down, there's no par-ticular need of me," he finished glibly.

"You might consider doing something useful," Gervase suggested.

"I *might*," Augustus conceded, favoring Gervase with a smile of such charm that the earl was certain his cousin had been wearied to death of this matter in the not too distant past. "But what? I ask myself, Gussie-my-lad, what occupation is there upon this swiftly tilting globe that is worthy of you? Your charm, your intelligence, your wit . . ."

"Marriage, perhaps," suggested the earl. "It's time you took a wife as well. But that's neither here nor there," he added, ruthlessly turning the subject. "You haven't yet said you would bear me up through the Season. When I think of the parties, the routs, the assemblies . . .''

''You'll give a ball, of course?''

''Of course. For both girls, here at Coldmeece House. We'll start the Season with it. I fancy we can be assured of a proper turnout.''

''A proper turnout? I *should* say! Coldmeece House hasn't been opened for a ball since before I was born. You'll do famously, and of course I'll be delighted to do my small bit to bear you up and turn all the matchmaking mamas green that they haven't snabbled you for *their* daughters. I'd forgotten what it's like here at home.''

''You needn't tell me the net wasn't spread for you abroad, Augustus, for I know better.''

''Oh, it was, but I am as subtle as the serpent, and more guileful. But here—what do you mean, 'both girls'? And who's to play your hostess, if Caroline's not presenting this Celia chit?''

The earl looked ever so slightly uncomfortable. ''As to that, I have not yet made up my mind. Caroline's fragile health, *as you know, Augustus,* makes it out of the question for her to bring Celia out.''

''Oh, by Jove,'' said Augustus appreciatively, ''don't it just! No, no, there's no need to glare at me, Gervase, I know how to keep mum.''

The earl did not look convinced of this, but continued. ''And so I have asked Lady Mulford to sponsor Celia, and of course we shall give Lady Louisa a Season as well.''

''Give Louisa a Season?'' gasped Augustus in awed delight. He began to laugh, forcing Gervase to rescue his wineglass and set it on the side table. ''Oh, dear,'' said Augustus between peals.

Gervase waited patiently for him to subside. ''Is the girl really so ineligible, Augustus?''

Augustus wiped tears of mirth from his eyes. ''Oh, not at all, Cousin Coldmeece. No, no. In fact, I am sure she will do you credit.''

The earl regarded Augustus narrowly. ''Something must be done with her, after all, and as she is twenty-three, dowerless, and of an—unusual background, let us say, what better course than for her to share the come-out of the future Countess of Coldmeece?''

"Where the Darwen name can cloak her sins in a mantle of English virtue," Augustus caroled happily. "Oh, if only I could have been there when Aunt Josie told her they were staying in London! Oh, my dear Cousin, you are too good to us all, really you are!''

"All right," the earl demanded suspiciously, "what's wrong with the girl?''

"Wrong?" said Augustus, with an expression of pellucid innocence. "Nothing in the world, I assure you!'' He paused as if to consider, then added in the bright tones of one telling an absolute bouncer, "It's just that poor dear Lou's most dreadfully *shy*, you know, but other than that . . .''

The earl settled back in his chair with a disgruntled expression. Judging by Augustus's reaction, Lady Louisa was a regular out-and-outer, who had not put off one whit the scandalous behavior she must have learned in Turkey. He must find out how outrageous the girl actually was; he had assumed from Lady Mulford's letters that his cousin Louisa was at least presentable, but now . . .

He would have to call on Lady Mulford at the earliest possible moment. Louisa Darwen's unfortunate history was currently known only to a few, but if the girl were completely ineligible the whole appalling story would be bound to come out. There would be no getting her married off then—what man would choose a bride reared in the seraglio of the Grand Turk, however virtuous she might actually be? Lady Mulford had indignantly defended her niece, but Augustus's maliciously gleeful expression argued ill for Lady Louisa's virtues. Well, it should not become a tale for all the town if he could help it.

"Since you're staying," he said to Augustus, "you may as well get yourself out of those wet things and send a message to your man to bring your traps here. You shan't weasel out of your family duties with a cold, that I promise you.''

"No," said Augustus virtuously. "Certainly not. A London Season. Oh, dear."

The object of all this exercise sat, the following morning, in her aunt's breakfast parlor, regarding the sun streaming in the windows with deep relief. If it had rained another day, she felt, she would surely have gone mad, but she did not trust the sun to remain past the point at which it beguiled her out of doors. Idly she toyed with the stiff billet of cream-colored vellum that lay beside her plate. Under the Coldmeece crest Augustus had written to tell her that he was staying at Coldmeece House to escape the measles, and would she ride with him at three. She had already dispatched her acceptance, and was quite looking forward to seeing Augustus again, but there was still the morning to be dealt with.

The previous seven days had been a mad whirl of activity. Mulford House was still being cleaned top to bottom and made fit for occupancy. There had been appointments with the modiste, where Louisa had argued heatedly against her aunt's plan to garb her in the die-away pastels suitable to a young girl's first Season. There had also been far too many social calls on Lady Mulford's London acquaintance, which Louisa had found numbing beyond words.

On the brighter side, the horses—including her own dear Corsair—and Lady Mulford's carriage had arrived, so they were not obliged to go on foot or in a job-chaise, and Lady Mulford had written to the abominable earl's unknown betrothed, bidding Celia come to them for the Season. Louisa hoped that Celia would shield her from the worst of the deadly social rounds, and in truth, she looked forward to having another girl in her aunt's establishment. Louisa had never lacked for companionship in the harem, but among the Franks, save for her cousin Augustus, she had met few persons her own age. Lady Celia would be welcome company.

She had just poured herself a cup of tea when her aunt appeared in the doorway. "Louisa?" she said in amazement.

"I was, the last time I looked," Louisa said pertly.

Lady Mulford subsided into a chair and gazed at Louisa, who was garbed in a serviceable but sadly outmoded gown of blue wool challis, cunningly accessorized by not one but three thick wool paisley shawls. "But, my dear child, whatever are you got up as?" she asked weakly. "I did not think to find you awake before noo—at this early hour. But since you *are* up, you may come with me to see Lady Vane—but not dressed like that!"

Louisa grinned at her scandalized aunt and wrapped the topmost layer of shawl more securely about her shoulders. "Now, Aunt Josephine," she said, "if you expect me to inventory the linens, turn out the closets, and air the guest rooms in one of my ball gowns, I must disabuse you of the notion."

"Turn out the—oh, Louisa, no! It is true Madame Francine will not have the first of your new wardrobe ready for another week, but your amber walking dress is *more* than suitable for an informal call of this nature."

"I could not ask such condescension from Lady Vane," said Louisa hollowly. "Besides, isn't she the one with that appallingly dull-minded son? Really, Aunt."

"Well . . ." Lady Mulford admitted with a sigh. She fiddled with the snugly fitting cuff of her morning dress. "But really, my dear, why don't you let Mrs. Files attend to those horribly tedious chores? Whatever is a housekeeper for? It is the first sunny day in a week—do come with me, love."

Louisa laughed and shook her head. "No and no and no. You'll not take away my excuse to avoid those dreary calls so easily. Besides—"

"My dear Louisa, do you mean to tell me that you are planning to indulge in actual physical labor merely to avoid the tedium of a social call?"

Her unregenerate niece regarded her with round, soulful eyes. "*I*, Aunt?"

Correctly interpreting this as an affirmative, Lady Mulford sighed deeply. "Brain fever. I knew how it would be. The voyage home and the strain of the coming Season. I shall have to call in Sir Henry to examine you, but I know what he'll say. Brain fever.''

Louisa smiled and reached for a muffin. ''Now, dearest, you know you simply cannot leave the task of making ready a house that has been closed for donkey's years to poor Mrs. Files. One must always consider the sl—the servants. The day-to-day chores, yes, but there are major decisions to be made, and if one of us is not here . . .''

''Mrs. Files may take offense, and feel we do not trust her,'' suggested Lady Mulford hopefully.

''Who do you think brought the matter to my attention in the first place?'' Louisa asked.

''Well,'' said Lady Mulford doubtfully, ''if it is that much of a task, perhaps I should stay and—''

''*No!*'' said Louisa instantly. ''That is, I had much rather make myself *useful* here, while you bang the drum for Lady Celia's arrival. It wouldn't do, you know, for her to find her Season flat—any more than it would for her to find no bed ready for her.''

Lady Mulford was forced to admit the truth of this, and of the fact that she was as much suited to 'bang the drum' as Louisa was to ready the bed. Louisa loved comfort, ease, and order, and in matters pertaining to their arrangement she was the most efficient and organized of mortals.

''But,'' Lady Mulford protested feebly, ''I brought you to London to have *fun*, darling, not to slave away in the attics!''

''Dearest and most totty-headed of aunts! I shan't be slaving away in any attics, I assure you. Besides, Gussie has come up to Town to stay with Coldmeece, and I am engaged to ride with him at three, so you see, I shan't be working all the day.''

Lady Mulford reached out and patted her niece's wrist. ''I see that you are right, Louisa, but that reminds me . . .'' She looked vaguely guilty. Louisa raised quizzical brows. Lady Mulford took a deep breath and continued. ''It is about Augustus. I'm sure I need not tell you that London is different from any place you have ever been, and certain standards apply. Things that are perfectly acceptable in foreign society are not looked on at all the same way here. I'm certain it would not harm Augustus's reputation—men are different, darling, as you know—but it would not *look* well, and really, as much as you may frown at me, there is Celia to consider. Gervase trusts me to see that all is brought off well, and so many people are likely to be jealous of poor Celia that they will seek any opportunity to brew scandal-broth. You see that it is a delicate situation.''

"I'm sure I would see that, Aunt, if I could but figure out what you are talking about," Louisa said perplexedly. "What is wrong with Gussie's behavior?"

"It is not so much *his* behavior," Lady Mulford admitted reluctantly, "as it is—forgive me, darling—yours. Everyone has seen how you hang on his sleeve, and you must not do that here!"

"But Augustus is my dearest friend, Aunt," Louisa said in bewilderment. "I can't pretend not to know him. I *won't*!"

"No one is asking that you give Augustus the cut direct, Louisa, only that you behave conformably with—with the decorum expected of a young lady of Quality, my love. And, my dear, you must be careful for Gussie's sake as well as your own."

"You said he hadn't any reputation to lose," Louisa muttered mutinously.

Lady Mulford look shocked. "I never said that," she protested. "Only think how it would reflect on his character, to seem to encourage a young, unattached lady of good family to sit in his pocket—be she never so much his cousin."

"Augustus hasn't got any character," Louisa said, but she knew she was beaten. If Aunt Josephine said that was what people would think, well, then people would think that. But it seemed hard to lose her dearest—her only—friend to the conventions of Society. She felt more alone than ever.

Lady Mulford stood and patted Louisa's cheek. "There, there, dear, do not look so sad, I beg of you. You may find someone this Season you can like better than Augustus, and I know neither of you would wish to stand in the other's way. All will right itself with time, and you will laugh at this, you'll see.''

Her aunt's words stayed with Louisa as she and Mrs. Files attacked their monumental task. She had thought herself well able to weather whatever the London *ton* saw fit to hurl at her, but only because she had imagined Augustus would be at her side.

She was just about to change for riding when a breathless housemaid knocked to disturb her and announce that there was a caller in the morning room, and (in tones of greatest awe) that "It's an *earl*, miss!"

"An earl!" said Louisa in some surprise. "Well, tell Royton to inform him that my aunt is out, and that"—the devil fly away with London Society!—"I am not receiving this morning."

The maid bobbed another nervous curtsy. "I'm very sorry, mum—miss—m'lady, but Mr. Royton says as 'tis the earl of Coldmeece, and . . . and . . ."—here the maid's voice took on the stilted accents of one attempting a direct quote—" 'And as Lady Mulford's not t'home, his lordship will be pleased to wait,' miss—m'lady.''

"Oh, bother!" It was obviously impossible to leave the man twiddling his thumbs until her aunt returned. Aunt Josephine seemed fond of her godson-nephew, and Louisa had promised to try to behave in a convenable fashion. "Well," she said aloud, "I suppose I must go and entertain the man. You—Campbell, isn't it?—go and tell Royton to take sherry and biscuits to the morning room, and that I shall be down directly."

The unfortunate Campbell bobbed again as she shut the door behind her, and Louisa turned to the mirror, reaching for her hairbrush. She pulled off the snood and stood brushing out her hair in short, impatient strokes. Bother Cousin Coldmeece! What was his business turning up here? Probably he wished to make sure everyone had hopped to his piping. Intolerable man!

Deftly, Louisa whipped her sandy hair into a thick braid and wound it around the crown of her head. She flung a corner of her topmost shawl over her head; even after five years outside the harem walls, it still felt a little queer to be receiving a strange gentleman at all, let alone unchaperoned. She told herself that the earl was, after all, her cousin, so everything was quite convenable, and then swathed herself more securely in her shawls and swept out.

Gervase rose to his feet as the morning room door opened and his eyes widened in surprise. A muffled figure in a rather shabby blue dress and layers of miscellaneous coverings came forward and held out its hand.

"Good morning, Lord Coldmeece," the veiled apparition said. "I am Louisa Darwen. I hope you have been made comfortable."

"Quite," said the earl, bowing over her hand. As Lady Louisa had for some unaccountable reason thrown a shawl over her head and then wrapped it round her throat, there was little opportunity to determine what lay within its folds, but the overriding impression was of a sort of rabbity meekness, an impression bolstered by the care she took to seat herself as far as possible from him.

It was obvious to the earl that Augustus had been ragging him; instead of the dashing, voluptuous *houri* Gervase had been led to expect, his cousin Louisa, poor thing, seemed to be painfully shy and retiring. Much good a London Season would do *her*—she had apparently made up her mind to cloak the lurid sins of her past in a life of spinsterhood. No wonder Lady Mulford hadn't been able to fire her off—the wonder was that his flutterbye godmama had stood her niece's company so long.

Gervase felt positively sorry for his unfortunate cousin Louisa; when the Season was over, he would take good care to see her suitably established. Perhaps a country vicarage? Mr. Bewley, who had the living at Coldmere, was a sober, reliable widower with four young children. Doubtless he would welcome a grateful wife. . . . But that was a matter for the future; for now, he must strive to get through this morning call as best he might. "I hope," he said gently, "that I have not unduly inconvenienced you?"

Louisa's first impression of her cousin Gervase the earl

was one of sheer size. All her young life she had towered over her companions in the Turkish *hareem*, and even in Europe Louisa, at five feet eight inches, was as tall as most of the men she had met.

This cousin was a different matter. In fact, thought Louisa with faint approval, he didn't look quite English. He was not in the least pale and moonfaced, but had strongly boned features, a full sensual mouth, and curling chestnut hair. There was the glint of mocking good humor in the changeable sea gray eyes, and the lines about the mouth of a temper held firmly in check. He looked masculine, and supremely competent, and was quite the most attractive man she'd seen in ages.

When he rose to his feet to greet her Louisa became aware that while the earl was not *vulgarly* tall—not much taller than Augustus—he was more solidly built, with the heavy stallion muscle of maturity bulking his chest and shoulders. And his legs, clearly displayed by his glove-tight inexpressibles, were well formed and well muscled. How could the man bear to expose himself on the street like that? Louisa wondered, struck, not for the first time, by the sheer indecency of Frankish clothing. Why, he was very nearly undressed! And heaven knew it didn't show him off to the same advantage proper Turkish dress would—

Here, Louisa, suddenly painfully aware that she was gawking at the Earl of Coldmeece as if she were fresh from the seraglio, finally rallied her apparently disordered wits.

"Inconvenienced?" she managed. "Oh, not in the least. And I'm sure my—our aunt will return soon."

Louisa allowed the shawl to slip from her hair onto her shoulders, and yet another of the earl's convictions underwent a sea change. Lady Louisa Darwen was not only shy and dowdy, but plain; far too plain, in fact, to have remained anything but virtuous, even in the harem of the Grand Turk. A charitable observer might have described her colorless eyes as gray; not even the most charitable could honestly call her hair anything other than red, the faded, foxy red that marked so many of the Darwens.

Gervase felt vaguely—and most unreasonably—disappointed.

"And tell me," he went on with avuncular heartiness after a moment, "how do you find London?"

The earl's unconcealed look of astonishment when she'd entered the room, and his more controlled surprise when she'd unveiled, had told Louisa everything she'd needed to know. For some reason, anyone who knew about her past expected her to be arrayed like something out of Byron, wearing two wisps of silk and a spangle and reclining on a divan amid clouds of incense.

Alternately, of course, there were those who seemed to feel that she was making a good job of sweeping her sins—*her* sins, Louisa had been given to understand, although she had supposedly been a helpless victim of the (no doubt) lustful Turk—under the rug and simply wished to lead a blameless life and forget her past. As they were usually basing this opinion on the plainness of Louisa's face, this conclusion was no more accurate than the first. Louisa had quickly seen that her cousin belonged to the sweeping sins school of thought, and, impelled by her perverse imp of mischief, decided that Lord Coldmeece should not be disabused of his quaint notions of her character—at least, not until she was good and ready.

"Oh," she said, schooling her features to the sort of guilty ingenuousness she felt was expected of her, "I do find London beyond anything great! There are so very many people here"—as if Constantinople weren't the largest city in the East, and both Vienna and St. Petersburg 'more cosmopolitan than this foggy rock!—"and so much to do! The museums, the parks . . . Really, Lord Coldmeece, there are so many sights of uplift and interest that one is quite confounded!" She then shrank back in her chair slightly, hoping to look crushed.

"Yes," said the earl kindly. "If there is anything I might do to make your stay here more enjoyable, please do not hesitate, Cousin, to call upon me."

Louisa suddenly regretted that the earl's empty civilities were only that. Her so respectable cousin undoubtedly hoped never to see her—or rather, the person he thought her to be—again.

She concentrated on projecting the image of a grateful yet penitent spaniel. "Oh, thank you, Cousin," she murmured almost inaudibly.

The earl bestowed an encouraging smile upon her. "But I do not mean to take up all your morning," he added briskly. "As one of the family, I can certainly entertain myself until Lady Mulford returns."

Louisa stifled an urge to giggle at this obvious attempt to gently dismiss her. "Oh, dearest Aunt Josephine would *never* wish me to be backward in *any* attention to a guest," she said in a breathless rush. "She has always said to me, 'Louisa, when one is—' That is, my lord, she has always given me to understand that Frankish manners—I mean— Oh, dear," she said mournfully, raising her hands to her lips to hide their upward curve.

"That's all right," said the earl quickly. "I quite understand."

"My aunt would never forgive me if I did not do my duty and keep you entertained," Louisa said with prim determination. "Her dearest godson. Do have some sherry, my lord. I am certain she will be along directly. She is making all ready for dear Lady Celia's arrival."

"Ah, Lady Celia," said the earl. "I hope you will find her company agreeable, Lady Louisa. She has lived quietly in the country all her life, so you need not fear that she is—fast."

Such a generous heart deserved a provocative answer. "Oh, my lord earl, you are too kind! Naturally I look forward to welcoming my poor, dear little cousin into the bosom of our hearth and home, but truly, I *had* feared to be dragged from the quiet of the printed page. Do *you* not find books the most satisfactory of all companions?" From the expression on the earl's face, Louisa rather thought he didn't, so she blithely continued, "Many a happy hour have I spent poring over their pages! The poets! The playwrights! . . ."

"The novelists?" suggested the earl helpfully, with the

air of one who knew every turn of the conversation far in advance.

"Of a certainty, the novelists," Louisa agreed, adding primly, "I speak, of course, of the *improving* novelists, my lord." In point of truth, Louisa's taste in literature ran distinctly to the flamboyant; she had a liking for dashingly absurd romances and Gothic horrors.

"Of course," the earl agreed.

Louisa clasped her hands before her and, quaking with inward mirth, delivered an effusive speech. "Yes, I have learned oh, so much of this happy, happy land through its literature! And now to be here, here on this 'emerald jewel set in a silver sea,' as the dear Bard has it—well, I can hardly believe it!" Lips tight over laughter, Louisa eyed Coldmeece as the man's brows slowly rose in patent disbelief. Yes, that misquote had definitely been a brilliant touch. She poured out a glass of sherry and offered it to the earl, ruthlessly continuing. "And oh, but the chance, the priceless opportunity I shall now have to see those places hallowed by the feet of literary greatness! Why, only think of it!"

"Yes," drawled the earl noncommitally, "only think of it, Lady Louisa."

She blinked her eyes twice in a display of innocence, cudgeling her brains for the name of that lady novelist Aunt Josephine had urged on her in early days. "Why, I shall be walking the very streets where trod the feet of Maria Edgewater!" she gushed rapturously.

"I see," said the earl. "May I say, Cousin Louisa, that this conversation has come as a revelation to me. I almost feel as if I know you—though of course that is hardly possible on such short acquaintance."

Perhaps, thought Louisa, the earl was not altogether made of wood. She looked forward to standing up with him at the ball and giving him the opportunity to appreciate the figure she cut in evening dress.

"You are all kindness, my lord Earl," she murmured sweetly. "But it is all of a piece! Such warmth, such courtesy have we received since first we set foot onto English soil." Which she was no longer as anxious to leave as she had been that morning. She dredged up one more sigh, aware that she was behaving quite shockingly. "Why, I can hardly credit that I shall have time to see all that I would—the Tower, St. Paul's, the Abbey, the—the Castle of Otranto!"

The earl's lips twitched, and he was overcome with a brief fit of coughing. Louisa firmly schooled her features to idiocy and peered at him hopefully. "Perhaps we shall even have the pleasure of your escort, sir? I know my dearest aunt—and of course she is your dearest aunt too, is she not?—is prodigious fond of you."

"My dear cousin," said the earl, in tones made slightly hoarse by his recent coughing fit, "I fear that such escort may well prove beyond my power, whatever my wish. However—"

The sound of carriage wheels on the bricks outside heralded Lady Mulford's return. The earl, sounding rather regretful about it, said, "I fear that Lady Mulford has returned, and we must perforce cut short our conversation. However, I must thank you, Lady Louisa, for a most illuminating morning. You have made me see English literature in an entirely new light."

"Oh, *thank* you, Cousin Coldmeece," said Louisa, sweeping to her feet in a confusion of shawls. She ached with holding back a fit of the giggles, and was certain she must present a peculiarly stricken countenance to the earl's gaze. "It is always so *heartening* to feel one has been of some use. I would not rush off like this, but I have a pressing appointment—which is of course to be held at naught beside the specter of family duty!"

"Naturally," said the earl, also rising.

Louisa backed toward the door, and when she had its knob securely in hand, she delivered her parting shot. "And if I have, in some small measure, compensated you for foregoing the joy of having me sewn in a sack and dropped in the Bosphorus, then you may only imagine my delight!" On that note, Louisa dropped a hasty curtsy and fled.

A quick glance at the hall clock told Louisa that Augustus must already be waiting for her. She hurried for the stairs, only to be stopped by Lady Mulford, who was just coming in the door.

"Louisa, my love," Lady Mulford called, "wherever are you off to? Augustus is waiting outside—on the most *peculiar* animal—he told me to tell you to hurry, or he could *not* be responsible."

"Gussie's never responsible!" Louisa said cheerfully. "As for me, I have been most virtuously entertaining your godson. He is in the morning parlor, and he says he is *not* sorry I came to England instead of being drowned at his command."

"What?" Lady Mulford gasped. "Oh, Louisa, in *that* dress?"

Louisa waved and ran up the stairs on winged feet, heartlessly leaving her aunt to cope with his lordship of Coldmeece.

Chapter
FOUR

"Good God!" said Louisa, coming down the steps of Mulford House. "Is that what you wanted to show me? What a beauty he is, to be sure!" She gazed at the gleaming bay stallion in cautious admiration.

"Yes," said Augustus smugly, "he is, isn't he?" A waiting groom seized the horse's headstall and Augustus swung down from the saddle. "Shall I buy you a match for my Prometheus, Louisa?"

"You couldn't get me on his back for a thousand pounds," she said frankly. Augustus grinned, then tossed her lightly into the saddle of her placidly waiting gray mare.

"You need a horse to match those riding habits of yours," he told her severely, eyeing her opulent costume. "Something with a bit of dash and spirit."

"I do not *want* a horse with 'dash and spirit,'" said Louisa. "I want a horse that will do as it is told. I'm quite happy with my sweet slug, and well you know it."

"Corsair!" Augustus regarded Corsair with disgust. "*What* a name for a horse like that—and a mare to boot! And you needn't tell me again you named her out of fondness for that everlasting Byron fellow, for well I know it! I'd still like to see you on something decent."

"I wouldn't be on *your* idea of something decent *long*, now, would I?" retorted Louisa as Augustus remounted his skittish bay. "Now, are we going to the Park, or are we going to stand here all day admiring the perfect picture you present?"

Augustus half bowed and waved his hand expansively. "After you, m'lady."

The Park was reached without incident, and after a brisk canter, Augustus's devil-to-go quieted down enough to permit conversation.

"So," Augustus said, "how does it feel to be home?"

Louisa slanted a mocking glance at him from under the brim of her hat. "I ought to ask *you* that question, my angel. This is your home, not mine. I haven't been in England since I was ten years old."

"But, oh, the call of the ancestral blood! The shriek of the hoopoe, and all that rot. Don't it *speak* to you?"

"Yes. It says, 'Louisa, get out of this godforsaken swamp.' But I suppose we are fixed here until the end of the Season, if only for Lady Celia's sake. Poor child, I already feel sorry for her."

"Sorry?" asked Augustus, pulling Prometheus to a slower walk. "What for? You can't expect Dowager Caro to make that much trouble for her. I mean, dash it all, there *are* limits. Or do you think Aunt Josie'll play propriety and trample her girlish high spirits?"

The thought of Aunt Josephine intimidating *anyone* caused Louisa to chuckle. "Hardly. But really, being dragged up from the country will-she nill-she to marry a man she's never met and doesn't know a thing about— well, think how awkward for her when she refuses him."

"Refuse him?" said Augustus, baffled. "Never seen? Of course she's seen him! Betrothed for years! Told me so himself. Why would she cry off now?"

"Because she never *has* seen him, and furthermore, she hasn't the least notion he's to marry her. Aunt Josephine told me so *her*self, and *she* had it from the earl."

Augustus was quickly put in possession of the facts, and he turned a look of outraged dignity on his cousin. "I've never heard anything so idiotish! I *told* him the earldom wasn't good for him—given him all manner of totty-headed notions. Why, he told *me* the matter was as good as settled. Imagine bamming me like that! He'll hear about it before he's very much older, I promise you!"

"Oh, don't!" Louisa begged. "You know very well he won't listen to you—and I think Lady Celia ought to come to Town and make up her own mind," she finished virtuously.

"Ho!" said Augustus. "You just want to put Coldmeece out of countenance. A fine thing, after I was at such pains to give him a good report of you."

"Oh," said Louisa, turning upon her cousin with a martial light in her eye, "so it was *you* who was talking to him. No wonder he stared at me this morning—he expected to see the collected works of Byron."

" 'Now melt into sorrow, now madden to crime,' " Augustus agreed. "And found instead?"

"The most *quakerish* of creatures," said Louisa mirthfully, "dressed in sober woollens and reading only the most uplifting of literature—'I do find books the most *satisfactory* of all companions, don't you, my lord Earl?' He very kindly took the greatest pains to assure me that Lady Celia was of a quiet and modest disposition."

"Better watch out," Augustus advised. "He'll have you married to a country vicar next—it's all the crack this Season, it seems."

"Gussie! Never tell me your mama wants to marry you to a country vicar!" Louisa said.

"No, but the next best thing. Everyone prosing at me to *make* something of myself—even Coldmeece thinking I ought to get myself spliced. It's the outside of enough!"

"I don't see why you should be spared what I am not. At least, they are not asking you to hire a maid, too; you have Sasha, while I am forever being presented with this whey-faced miss or that, *and* lectured that I must be on the catch for a husband, and not ruin *your* reputation while I am at it. Oh, England is so *complicated*!"

"My reputation?" said Augustus. "What about my reputation?"

"Oh," said Louisa crossly, "some nonsense that I should not dangle after your pocket—although I am sure I never gave *anyone* reason to think I was *fond* of you!"

"Sweet angel," said Augustus fulsomely. Louisa flicked the end of her reins at him.

After Augustus regained control of Prometheus, he pulled up beside Louisa again. "I don't see why *you* must marry," he said, continuing the conversation as if there had been no interruption. "It's not as though you had any property, say."

"That's just the point. Aunt Josephine is worrying again, poor dear, about what will happen to me when she is gone, which I've told her and told her is absurd. Why, she'll probably outlive me!"

"Very likely," agreed Augustus, "since I confidently expect someone to strangle you in a fit of fury one of these fine days."

"Yes, but you do see?" said Louisa, smiling at him.

"Oh, by Jove, yes." Augustus smiled back. It was one of life's great mysteries that Louisa had never felt the least heart-flutter in his presence, but at least this shocking lack of sensibility had allowed her to form a deep and long-lasting friendship for him, which, being practical, she valued far more than a romantic entanglement.

"What *I* don't see," said Louisa aggrievedly, "is what all of this marriage rubbish has to do with me. I think Aunt Josephine's chasing moonshine, though I suppose I must marry sooner or later. Only why must *I* have to choose the man?"

"Quite true. After all, Lady Lou, you're only the bride-to-be. Why you should have any say in your groom is beyond me."

"You fiend!" said Louisa at the use of the detested nickname.

"Besides," Augustus went on, "ain't you the one who was just ranting about poor little Celia, forced to marry a man she'd never met? Try for a little consistency, Coz, do."

Louisa stared at him wide-eyed. "But that is quite different! Celia is an *English* girl, Gussie, and has been raised to do as she pleases. But I was *not*. What, pray, do I know of selecting a proper husband? Why, it is almost as important as the selection"—Louisa grinned maliciously at Augustus—"of the proper horse."

"Now, dash it all, Lou . . ." Prometheus took advan-

41

tage of his rider's momentary inattention to sniff at Corsair's neck; the little mare sidled out of reach, ears flat.

"But seriously, Gussie," Louisa went on, stroking Corsair's satiny neck, "after all I have been told of English ways—well, if I am to have an English bridegroom, I'm sure I should be much better served if he were chosen by someone more qualified than I to judge his English merits. Only think how vexatious if I were to choose wrongly."

"Aunt Josie wants you to be happy, Louisa. She'd never dream of picking your husband for you, just because you're too lazy to do it yourself."

"Well, someone must, for I know nothing about the matter. And *I* won't marry a country curate and be buried in the country!"

"No curates need apply," said Augustus cheerfully. "Well, what sort of husband *do* you want? I mean, really, girlish daydreams and all that rot. You must have some notion about this hypothetical chap."

"Yes!" said Louisa defiantly. "I want an indolent, agreeable—and *rich*, if you must know—amiable husband, who isn't averse to travel and won't be forever ringing an odious peal over me for what Aunt Josephine calls my 'Past.' I haven't a Past, have I, Gussie?"

"Not a bit of it," said Augustus loyally. "Which is hardly what any of the Society mamas would believe—especially after one look at you in a ball gown."

Louisa preened. "I do look rather well in evening dress, don't I, Gussie-my-angel. But there's the problem. I have my standards—"

"Low though they may be."

"—but I can't just go around asking people if they fit them! Perhaps I should place an advertisement in the *Gazette*."

" 'Wanted: One husband; Indolent, Amiable, and Rich, to wed Darwen with a Past.' No, I see it wouldn't do. You'd better toddle along with Aunt Josie's first idea and marry a Darwen."

"What?" said Louisa, diverted by the novel concept of Aunt Josephine's having had an idea.

"A Darwen," Augustus explained. "Darwens always

marry their cousins—except Edmund, who was fool enough to marry that Everhill jade—''

''*Dear* Caro,'' Louisa supplied.

''—and Mama, who married for love,'' went on Augustus, daring Louisa to comment. ''And Aunt Sophronia, who ran off with that American. But still. That way, of course, you know what everyone's worth, in strictest confidence and straitest propriety, because it's all in the family. Or just pick one at random and marry him.''

''I don't know how many cousins I've got, let alone which ones are unmarried, Gussie.''

''Well, let's see. Mama had the genealogy out while I was home, so I ought to be up on things. There's Gervase, and Aunt Sophronia had a son, but he's in the colonies, and there's me—''

''That's the best idea you've had yet,'' said Louisa with a smile. ''It's a pity you don't mean it.''

''Mean it?'' Augustus looked blank. ''Mean what?''

''That I should marry you, of course. Let's see—yes, you're rich, agreeable, like to travel, a cousin . . .'' Louisa grinned at her cousin. ''Really, Gussie, that expression. *So* flattering, my love.''

''Marry you?'' said Augustus, staring at her. Then, in a different tone, ''Well, why not?''

It was Louisa's turn to stare. ''Gussie, you're not serious!''

Augustus looked defensive. ''I don't see why I shouldn't be. Since, as you have so kindly pointed out, I *am* a matrimonial prize of no mean order, it's my civic duty to bestow myself with all deliberate haste. Therefore, dear Cousin Louisa—''

''Oh, Gussie, no! Be serious!''

Augustus regarded her, a mocking light in his brilliant blue eyes. ''Oh, but I am, sweet Coz. I don't know why I didn't think of it. I must have done eventually, but the sooner the better. Consider, sweetheart. You get a rich and amiable husband who doesn't care a fig for your scandalous past. I get a convenable wife, and Mama can't say I'm throwing myself away, because after all you *are* a Darwen, my cousin, and absolutely top drawer. Aunt Josie's happy,

Mama's happy, yours truly is saved from the snares and pitfalls of the coming Season. . . . Make me the happiest of mortals!''

"You're going to be very mortal," Louisa said dryly, "if he gets that bit between his teeth." She nodded at Prometheus.

Augustus settled the bit and the stallion tossed his head. Louisa looked down at her hands, trying to sort out her feelings. She felt an overwhelming sense of relief at the thought of marrying Gussie, someone she knew and trusted. It would be so good to have the matter settled for all time.

In the harem she had been raised to the idea that a suitable husband would be found for her. But when Aunt Josephine had come and taken her away, nothing had been said about a husband for Louisa. Apparently, Louisa had decided unhappily, her family did not wish her to marry.

But the moment they touched shore at Dover, Aunt Josephine had started telling Louisa that she must marry, and soon, *and* find the husband herself, and Louisa felt both unsuited to the task and indignant at being asked to do it. It was, she thought, smiling to herself at the pun, rather Turkish treatment to receive from one's own aunt.

"Changed your mind, Coz?" Augustus asked softly. "Because you needn't marry me if you don't wish, but I'm sure we'd deal extremely."

Louisa gave him a grateful, slightly shy, smile. "Thank you. I am sure we shall." In spite of herself, she shivered.

"Cold?" said Augustus, changing the subject.

"This English climate! Oh, Gussie, when we are married, may I have a *stove*? A closed stove, such as they heated the Tsar's palace with? I am always cold here, and I have asked Aunt Josephine to buy one, but I know she will not."

"I've a much better idea. Why don't we just go back to Russia? I'll wager I could even get something in the diplomatic line—always fancied myself a diplomat. I can have Gervase put in a good word for me at the Foreign Office. Mama'll go into raptures. Now, about the announcement—"

"Gussie," said Louisa, a trifle uneasily, "oughtn't we

to talk to your mama first? Before we settle everything between ourselves, I mean. It may come as a bit of a shock to her.'' Louisa somehow doubted that Aunt Euphemia would go into quite the raptures Gussie thought she would at the news of his matrimonial plans.

''Nothing of the sort!'' Augustus said cheerfully. ''Mama's got pluck to the backbone! I'll just ride on down tonight and—blast!''

''What's the matter?''

''Measles. I forgot to tell you, and Mama locked me out in the Dower House when everyone else came out all over spots. Wouldn't let me in the front gate. Well, I'll just have to send her a message.''

Louisa had no faith in Augustus's ability to tactfully word a billet that would explain all to a doting mother who had five children ill with the measles. ''That's all right,'' she said soothingly. ''Let's keep it a secret just now, and tell your parents when they come up to Town. After all, you may fall madly in love with someone else in the meantime and wish to cry off, you know.''

''Don't trust me to come the pretty with Mama, eh?'' said Augustus with dismaying accuracy. ''Well, p'raps you're right, but that's no call to go inventing Banbury tales about true loves. We're not the falling-in-love kind, either of us—that's one of the reasons we'll deal extremely together.''

Louisa nodded. Augustus was quite right. Oh, it would not be a love match, one of those exhaustingly romantical idiocies so beloved of lurid novelists; they had affection and friendship, and it would be enough. And, she dared swear, far more lastingly satisfying.

''Thank you, Gussie-my-love,'' she said. ''I knew I could depend on you.''

''So I should hope,'' he told her severely. ''I'm just glad you had the sense to ask me, my pet.''

''To *ask*—Augustus!'' She glared at his back as he prudently cantered away.

Following his errand to Lady Mulford, the earl turned his steps homeward, where he was disconcerted to find

45

the carriage belonging to the Dowager Countess of Cold-meece drawn up before his door.

"Darling Gervase, how wonderful to see you again!" Caro Darwen rose gracefully to her feet as her brother-in-law entered the library.

At five-and-twenty, Caroline Darwen still retained the striking good looks that, with her shrewd eye to the main chance, had made her the countess of the ninth Earl of Coldmeece six years before. Pale, shining blond hair framed an oval face graced with a classically lovely nose, a rosebud mouth that could be prim or inviting by turns, and wide, faintly tilted blue eyes that had been compared to ocean waves and forest pools by the numerous suitors of her maidenhood. This golden beauty was exquisitely set off by her dress, an elegant confection in sky blue silk trimmed at the hem with knots of ribbon in a deeper hue. Her bonnet, fur-trimmed pelisse, and matching muff had been thrown over a nearby chair, as if to offer mute testimony to the haste and urgency of her visit.

"Caroline," Gervase acknowledged. "*Dear* sister." He took the proffered hand and bowed over it punctiliously. "Do sit down. You must be tired after so long, and un-expected, a journey."

The dowager countess sank as gracefully as she had risen into a straight chair upholstered in plum-colored brocade. She looked demure. The earl rang for tea to be brought, and they spoke desultorily on Town topics until the foot-man had delivered the tea tray and departed. Then the earl leaned forward in the chair he had drawn up opposite his sister-in-law's.

"Now, what brings you to Town, dear Sister? I had thought you safely established at Bath for some weeks yet."

Caro wrinkled her nose prettily. "I *do* wish you would not call me that, Gervase. It puts me quite out of temper to be so—so *relegated*."

The earl raised one jovian eyebrow. After a moment, seeing that he was not to be drawn, Caro went on. "As for Bath—well, my love, one cannot rusticate forever."

"Indeed," he said blandly. "I am surprised you stayed as long as you did."

"*I* am surprised," she said sweetly, "that *you* should have come to Town so early. You did not use to find London more attractive than Coldmere."

"And you have never found Coldmere attractive at all, so I should hardly be surprised that you are here, rather than fixed at the Dower House. If it is about your allowance, Caroline, you will not find me in a mood to increase it. Good and sufficient provision has been made for you, and I see no reason to further encumber the estate to pay for your pleasures."

Caro pouted, an expression frequently described by besotted admirers as enchanting. "Gervase, really! The way you go on, anyone would think the only thing I ever wanted from you was money, when I am sure I have worked as hard as anyone to bring Coldmere around!"

The earl surveyed her coldly. "If by hard work you mean that you took yourself to the Continent before you were out of mourning to leave me a clear hand with the bills, then you are quite correct, Caroline, and I felicitate you."

Caro sighed theatrically. "Well, I see there is nothing to be done with you today, Gervase—oh, don't eat me, it is no more than the truth, and what *am* I to do when you frown so? It makes my very bones shake! But still, I have come on family business, and I will have my say." She paused dramatically.

"Go on," the earl said.

"I have heard—talk—that you are presiding over a come-out this Season, Gervase—or two, rather. Orelton's daughter and that impossible niece of Lady Mulford's. Really, you'd think she had better sense than to bring the girl here! Am I right?"

"May one ask," said the earl noncommittally, "how you came to be in possession of this information?"

"Why, Gervase," she purred, "Salvington is *my* solicitor too, and very happy to explain the practical reasons you couldn't be bothered increasing my allowance this year. He said you would have a great many calls on your resources this season."

"And so you hastened to Town to commiserate with me. How touching."

"Oh, don't be so cold to me, Gervase! Salvington told me all. Surely we two, we who have been so dear to each other, can discuss it, you and I?" She reached out and took his hand.

The earl carefully withdrew it and stood, moving away from her chair. "I see I must speak to Salvington. He was told to hold the matter in strictest confidence."

"Oh, don't be cross with the poor man, Gervase. I told him I already knew all, and only wished to determine precisely what arrangements had been made."

"I see," said the earl. "Surely you did not feel I must needs consult you in the matter?"

Caroline turned away and pressed her handkerchief to her lips. It was as well for her that she could not see the expression of contempt on Gervase's features at that moment.

"I had hoped," she said, "that you had forgiven me at last. Instead I find that, so far from it, you are punishing yourself with a hasty marriage to a chit just out of the schoolroom. Oh, Gervase, how could you do such a thing!"

"The marriage," the earl drawled blightingly, "was arranged by my father and hers the year she was born—as Salvington must also have told you."

"And so," said Caro, "now that this girl is of an age to marry, you intend to honor this—this obligation?" Her eyes gleamed with an emotionless malice.

"Why not?"

"The brat's complete unsuitability, that's why not!"

The earl frowned. "Lady Celia's birth is unexceptionable, as you well know. Orleton was quite a well-respected man, and his wife of sound stock. Lady Celia is a distant cousin of mine, as a matter of fact. What, my dearest sister-in-law, could be *more* suitable?"

"Which is, of course, why you are rushing her into a come-out, giving a ball—*without telling me*—before anyone at all is in Town, and, I daresay, planning to marry her from the ballroom floor and bury her on the ancestral estates. I'm told the girl is rich, but is the earldom in such sad straits that you must needs kidnap an heiress?"

"Nothing of the sort," he protested. "Lady Celia will have her Season and marry me at the end of it, a very common arrangement. And do make up your mind, darling, whether Lady Celia is no fit bride or I am no fit husband. A sweet consistency, you know, is held a virtue."

Caro began to toy with an ivory box on the side table. "No," she announced decisively, "it won't do, my *dear* brother-in-law, it just won't do. You are marrying this girl out of the nursery, behind everyone's back, in a skimble-skamble fashion—solely for the money to clear your debts! That's what everyone will say. You can hardly expect to flummox the rest of the *ton* as you did the feather-pated Lady Mulford."

"Such language," said Gervase. "And from a doting mama, too."

A flash of anger marred Caro's perfect features. "Say what you like to me, but others will talk. They *will* talk. And so, my dear, to keep you from making a complete fool of yourself"—Caro rose and drifted gracefully over to where the earl leaned against the mantelpiece—"I came as soon as I heard the news of the ball."

"Your resiliency, my dear Caroline, never ceases to amaze me. What scheme have you so generously devised to keep me from 'making a fool of myself'?"

"Why," said Caro simply, "*I* shall play hostess at your ball. Sweet Celia will make her come-out and with my blessings, and no one can say you are wearing the willow, when I—when I am there, as I should be, to lend my countenance and make all serene. And of course I shall do my best to quash all tales that you are fortune hunting. We will put it about that the girl is your ward, nothing more."

"You fascinate me," said the earl. "Do you think none of this has occurred to me? Nevertheless, Lady Mulford can act as hostess."

"She *could*," Caro said meditatively, "when I was

49

known to be in Bath. But now I am here, and here I mean to stay."

The earl took a half step forward, and Caro swayed lithely out of his reach. "Oh, no, Gervase. You cannot again bundle me off to rusticate as you did when Edmund died and I was *enceinte*. I do not mean to retire from *this* Season for reasons of ill health. I shall stay in Town, and if you are wise, you will seek my cooperation."

"And if I am not . . . wise?" said Gervase slowly.

"Oh, Gervase!" said Caro. "Please, let us be friends. You are to marry at last, and I wish you very happy, both of you. May I not help? I swear I mean no harm—you are very cruel to think otherwise—and all I wish is . . . is to make her engagement Season as happy as . . . as mine would have been. Oh, what can I say to convince you?"

"Take heart," said Gervase caustically. "You *have* convinced me. You have convinced me, dear Caroline, that you will be a great deal of trouble if you are not allowed to—shall I say 'help'? I suppose you would insist on conducting these Cheltenham tragedies in public?"

"Oh, only at the most select gatherings," said Caro sweetly. "By the time of the ball neither you nor that little chit from the country would dare show your faces anywhere, and you may also be certain that I would make Lady Louisa's past quite, quite public as well. The Darwen family has so many interesting secrets, has it not? But do be reasonable, darling. Am I asking so very much? It is not so long since *my* first Season, you know."

Her words were lightly mocking, but in her eyes was a wistfulness that belied her tone.

"You are, as always, dear sister, exquisitely reasonable," the earl said as Caroline drew on her gloves. "But pray do not let me keep you. I am sure with the press of the Season coming on that you will find yourself quite busy."

"Oh, yes," she said, as he assisted her on with her pelisse. "I shall be well occupied."

The following morning found the earl alone at his breakfast table. He had already written to inform Lady

Mulford that Caro was in Town and would be acting as hostess for the ball, but he had no intention of allowing Caro to make any of the preparations. Not only was he sure his godmother would be glad to assist him with preparations for the ball, but he could suggest to her the matter of Mr. Bewley, the vicar, as a possible solution to Lady Louisa's difficulties when he saw her later this afternoon—although he was no longer as certain as he had been that this match would serve. Lady Louisa seemed possessed of a sly sense of humor, and Mr. Bewley, as befitted a widowed vicar with four small children, was of a reserved disposition. Well, there would be time enough after the ball to settle things. Thank heavens he no longer needed to worry about Augustus, as the boy seemed to have settled on a career in the diplomatic corps.

Just as the earl's ruminations had reached this agreeable pass, Bracken intruded himself to announce the presence of Mrs. Raxton.

On being told to produce Mrs. Raxton, Bracken stood aside, and a stout lady of some forty years of age came bustling into the earl's presence and dropped a curtsy upon beholding him.

"Very sorry to have disturbed your lordship at breakfast, I *am* sure!" she said. "But it's little Lady Charlotte, my lord, and how it could have happened I'm sure I don't know, but pray the good Lord the little lamb hasn't come to harm, though how could you be certain of such a thing with that woman and a most unnatural parent meddling in the matter I'm sure I couldn't say, and I would have been here yesterday—it having happened along of the forenoon, you see, my lord—only the carriage lost a wheel. But your lordship will be wanting to know exactly what happened."

"Yes," said the earl firmly. If the Coldmeece nursery governess had faults, they were an inability to see ill in her charge and an even greater inability to come to the point quickly. Her rambling conversational style had not been improved by the rigors of what the earl guessed to have been a precipitous journey from Coldmere to London.

"Well, my lord," she began, "it was but yesterday, and

a fine morning, though *not*, I must say, for goings-on of that sort, which I never did hold with—such an unnatural woman—''

''When Lady Coldmeece came to Coldmere,'' the earl interjected presciently.

Mrs. Raxton's broad, honest features reflected stunned surprise. ''Why, my lord, however did you know? I had just looked out to see her ladyship's carriage pulled up in the drive—we were all *that* surprised to see her, what with thinking her ladyship at Bath as she was, when who but her ladyship herself should come up the stairs and into the nursery—without, moreover, so much as a by-your-leave to myself, which, all things considered and it no longer being my lady's house, she might well have done, begging your lordship's pardon, to be sure—and take little Lady Charlotte away with her! Such shrieks as were never heard, and my little lamb a-crying and a-screaming until it was in a fair way to have broken your heart, not, as you could see if you had been there, my lord, that it afflicted that woman—her ladyship, I *should* say—one whit, with her saying to me, bold as brass, that she would be a-taking the little one away with her for to live in London with her mother as any good child should, which, to my way of thinking, my lord, was fine talk from one who hadn't troubled to drive across the park the whole twelvemonth to see the wee tyke, no more she would come home from those nasty foreign places like a good Christian woman—begging your lordship's pardon, I'm sure!'' Mrs. Raxton stopped abruptly.

''Caroline brought Charlotte to London with her,'' the earl said.

''Yes, my lord; and myself no further behind than the time it took to order young William to bring round the carriage, which I made so free as to do, begging your lordship's pardon, and myself to see that some of my little lamb's things were packed for her. Imagine taking Miss Charlotte to London, sir, without her doll nor yet any of her things! It's unnatural, it is, my lord, which I say and I always *have* said, and I would have been to see your lordship yesterday, only as I have said, the wheel came off and I was obliged to wait while it was put back.''

"Yes, yes, Mrs. Raxton," the earl said. "But she is in London now, and I think it best that she stay here. I shall have Mrs. Leadbury open the nursery suite," he continued, rising from the table, "and I trust I may count upon you to remain here to see to the child?"

"Never doubt it, my lord!" she said stoutly. "As if I would turn my back on my lamb in her hour of need!"

But his lordship did not stay to hear the end of this edifying speech, and in a very short time his town carriage was making its brisk way toward Lady Coldmeece's house in Half Moon street.

That residence was in very fine trim indeed, ample evidence that Caroline had planned her impulsive trip to Town in some detail. Despite the earliness of the hour, he saw Lady Jersey's carriage standing in the street before the door, and as his own vehicle drew near, Silence herself emerged from the town house and mounted into her carriage.

There, thought the earl grimly, went any chance of keeping Caro's arrival a secret. He only hoped his sister-in-law was sticking to the bargain she'd driven, but there was no hope that she had not filled Lady Jersey's ears with news of the ball she would be hostessing in Coldmeece House. No chance now to pack Caro quietly off, for what Lady Jersey knew now, all the *ton* would know by teatime.

The earl strode up to the door of the fashionable residence and pounded furiously. The door was opened by Caro's butler, whom the earl brushed past without a word. Gervase knew well where to find Caro here. She would be in the small and intimate salon that had been designed as a fitting setting for her fair beauty.

He thrust open the gilt and ivory painted doors. Caroline looked up with a studied air of surprise that changed to real consternation when she saw who it was.

"Did you truly think," Gervase said, "that Mrs. Raxton would contrive to keep your secret?"

A faint frown appeared on Caro's perfect brow, then was smoothed away as if by a master hand. The earl strode

53

into the room and stood before her. "Hear-me, Caroline. I made myself quite clear a year ago and I will repeat myself now. You are to have nothing to do with Charlotte. You may visit her, if you like, but she is a Darwen and deserves better of life than to be raised under your roof."

Caroline went pale with anger. "How *can* you say that!" she began heatedly, but the earl held up his hand.

"We have had this discussion," he said with suspicious mildness, "and when last we talked you were very satisfied with the terms. What, I wonder, can have changed your mind now? Could it be," he said lightly, "that you had hoped, were you unable to convince me you should play hostess at Celia's ball, that my darling niece would succeed where you had failed?" Caro still said nothing, but her small white teeth were set against her lower lip, and her fingers fretted the frame of the embroidery hoop in her lap.

Gervase smiled broadly, but his eyes were cold. "Dear sister, how interesting you do make Town, to be sure. However, your amiable aim being achieved, you have no further need of my niece."

Lady Coldmeece bared her teeth in what was meant for a smile but more closely resembled the snarl of a trapped animal. "Take the brat, then, and welcome to her," she said ungraciously. "I don't see—" She broke off and rose to her feet. "Come, then."

The nursery was an old-fashioned room, set at the back of the house. Lady Charlotte Darwen, only issue of the late earl's marriage and just three years of age, looked up as the door opened.

"Nuncle!" she shrieked delightedly, tottering to the earl as fast as her chubby little legs would carry her. She clasped him about the knees of his exquisitely cut white buckskin breeches and burst into tears. The earl tousled her glossy dark brown curls an instant before lifting her into his arms. "Bad!" wailed the child.

"Darling!" began Caro sweetly, reaching out to her daughter, but further and louder shrieks forced her to desist. "It is only that she is tired," Caro explained distractedly. "The long ride up to Town, the ride—"

"Yes," the earl drawled, patting Charlotte's back soothingly, "I daresay. Perhaps you would be so good, madam, when in future you wish to indulge your maternal instincts, to do so with my knowledge. You do not look well when you are put out of countenance, you see," he added maliciously, "and I would prefer to see you at your best."

Caroline dropped him a curtsy, her eyes snapping sparks.

The earl bowed, not hampered in the least by the presence of the hiccupping child in his arms. "Oh, and one other thing," he said. "I am sure I need not tell you, but I expect the rigors of the Season will keep you far too busy to make any overtures to Lady Mulford or to any member of her household. In fact, I should not be surprised to find, should you overextend yourself by visiting them, that you had suddenly been taken most gravely ill and forced to repair to the country for an indefinite period of extreme quiet." There was no mistaking the meaning in his voice.

"As you wish," said Caro, curtsying again, and the earl turned on his heel and left the house.

Lady Charlotte recovered her spirits amazingly on the drive back to Coldmeece House, a circumstance attributable to Gervase telling her that both Mrs. Raxton and her favorite doll were within its walls. The earl alighted from his carriage at the front steps and walked into the house with Charlotte in his arms. He rather thought it would be the talk of fashionable London within the day, and wondered what use Caro would make of this escapade.

Augustus greeted him as he entered the house, and upon catching sight of the child, came closer, his eyebrows raised in interest.

"Hello, what's this?" he asked, inspecting Gervase's burden. "Picking up children off the street, Cousin?"

Charlotte, fascinated by the sight of this peculiar person in a dressing gown of more than oriental splendor, goggled at him round-eyed.

"This," Gervase said dryly, "is my niece, and your cousin, Augustus. But I forget, you were in Europe when she was born, and so were never properly introduced. Lady Charlotte, may I have the honor to present to you your second cousin, the Honorable Augustus Leslie Templeton.''

Augustus bowed low, with a great swoop of mandarin sleeves, and Lady Charlotte giggled and hid her face against the earl's neck. Unfortunately, Augustus was not so easily diverted.

''Caro and Edmund's daughter, eh?'' he said, walking around Gervase and staring until the earl began to feel like a public monument. ''Don't look much like Edmund, do she?''

Lady Charlotte tossed her dark curls and flirted her pansy brown eyes at Augustus.

''Don't look much like her mama, either. I *say*, Gervase . . .'' Augustus began, as an idea that had forcibly occurred to Gervase three years before took violent possession of him. ''I *say*—''

''Augustus,'' said the earl firmly, ''don't make an idiot of yourself.''

''But I say . . . But I say . . . But *surely* . . . All *I* can say is, it's a good job you were a girl, not an earl, wasn't it, your ladyship?''

Lady Charlotte decided she had had enough of this peripatetic lunatic.

''*Bad* man,'' she pronounced oracularly. ''Nasty man!''

Augustus drew back in affront. ''Well, I daresay you're a very nasty little girl, too!'' he said roundly.

''Oh, for heaven's sake, man,'' the earl muttered, but it was too late.

Charlotte stared one instant, round-eyed and speechless with shock, and then filled the air with shrieks. Augustus retreated in hasty disorder, and the earl sought out Mrs. Raxton to bestow Charlotte upon her. Mrs. Raxton's bustlings in search of hot bricks, hot milk, hot baths, and suitable nightdresses for the Lost Who Has Been Found, soon drove Gervase from his home and to his club, where he had hopes of finding both solitude and refreshment.

Chapter
FIVE

Lady Louisa sat in the bow window of Mulford House, watching the street. A passing tradesman's cart provided momentary diversion, and Louisa was glad to be distracted from her novel. Lady Mulford had gotten it from Hatchard's especially for her, but she found the writing unexciting and the plot dull. She glanced at the title page. *Mansfield Park*—well, she would know better than to read one of Miss Austen's books again. She had just set the rejected volume aside when a lumbering carriage turned up Curzon Street.

It was a large, old-fashioned traveling coach. There was a crest on the door panel, but the coach was so splashed with mud that the device was impossible to make out. And it was bound for Mulford House, for the carriage stopped before the steps and the coachman stepped down to open the carriage door.

Louisa flew on winged feet to the front door, ducking neatly under Royton's arm to open it just as the door knocker sounded. The caller was a short female, dressed in black and heavily veiled.

"Yes?" said Louisa.

"I—is this Mulford House? I am expected."

"This is Mulford House," conceded Louisa. "What are you expected to do?"

"Do? I . . . that is to say . . . Excuse me, please, but may I speak to Lady Mulford, or to Lady Louisa Darwen?"

"But of course you may!" said Louisa, as the light be-

57

gan to dawn. "I am Lady Louisa, and *you* must be poor dear little Celia! But we weren't expecting you for *days*— whatever are you doing *here*? Come in—Aunt Josephine is out right now, but we shall have tea. And let me take your bonnet."

Louisa pulled her inside. "Royton will see to your trunks. How wonderful that you are here at last; I was getting dreadfully bored, and now there will be someone to share the Season with!" Louisa ruthlessly removed Celia's black bonnet and attendant veiling and turned back to take a good look at her new cousin. What she saw quite literally took her breath away. Well, I said Lady Celia would make me look all no-how, and I was *right*, was her resigned—and envious—thought.

Lady Celia Darwen-Neville was seventeen years old and an heiress of considerable fortune. In addition to these assets, a playful Providence had seen fit to invest her also with flawless skin of roses and cream, sky blue eyes fringed with long dark lashes, thick silver-gilt curls, a rosebud mouth, and a kitten face of almost unbearable sweetness. She was small, her head barely reaching Louisa's shoulder, but she was every inch a "Stunner," as Augustus would say, and if she did not capture every heart in the Marriage Mart, well, then Louisa was no judge.

"Oh, my," said Louisa, quite inadequately.

"I—I am sorry to be so beforehand," Celia said shyly, looking down and turning pink. "I hope I am not in the way, but Miss Pymm—my governess—was to take up a new position here in London, so I thought perhaps you would not mind . . ." Her voice trailed off, and she stood worrying at a large, black-bordered handkerchief.

"Not at all!" Louisa said cheerfully. She had not understood one word of Celia's explanation, but she would leave small matters of that nature to Lady Mulford. "But you must be dreadfully tired from your journey. Your room has been ready for days—it's right next to mine. We could take our tea there, unless you feel you should like to lie down for a while first?"

"Oh, no," Celia said. "We were only on the road a

few hours this morning. But I should be glad of a chance to wash up, Lady Louisa.''

"If we are to be sharing a London Season, you must call me Louisa, and I shall call you Celia," Louisa said firmly. "And I am sure we shall have a splendid time!"

The two young ladies repaired to Celia's room, and Celia busied herself unpacking the two large trunks she had brought with her. Even in her sadly outmoded black dress, she was every bit as flawless as she had first appeared.

"I thought as much," said Louisa darkly. "My very dear cousin, was it *quite* necessary for you to be so *very* beautiful?"

Celia looked at her in surprise, her blue eyes very round. "B-beautiful? I?" she stammered, looking stunned by the concept.

"Why, of course, you," Louisa said. "For the love of Allah, child, haven't you ever looked into a mirror?"

"Yes," said Celia in gloomy tones. "But one should do so only to ensure personal tidiness, and not for purposes of vanity and wasteful considerations of one's appearance. What is 'allah,' Lady Louisa?"

"Oh, just an expression," said Louisa hastily, belatedly recalling her promises to her aunt. "But never mind that now. And you are to call me Louisa, remember. Good heavens, child, do stop worrying at those trunks, one of the maids will do that. I take it you haven't brought your maid with you?" As she spoke, Louisa was trying to peer around Celia, the better to see the contents of her trunks. It seemed that every single item Celia had unpacked, with the possible exception of nightdresses, was black. This struck Louisa as a very odd wardrobe for a schoolroom miss about to enter on her first Season.

"Oh, no. I have no maid; Papa thought it was foolishness and unnecessary luxury, and that a woman should be able to dress herself without assistance."

"Oh," Louisa said. "Well, I suppose you will find us all very foolish here, but your papa could not disapprove of your being turned out in a fashionable style, could he?"

An irrepressible dimple peeped out at the corner of Celia's mouth as she answered, "Yes!" Then she resumed her expression of gravity. "What I mean is, with no disrespect to you, or to Lady Mulford, or to the Earl of Coldmeece, who stands as my guardian—"

"The abominable earl," Louisa broke in, "has not yet stood for as much as he is going to. But Celia, where are the rest of your things? Were some of your trunks lost? Everything here is black!"

"Yes," said Celia. "I am in mourning for my papa."

"But—forgive me, Celia—did not your papa die two years ago?"

"Two and a half," pronounced Lady Celia. "But Miss Pymm said that nothing was so shocking as a want of family feeling in a young girl, and we did not like to apply to Mr. Tudball for the money to have other gowns made when these were perfectly serviceable."

At this, Celia looked so woebegone that Louisa jumped up from where she had been sitting and hugged her tightly. Celia squeaked in startlement.

"Well, they are *not* perfectly serviceable," Louisa announced vigorously. "And two years is more than enough time to put off your black. This is to be your come-out, and you must have dresses, and fans, and slippers, and shawls—a whole wardrobe. Oh, Aunt Josephine will be ecstatic—she adores dressing people—and you must come along at once to see what *I* have that Rigsby can make over for you by tomorrow, for what you have isn't even fit to go to Madame Francine's in, and that's the truth with no bark on it."

"Oh, *thank* you, Louisa!" said Celia, her eyes sparkling with tears of happiness. "I *knew* I should be happy here!"

Lady Mulford was just as shocked and indignant as Louisa had prophesied by the dreadful state of Celia's wardrobe. It was incredible that so rich an heiress as Lady Celia Darwen-Neville should have lived in such shocking poverty, but the late Earl of Orleton had been an airdreamer with nip-cheese habits, and matters had not improved much under Miss Pymm's wardenship.

Thus there was a second hurried visit in as many weeks

to Madame Francine's, for the ordering of another complete wardrobe.

"This is Lady Celia Darwen-Neville, a young cousin of mine," Lady Mulford announced. "She will be making her come-out this Season, and she will require a full wardrobe at once. In particular, she must have a ball gown for her come-out ball at Lord Coldmeece's in three weeks."

"Very good," Madame said briskly. "Now, if Lady Celia would care to look over these pattern books, I'll have Brigit bring out Lady Louisa's gowns."

Three quarters of an hour later, Celia sat dolefully in front of a table piled high with pattern books and swatches. Lady Mulford was in a prime dither, and Madame Francine looked extremely grim.

"Oh!" said Celia, looking at the pattern books as though they were a pile of serpents. "But they are all so wasteful—and that balldress! The *ankles* are exposed! Dear Lady Mulford, I am persuaded *you* could not wish me to wear such a garment."

"But, Celia," said Louisa rallyingly, coming to her beleaguered aunt's rescue, "I have *told* you we are all frivolous here in London. You will just have to accustom yourself to our ways, for if your papa did not wish that, he would hardly have left you to the Earl of Coldmeece, now, would he?" Louisa finished reasonably.

Lady Mulford stared at her. "Now, Louisa," she began, "I am not perfectly certain that—"

"Oh, Louisa!" cried Celia, moving aside on the bench to make room for her cousin, "I shall *try* to be good, but there are so *many* dresses! I cannot choose!"

"Take them all, then," Louisa suggested.

Celia's cerulean eyes widened in horror. "I could not do that! Dear Louisa, only *think* what a shocking extravagance it would be!"

"And," added Lady Mulford helpfully, "some of them would be *sure* not to become you, Celia dear."

Louisa patted Celia's shoulder comfortingly and considered the matter. *She* was perfectly willing to spend Celia's money and choose her wardrobe for her, but she was not quite certain of her ability to turn Celia out in the first style of English elegance.

It was at this pass that Providence itself came to her rescue.

"Good afternoon, ladies. I saw your carriage standing in the street and hoped I would find you here," drawled a charming masculine voice behind them.

"Gussie!" Louisa leapt to her feet, a smile of relief lighting her face. Ignoring Lady Mulford's minatory frown, she held out her hands in welcome. "Oh, thank heavens you are here. We are in the most dreadful muddle, and you are just the one to solve it."

Augustus swept forward, possessed himself of her hands and kissed them, then turned an inquiring glance on Celia, brows raised. Taking the hint, Louisa said, "Gussie, this is little Celia. Celia, this is your cousin Augustus—you mustn't mind him in the least."

"I am charmed, Lady Celia," Augustus said gallantly, as Celia murmured something inaudible. "But as our rag-mannered cousin Louisa neglected to inform you, I am a Templeton by birth, and a Darwen only in the smallest way."

"His mother, you are to understand," Louisa said, "was Lady Euphemia Darwen—only the merest connection."

"And in what fashion, fair damsel, may I aid you—for on seeing you, glorious flowering of a venerable tree, I publish myself ready to fling my life at your feet!"

Celia began to look seriously alarmed, and Lady Mulford made disapproving noises. Louisa said tartly, "Oh, for heaven's sake, Gussie, cut line! It is only that I thought you might be useful in dressing Celia, for her wardrobe is in as sad a state as mine once was."

"Oh, Louisa," gasped Celia hurriedly, "I am sure that Cousin Augustus would know nothing about the dress of females!"

Louisa and Augustus's gazes locked over Celia's head with identical expressions of amusement. What Augustus did not know about turning out a female in the first style of elegance was not worth the knowing.

"You may be right, Lady Celia," said Augustus, "but I flatter myself I may be a little more accustomed to Town modes than you, and if I might offer a few poor and humble suggestions . . ."

Louisa got to her feet to make room for Augustus on the bench, and he soon had Celia's wardrobe well in hand. Matters were all but settled when he rose to take his leave, and Lady Mulford decided that they, too, would go; it had been a longer morning than she had anticipated, and Celia could come back to be fitted after luncheon.

They had just reached the door when sounds of equine displeasure reached them from outside. "Oh, Lord!" Augustus muttered.

He had been riding Prometheus when he chanced to stop at Madame Francine's, and the great bay stallion had taken exception to the urchin Augustus had paid to hold him. Augustus rushed to Prometheus's head and was putting his excitable mount into a better temper as the ladies came down the steps.

"Oh, what a *beautiful* animal!"

Louisa turned, startled by the first real warmth she had heard in Celia's voice, but her cousin had slipped under her arm and was standing at a respectful distance, gazing adoringly at Augustus's fiery steed.

"Oh, Cousin Augustus, he is the dearest thing!" said Celia, and then embarked on a glowing panegyric in which encomiums on the length of Prometheus's back, the depth of his chest, the soundness of his bone, the smoothness of his limbs, became quite tangled with observations on Augustus's great good sense in possessing such a wonderful beast. Celia's passion, it appeared, was for horses, and upon learning that Augustus's father bred horses and that this magnificent animal before her was a product of the Templeton family avocation, her admiration passed all bounds, until Lady Mulford intervened.

"Yes, dear, and I am sure that is all very well, Celia, but you must not forget, we have a great many things to do today, and you must not be keeping Mr. Templeton standing in the street."

"No," said Celia, reaching up to stroke Prometheus's

satiny nose, while Augustus firmly held the stallion's head down to permit it. "I know I must not. But, oh, he *is* a bang-up piece of blood and bone!"

Louisa gave an unladylike snort of laughter. "Celia! Wherever did you pick up such a dreadful piece of slang?"

"Oh, dear," said Celia mournfully. "Miss Pymm always said I was the greatest mortification to her, and that I should not spend so much time in the stables. She said it had an unfortunate coarsening effect on the character."

"Now, I say!" began Augustus indignantly. He was distracted by Louisa's barely suppressed giggle. "Well," he began again, "why don't you come for a turn in the Park with me tomorrow, Cousin Celia? Did you bring your horses up to Town with you?"

"Oh, no. The stable was sold after Papa died, and—"

"Well," said Louisa practically, "I'm sure Cousin Gervase—"

"Will find something in his stables to suit you, Celia," Lady Mulford interrupted loudly, causing everyone to stare at her. "At any rate, I am sure I have no objection to your going riding tomorrow, providing we finish all our errands today."

With this stern reminder, Lady Mulford shepherded her charges into the waiting carriage and bore her young relatives off home to luncheon.

The morning's ride was not a success. The gentle lady's hack provided by Coldmeece for her use was not at all to Celia's taste, and was roundly castigated at sight by Augustus as "a slug." When Louisa later came down to join them in the morning parlor, she found the two of them hotly discussing horses.

"But spirit is the most important thing of all in an animal, surely," Celia protested.

"It don't signify if the beast's forever throwing out a splint! Oh, hello, Louisa. I say, don't you think I ought to have m'father send Oriflamme up from the farm for Celia? That Buttercup Coldmeece sent don't suit her above half."

"Not if Oriflamme's the mare you told me about who likes to go *through* fences and had the vicar off in the duck pond at Temple Down," answered Louisa, and Celia giggled.

"Well," said Augustus, affronted, "but the vicar hadn't any seat! You've just got to cram her at the fences; she'll go over."

"*I*," said Louisa, "am not likely to do any such thing. She may go *under* the fences if she likes, for all of me." The other two promptly ignored her and her heretical opinions on matters equine and equestrian, and continued to wrangle companionably.

It was some minutes later before her attention was again summoned, this time by a note of anxiety in Celia's voice.

"Oh, but it will never do!" Celia was saying. "I knew about the ball, of course, but I never thought—I cannot possibly dance!"

"Not dance?" chorused Augustus and Louisa, both staring at her.

"Why not?" continued Augustus.

"Oh, Celia, don't tell me Papa did not approve of that as well?" said Louisa.

Celia raised her chin defiantly. "I do not see that dancing is any particular accomplishment. Surely it is not necessary to one's social success. Persons of refined character would never judge one on one's ability to dance," she added firmly.

"Can't dance," said Augustus knowledgeably.

Louisa sighed. "What could the man have been thinking of, Gussie-my-angel? If this is an example of vaunted English foresight, then . . . Well!" She cut glances with Augustus, and a sly smile tugged at the corner of her mouth. "You've only three weeks, my love. Do you think you can contrive?"

Augustus grinned back. "If I could teach you to dance in two days, my cow-footed *houri*, I can certainly contrive."

"*Cow-footed*—" began Louisa wrathfully, but Celia was looking at both of them in dread.

"What will you contrive?" she demanded uneasily. "Oh, I knew I should not have allowed myself to be seduced by worldly vanities! I shall have to tell the Earl of

65

Coldmeece that a ball is quite impossible, and—and I shall not attend.''

"What?'' said Louisa, "and deny us the incredible felicity of seeing him when he must stand up with you at the ball? Never say so, Celia!''

"Instead," said Augustus, "you shall learn to dance, and no one shall ever know you were not born to it.''

"But—but—but—'' stammered Celia, "I am in mourning for my papa!''

"I am sure,'' said Louisa virtuously, "that your papa would have wished you to acquit yourself favorably.'' She rose to her feet and went over to uncover the pianoforte.

And so it was that Lady Mulford, on returning to the household at two of the afternoon, found Celia whirling about the drawing room in Augustus's arms, while Louisa accompanied the dancers with great enthusiasm and no particular skill upon the pianoforte.

"And oh, Lady Mulford,'' said Celia, turning to her with flushed face and radiant expression, "while Papa did not exactly disapprove of dancing as a form of exercise, he did caution me most sternly against it—and he was right! Such excercise *does* lead to lascivious thoughts!''

Louisa and Augustus had collapsed in laughter, while Lady Mulford had recourse to her vinaigrette. Later, when Louisa and Augustus had stolen a few moments alone together in the front hall, Louisa said, "I don't mean to speak ill of anyone's family, I'm sure, Gussie, but Celia's papa sounds like the world's chilliest prig!''

"Well, that he may very well have been, but it don't signify now, do it? Once Celia's on the town, she'll forget all her papa's crack-brained notions and deal extremely. You'll see.''

"I suppose so,'' said Louisa doubtfully. "And, oh, Gussie, I wish I may be there when she meets her future husband, the earl, and proses on at him about his luxurious frivolity!''

"She won't be able to do that for a fortnight,'' said Augustus. "He was called down to Coldmere, and won't be back until April tenth. Besides, Coz, you're being too hard on Celia; she don't prose on at people." Louisa raised her brows, but Augustus took no heed of this silent comment. "It's only that she's been buried in the country for ever so," he went on. "Celia's a trooper. She'll outshine them all once she knows what she's about."

Here Louisa was able to agree wholeheartedly. "She *is* a little beauty, isn't she," she said, and grinned at him. "Do you know, Gussie, if the Darwens ever wanted to make amends to the Sultan for their scaley behavior, they should send him Celia. She'd be a gift that would turn anyone up sweet."

"Louisa!" Augustus apparently failed to see either the sense or the humor in this suggestion. "For heaven's sake, Coz, mind your tongue, will you? I mean, *I* know you don't mean anything by it"—a statement Augustus's stern expression flatly contradicted—"but other people wouldn't."

"Well, I'm hardly likely to be saying it to other people, now, am I?"

"The fact is, Lou, there's never any telling *what* you'll say!" said Augustus. "Just don't say it to anyone but me, that's all I ask."

Louisa glared at him. *"Don't* call me 'Lou'!" she snapped. "Have you any other instructions for your humble slave, O lord and master?"

"As a matter of fact," said Augustus cheerfully, "I have. Stop talking about sultans, stop using those scaley slang expressions, and stop glowering at me like that, Amber Pearl. You'll give yourself nasty lines."

"Ho!" said Louisa. "I shall give myself as many lines as I like."

"Not if you're to marry me, you won't," said Augustus, reaching out to tug at one of her braids. "I don't like 'em."

Louisa hated leaving Augustus with the last word in an argument, but this opening was too convenient to ignore. "And speaking of marrying, Gussie-my-love . . ."

"Ah, I'm back in favor, I see," said Augustus, giving her braid another tweak.

"You are *not*, and if you pull down my hair Aunt will

have a *spasm*," said Louisa primly. "As I was saying, speaking of marriage, Gussie, don't you think we ought to warn Celia about *her* betrothal? Everyone knows—you, me, Aunt Josephine, even Madame Francine hinted at it. And I'm certain Caro knows. Ought we tell?"

Augustus frowned. "Gervase said he didn't want me spreadin' it about. . . . Dash it, Louisa, *I* haven't a clue, I'm sure. Why don't we wait until Gervase gets back from Coldmere?"

"Mm," said Louisa noncommittally. "We'll see, Gussie. Will you visit us tomorrow?"

Augustus laughed. "Try to keep me away! I may have taught *you* to waltz overnight, but our cousin Celia wants far more schooling." With that, he dropped a light kiss on Louisa's brow and took his leave.

Louisa walked slowly back to join Celia and Lady Mulford in the parlor. She was sure it was not right to leave Celia in happy ignorance of her impending marriage to Coldmeece—and how dare Gussie prose on at her in that puritanical fashion? Really, there was nothing to choose between him and Celia's papa! Louisa frowned harder, lines or no. This London Season was proving more complicated than expected.

"Aunt, do you seriously mean to tell me that even though Cousin Coldmeece did not have the courtesy to ask you to hostess his ball, he is still asking you to do all the work?" Louisa paused with the toast point halfway to her mouth, staring at her aunt. Lady Celia was absent from the breakfast table, having risen at what Louisa regarded as an appallingly early hour and gone for a canter on the much maligned Buttercup.

Lady Mulford smiled at her affronted niece. "Of course, darling—how could he possibly arrange anything from Coldmere? You *know* how inconveniently placed it is, though I'm certain the family had no idea of it when it was built, of course, as that was ever so long ago. And of *course* poor Gervase didn't dare have Caroline arrange matters—why, Coldmeece House would be all over wax lights and silk festoons and hothouse flowers and French wine in the *most* ineligible fashion before the cat could lick her ear! You mustn't mind for me, darling, I haven't had so much fun in years.''

"Well, I still think it's infamous!" Louisa said. "Here we are with Celia to turn out—that prosing papa of hers is the outside of enough, Aunt—and—''

"Louisa!" said Lady Mulford in automatic reproof.

"Well, I do!" Louisa repeated stubbornly. "He sounds the most complete rotter, you know. I have noticed, if you have not, that all of Lord Orleton's vaunted economical notions seem to have centered on *Celia.* He certainly did not stint on himself, from all she says, although poor Celia's too sweetly stupid to realize it. Why, what his horses alone must have cost, and Celia with hardly a gown to her back—and all of them *ugly*!''

"Oh, dear," said Lady Mulford. "Now, Louisa, even if you are right, and I daresay Lord Orleton, poor man, simply didn't know how to go on—a mother's touch is *so* important to a girl, after all—but you should not *say* so. One must not," she continued firmly, "speak ill of the dead.''

"Why not?" said Louisa. "It's Orelton's fault that you must transform his daughter in less than a month, and Coldmeece's that you've a whole ball to arrange in the same time.''

"Perhaps," said Lady Mulford consideringly. "And you are right, my love. Scant three weeks *is* barely enough time. I am *so* glad I was able to engage Madame Francine and Belvoir before word got out—already not a modiste or coiffeur in Town is free.''

Louisa darted a suspicious glance at her aunt. "No," she said flatly. "I will not let my hair be chopped and primped and hardly used.''

"But my dear, Belvoir is coming today for Celia. He is the most talented hairdresser—''

"Oh, Aunt Josephine, Celia is not cutting all that beautiful hair?" Louisa demanded in horror.

"Not everyone is as old-fashioned as you are, miss! Celia will look charmingly, quite in the latest style.''

Louisa sighed over the loss of her cousin's glossy silver-gilt mane, but realized it was futile to object. "Let him make a head for you, Aunt, and Celia will no doubt look charmingly in a crop, but I am well content as I am. We cut my hair once, and I vowed then—never again!"

"Well, then, my love, you may do with your hair as you wish. But what of your dress? I had forgotten you had not ordered a balldress from Madame Francine, until she reminded me yesterday."

Louisa made a wry face. "As if the woman needed more business, and at this time. Fear not, dearest and darlingest of aunts, I have my ball gown well in hand."

"Louisa," said Lady Mulford with foreboding, "you are up to something."

"I, Aunt?" Louisa said piously. "Perish the thought!"

"Oh-h-h!" breathed Celia in awe some time later.

Louisa went over to where Celia was still gazing at her reflection in the mirror. For the coiffeur's attentions, Celia had been swathed in a pearl green robe of tabby silk with a cream Vandyke collar in seven tiers, a gift to her from Louisa's wardrobe. That, along with her new hairstyle, made her look totally unlike herself.

"Augustus will never recognize you," Louisa said admiringly. "Oh, Celia, how you *will* outshine me at the ball—and everyone else, for that matter!"

Celia turned to face her anxiously. "Will I? Will—will you mind, Louisa? Lady Mulford has told me that you were to have a Season by yourself, before the earl prevailed upon her to take me as well on account of the poor dowager countess's delicate state of health, and now I am here to ruin everything for you."

"Ruin everything?" scoffed Louisa. "Never that, Celia. I was bored to tears until you came, and since you can hardly dance every waltz with Gussie, you couldn't possibly ruin the ball for me, so put such idiotish thoughts out of your head."

"Oh, he is very kind, is he not, Louisa?" Celia said. "Mr. Templeton, I mean to say. He is taking such pains for me that people will think I have been upon the town all my life, not less than a month,"

It was on the tip of Louisa's tongue to say that Augustus could hardly do any less for his cousin's wife-to-be, but she sternly restrained herself.

"But even kinder, I think, must be Lord Coldmeece," went on Celia happily. "For he, you know, has never even met me, and I am sure I must be a shocking charge on him. Even if he *is* one of my trustees, and in some sense obligated, I think it very kindly of him to go to all this trouble for me. Have *you* ever met him, Louisa?"

"Yes, I have," she managed to say at last, "and I think I must tell you, Celia, that I have reason to believe the earl's motives are not so disinterested as you think."

Celia looked at her with wide-eyed interest. "Why, whatever do you mean? What sort of a man is he, then?"

"Well, he—he is well enough, I suppose," Louisa said, hastily seeking something innocuous to say that would still satisfy Celia. "As far as his character, the earl has a sound mind, I fancy, and—oh, everything that goes with fortune, I daresay. Pray excuse me!" She shot to her feet and rushed from the room, leaving Celia staring after her in confusion.

Louisa pounced upon Lady Mulford as soon as she found her and virtually dragged her unsuspecting aunt into the front parlor.

"Oh, Aunt Josephine!" she wailed. "That infamous man! How can you bear to deceive Celia so?"

"Infamous man?" said Lady Mulford. "Deceive Celia? Why, Louisa, do sit down and explain yourself."

Louisa flounced loose-limbed into a chair and gazed fixedly at her aunt. "All the town suspects, and half of it knows, that Celia is to marry Coldmeece, but *she* remains in ignorance! She has just been telling me how *good* he must be, to be giving her this Season out of the purest disinterested kindness, and I could not *bear* it! Celia has had no life of her own, and now to be sold like a horse at auction—"

"*Louisa Darwen!*" gasped her aunt. "I'm certain Gervase has no such plan in mind! *Selling* . . . Oh, dear, such *language*—" Lady Mulford composed herself with an effort. "I am sure you do not mean to imply such things of

71

your cousin, Louisa. I am certain he has the very best of intentions towards Celia.''

"If that is the case," said Louisa, pouncing, "then she might, perhaps, be told what half of England already knows—that she is to be married out of hand to Cold-meece—don't you think? Or must she be left to discover it from the coachman?''

"Now, Louisa, I am certain Gervase has matters well in hand, and would not thank us for meddling with him—''

"No more he would," muttered a rebellious Louisa.

"—and as soon as he returns from Coldmere I shall ask him when he intends to declare himself to Celia. Now, darling, do run along. Augustus will be here soon and I have a thousand things to do." Lady Mulford kissed her seething niece's cheek and bustled off.

Louisa sat in the parlor a while longer. Lord Orleton had obviously had no more sense than had her own late papa, and his daughter had not had the benefits of Louisa's own upbringing. Yes, Lady Celia was obviously in need of protection.

Louisa had not yet decided what form this necessary protection should take, when Augustus arrived for Celia's dancing lesson. His eyes widened in surprise as he beheld Celia, then he made her a sweeping bow.

"Fair goddess!" he exclaimed. "Never have I seen you look so radiant!"

"Oh," said Celia awkwardly. "It is only a new way of dressing my hair, Mr. Templeton. Do not refine upon it so!''

"Your lightest wish, goddess," said Augustus piously, "is my command. But do you not think, Cousin Celia, that since Louisa has made me free of your name, you might presume to address me by mine? I am only a cousin, you know, a poor wretched thing, and certainly not worth taking pains over.''

Celia blushed. "Very well, Augustus. If you wish it."

At the end of half an hour's exertions, both dancers

were ready to call a halt. The three sipped lemonade in a peace that was shattered by a question from Celia.

"Augustus, is it true that Coldmeece has had me brought to Town to make away with my fortune?" Celia said artlessly.

Augustus, who had been gingerly essaying a glass of the lemonade, choked violently.

As he was recovering himself, Celia turned her pellucid gaze on Louisa. "*Is* it true, Cousin Louisa? I know you will tell me the truth, for I know that yours is too noble a spirit to bear the thought of deception."

"*Is* it?" said Augustus, enraptured by this view of Louisa's character. "Celia, wherever did you get a woolly-pated notion like that—about Coldmeece, not Louisa. Coldmeece ain't after your blunt!"

"Oh," said Celia doubtfully. "I had thought perhaps he had impoverished my estate through his guardianship, and that was why he had set me upon the town—so that I might find a suitable husband before my ruination became known."

"Where did you get a crack-brained notion like that?" Augustus thundered, glaring suspiciously at Louisa, who shook her head.

Celia raised her chin and regarded Augustus with haughty superiority. "I am not so green as you suppose, Augustus. It has been borne in upon me that the earl's behavior toward me is the mark of a signal condescension that cannot be explained merely by familial ties." She looked at Louisa and blushed. "Forgive me, Louisa, I do not wish to betray a confidence, but when you hinted that the earl must not be disinterested in my case . . . Everyone has been looking at me as if I were a prize bloodstock mare since I came to Town, and I do not understand it."

"It is very simple," said Louisa calmly, before Augustus could protest. "Your father betrothed you in your cradle to the earl of Coldmeece, and now the earl means to honor the bargain and marry you. It was meant to be a secret for a while longer, but I don't see why you should not know."

Augustus sighed in resignation to the inevitable and took

73

Celia's hand. "That's the truth, Cousin. But really, Gervase ain't after your money—fact is, he's got plenty of his own." Feeling that he had now settled any possible misunderstanding, Augustus patted Celia's hand, and sat back, looking pleased with himself.

Celia withdrew her hand, staring at him. "But—but why did no one *tell* me?"

Louisa, who had wondered the same thing herself, kindly tried to put what she felt would be the most charitable interpretation on it. "Perhaps Coldmeece wished to tell you himself, Celia. He was called away unexpectedly. Perhaps he wished it to be a surprise." This seemed a singularly inadequate argument even to Louisa, but it was the best she could do.

Spots of angry temper flared in Celia's cheeks. "Well, it *is* a surprise! Oh! And I do not *like* it! To—to *lure* me to London under the pretexts of friendship, only to bait a trap for me in this *odious* fashion! And to force you—my *dear* friends—to connive with him! He might at least have mentioned it when he sent for me—and now I have sent Pymm away, and there will be no one to care for me, and I think he must be most abominably arrogant!"

"Yes," said Louisa, moved to sympathy. "He tried to have me drowned once, you know."

"Yes!" said Celia stormily. "That is just the sort of thing he *would* do!"

"Louisa!" said Augustus sharply. "There's no call to be telling Celia all sorts of nonsense! Coldmeece never wanted to drown you—though I wouldn't be surprised if someone didn't, one of these days."

"I must leave at once!" declared Celia. "Oh, whatever can I say to Lady Mulford? She has been all kindness. But to stay under her roof one moment longer as a party to deception—no, that I cannot do!"

"Drowned," said Louisa hollowly, to show Augustus he could not dictate to *her*. She was quite surprised at Celia's unexpected flash of temper. This was no milk-and-water miss, to be sure. Yes, definitely the earl should meet dear little Celia. Augustus glared at her and Louisa glared right back.

"He is an abominable, dissipated *roué*!" announced Celia, just as Lady Mulford walked into the room.

"A *roué*, dear?" Lady Mulford said quaveringly. "Augustus?"

"No," said Celia, "the Earl of Coldmeece."

"Oh, *dear*!" gasped Lady Mulford, subsiding onto a sopha with her hand to her throat.

Hartshorn and water was called for and administered, and tempers were given a chance to cool while Lady Mulford was being revived.

"Now," said Lady Mulford, at last restored, "begin at the beginning, if you please."

Celia revealed how the abominable Earl of Coldmeece—"and truly I beg your pardon, Lady Mulford, for you have been kindness itself to me and he is your godson, but I am sure you have been grossly deceived!"—had lured her to London without telling her she was betrothed to him, and how his duplicity had rendered the polite world as dust and ashes—or perhaps gall and wormwood, Celia wasn't quite certain on this point—and that therefore, with no disrespect to her hostess, she wished to return to Thornage Hall at once. She then remained regretfully adamant for three quarters of an hour against their combined entreaties that she remain, until Lady Mulford shot the telling bolt.

"But Celia, darling," she said tragically, "it was your father's wish that you and Gervase be married! Why, *he*— Gervase, that is, you know, dearest—was only a boy at the time, and not conniving at all!"

"Oh!" Celia gulped. She stopped looking defiant and looked miserable.

"But you needn't regard that," Augustus reassured her bracingly. Louisa kicked him sharply on the ankle. "What I mean is—" he began.

"What he means is," said Louisa firmly, "that even the sternest of fathers and the most abominable and dissipated of *roués* would not try to force you to do anything you did not particularly wish. I am certain your papa only wanted you to be happy."

"Do you think so?" said Celia, who did not look in the least convinced of this. "Oh, Louisa, truly?"

"What *I* think," said Lady Mulford decisively, "is that there has been quite enough rumpus for one day. And at any rate, Celia, you can make no decision until after the ball."

This fiat having been delivered, Lady Mulford bore Celia off with her to drink a soothing draught and lie down for a while.

"My," said Louisa inadequately, when she and Augustus were alone, "that *has* let the cat well out of the bag, hasn't it? I was sure Celia was set to post home to Dreadfulshire immediately."

"Yorkshire," Augustus informed her absently. "Really, Louisa, whatever possessed you to be telling her crackbrained tales about Coldmeece trying to murder you? I thought you had a *little* common sense, at least."

"Oh, certainly as much as *you* do, telling her she mustn't regard her papa's wishes! If she weren't regarding her papa's wishes, she'd have gone off to Thornage at once! I think it was ever so clever of Aunt Josephine to mention that."

"Well, if you wanted her to marry Gervase anyway, why didn't you just keep mum about the whole thing?" Augustus demanded. "If *you* hadn't taken to dropping mysterious hints—"

"*I?* Wish her to marry the odious earl?" Louisa blinked at him in surprise. "Don't be silly, Gussie!"

"Well she will, you know. Once she's got a maggot into her head that that's what her sainted papa of sacred memory wants, that's what she'll do, and nothing will stop her."

"Oh, yes it will!" said Louisa, taking up the challenge. "She won't marry the earl, and she won't go for a spinster buried in the country. We'll just have to bring her to see that Coldmeece *deserves* to be refused—I'm sure it will have a salutary effect upon his character."

The cousins grinned wickedly at each other, in charity once more. Louisa did not quite understand the cause of

Gussie's ill humor, but was glad he was his amiable self again.

He possessed himself of her hand and kissed it. "Sweet Cousin. The very pattern mold of virtue. Our noble cousin will rue the day he fell afoul of you!"

"Yes," said Louisa complacently. "Won't he just?"

Chapter
SIX

In the following fortnight, dresses came from the busy
needles at Madame Francine's in droves, and a most superior dresser, one Teale, was engaged for Celia and
Louisa. Teale had sniffed disapprovingly at the sight of
Louisa, but had taken Celia to her bosom like a hen with
one chick. Lady Mulford beamed, Celia quaked, and
Louisa fell back on the services of Campbell, an upper
housemaid.

In the matter of the measles, although Augustus had
initially been pleased to report that matters were on the
mend, his half brother Harry had come home on leave and
had managed to come out all over spots even though he'd
been billeted in the despised Dower House. Harry's condition was serious; he had been moved up to the main
house so Euphemia could nurse him, and it now looked
as if nothing would be seen of the Templetons in Town
until late in the Season, if at all.

On a slightly more cheerful note, though one equally
distressing to Augustus, Celia had been up on every horse
he could find to put at her disposal and none of them had
been to either Augustus's or Celia's taste.

Celia had been quite mournful for several days after her
impending marriage had been disclosed to her. Louisa and
Augustus strove mightily to convince her that she was perfectly free to refuse to marry the earl. Celia must not feel
that her father could expect her to marry any man whose
delicacy of character did not match her own, and who
knew what degenerations Gervase's character might not

have undergone in seventeen years? Celia conceded gravely that this was true, while Louisa was very hard put to keep a straight face through Augustus's reasonings. Louisa did not find London quite as horrible as she had expected. Still, she owned that she would be well pleased to forsake her so-called native shores for the comfortable warmth of a Russian palace. If only Augustus's wretched family would not keep coming out in spots!

Such halcyon conditions could not be expected to last forever; Gervase returned to London and decided it was really high time he met his bride-to-be. Accordingly, a riding party was arranged for the next morning.

The morning dawned mercifully clear. Louisa was still at her dressing, although Lord Coldmeece had arrived half an hour before and was closeted with Lady Mulford, and Celia and Gussie were undoubtedly out with the horses.

Lady Mulford had wished more particularly to speak with Gervase before he encountered Celia; when he had arrived, she had broken down and told all.

"Well, I suppose it was too much to hope to keep it secret until after the ball," said the earl resignedly. "Still, it is awkward. Drat the boy!"

"Oh, no," Lady Mulford protested. "Gussie has been *such* a help to me—he has turned out Lady Celia with the greatest credit to you. Really, Gervase, you make troubles out of nothing. If Celia does not think that *you* know *she* knows, she will not let you know, you see."

The earl put his hands to his head in mock protest. "Enough, Godmama! I don't think my poor head can encompass any more of your explanations. I shall deal with Lady Celia in my own good time. Now tell me, how is Lady Louisa getting on? Is London to her taste—and more to the point, has she an eligible *parti* in train?"

Lady Mulford sighed. "Oh, Gervase, I do not know *what* I am to do."

"Godmama, I've been thinking. I had thought at first I might put Lady Louisa in the way of an eligible match, but I have come to see that it will not do at all, so I had thought that perhaps the best thing to do would be to settle an income on her. The estate can easily afford it, and—"

"No! Never!" said Lady Mulford vehemently. The flat velvet box she had been nervously toying with came open in her hands, casting a spill of blue fire to the Turkey carpet. "I—oh, dear!"

Gervase stooped to retrieve the jewels—a necklace, a ring, and a pair of very fine bracelets, all of sapphires. He held the necklace up to the light. Stones of the first water, too; he could see the blue fires lurking in their depths, and knew they had come dear.

"You should have these put under lock," he said mildly, raising an interrogative eyebrow at Lady Mulford.

Lady Mulford faced him squarely. "Yes, and they will be, but they were delivered just this morning. They are a gift for Louisa, for her come-out."

Gervase replaced the jewels in the case, closed it, and handed it to her. "Your trustee will have a spasm when he receives *that* bill."

"Let him! Mulford's money is mine to dispose of so long as I am alive," she said defiantly.

"And so you are providing for Lady Louisa as best you may—her matrimonial prospects being dim. Why will you not allow me to do the same? I *am* head of the family, you know, and responsible for her, in a sense."

"And leave her your pensioner," Lady Mulford retorted hotly, "racketing about on the Continent, or moving from Darwen to Darwen here in England, with no true home of her own? Louisa is too shy for her own good, and if she does not feel that she *must* marry, I know she will leave it until it is far too late. No, Gervase, I am sorry, but I must absolutely forbid you to hand Louisa an income of her own."

The object of all this lucubration, serenely unaware that her future was being determined for her, opened the front door of Mulford House, took three steps down to the street, and froze, transfixed with horror.

Her dear Corsair was waiting patiently, and so was a big-boned, roman-nosed chestnut that she guessed to be the earl's. Augustus's flashy bay stallion Prometheus was also there, and Celia's saddle was on his back. A groom stood at the restless stallion's head, and Augustus was waiting to toss Celia into the saddle. Prometheus's ears flicked nervously, and his eye showed white.

Louisa turned and fled back into the house.

Gervase had just come out of the library; Louisa ran into him with a thud and clutched at his lapels for support.

"Come *quick*!" she gasped.

Louisa realized later that she lost her heart to the Earl of Coldmeece in that instant, for instead of asking why, or commenting on her dress, or, in short, doing any of the things Augustus would have done, he simply took her firmly by the arm and came.

When they arrived on the front step, Augustus had just settled Celia onto Prometheus's back; without seeming to hurry, Gervase released Louisa, strode over to the stallion, brushed past Augustus, and plucked Celia down from the saddle.

Gervase's first thought, on sight of her, had been that Augustus had run mad and was putting a small child up on his bay. When he had a better look at her, he realized who she must be, and was quietly appalled. Seventeen! The chit looked nothing of seventeen! She looked as though she oughtn't be out of leading strings yet. Was this his betrothed? This *child*?

She was, Gervase conceded, quite beautiful, in spite of her extreme youth. "Who are you, sir?" this enchanting vision demanded. "And what do you mean by this abominable mishandling of my person?"

Behind her Augustus reached out a minatory hand. "Ah, Celia—" he began.

Gervase smiled, struck by the absurdity of the situation. "I have the honor to be the Earl of Coldmeece, and I apprehend I am addressing Lady Celia Darwen-Neville?" He arched his eyebrows politely.

"Oh," said Celia, stricken. She blushed a fiery scarlet. "Oh, *no*."

Behind him, Gervase heard a gurgle of laughter, and

turned to frown in mock menace at an unrepentent Lady Louisa. Then he bent his attentions on his erring heir.

"Do be so good, Augustus, as to favor me with an explanation of why you were putting Lady Celia up on this horse."

"There's no call to be talking about Prometheus like that!" Augustus said, aggrieved. "I'd never have done it if there was the last danger, Gervase, you know that. Celia's a bruising rider, and that Buttercup just ain't up to her weight."

"Nevertheless," said the earl, "you will oblige me by having Lady Celia's saddle put back upon Buttercup, and reserving Prometheus's favors exclusively to yourself in future."

Augustus shrugged a bit sulkily. "Oh, very well," he said ungraciously, and led Prometheus off in the company of the groom.

The earl turned to his betrothed. "I am very sorry to have discomfited you, Lady Celia. Had I known you were experienced in the saddle, I would have taken care to provide a mount more to your liking."

"I am sure I could have ridden Prometheus, Lord Coldmeece," said Celia. The color surged and ebbed in her cheeks, and her stirring rejoinder lost much of its force, as it was delivered to the tips of her riding boots.

"Perhaps," said the earl. There was an uncomfortable silence, which was broken by Augustus's return. Augustus rather defiantly offered Lady Celia a hand up onto the despised Buttercup, and so the earl turned to assist Lady Louisa.

Now that he had the leisure to take note of her, he discovered that Louisa had chosen to ride today in a dashing plum and black costume liberally trimmed in fur and goldwork. Her sandy-fox hair was brushed neatly and sleekly back into its snood, and though the entire effect was strikingly un-English, it was not unbecoming. Gervase discovered that he had been quite looking forward to seeing his foreign cousin again—and if she did not blend in with all the other English misses in London, well, he supposed it had been a forlorn hope that her scandalous past would remain decently buried. At least this comic-opera costume of hers was as modest—if not as restrained—as anyone could wish.

"Ah," said the earl, looking pointedly at Louisa's sleepy little mare, "I see that you are a very centauress in the saddle—one of those neck-or-nothing riders, I have no doubt." He wondered if the animal would be able to summon up the energy for a canter.

"Not-at-all!" Louisa replied, in the self-deprecating tones of one who makes light of the obvious truth in a compliment. "I am competent in the saddle, no more. However, I *am* fond of horses, and enjoy a pleasant canter." Here she leaned forward to stroke her mount's satiny neck. Reaching into a pocket, she pulled out a small sugary square and offered it to the mare, who craned her head around to take it. Louisa then popped one of the sweetmeats into her own mouth.

"*Rahat lokum,*" she explained kindly to the earl. "Turkish delight. Corsair is fond of it and so am I; I've rather a sweet tooth, I'm afraid. What is your horse's name?"

"Champion," said the earl, as he gracefully swung up onto his chestnut gelding. Louisa produced another piece of Turkish delight and offered it to his horse on the flat of her gloved hand. Louisa scratched the chestnut's nose, then turned to the earl, who wondered in alarm if she were going to offer *him* a piece next.

Instead, she said, "I hope you will not be cross with Lady Celia, my lord—she is the most *timid* creature, and does not like anyone to be angry with her." Louisa bent upon the earl a look of soulful innocence.

"Yes," said the early dryly, "she does look it." He gathered up Champion's reins, and soon the little party was clattering down the street in the direction of the Park.

The earl gallantly attempted to make conversation with his betrothed, to which Lady Celia returned short, embarrassed answers. He and Augustus, with occasional assistance from Louisa, kept the conversation from foundering, but the earl was glad enough, when propriety permitted, to drop back and ride beside Lady Louisa. He supposed that anyone might shine as a conversationalist when compared with the mouse-mum Celia; still, it was a relief not to fear alarming one's companion with the most innocent of remarks.

"I fear, Cousin Louisa," he began, as he slowed Champion to ride beside her, "that I owe you an apology."

"An apology, Cousin Coldmeece?" said Louisa, brows arched.

"An apology," he repeated firmly. "I now feel it would have been a grave error to have had you drowned in the—what was that river?"

"The Bosphorus," Louisa informed him with a giggle. "And it is a strait, you know, between the Black Sea and the Sea of Marmara."

"Ah, yes," said the earl in mock sobriety. "You cannot conceive, Cousin, what a pleasure it is to converse with a female of your intellectual accomplishments—not to mention your literary tastes."

"Quite a rare treat, in fact?" suggested Louisa.

"But of course," he said, smiling at her. "And so, in atonement for my past murderous inclinations, I have arranged a rare treat for you, Cousin: Mrs. Edge*worth* will be more than pleased to pay Lady Mulford and Lady Louisa Darwen—and Lady Celia, too, of course—a morning visit on Thursday next."

"You what?" gasped Louisa, startling her mount.

"No, no, don't thank me," he went on smoothly, holding up a minatory hand. "It's just by way of an apology, you understand." Then he grinned at her, amused by the thunderstruck expression on her face. "And by the by, just in case you haven't read her novels, I'll have a set sent around to you tomorrow."

Louisa struggled with her emotions, lost, and laughed. "That, Cousin, is one of the most—most thoroughly fiendish things I've ever *heard* of!"

"One does one's poor best," murmured the earl. Then he grinned again, his gray-blue eyes glinting. "Tell me, Cousin, *have* you read any of the woman's wretched scribblings?"

Louisa choked down the last of her laughter and nodded. "How can you doubt it? I was *most* struck by the manner in which her heroine turned red and white at one and the same instant." She shook her head mournfully. "I have tried and *tried* to let my sensibilities so overcome me that I simultaneously flush and pale, but in vain. I have come to the regrettable conclusion that there is some secret knack to it." She considered this a moment. "Either that, or I lack the proper sensibilities, which seems a great deal more likely. But in any case," she went on, "you can see that such considerations quite distract one from the sense of the book."

"I am certain," said the earl, "that you have quite as many sensibilities as the occasion requires." He was pleased to find that his cousin wasn't the timid idiot she had seemed to be on their first meeting. She apparently possessed a ready tongue and a ready wit. Possibly a touch *too* ready, but certainly he should be able to hint her into a proper mode and then find her a husband. And *not* a country parson, he rather thought. He must somehow find her someone of a suitable rank and position in Society; it would be a great pity to lose touch with her after her marriage.

"Dare I ask," he went on, hoping for another of her diverting literary comments, "your opinions on the poetry of Byron?"

Louisa regarded him consideringly. As before, the sight of the earl aroused in her a nigh uncontrollable desire to reach through the so polite barrier of Frankish deference to the man beneath. But was it wise, when she wished to rob him of his affianced bride and elope with his heir? If he discovered either of these plans, Louisa felt he could only disapprove, and while she was fast coming to believe him far more attractive even than Augustus, she did not wish to care a fig for the earl's feelings.

"No," she said at length, "I rather think not. Another time, your lordship." Then, seeing how far they had fallen behind the others, she prudently cantered ahead to join them.

At length the party returned to Mulford House, where the ladies went upstairs to change before luncheon. No sooner had Louisa and Celia gained the seclusion of their rooms than Celia threw herself down on the bed.

"I cannot!" she wailed. "No! Not even for dear Papa's sake! Oh, it is too horrible!"

Louisa, alarmed, sat down beside her cousin.

"I cannot love a man named Coldmeece!" Celia tearfully declared. "Nor marry him, either! Oh, Louisa, was it not dreadful for you too? His forbidding glare, his hideous countenance—When he looked at me, I felt sure I would sink! And—and—and I do not believe he cares for horses overmuch!" she concluded, sniffing militantly.

"But Celia, darling," said Louisa, considerably startled by this description, "he didn't glare at you, indeed, he did not. Or if he did," she amended tactfully, to cater to all opinions in the matter, "I'm sure he did not mean it. He was doubtless only upset at seeing you on that impossible beast of Gussie's."

"Oh!" Celia wailed, fresh tears springing to her eyes. "I daresay he will forbid me to *ride*, now. It would be just like him. And—oh, Louisa!" she wept, flinging herself into Louisa's arms.

It was just like Celia, thought Louisa with exasperation, to look beautiful even while crying. Life, thought Louisa, who looked perfectly dreadful when *she* cried, was not fair. She sighed, and concentrated on consoling her unhappy cousin.

"Well," she said, "if you cannot like him, you need not marry him, you know. It is just as Augustus said, and undoubtedly your papa would not wish you to marry the earl if you have taken him in *particular* dislike."

"Oh, yes!" said Celia between hiccups. "It is my duty. And even if he is not *really* elderly, I just *know* he is a vile man!"

Louisa felt more partisanship for Coldmeece the more Celia refined upon his faults.

"Perhaps you are right," she temporized, "but as I have said, there is not the least need for you to refine upon it, as there is not the least need for you to marry him.

Poor darling! I am persuaded you must have the most shocking head—I will send Teale in to you.''

"Oh, Louisa," sighed Celia, "must you go?"

"I am afraid I must," said Louisa. "Someone must make suitable excuses."

"What *really* happened?" demanded Augustus the instant he had Louisa alone.

"I shall tell you that if you will favor me with his lordship's true opinion of his blushing bride. Oh, lord, Gussie—do you know we are to be honored by a visit from Maria Edgeworth Thursday next?"

"Gervase's doing, I'll wager. Well, it will serve you right to have to read all her books in a week."

"But I am not the least interested in the Irish Question!" wailed Louisa. "If anything, the Irish are more incomprehensible than the English, and their climate worse!"

Augustus laughed. "Always fair. Well, to be cruel, Gervase is as fond of Lady Celia as you are of the Irish. Oh, not that he don't care for the girl, but he thinks she's by far too young, and it's his opinion that his father, her father, and their solicitors were a prime collection of crackbrains, and he won't hold her to the agreement."

"Did he say so?" asked Louisa instantly.

"N-no . . ." admitted Augustus. "He was too busy giving all the reverend ancestors the rough side of his tongue. But that's the truth of the matter, I'll lay a monkey."

Louisa heaved a sigh of relief. "Oh, Gussie, I'm *so* glad! The poor little thing was in hysterics. 'Oh!' she said, 'I cannot love a man called Coldmeece—or marry one either!' '' Her impersonation failed to bring a smile to her cousin's face, however.

"Poor little thing," he repeated. "I say, Louisa—why don't you go on up and tell her she's got nothing to fear? I'd hate to think of her worrying. And I've got to be pushing off, anyway—there's a horse I want to have a look at."

"Thy slave, O caliph, is thine to command," said

Louisa in flawless Turkish, salaaming herself backward out of the room.

"Louisa!" began Augustus, laughing—but she was already gone.

Upon ascending to Celia's room Louisa found her little cousin sound asleep. Teale had coaxed her out of her riding dress and into a negligee, and she looked really absurdly young. Well, Louisa would save her glad tidings of earlish forbearance for later.

As things fell out, she never did tell Celia the earl's private opinion of his bride-to-be. The events of the next day drove the conversation with Augustus clean from her mind.

The following day saw Augustus once again at Mulford House for Lady Celia's dancing lesson. Celia preserved a clam-like silence on the subject of the Earl of Coldmeece, and perhaps his far from warm welcome, Louisa thought regretfully, would induce the earl never to visit again—a pity, that would be, as she was in the midst of refining a scheme to properly recompense him for that Maria Edgeworth business.

Augustus Templeton had been unconsciously dreading Celia's first meeting with Gervase, for he was well aware that there were a number of women who—inexplicably—preferred his cousin to himself, and he had cherished hopes that Celia would not be one of these unaccountable ladies. Since she had demonstrated yesterday that she most emphatically was not, Augustus felt that all the kingdoms of the earth had opened up before him.

The dancers were sitting down to elevenses in the little drawing room just as Royton was opening the front door on a caller. Royton might have mistaken him for Mr. Templeton himself, were the butler not perfectly aware that Mr. Templeton was already within.

On a second glance, however, the differences between the two men became obvious. Augustus was a little taller, the stranger was older, and his face was dark-tanned, as by strange excursions beneath faraway suns. His eyes were green to Augustus's blue, and a lock of hair fell unruly over his forehead. Yet, when all was said, the two men were more alike than not, and shared a strong family resemblance.

"Hello," said the stranger to Royton. "Is Lady Mulford at home? I've come to pay my respects—she should be expecting me."

The stranger produced his card to be sent up, and was soon rewarded by the appearance of Lady Mulford.

"Aunt Josephine!" he said.

Lady Mulford stopped short. " 'Aunt Josephine' ?" she echoed in bewilderment.

He bowed. "I am here at last—come all the way from America to pay my respects to the English branch of the family tree." At her look of confusion, he frowned. "But—did you not receive my letter? I sent it nearly two weeks ago! I am Kennard Upshaw, nephew, and very much at your service, dear lady."

At that hint Lady Mulford's brow cleared. "Kennard!" she cried, enveloping him in a lilac-scented lavender gauze embrace. "Of course! *How* is dear Sophronia? But whatever are you doing *here*, dearest boy! Come along—you must join us in the parlor."

In the little drawing room, Augustus had set himself to teasing Celia out of her mopes and was soon rewarded by the return of her peculiar prosing ebullience. Without him to take some of the burden of entertaining Celia from her shoulders, Louisa felt she would have gone mad in a week. Must Celia have such passionate opinions on everything under the sun? It was very awkward, especially now that Celia was driving herself to a fine fit of the vapors with her belief that her papa would have wished her to marry the abominable Earl of Coldmeece. Louisa was very tired of Celia's late papa.

Celia, serenely unaware of the concern she was causing both her cousins, was at that very moment occupied with the weighty matter of What Would Papa Wish? Ought she to marry the odious Earl of Coldmeece, a most forbidding person, who was well known to be a violent scoundrel and a monster of duplicity? Or ought she to do as her cousins urged and bestow her affections elsewhere? Here she stole a quick glance from beneath her lashes at Augustus and turned a becoming shade of pink. Fortunately, that gentleman appeared unaware of it.

It was at this pass that Lady Mulford returned.

"My dears," she said from the doorway, "I have the loveliest surprise for you! This is Mr. Kennard Upshaw, your cousin from America!"

Louisa and Augustus gazed at this unexpected addition to the family circle. It was left to Celia, staring just as hard, to voice the obvious. "Why," she exclaimed, "you look just like—" At a strangled gasp from Lady Mulford, Celia subsided, blushing.

Kennard smiled at her. "Anyone else, little cousin? Well, it's no wonder; I left war paint and feathers at home, you see."

To Louisa it looked very much as if Mr. Upshaw possessed a practiced charm and expected to enthrall his female relatives. She promptly determined to be unimpressed.

Recognizing the battle-light in Louisa's eye, Lady Mulford admonished them all to please consider themselves, made formal introductions, and rang for tea to be brought. Before long, all five were seated again, Mr. Upshaw with a glass of wine at his elbow. He did not seem in the least put out by the magnificence of his surroundings or the eager curiosity of his hosts.

"I must say," he began, sipping his sherry appreciatively, "this is the first piece of good fortune I've had in a fortnight. I hardly know how to apologize, Aunt Josephine, bargin' in on you like that—I was certain you'd gotten my letter—Mama had entrusted me with letters for Aunt Euphemia and Uncle Augustus—and yourself, of course—but I'm afraid they were lost with my trunks. I'm told it was the greatest luck my finding you in London at all. The tattle is that you've become a great traveler."

It was then necessary to commiserate with Mr. Upshaw on the loss of his luggage in a stupid accident at sea; to explain to him that his Uncle Augustus had passed on some

90

years before; to discuss in exhaustive detail the events surrounding the devolution of the earldom of Coldmeece upon his late Uncle Augustus's younger son, Gervase. Lady Mulford then inquired after news of her sister, relating her history for the benefit of the younger generation.

"Not to make too long a tale of it, dearests, years and years and years ago, my baby sister, Lady Sophronia Darwen, married a gentleman from America—the Colonies they were then, though I hope dear Kennard won't take offense at my saying so—and went away with him. She was quite young at the time, and Papa was quite livid about it, and actually forbade us all to write to her, and then there was that dreadful war—and now here is Mr. Upshaw, all the way across the ocean to renew the connection! What a delightful surprise!"

Mr. Upshaw was unfortunately vague on the matter of his mother's present state. He had taken a fancy to come to England, he said, wishing to see the family his mama had spoken of so fondly. And here he was. He turned his charming smile on them once more. Lady Mulford beamed at him fondly; Celia smiled shyly back.

"I wonder, Cousin Upshaw," said Louisa brightly, "why you languished so long in confusion instead of applying for information directly to the head of the Darwen family. Lord Coldmeece currently resides in London, as you must know."

Aunt Josephine directed a quelling look at Louisa, but Kennard said self-deprecatingly, "But, Cousin Louisa, from all account the earl is a very busy man, with no time for an American connection of no particular importance. Had I known that he could direct me to the best of dear Mama's sisters . . ." He shrugged.

"We will say no more about it," said Lady Mulford with decision. "You are here now, and we mean to see much of you during your stay. Or do you mean to make your home now in England?"

"As to that, Aunt Josephine, I couldn't say. I am here on business, in a manner of speakin', and my plans are not yet settled."

Talk then turned on the upcoming ball, and nothing

would do but for Lady Mulford to invite him to the event, an invitation he accepted with pleasure. It was agreed that he would call for them at Mulford House the night of the ball and ride over with them in Lady Mulford's carriage. Augustus graciously offered to assist Mr. Upshaw with any advice he might feel in need of on coatmakers or dress; Mr. Upshaw assured Augustus that he had suitable evening attire, and took his leave. Lady Mulford retired to her room after adjuring Augustus not to stay *too* long, and the three cousins were left to discuss their recent visitor.

"What a cake you made of yourself, Gussie, to be sure!" Louisa said unkindly. " 'Mr. Upshaw, if there is any way in which I may oblige you in the peculiarities of the situation—' "

"Oh, cut line, Lou!" Mr. Templeton snapped, and Louisa rose to do battle when Celia intervened.

"Oh," Celia breathed, "I think he is beyond anything handsome—and, one may depend, a true libertarian!"

"A what?" said Augustus blankly.

"One who espouses the principles of true equality, of manifest destiny, and a fundamental belief in—"

"What *I* have an ultimate belief in," put in Lady Louisa wickedly, after a cheering look at Mr. Templeton's countenance, "is that if we do *not* leave off jabbering and go about our errands this very instant, we will have left it too late, and the consequences of *that*"—Louisa dropped her voice dramatically—"are Too Dreadful to be Borne."

"Oh! Of course!" said Celia, leaping up. Augustus rose and bowed his own way out, carrying each damsel's hand to his lips with no evidence of partiality.

The earl, preoccupied with other matters, was not as interested as Augustus had hoped in the full particulars of Kennard Upshaw's arrival in London, and his projected attendance at Gervase's ball, merely remarking that it would be amusing to make the man's acquaintance.

In fact, Gervase's main concern, as the weeks before the ball dwindled to days, was Caro Darwen's quite extraordinary amiability. The Dowager Countess of Coldmeece had been a pattern card of virtue in the past month. Such saintly forebearance could only be the precursor to a truly outrageous demand, and it would have eased Gervase's mind considerably to know what it was going to be.

As it happened, it was not Caro but another of his female connections that was to cause him immediate worry.

He had prudently absented himself from the Mulford household for several days after the ill-starred riding party. He did not hunger for the sight of his betrothed's face, and he could not lack for news, with Augustus visiting there every day. This close to the ball, however, he felt he had better reopen diplomatic relations. He was dressing to pay an informal morning call upon Celia when Bracken brought him the news that Mr. Salvington awaited, urgently desiring an interview.

"Put him in the library," the earl said, dismissing his proposed morning call with a guilty feeling of relief. Personal matters must always take second place to family business.

He found Salvington pacing the library, and at his entrance the elderly solicitor summoned up a wry smile.

"Lord Coldmeece! How good to see you again, my lord—though I fancy you won't be able to say the same of me once you've heard what I have to tell you."

"I had not known you to live in terror of my displeasure," the earl said. "Take some refreshment, and tell me what brings you to these hallowed precincts so short a time before hell is due to break upon them."

"It has to do with her ladyship, my lord—Lady Mulford, that is to say. Her trustee—that would be Lord Mulford's man of business—took the unusual step of writing to me because of certain irregularities in her ladyship's finances, which, it was feared, might become so serious that your lordship would be called upon to intervene."

"I take it Mr. Dumbarton did not consider the obvious step of mentioning these matters to Lady Mulford?"

Salvington coughed discreetly. "As I fancy your lordship is aware, her ladyship and young Dumbarton are not on the best of terms. The peculiar entitlements of the late Lord Mulford's will, allowing her to draw at will upon the

93

estate for funds, is rather a sore point with the Mulford family.''

"And has she been?" the earl asked, taking a glass of wine for himself and lounging indolently back in a large chair.

"Well." Salvington regarded the middle distance. "It is Mr. Dumbarton's contention that, since her arrival in London, Lady Mulford had been making such heavy demands upon the estate that, should she continue in this fashion, some, ah, capital readjustments may have to be made."

"In other words," the earl translated, "he might have to sell off some of the property."

"Quite." Salvington adjusted his pince-nez.

Gervase was quite familiar with Lady Mulford's financial situation. If the estate were really in serious difficulty—or about to be—Aunt Josephine must be spending in quite a high-flying style. He thought of the sapphires, and his mouth gave an uncharacteristic twitch. There might well be the cause of Dumbarton's anxiety—and who knew how many other lavish presents Lady Mulford had recently made to her niece? But if these extravagant gifts continued to drain the estate, Dumbarton might be driven to legal action, which would be quite unpleasant.

"Salvington," the earl said suddenly, "you recall that I told you to set aside the plans to make over an income to Lady Louisa Darwen?"

"Yes, my lord," said his man of business, unruffled by the apparent change of topic.

"Cancel the cancellation. Lady Louisa is not a minor, and there is no guardian to consult."

"Yes, my lord. It will be put in train at once. And the other matter?"

The early airily waved a hand. "Oh, tell Dumbarton you found me far too busy with idleness and dissipation to pay you the least attention."

Salvington bowed, not quite concealing a smile. "As you wish, my lord."

Chapter
SEVEN

The days until the ball dwindled to mere hours, and the afternoon of the day itself found Lady Louisa regarding her reflection in the mirror with unhappy honesty.

It had not been so very bad when it was only she and Gussie and Aunt Josephine junketing all over Europe with only each other for real company. Gussie didn't care a fig if she wasn't pretty. But here, in London, she was facing her come-out at a great ball in tandem with a maiden who was everything she, Louisa, was not. Louisa would have been made of stone if the prospect did not depress her at least a little, and a great fool not to admit it.

Oh, dear, she thought, picking up the ornately scrolled silver hairbrush and shaking out her hair prior to brushing it. But there's nothing to answer to it, now, is there, my angel? Oh, how vexing—if only I were a blank canvas and one of those Italian fellows around to paint me!

To paint . . . Her hand paused halfway through a brushstroke. "Paint," Louisa repeated aloud, setting the brush down with a bang. "*Paint!* Gussie won't care, and Aunt Josephine won't *dare* squeak, and *that*"—she snapped her fingers at her reflection—"for the fusty fossils of the London *ton*! Rigsby! *Rigsby!*" she called at the top of her lungs. "Bring me my traveling case!"

The disapproving abigail appeared as if by magic, and after some minutes' search, Louisa's traveling case was unearthed in the dim recesses of a wardrobe and presented for Louisa's attention.

"And what will you be wanting with *this*, now, Miss?"

Rigsby asked suspiciously. "With that fine ball tonight you can't be thinking of traveling, surely?"

"Oh, of course not, Rigsby," Louisa said distractedly, opening the case. "What a silly idea."

Patchouli and sandalwood scented the room as she lifted the lid of the silver-trimmed Nile green dressing case. Tucked down behind everything, wrapped in a scarf of paisley silk, was the bundle Louisa had been searching for. She pounced upon it and spread its contents out lovingly upon the table.

"*Miss Louisa!*" Rigsby gasped, outraged. Words failed Lady Mulford's faithful maid as she stood glaring at Lady Louisa. "You're never thinking of . . ."

The little lacquer and ivory boxes looked pagan and gaudy on the prim English dressing table. There was rose-petal salve to color the lips and cheeks, kohl and lapis and malachite for the eyes, henna for the hair, musk and sandalwood and patchouli, oil of frankincense . . .

"*Painting,*" said Louisa with wicked relish. "Well . . ." She affected to consider the matter for a moment. "Maybe I am, and maybe I'm not."

"But, *Miss!*" Rigsby protested. "It's the Earl of Coldmeece's ball!"

"Yes-s," Louisa said, poking an experimental finger into the rose-petal salve. "It is, isn't it?" She looked up at the abigail. "That will be all, Rigsby."

The irate servant marched stiffly to the door, then turned to deliver her final enfilade. "I'll tell your aunt, Miss Louisa, never you see if I don't!"

"Why," asked Louisa, "when you know it won't do any good at all?"

Rigsby stormily withdrew. Louisa sat regarding her colorful horde with deep delight.

"Oh, I shall enjoy this. I was taking far too much notice of London conventions!"

The evening of the ball, Celia spent all the time Teale was fussing over her wondering whether she could borrow enough money from Lady Louisa or Augustus or even from

Mr. Upshaw to hire a chaise to take her back to Thornage Hall.

She was but a miserable dab of a girl, and the Coldmeece ball would unveil the cream of the Season's young ladies. Even Augustus would discover that he had treated Orleton's daughter with far too much particularity—she would stand revealed as a rag-mannered country mouse, and he would scorn her utterly.

" 'Tis all done now, Lady Celia," Teale said. She made a last-minute adjustment to Celia's gown, then stood aside, an almost fatuous smile of beaming approval on her face.

Hardly daring to breathe, Celia faced the cheval glass and was struck speechless with delight. Could that exquisite stranger really be she?

Never had she dreamed she could look like this. From artlessly arranged jonquil yellow curls to blue satin dancing slippers, she looked like a dream princess. Her gown, seafoam blue *broderie anglaise* over a soft blue satin underslip, was cut in the modest lines appropriate to a young girl in her first Season, and the luxurious richness of the material was completely new to her. And to set the seal on her happiness, her toilette was modishly completed by matched pearls at throat and ears, and palest blue kid gloves that almost met the tiny puffed sleeves of her gown.

Almost glowing with joy, she whirled and gave Teale an impulsive hug. "Oh, Teale, thank you. *Thank* you!" Then, with a flash of skirts, she was out the door and off to Louisa's room.

Louisa stood admiring the lovely picture she made in the mirror. She had had Teale in to her earlier, to coil her fox-red hair around her head and secure it with a myriad of diamond pins. Later she had summoned Campbell to do up her dress, but in the main her transformation had been accomplished in solitude.

Winter's white for the die-away debutante, she had said mockingly when her aunt had told her how *necessary* it was that she be seen at Coldmeece's ball in that color. But she had promised her aunt, and so here she was, obediently clad in that virginal hue from top to toe—despite

Lady Mulford's dazzling gift of sapphires earlier that evening.

The gown was white, true, but it was of a diamanté pallor that caught the light and glistened; its *décolletage* was cut *just* at the limit of propriety, and the slightly gored skirts clung lovingly to Louisa's slender curves. It was the first time she had actually dared wear the dress, other than in the privacy of the modiste's Paris atelier, and even she was rather surprised to see how very far from modest and maidenly a white gown could look.

There came a timid knock at the door. "Come in, Celia," Louisa called.

Her little cousin, *une jeune fille* vision in palest blue, came tripping into the room, took one good look at Lady Louisa Darwen, and stopped dead. She opened and closed her mouth several times, while blushing an excited scarlet to the roots of her silver-gilt curls.

"Oh, *Louisa*," she said at last, in a tone halfway between admiration and censure, "you have painted your face and defamed your natural beauty."

"Yes, I have, rather," Louisa admitted cheerfully, peeking over her shoulder at the painted vision in the mirror; a vision who, unlike Lady Louisa Darwen *au naturel*, had well-defined brows and dark lashes, vivid gray eyes set off by delicately tinted lids, glowing pink cheeks, and a rosy-lipped mouth. Not quite in the style of the Grand Seraglio, but Louisa fancied she had done a good job of capturing the *style anglais*.

"Oh, but *Louisa*!" said Celia again.

Louisa advanced and placed a kiss upon her cousin's cheek. "Celia, my angel, you are truly ravishing. All the men will be swooning over you, you abominable child."

"Oh, no," said Celia with grave veracity. "They won't notice me while you're around, Louisa. You are just like Babylon, you know."

Louisa wisely forebore from tracking Celia's biblical reference to its source. "I shall take that for a compliment, darling—now let us away, for I am *sure* Aunt Josephine thinks we will be late and she will never be let to dance." She collected fans, gloves, and reticule. "I cannot wait to see Gussie's face when he beholds you, my love!''

At the bedroom door Celia hung back, suddenly unsure again. "Louisa, you—you *do* think I look . . ."

Heedless of silken finery, Louisa hugged her reassuringly. "My dearest Cousin, you are so *very* ravishing that the abominable earl will without a doubt be struck by a *coup de foudre* upon beholding you, fling himself at your feet, and renounce all his evil ways will only you be his. Several of the younger men will put a period to their existence in despair, and Gussie—''

"There are times, Louisa," Celia said severely, much relieved, "when you are very *silly*.''

Coldmeece House glowed in the reflected glory of thousands of scented candles. An army of retainers had labored unceasingly, and now all was in readiness for the first ball of the Season.

The dinner before the ball was to be at eight, and would seat thirty. By seven thirty Caroline, companion in tow, had arrived at Coldmeece House.

"Dearest Gervase," she said languidly. "So kind of you to take this much trouble for your dear little . . . ward. And she just in from the country, too.''

The earl's answering smile was openly mocking. There were already rumors of the betrothal, and jealous gossips whom Caro had alienated were waiting to hone their tongues on her misfortune. Well, he had done all he intended to to ease her way by letting her be his hostess at this ball; afterwards she could stew in the scandal-broth of her own brewing. "I know I can depend on you, Caroline, to do all you may for Lady Celia, and see to her . . . ease of entry?''

Caroline raised ice blue eyes to his face and gave a delicate sigh. "But of course, my darling Gervase. Did I not agree to serve as hostess here tonight?" Caro put a small, proprietary hand on his arm. He looked at the offending member coldly, but she did not release him.

"Don't overstep yourself, my darling Dowager Countess," Gervase murmured.

"Ah, but of course, you remind me that as your late brother's wife it is my *duty* to serve as hostess for an entertainment such as this, and I am the *slave* of duty. But no, dear Gervase, a duty such as this is *sheerest* pleasure!"

She tilted her head, flirting her eyes at him, and the earl was forcibly reminded of how beautiful he had once thought her. She was beautiful still, if one regarded only beauty of face and form. He sketched her a bow, and she moved off, toying prettily with her fan.

The guests were beginning to arrive, and Augustus appeared as if by magic at Gervase's elbow, performing the task of ushering the guests on to the antechamber. Gervase greeted each arrival in a manner calculated to please. Even if he were not to marry Lady Celia, it was no excuse not to do the pretty and launch the child gracefully into Society.

By five minutes before eight, the dinner guests, with the exception of Lady Mulford's party, had all made their appearance. Caroline, facing the stairs, tensed as Lady Mulford's party was announced and a look of sudden chagrin crossed her face. Curiosity piqued, the earl turned toward the staircase.

His delightful godmama, arrayed in flowing lavender draperies, was slowly mounting the stairs. After a moment's reflection, Gervase realized that her handsome escort must be that American connection Augustus had been in such a lather about. The American was very like Augustus, even allowing for the difference in age and a certain lack of true exquisiteness in Mr. Upshaw's person.

He next turned his attention to the two young ladies for whom this party was being given. The pretty little blonde in the soft blue gown, so obviously a schoolroom miss at her first ball, was Lady Celia, and quite lovely she looked, too. He flicked a careless glance at her companion while looking curiously about for Lady Louisa, then stiffened. He was vaguely aware that his mouth had dropped open in shock. So *this* was why Caroline had pokered up so!

The tall woman in the shimmering, clinging white gown *just* this side of proper could only be Lady Louisa Dar-

100

wen. She looked as if the closest she had ever been to a book in her life was when she strolled past Hatchard's on the way to the modiste; and furthermore, Gervase was very well aware that those rose-petal lips and lustrous black lashes had not been hers when he met her in Lady Mulford's morning room. She looked, in fact, quite as fast as Gervase had originally suspected her of being, and Gervase ruefully acknowledged that he had been taken in indeed. While Louisa had not been miraculously transformed into a beauty, she was one who, as the saying went, "paid for the dressing."

Gervase looked over at Augustus, and was surprised to note a stormy look plain upon his features. It comforted Gervase somewhat to know he was not the only one Lady Louisa had stolen a march on. He bowed to Mr. Upshaw, then turned a benign smile on Louisa.

He sketched a bow and said, "I am pleased to make your acquaintance, Lady Louisa—at last."

The gleam in Louisa's eyes acknowledged the hit. Gervase's smiled broadened, and he added, "Augustus has told me so much about you, but I see now that he failed signally to do you justice." Prudently allowing her no time to respond, Gervase handed Lady Louisa on to Caroline, who reluctantly relinquished Mr. Upshaw and radiated censorious disapproval on Lady Louisa.

An appreciative smile still on his lips, the earl then turned his attention to Lady Celia. He bowed gracefully and smiled charmingly, but the lady's severe expression did not alter one whit. She dropped him a precise curtsy and inclined her head to the smallest degree consonant with good manners. She then held a charming posy of blue flowers to her nose and studied him over its petals.

Gervase knew he had ordered Brendan to send Lady Celia a large nosegay of white rosebuds and deduced, therefore, that he had a rival. He was somewhat nettled by Celia's out of hand dismissal of what he felt to be his not inconsiderable charm, address, title, and other amiable qualities, and resolved that by the end of the evening he would have presented himself to Lady Celia in an entirely new light.

The last guests entered the drawing room, and Gervase offered his arm to Caroline.

Lady Louisa sailed past Lady Coldmeece and into the drawing room on a wave of unmaidenly glee. The look on the face of the abominable earl when she had been presented to him had been quite, quite worth her poor aunt's palpitations. The diamanté gown was not, after all, so *very* daring. Why, if she didn't have a carefully hidden Past, and weren't supposed to be *une jeune fille anglaise* in her first Season, her dress wouldn't have caused the least comment! And after all, nothing she might do here tonight could injure Celia's consequence in the slightest—not with both of them appearing under Coldmeece's aegis. So *she* intended to have a good time.

"Louisa, may I have a word with you?" The voice was Augustus's, but the reproving tone was entirely unlike him. Surprised, Louisa turned to face her cousin. His lean, handsome face and dark hair, stylishly disordered *à la brigand*, made him look quite the corsair, but his expression more closely resembled that of a particularly prim country vicar.

"Gussie?" said Louisa. "What's wrong?"

He offered her his arm and soon, to all appearances, they were passionately involved in study of the landscapes that graced the far wall.

"I suppose it amuses you to come here rigged out for a masquerade!" Augustus began in a savage undertone.

"Whatever do you mean, *dear* cousin?" Louisa retorted, confused but unwilling to be insulted.

"That . . . dress."

"White is usually considered proper for one's come-out ball," Louisa informed him blightingly.

Augustus grabbed her arm rather forcibly and turned her back toward him. "Not like that it ain't! What makes you think you can ruin Celia's ball for her like this—and as much as she's looked forward to it, too?"

"And what makes you think I can't? I mean, what makes you think I *want* to? It's only a dress, Gussie, and not as daring as some you've been pleased to approve, my love. I remember once in St. Petersburg—''

"Well, this ain't St. Petersburg, Louisa—it's London, and to show up at a ball tricked out like a bird of paradise and painted like a . . .''

Louisa stared at Augustus. This couldn't be Gussie saying these things to her—he had always supported her every rig and row. This was nothing more daring than she'd done a hundred times before with his encouragement.

"You and Aunt Josephine," she said bitterly. "Both of you determined to turn me out like all the other missish little mice on this sacred Marriage Mart of yours. But I'm not on the catch for a husband, Gussie—at least, I hadn't thought so! You never used to mind when I painted—you said I should keep it up, when all Aunt Josephine wanted to do was throw away my paints. You said it made me look as if I had a face. Lots of women paint; I've seen them.''

"But that wasn't London!" Augustus repeated stubbornly.

Louisa's temper boiled over. She had been looking forward to an amusing evening, and here was her lovable, scapegrace cousin ringing a peal over her in the most unexpectedly prudish manner possible! "No," she whispered back fiercely, "it was St. Petersburg, or Rome, or Paris, or Vienna—all cities with a great deal to recommend them, all far more graceful, charming, witty, and cosmopolitan than this dismal swamp, and all of them possessing the sterling advantage that they did not turn my cousin into a sheep-witted *blanc mange*!''

Augustus started to speak, but she overrode him. "I have had more than my fill of watching you come the model of propriety with Celia—but if you enjoy it, far be it from me to impede your strange pleasures. But do *not* try to reform me! I do what *I* wish, and I am *tired*—'' Suddenly, humiliatingly, she felt tears come springing to her eyes, and forced herself to take a deep, unsteady breath.

At first Augustus seemed shocked by her tears; she was Louisa Darwen, and Louisa never cried. Then his expression softened to tenderness, and he reached out one immaculately gloved hand to touch her cheek. "Poor Coz," he said soothingly, "you've had a wretched time of it, haven't you?"

"*I hate you!*" snarled Louisa from the depths of her soul, and stalked off, now dry-eyed and shaking with fury.

Mr. Kennard Upshaw was a man well content. It had been no difficult matter to persuade the wealthy and soft-hearted Lady Mulford that his trunks had been lost, and she had agreed to hold his bills until the draft on his American bank came through. He had suffered no qualms of conscience over this; he had done his research well, and it was a sure thing that the Earl of Coldmeece would absolve Lady Mulford of these debts before they became an embarrassment. Who knew—Kennard might even pay them himself, if matters fell out as he hoped. His dear mama could not be the only impressionable English belle whose head could be turned by an American of smooth address. Perhaps an heiress might be induced to throw herself away on him, though he had his doubts. Kennard Upshaw was a most particular man, and the heiresses that *weren't* butter-toothed, Friday-faced, wrinkled old ape leaders were as rare as hen's teeth. On the other hand, he told himself, noting Lady Celia's radiant butterfly progress with approval, they weren't nonexistent. Perhaps an opportunity would present itself for wooing the divinely desirable Celia away from that young pup Augustus.

His musings were interrupted by the arrival of Lady Louisa Darwen, who swept up to him, her color high and her bosom heaving, and firmly engaged him in sparkling chat. As he was regaling her with a wholly fictitious tale of an attack by Savages on his ancestral home, her mouth quirked beguilingly, and Mr. Upshaw thought it looked an uncommonly kissable mouth for all its owner's plainness. That outrageous rag of a dress suited her tall figure uncommon well, too, and tonight she even had a bit of color.

"A penny for your thoughts, Cousin?" he said, and Louisa smiled more determinedly.

"I was just thinking, Mr. Upshaw," she said glibly, "what a dreadful disappointment it will be for these coming mamas when they find that you're not Augustus. The two of you are very alike, you know. It is enough to confuse anyone who doesn't know Gussie well, and mamas are always on the catch to snabble him up for their daughters."

"I should think," said Mr. Upshaw, "that Mr. Templeton is in no danger of being snabbled up by any mamas—at least, not this evening."

Louisa followed the direction of Mr. Upshaw's gaze, to see Augustus making conversation with Celia near the door. As Celia spoke, she raised her posy of forget-me-nots to her face, and Louisa wondered if it were more than simple mischief that had made Gussie send it and Celia carry it.

"Nonsense!" said Louisa tartly. "Gussie taught the child to waltz!"

What reply Mr. Upshaw would have made to this masterly argument she was never to know, for at that moment Bracken bid all the company in to dinner.

Lady Celia Darwen-Neville was too enraptured by her first experience of London society to much notice the sumptuous repast set before her. Covertly she glanced at the earl, only to find him regarding her. Her chin rose, and her kittenish face assumed an expression of glacial disdain. Perhaps he was not quite so odiously dissipated and elderly as she had first assumed him to be, but he was still obviously a vile and abominable person, as well as a rake attempting to force her into marriage, and she would treat him with all the genteel reserve such upstart behavior warranted.

"Do you not find the dishes to your liking, Lady Celia? You seem scarcely to have touched your dinner," observed his lordship, and Celia hastened to assure him, with perhaps a bit more genteel reserve than she had intended, that she found no fault with the dinner. The earl's mouth quite unfortunately quirked, but Celia was saved the necessity of formulating a sufficiently dignified and damping reply by the presentation of the second course.

At length the guests rose from their chairs to make their way to the ballroom. Before Celia had quite time to understand how it had come about, she was on the earl's arm being presented to Lady Jersey; Silence archly gave permission for Celia to waltz.

Dancing with the earl was nothing at all like dancing with Augustus, though the long hours of his tutelage now stood her in good stead. "Tell me," he murmured, looking down at her with an expression she interpreted as grim in the extreme, "what have I done to cause you to take me in such evident dislike?"

Had the earl not then swept her on around the ballroom floor, Celia would very likely have stopped dead. She opened her mouth, searching for a polite evasion, but as usual when Celia was faced with a choice between truth and tact, truth won.

"You—you are the most arrogant man!" she burst out, following this disclosure with a mortified squeak.

The earl raised his brows slightly. "Tell me, my child, has Lady Louisa been giving you notions of my character?"

Celia was quite pink by this time. "She said you wished to have her drowned. She *did*!"

The earl nodded, as one to whom all has been made clear. "I thought that might be the case. But she tells me she has forgiven me that, so naturally I assumed you also to have—but pray do forgive me, Lady Celia, for an *elderly* cousin's presumption."

"Elderly?" Celia repeated, flushing anew. "But Louisa said it wasn't rag-mannered, as long as you only called people names behind their backs."

"And so I was not to know that I am regarded in the light of an 'elderly *roué*'?" said the earl teasingly. "But you must blame my godmama for that; it was she who let the cat out of the bag. Now, as for your dear cousin's ideas of proper behavior—"

"Oh, pray do not be angry with Louisa!" pleaded Celia. "It is *not* her fault! Do you know, Lord Coldmeece, I fancy there is something 'shady' about Louisa's past, though she will not speak of it, and neither will Lady Mulford. It is very vexing to be treated as if one were the merest *child*!''

The earl gravely agreed, and by the time he returned his young partner to the sidelines, Celia was very nearly in charity with the once abominable earl.

Augustus kept trying to see her alone, but the press of people and Celia's own rapidly developing sense of coquetry did not permit it. At last, exhausted from dancing with what seemed an endless series of gallants, she looked for him in order to relent, but did not see him anywhere. In search of him, or at least of an out-of-the-way place, she pushed open the door to one of the rooms letting off the main ballroom. As soon as she had done so, she realized that this was not one of the rooms that had been opened for cards or other divertissements, but in the end practicality won out, and she settled with a sigh upon the velvet cushions of a waiting sopha.

''May I disturb you, Cousin?'' Caroline, Dowager Countess of Coldmeece, entered, carrying a candle. Celia envied the older woman her cool sophistication, certain it was far more captivating than her own inexperience.

''Yes,'' said Celia dutifully. ''Please do come in, Lady Coldmeece.''

Caro made a small moue of distaste. ''Please, dear cousin, call me Caroline, and I shall call you Celia. If we are to be sisters, then there is surely no need to stand upon formality.'' She seated herself beside Celia. ''When I saw you slip away from the dancing, I thought there might be something wrong. Is anything amiss?''

''Oh, no,'' Celia said. ''The ball is beyond anything great—I think I must have danced with nearly everyone here! But please tell me, ma'am, why you say that you and I are to be sisters?''

''Why, when you have married Gervase, you shall be my sister, as I am his.'' Celia's determined chin came up, and Caro added quickly, ''Oh, please forgive me—I know it was to be secret between you two for a while longer, but Gervase tells me all, and I could not help . . . This is in part why I followed you, so we could talk with no one to see.''

There was a long silence, during which Celia wondered miserably just how many people in London knew of her supposedly secret betrothal to the Earl of Coldmeece. At last she was moved to say, ''You said you wished to speak to me, ma'am—Caroline.''

''Yes,'' said Lady Coldmeece starkly. ''It is about Gervase. I had to talk to you now, before you chanced to hear any of those things that people say. I hope to spare you great disappointment and future pain.''

Celia's brow wrinkled in pretty confusion. ''What could you mean?''

''What I mean is—oh, my dear! If only it could have been different!'' Having taken her audience well in hand with these dramatic overtures, Caro expanded upon her theme. ''You may wonder, my dear Celia, why it is that a man as old as Coldmeece, with his family and position to think of, has never married?''

Celia, who had not wondered any such thing until this very moment, nodded, round-eyed.

Caroline patted Celia's hand and sighed tragically. ''It is a long story, my dear Celia. It goes back to the time of my marriage to his elder brother Edmund. When I married Edmund, I hardly realized that Gervase had formed a violent *tendre* for me during his brother's courtship and was now stricken with grief at my marriage.''

''He was?'' said Celia, who could not imagine the earl stricken by any emotion whatsoever.

''Yes!'' Caroline declared. ''Oh, Celia, had I but known his true feelings before I had accepted Edmund! But it was my family's dearest wish that I marry him, and who was I to go against the sacred dictates of family?'' Caro broke off, clasping Celia's hand agitatedly; then, with a sidewise glance at her entranced listener, continued. ''But it was done. I tried to make Gervase see that we could still be friends, but he would have none of it—he fled to Europe and never set foot in England again until the day of his brother's death.''

"Oh, how dreadful!" said Celia, much moved. Having read few novels, she did not recognize the extremely standard plot of this affecting tale.

"He returned," Caro continued, "under the delusion that—that my affections might now be his. But during our marriage I had grown to love Edmund deeply, and so to find that Gervase had returned to England only for the purpose of—of renewing his suit . . . Well, the shock was too much for my nerves. We Everhills have always been of a very delicate constitution, you know, and I was forced to retire into the country."

"But what has all this to do with me?" asked Celia.

Caroline leaned forward over their clasped hands. "My dear, it is very painful for me to say this, but I fancy I know the earl's mind better than anyone now living. It is plain to me that he has not put off the willow—in fact, you may have heard how he came to see me the very first day I was in Town, and begged me to support him at your first meeting. He taxed me with . . . with the fondness we had once held for one another, and told me that *I* would now see what it was to have the one I loved marry another while I stood by, powerless to intervene! This betrothal of yours is only a spite match. He means to hurt me—but I think it will hurt you more. He does not care that you will have to marry him, and live year after year with the knowledge that he thinks only of . . . Another . . ."

Celia sat staring through Caro as if she possessed no more substance than the moonlight filtering through a chink in the draperies. The truth had at last been revealed to her. The earl was not an elderly *roué* after all, but a man who had been young once, young and bitterly disappointed in love. And she, Celia, had meant to reject him, to leave him twice rejected, when all London knew of their betrothal. Oh, how could she had contemplated it, however unknowingly?

"I—I must think," she stammered, pulling her hand free and leaping to her feet. Their weariness was forgotten as she fled to the door, stopping long enough to bob Caro a hasty curtsy. "Oh, *thank* you!" Celia gasped, and vanished.

Caroline leaned back against the cushions and allowed a smile of self-satisfaction to spread itself across her perfect features. The chit had swallowed the tale whole—and it contained enough facts to make it plausible indeed. Why, Caro herself found it quite a touching story, and so *very* nearly true!

And little Lady Celia certainly would be discouraged from prying further into the matter. Dear Gervase would be unlikely to unburden himself to any unbecomingly pert seventeen-year-old miss; and the Turkish treatment Celia would get would surely convince any schoolgirl that his feelings were indeed deeply wounded. With any luck, one week's time—a month at most—should see Lady Celia Darwen-Neville safely back in the country, and the earl in a position to be brought round Caro's finger. She knew as well as anyone that Gervase must marry, and soon, and she would make him a comfortable wife. Indeed, Gervase would have cause to be thankful he had asked her to act as hostess this night.

Celia rushed back to the dance floor flushed and breathless, her mind in a whirl from the extraordinary interview just past.

"Cousin Celia?"

Startled, she raised her eyes to behold Augustus, who was regarding her with a hopeful gleam of mischief in his slanting blue eyes. "At last, fair torment, I find you alone—and while my abominable cousin is off with my other abominable cousin, I shall take the opportunity of bespeaking your company at supper tonight."

Celia wrinkled her nose prettily. "I had much rather go in with you than the earl," she confided, "and since he has not asked me yet, I suppose I may. There is something I particularly wish to know from you, Mr. Templeton."

Augustus raised his eyebrows with a look of mock affront and took Celia's hand. " 'Mr. Templeton,' is it now? And I thought we had been on less formal terms—or have you been dazzled by the earl into forgetting all lesser mortals?"

"I most certainly have not—Gussie!" Celia retorted, and Augustus gave a sharp bark of laughter.

"I hope not, Cousin, and speaking of cousins, the cousins I was speaking of are your cousin Coldmeece and your cousin Louisa—and mine too, for that matter. Dreadfully clannish, we Darwens . . . In any event, he's dancing with her, while I am hoping to dance with you, and depress his pretensions behind his back. Isn't it wonderful that you particularly wish to talk to me, for I particularly wish to talk to you, you know. Say you'll be mine, O Earthly Goddess, and you shall have champagne!"

Celia's eyes lit up. "Oh," she breathed in rapture, the earl momentarily forgotten, "but Papa would not approve—and Aunt Josephine said I was not to drink anything stronger than lemonade, not being used to parties."

"And how," inquired Mr. Templeton, "are you to *get* used to them if you never experience any of the manifold delights and uplifting raptures of the glorious, transcendent—"

"Pooh," said Celia with decision.

Lady Louisa was finding dancing with the earl an even more enjoyable experience than she had anticipated. For all his size, he was an excellent dancer; moreover, he was a large enough man to allow her to feel that she was not in imminent danger of oversetting him and sending them both crashing to the floor. He augmented his truly superior waltzing with the sort of barbed verbal fencing she most enjoyed and rarely experienced.

For all her misgivings about developing any particular fondness for her handsome and high-handed cousin, Louisa felt that tonight must be different. Tonight she might treat him as she liked, for surely no one paid any mind to what was said and done at balls. He and Celia were in charity with each other, as all could see; tomorrow Celia would cry off the engagement, and go on to enjoy her Season. And then . . . But Louisa firmly put all thoughts of what the future might bring from her mind, and set herself to enjoy the present.

So she had swept him one of her very best—and very

lowest—curtsies, and the earl had carried her masterfully into the whirls of the dance. After a turn or two, he began. "As I have said before, Lady Louisa, it is a pleasure to see you showing—dare I say your true colors?—at last."

Louisa looked at him through her darkened lashes in her most provocatively innocent manner. "You do not consider, then, Cousin Coldmeece, that I have defamed my natural beauty?"

"Not at all," said Gervase truthfully, and rather to his own surprise. "Had I not had the pleasure of previous acquaintance, I would simply account you a tolerably well-looking girl. As for the rest, surely Aunt Josephine has told you the Darwen name can carry all, even in the face of what I deduce to be Lady Celia's disapproval."

"Oh, yes, dozens of times," Louisa told him, smiling. "But I've discovered it will only carry all Aunt Josephine wishes me to do, as she has *also* told me that the veriest nothing will put me quite beyond the pale. It is the *oddest* thing! Do you not think so, Cousin?"

"Very odd," the earl agreed. "Particularly, dear cousin, your definitions of the 'the veriest nothing'!"

Louisa dimpled, but went on, as if endeavoring to be truly fair-minded, "Of course, you English are all so . . ." Louisa shrugged her shoulders—a supple maneuver no English miss would have tried while twirling in the waltz, but, as Louisa thought maliciously, the veriest nothing to one who had been taught to dance in the harem. "It is all very difficult."

The earl's stare was most gratifying, but he recovered himself well. "Difficult as it may be, can I persuade you, do you think, to venture your opinion on the particular, as opposed to the general? In short, Lady Louisa, perhaps you will be good enough to favor me with *your* views on my character, as Lady Celia was able to offer only the most fragmentary discourse on the subject. You must know that *I* do not hold that it is, ah, 'rag-mannered' to express oneself frankly on such intimate topics, providing one is waltzing with one's victim at the time."

Louisa smothered a most unmannerly chortle of mirth. "I knew it would come to that, Lord Coldmeece," she said with a fatalistic air, "but at least it was not the Corn Laws." She stifled a small and wholly artificial sigh.

"The Corn Laws?" the earl said.

"Oh, la, my lord," Louisa began with a girlish simper, then gave a muffled yelp. "You brute! You stepped on my foot!"

"And so I shall again, should you recommence that appalling masquerade. I have seen enough deception from you, ma'am, and require no more. Even that, however, will not serve to distract me from the connection between the Corn Laws and my character," he informed her imperturbably.

"I am not, myself, precisely certain of the connection," Louisa admitted, "but Celia is quite taken with them and will discuss them for hours. I *think* it has to do with universal sufferage—but if you know better, I pray you will not enlighten me!" She sighed again, genuinely this time. "Everything seems to come around to them, soon or late. It was not merely that you were elderly, and dissipated, and had embezzled her fortune, and did not like horses, but that your views on the Corn Laws were not at all what she could like. Not," Louisa went on hastily, seeing the earl's face, "that I am inquiring into them in the least, whatever they are. You may keep them undisturbed, for all of me."

The music ended, and Gervase bore Louisa off to one of the dainty gilded chairs lining the walls to continue their conversation. He then took the opportunity to ask if Louisa had enjoyed Mrs. Edgeworth's recent visit to Mulford House.

"Oh," said Louisa ingenuously, "I enjoyed it quite as much as I ought—and you, sir, are an unspeakable monster!"

The earl beamed at her in perfect charity. "I trust that Lady Celia also enjoyed the visit?" he asked.

"Oh, yes," said Louisa recklessly, "but unfortunately Celia is not at all bookish *either*, and so could not be expected to have read and appreciated Mrs. Edgeworth's creations as perhaps she ought."

"Really?" said the earl, lifting his brows. "I would

have thought the child to be, oh, quite as bookish as you once appeared to be."

Louisa gave him a sidelong, provocative look. "Oh, no, my Lord, Celia's accomplishments are all ladylike, and do not include books. I, on the other hand, am possessed of a number of accomplishments, none of which are in the *least* ladylike."

"You astonish me," said the earl gravely. "And since you so obviously wish me to ask you what they are, I shall. If you do not do needlework, or watercolors, or converse in the Italian tongue, Lady Louisa, how do you distinguish yourself?"

"Well," said Louisa, as if considering. "I can read and write Turkish—and French and English, of course—and play upon the zither—and the pianoforte, badly—and compound sweetmeats and perfumes, and dance—a little."

"So I have observed," said the earl. His eyes gleamed, and the color inexplicably heightened in Louisa's cheeks.

"Gussie can speak Turkish too," she went on hastily. "We have always found it most useful, when we do not wish to be overheard, and perhaps I should not tell you any of the rest, or you will disinherit him and cast him upon the waters."

"My dear, I am quite certain you have Augustus confused with a piece of bread!" said Lady Mulford, appearing from the midst of a knot of dancers. "Although I do not believe he would return tenfold, one can never be too certain." Having settled the matter in her own mind, she turned decisively to the earl. "Gervase, you are quite neglecting poor dear Celia. How can she be expected to form a good opinion of you if you are nowhere to be found?"

"If you call the middle of the ballroom nowhere, Godmama, then I must plead guilty," said the earl. "And, sorry as I am to neglect Lady Celia, I must confess I have been quite absorbed by Lady Louisa's conversation." He smiled blandly. "I find the useful accomplishments she and Augustus possess between them quite fascinating."

A look of forboding was seen to cross Lady Mulford's plump features.

"Yes, Aunt," Louisa said brightly. "I was just telling Lord Coldmeece what I learned in the *hareem*."

"Oh, *Louisa*," Lady Mulford moaned, groping for her vinaigrette.

"Ah, yes, the *hareem*," said the earl calmly, unmoved by Lady Mulford's reliance on her smelling salts. "You were raised in one, were you not, Cousin? It is no wonder that you account Byron your favorite among the poets."

"Actually, I only spent six years there," said Louisa, vowing she would find some way to shatter his imperturbability. "And then Aunt Josephine came for me, over your protests."

"How obliging of her—and how brave," Gervase observed politely. "Dearest Godmama, are you ill?"

"You scapegrace! You are encouraging her! Gervase, I insist that you go and find Celia at once—I must talk with Louisa."

The earl rose and bowed himself away. Lady Mulford took a deep breath and rounded on her niece, but in a flash Louisa was on her feet and waving vaguely across the ballroom with her fan.

"Oh, Aunt Josephine, there's Mr. Upshaw, and I most especially promised him this dance. Pray excuse me!" Louisa dashed off in guilty haste, and Lady Mulford was left to compose for her own edification the lecture she would deliver to Louisa at the first opportunity.

Louisa had not, in fact, seen Mr. Upshaw—or, indeed, anyone she knew—across the ballroom. She certainly did not expect to bump into Augustus in a secluded alcove. She gave a small squeak of surprise and Augustus put out a hand in a steadying manner.

"In better spirits now, Coz?" he asked.

"Mm," said Louisa, engaged in studying the ballroom over his shoulder. It seemed that Gussie's volatile temper had suffered its usual sea change; she was no longer to be castigated for dressing like a bird of paradise. "Aunt thinks I'm dancing with our American cousin. I hope he doesn't appear to disabuse her of the notion."

"The last I saw of the noble savage, Caro Darwen was chasing him around the dance floor."

"Good. Then *she* can dance with him, and I hope he enjoys it. The woman's cow-footed."

"But," said Augustus, suavely drawing Louisa down onto a settee beside him, "if Caro does that, then Aunt Josephine will see that he is not dancing with you, and will come looking for you to deliver the scold you're so obviously avoiding."

Louisa gazed limpidly at her handsome cousin. "T'was ever thus. One attempts to bring a bit of culture, of enlightenment, to a backward country—"

"Telling Coldmeece all about the *hareem*, were you?" Augustus said, and Louisa grinned.

"Dear Cousin, I knew I could always depend upon you to see my actions in the most flattering light! Just for that, you may take me in to supper, and feed me grapes and champagne."

"They haven't any grapes, and anyway, I've already promised Celia," Augustus said, with no hint of apology in his cheerful tone.

"Then I shall have to fall back on the abominable earl. Oh, fate is too cruel," said Louisa placidly.

Augustus regarded her quizzically. "Satisfy my wretched curiosity, sweetest Cousin. Wonderful though it is to be able to approach you again without risking life and limb, I prepare to hazard all upon a question. *Why*, after being what dear Aunt Josie calls 'dreadfully-good-under-the-circumstances-after-all-dear-boy' for positive *weeks*, do you cut loose *here*? You know damn well that dress ain't the thing—I saw old Bulldog Drummond-Burrell positively freeze over when she clapped eyes on you, and if Aunt Josie don't do some fancy footwork, m'girl, you may never get to Almack's."

"Oh, Almack's." Louisa stifled a yawn, tapping her fan against her chin. "Who cares about Almack's? I'm sure I don't! *I* haven't any interest in cutting a dash in the English *ton*, and anyway, Coldmeece won't freeze me—not while Celia's under Aunt Josephine's roof—and where Coldmeece goes, can others fear to tread?"

"I hope you're not suggesting our esteemed cousin-the-earl is a fool, Louisa, 'cause you'll catch cold at that. If he wanted to bring you up short, he would."

Louisa tilted her head and regarded him sidewise, a dangerous light in her rain-colored eyes. "Why, Augustus, my martyred angel, could you possibly be suggesting that Coldmeece could find any fault in such an one as I, whom *you* have been pleased to approve in every particular?"

"You might think of Celia instead of yourself for once, Louisa," said Augustus reproachfully. "How do you think it will look for her, you bein' her cousin and all, and carryin' on like a Dasher of the first water? You may think London dull, but she doesn't—and Celia's got her heart set on Almack's."

It struck Louisa that Augustus was remarkably well informed about Celia's likes and dislikes, and she cast a measuring glance at him. A shade too casually, she said, "Well, then, I shall certainly exert myself to throw a sop in the way of Cerberus, for I would not wish to see Celia's happiness circumscribed. Do you know if she has made up her mind to speak to Coldmeece yet—or he to her? The two of you being so *very* close, you know."

Augustus took her fan away from her and rapped her over the knuckles with it. "Cat!" he said. "No, Celia hasn't told me what she means to do, but I think if Gervase don't speak, she won't either, and the matter can be let drop. All's well as ends well."

"Of course," said Louisa, unconvinced. Still, if Gussie wished to cry off, he'd have no hesitation in telling her so. She retrieved her fan and rose gracefully to her feet. "But before you take the earl's not-exactly-betrothed in to supper at the earl's ball, do dance with me, my angel. You may not be alive to do so later."

"Ho!" Mr. Templeton said, making her a sweeping bow. "Coldmeece don't believe in dueling."

"Perhaps not. But if he's such a master at bringing people up short, isn't it grand that you're not giving him any reason to?" Louisa said meaningfully, as Augustus led her onto the dance floor.

* * *

In another part of the ballroom, the characters of Lady Celia Darwen-Neville and the Earl of Coldmeece were also being discussed, though far more obliquely, by another pair of dancers.

Kennard Upshaw had been looking forward for some days to making the acquaintance of the ravishing Dowager Countess of Coldmeece. It had not been difficult to have himself invited to places where her scandalous history was freely discussed, and by the night of the ball he knew rather more about her than anyone might suppose. He knew she was just twenty-six, widowed nearly four years before from the ninth Earl of Coldmeece, possessed of a handsome allowance which she continually overspent, and of a flexible perception of the bounds of propriety, which she was nonetheless careful not to overstep. She had a weakness for deep play, showy horseflesh, and fast company, and though the strictness with which the current earl had managed her affairs since his brother's death was not-at-all to her taste, she showed no inclination to attenuate the connection.

Caroline, for her part, had not been idle since the arrival of the glamorous Mr. Upshaw. Upon hearing such of his history as was common knowledge, she had consulted friends lately returned from the West Indies, and upon such unhelpful information about Mr. Upshaw as they were able to provide she had built a towering edifice of fantasy—which was yet close enough to the facts of the matter to appall Mr. Upshaw, should he chance to hear of it. In Caro's simple universe, *any* mysterious American appearing on the town was a fortune hunter; that in this case she happened to be correct did not alter the entire speciousness of her reasoning.

Caro had hit upon an even better plan than the one she had conceived before the ball. Why be content to send Celia back to the country? The chit would still be Gervase's ward, and at any moment a romance might kindle between the two. How much better if Celia should be married off to someone Caro could trust to see *her* side of things and act accordingly. Since Lady Celia was both rich and titled, Caro could see no reason why Kennard and the child should not be very happy together.

Caro flirted her eyes at Mr. Upshaw as she moved with him through the graceful figures of the dance. He was quite an attractive man—rather like Caro's cousin by marriage, Augustus, but without Augustus's nasty smirking way of looking at things.

"Tell me, Mr. Upshaw," Caro said, "do you find England strange after your exciting life in the American—in the Americas?"

Kennard grinned down at the woman in his arms. "Well, Lady Coldmeece," he drawled, "it isn't so very different. We enjoy the same pleasures you do, after all. Dancin', and ridin', and . . . pleasant company."

Caro cast her eyes down and summoned up a blush. "Ah," she murmured, "I had feared you might find England . . . cold."

Kennard chuckled. "Now, Lady Coldmeece, where could you get such a notion as that, when I have all my cousins here to welcome me? Oh, but forgive me, ma'am; I had not considered that you, also, might be a relative of mine."

"Only by marriage," Caroline admitted. "But if you will allow me to presume upon a cousin's privilege, Mr. Upshaw, I will quiz you dreadfully, for I am positively dying to know what brings you to England."

Caro led her not unwilling partner off the dance floor and kept him by her side. She allowed Mr. Upshaw to beguile her with tales of the surprisingly sophisticated life of the Virginia plantation from which he had come, but never let him lead her entirely from the path she wished the conversation to take.

"But surely," Caro said, "you must have given some thought to marriage, Mr. Upshaw. You cannot be comfortable without a wife."

Mr. Upshaw tugged at his ear and displayed for Lady Coldmeece a most engaging grin, his white teeth sparkling brilliantly in his tanned buccaneer's face. "But, as surely *you* know, Lady Coldmeece, a marriage made without love lacks spice. At any rate, it don't signify. I doubt any of your English ladies would be willing to throw everything over for an American.''

Caro opened her pale eyes very wide. ''Now *there* I am persuaded you will find yourself in error, sir. In fact, Lady Ce—But I must not abuse a confidence, Mr. Upshaw, you will think it quite horrid of me.''

''Impossible,'' Kennard protested gallantly. He was prevented from anything further he might wish to say by the untimely appearance of the Viscount St. George, one of Caro's admirers.

Caro smiled sweetly upon St. George, and said in parting comment to Kennard, ''Perhaps, sir, if you would ride with me in the Park tomorrow at ten, we may continue a discussion which I assure you I have found of the utmost interest?''

Mr. Upshaw, recognizing his cue, assented to the plan, and Caroline was borne off by a satisfied St. George, leaving Kennard alone to wonder with amusement who the lady Lady Coldmeece so obviously intended him to marry was.

Celia paced on the terrace outside the ballroom. She wished Augustus would come. She had hoped to talk to him at supper, but there were too many people in the supper room for her to be private with him, and so he had suggested she slip away and he would meet her here.

A small sigh of frustration escaped her. Why didn't he hurry? She had thought when she came to the ball that she could simply renounce the earl's claims to her hand. But tonight she had found that the earl was not entirely repulsive to her; indeed, he was almost a fine figure of a man, even if rather old, and of course, now to find that the earl had been Previously Disappointed in Love—well! She did not know *what* dear Papa would have said.

Lady Coldmeece's story gave one a very lowering view of the nature of women—and if she, Celia, found it depressing, what must the earl think, finding himself scorned and courted by turns only for his title and possessions? And here she was, about to toss another engagement back at him, when all London—possibly all England—knew that the matter had been *completely* settled!

Her thoughts were all in a muddle, and she shivered in the April chill, wishing she had brought her shawl out with her. The idea of crying off the betrothal agreement had somehow become entangled in her mind with the sinfulness of confirming an odious person in his evil ways, and since Coldmeece was called upon to assume the aspects of both victim and villain in these cogitations, it was no wonder that Celia felt the first stirrings of a feverish headache. Oh, if only Augustus were here! He had such a reassuring way of looking at things, and he would surely know what Papa would have intended!

"Excuse me, Lady Celia, but could I perhaps be of some assistance?"

Celia turned at the sound of the voice and found herself facing the earl. Over one arm he carried her cream lace evening shawl.

"I thought you might be cold," he explained, "so I took the liberty of providing myself with it before I, er, sought you out. Allow me," he added, stepping behind her and arranging the shawl about her bare shoulders.

Celia knew that her hour had come. The earl was undoubtedly about to offer for her. "S-sought me out, sir?" she said in a trembling voice. "Why should you do that, sir?"

"We shall ignore for the moment the fact that I have a particular interest in your welfare," the earl drawled.

She glanced up quickly, but his face was cast in shadow. She desperately wished he would go away before he said another word.

Gervase, however, stood in ignorance of this. He had decided, after watching Celia with Augustus all evening, to speak to the girl and make sure she knew she was free to marry whom she pleased.

Therefore he smiled soothingly at Celia and patted her shoulder paternally. "I am glad to have this chance to speak to you privately, my child. Since I stand in so close a connection to you, I would not wish you to have any cause to think ill of me. Therefore, before matters progress any further, I would like to hear what you wish from this Season.''

"W-w-wish?'' Celia stammered.

The earl looked at her sharply, diagnosed exhaustion, excitement, and champagne, mentally consigned Augustus to perdition, and determined to cut this interview short. "I desire only your happiness, Cousin Celia, and whatever form it may take, I will stand ready to support you. As you know, many years ago our fathers were the greatest of friends; it was only natural for them to think along lines which need not concern you now. While your father had . . . certain plans for you, you've doubtless discovered this evening that young men will be overjoyed to throw themselves at your feet in great numbers, and—"

"No!'' said Celia with sudden determination. "I am going to marry you!'' Her head ached dreadfully, and her thoughts were fuzzy. She had not quite been following the earl's conversation, but had received the impression he was accusing her of jilting him, and hastened to thus disabuse him.

"I—My dear, such a decision, should you choose to make it, could only make me the happiest of men,'' the earl said, stunned. He took Celia's hands in his and felt their coldness and straightaway began to turn his self-proclaimed bride back to the light and warmth of the ballroom.

"I know all,'' Celia was declaiming with dreadful clarity, "and *I* will not throw you over for mere worldly happiness. I think—I think my Papa was a very wise man, and to go against his wishes is something I would in nowise countenance!''

"Very wise, I'm sure,'' said Gervase. He put his arm around her shoulders and urged her through the French doors. Once inside, he could see how flushed Lady Celia's cheeks were, and how overbright her eyes. He blamed himself entirely; he should have seen to it that Lady Mulford had kept a closer eye on her—and that rattle Augustus was no help at all!

"Hullo,'' said the rattle, appearing as if by magic. "I wondered where you'd gotten to, Cousin.''

"I am going to marry Lord Coldmeece," Celia recited, "and I shall strive to make him a comfortable wife."

An indescribable expression crossed Augustus's features; half disbelief, half fury. Gervase looked around quickly, but the damage had been done. Too many interested-looking people had heard Celia's reckless declaration, too many people already knew of that so-called secret betrothal. To repudiate Celia now would make it look as if he had brought her up to Town for the express purpose of looking her over, then had spurned her—nor could he call the poor child a liar in public, even to salve Augustus's wounded sensibilities.

"And I," Gervase added, before the silence that followed Celia's pronouncement had time to become awkward, "shall strive to be a tolerable husband. We wanted you to be the first to share our happiness, Augustus."

Augustus was very white about the mouth. "Charmed, Cousin. And *you* may wish *me* very happy as well—for I am to be married also." With that, he executed a furious and punctilious bow and stalked off, leaving the earl sole custodian of a young lady who showed a sudden marked desire to emulate a watering pot. Wishing fervently that he had never taken this ball upon himself, he and his weeping burden went in hasty search of Lady Mulford, and Celia was restored to her side.

"I understand I am to wish you very happy," Lady Mulford said uncertainly, with a measuring glance at her godson's face.

"It does look that way!" snapped the earl. "Allow me to suggest, Godmama, that both your charges would be the better for their beds, as the evening has been such a strain on all concerned."

"Yes," Lady Mulford agreed slowly. "Do have my carriage brought round, Gervase—I'll see if I can find Louisa."

"Allow me to be your servant in both matters, ma'am," he said brusquely. "I fancy Lady Celia has more need of you just now."

Augustus went instantly in search of Louisa. He found her at last in the supper room, listening with a dangerous

123

light in her eyes as a very young man expounded upon the English superiority to every other species of man. Augustus moved quickly to remove her from the young buck's provocative purview.

"Sweet Cousin, how do you find our cousin's—in all things such an admirable cousin!—ball, now that you have had time to savor the length and breadth and depth—depth most especially—of it?"

Louisa regarded him curiously, then frowned. "I think, dear cousin of cousins, I want some air."

Arriving on the terrace that gave out from the supper room, Augustus lounged on the rail, to the great detriment of his coat, and regarded her broodingly.

Louisa, recognizing all the signs of Augustus in the tiresome grip of Strong Emotion, sighed. "Well, Gussie?" she prodded at last.

"Sweetest and most constant of cousins, how correct you were! In token of my homage to Truth, let us away and be married over the anvil this very night! To Gretna, to pledge ourselves to sober propriety in wedlock, and quaff the draft of Constancy, foolish or no!" He seized Louisa's hands and pulled her close to him, gazing down at her with an expression of passionate intensity that quite disturbed her.

"Oh, certainly," she agreed caustically. "An elopement to Gretna would certainly make me the pattern-card of propriety. *Do* talk sense, Gussie. What's happened?"

Augustus released her abruptly with a muttered remark about the stars in their courses, and turned away from her to gaze out into the night. "Celia's accepted Coldmeece."

Louisa felt as if all the breath had been knocked out of her body. "She what?" she managed finally.

Augustus's voice was flat, and he spoke without his customary rodomontade. "She sent for me to meet her on the balcony, but I was late, and when I got there he was there with her. He said they wanted me to be the first to know. You know, Louisa, it's all very peculiar," he finished inadequately.

Coldmeece was to marry Celia? Louisa felt obscurely betrayed. "Poor Gussie," she said, taking his hand in both of hers and squeezing it comfortingly. Augustus, making a valiant effort to smile, enfolded his hands around hers and carried them to his lips. Just then a voice came from behind them.

"Do forgive me for interrupting you, Lady Louisa, but Lady Mulford sent me to find you. Lady Celia is feeling unwell, and your aunt thinks it best the girl be taken home."

Louisa turned, snatching her hands from Augustus, and found herself face to face with the Earl of Coldmeece.

"I'll take you to her, Cousin," Augustus said quickly, and rudely whisked Louisa off under Gervase's nose.

The earl stared after them, a horrid suspicion forming in his mind. Surely—surely Augustus did not mean that he had offered for *Lady Louisa Darwen*?

Chapter
EIGHT

At nine of the clock the morning after the ball, Gervase Darwen, earl of Coldmeece, was drinking coffee and eating sirloin in the breakfast room of Coldmeece House. The day had dawned fair, and a clear April sunlight sparkled off the napery and silver of the table.

Gervase's wakefulness at this hour was occasioned by his strong desire to speak to Mr. Augustus Templeton before that resourceful young gentleman found some way to avoid him. If what Augustus had blurted out last night—before far too many witnesses!—was true, then Augustus was pledged to marry his cousin Louisa, a woman who could in no way be considered a proper wife for Gervase's heir.

It was not that Gervase held Louisa in dislike; indeed, he had come to know her as a witty conversationalist, an excellent dancer, and a charming companion—when she was in the mood to be. Nor could he feel it was through any fault of her own that she had been raised in a Turkish seraglio. But now that he had seen her flying her true colors at Caro's ball, in a fashion more resembling a light frigate than a virtuous Darwen, he knew she was the last person on earth to make Augustus happy.

Gervase could not for the life of him see how, other than by force of blackmail, Augustus could in the first place have been induced to marry at all, and, in the second place, to marry a woman like that! Augustus might enjoy setting others by the ears, but he had little desire to be overset himself.

And as for Louisa, she needed a husband who would take proper care of her, or the day would come when she skated completely over the borders of propriety, ruining herself and those close to her in the process. Gervase could not feel that Augustus was the man to entrust with the guardianship of the exotic Louisa; Augustus thrived on raising havoc and leaving others to cope with the results. Those two headstrong Darwen cousins were fatally unsuited to each other. But how to make Louisa let Augustus go?

Gervase might have continued turning these worrisome puzzles about in his mind for some time had not Bracken entered to announce both that Augustus was at last awake, and that "Lady Coldmeece is here to see you, m'lord."

Intrigued, Gervase decided that Augustus would keep for the moment. What could possibly have dragged Caro out of bed before noon the day after a ball? He instructed Bracken to show her in, and absently tousled the dusky curls of his companion at the breakfast table and sternly instructed her to be on her best behavior.

Caroline sailed into the room looking far more radiant than could reasonably be expected of a lady who had been dancing 'til dawn. She was charmingly attired in a lace-trimmed frock of a daring shade of yellow, and a dashing bonnet trimmed with matching ribbons, which she removed as she entered.

"Gervase, darling," she cooed. "How *can* I thank you for all the pleasure you gave to all of us last night?"

"Do sit down, Caroline," the earl invited, ignoring this speech. "And tell me what you want."

"Want?" Caro pouted prettily, seating herself in the proffered chair. "Why is it that you always assume I want something when I come to see you, Gervase?"

"Because you always do," he replied. "And as I have provided you with a great many things recently, I cannot think what you want now."

"I want my child!" Caroline declared dramatically.

This stirring declamation had little effect upon the earl. Not moving from where he sat, he waved a lazy hand and indicated the seat beside him.

Lady Charlotte Amalia Darwen, dressed with consummate care and artistry by her nurse in pale pink embroidered muslin for the signal treat of breakfast with her uncle, sat spraddle-legged on the brocade cushion of her chair. Her face, her hands, and most of the front of her dress were covered with blackberry jam, to which the crumbs of a muffin clung most gratifyingly. Her chin was shiny with butter.

"Say good morning to your mama, Charlotte," the earl said, as Charlotte shrank back, round-eyed, from Caroline. To be fair, Caro recoiled nearly as much; the earl smiled upon them both, and said, "Charlotte," once more, in tones of stern warning.

Conscious of Gervase's mocking eyes upon her, Caroline leaned over and gave Charlotte's cheek a hasty peck, hoping devoutly that the brat wouldn't paw her. Remembering her mission, however, she said coaxingly, "How are you, darling? Do you want to come home with Mama?"

"No!" said Charlotte firmly, and turned her back upon Caroline.

"Charlotte," said the earl again, and rang the small silver bell at his elbow. When a footman appeared, he desired him to send Mrs. Raxton to the breakfast room at once. Charlotte seemed disposed to cry at this, and the earl reminded her gently that he had requested her to mind her manners in company.

"Mama's a *bad* lady!" tearfully insisted Charlotte.

"Perhaps," said the earl. "But one does not say so, child." He rose and picked Charlotte up, carrying her to the doorway, where he deposited her into Mrs. Raxton's arms.

Taking his seat once more, he regarded Caroline blandly. "To return to the topic at hand," he said, "I am afraid I must deny you my niece, as she does not seem to share the nearly universal partiality for your company you are so quick to provoke."

"How could she?" Caro shot back. "The way you persecute her?"

The earl raised an eyebrow. "Might I remind her doting

128

mama that in all the time Charlotte was at Coldmere—sixteen months—you only twice crossed the park to see her? And do not suggest it was fear of me that kept you away, dearest Sister-in-law, for as you well know, I was abroad much of that time.''

"She's my daughter!" Caro insisted stubbornly.

"A fact you never seem to recall until you want something from me," the earl riposted. "Which reminds me, Caro, you may wish me very happy. The date's not been set yet but Lady Celia and I are to be married." An uncharitable desire to do his annoying sister-in-law in the eye had warred with prudence; prudence, alas, had lost. Besides, if Caro had not already been regaled with the news a dozen times, he would be much surprised.

"But—" Caro protested, half rising from her seat, "but how could she?"

Gervase raised his brows. "And after all you had done to put her off, too?" he suggested.

Caroline flushed guiltily. "I am sure I wish you very happy—if you *will* be," she said darkly.

"I think I shall be tolerably well amused," he said offhandedly. "She assures me she will not throw me over for mere worldly happiness, so I do not expect to be—twice—confounded."

Caroline glared furiously down at her clasped hands for several seconds until he added genially, "However, you had come to demand your dear daughter, or failing her, some little service to make life bearable. I have told you before that Charlotte stays with me . . . so in what other way may I be of service, dear Caroline?"

The countess looked up quickly. "Oh, how you hate me, Gervase—but I swear, I would wish you happy in this match with all my heart if I thought *your* heart was engaged! You do not love the chit—why marry her?"

"Darwens always marry their cousins," said the earl lazily, "or nearly always. I have always noted it to work better that way. And now, Caroline, spare me any more foolish vaporings. I will gladly cede you all the maternal virtues, but the hour grows late and I have a number of pressing engagements, so if you will . . . ?"

"I want to give a ball," Caro said flatly. The earl leaned back in his chair. "A masquerade ball," she went on, and he frowned. "Here," she finished.

The earl sat up very straight. "No."

Caroline leaned forward supplicatingly. "Gervase, be reasonable! My tiny house hasn't the room in it to hold a ball! I should do all the work myself, and pay all the bills— you wouldn't even know anything out of the ordinary was happening."

"I doubt that very much," said the earl blightingly, "and the answer is still no, Caroline. Not a masque, nor yet any other kind of ball. One ball in this house this Season has been more than sufficient."

Caro stood and paced about the room, switching her demi-train as if it were the tail of an angry cat. "You are an *odious* man!" she announced furiously. "Quite impossible! I ask nothing of you—only that you do your duty by the family and lend me your ballroom just for one night! You are an insufferable man, Gervase, and being the earl has not improved you."

"Why, Caroline," said the earl mildly, "such frankness quite unnerves me."

Caro turned on him. "There is no use being on polite terms with you!" she snapped, and stood fuming as Gervase roared with laughter. When he was able to regard her silently, if not solemnly, she played her trump card. "Oh, you may laugh at me now, but you will not laugh when my masque—the masquerade ball of the countess of Coldmeece, *dear* Brother-in-law—is held in a public assembly room."

There was a pause. "You wouldn't dare," said the earl slowly. He could not imagine what had so possessed Caro that she must suddenly give a ball, and on the very heels of his own. Such precipitateness argued spite at the best. But whatever Caro's motives, he knew very well that his termagant sister-in-law would indeed stoop to renting a hall for her display—of temper, if nothing else.

"Would I not?" Caro smiled triumphantly.

"You talk to me of duty to the family, and yet you plan to make us a public spectacle?"

130

"As if anything I could do would gain more notice than your cousin Louisa at the ball last night!" snapped Caroline, with more venom than veracity. "And *Augustus*! The whole town is a-buzz with gossip, wondering who he is to wed. I might make a guess, dear brother-in-law mine, as to who—and why. Shall I?"

The earl knew he had been outmaneuvered. Whatever happened, there must be no more gossip about the Darwens this Season. If Caro were properly bribed she could be very useful in countering the stories already being retailed about Lady Celia's come-out ball. If she were not . . . Caro was quite stubborn enough to hold a masked ball in rented rooms, and he—if not she—did have the family to think of.

"And when do you contemplate holding this . . . small entertainment?"

"The invitations give the date as a month from now," Caro said with a coy smile. "That should give everyone enough time to arrange for costumes, don't you think?"

Gervase instantly assumed the worst. "I think, Caroline," he said grimly, "that you have already sent out those invitations, have you not?"

Caro opened her azure eyes very wide. "Why, Gervase!" she said in honeyed tones. "How *can* you say such a thing?"

"Because I know you, Caro, and I know that tone and that smirk," he told her bluntly.

"Yes, you and I know one another well," she agreed airily. "Do you agree, then?"

"You have my permission to hold your masquerade here," the earl said reluctantly. "But remember, Caroline, you will not always find me this . . . accommodating."

He rose to his feet and escorted her out into the hall, waiting as she tied the ribbons of her bonnet. She lifted her chin a trifle defiantly as she turned to face him.

"Why must we always quarrel, Gervase?" she asked plaintively. "I would so much rather we did not."

"Do we quarrel?" The earl raised his brows. "Caroline, you distress me to a degree I cannot express. Our relationship is simple: you come to me with demands, I gratify them. Such an elemental contract leaves no room for quarreling.''

''Oh, aren't you ever serious?'' she demanded.

The earl opened the front door for her and stood aside. ''Dear sister,'' he remarked as he ushered her out into the sunlight, ''the one thing you will learn in this life is that sincerity is the virtue that everyone praises and no one rewards. Good day, Caroline.''

And that, Caro reflected to herself as her footman helped her into her carriage, was as much as she would have to be content with. Still, he *had* granted permission for her to hold the masked ball at Coldmeece House—and what a perfect setting *that* would be for an elopement! She was certain Celia could be made to see it that way, at any rate. So romantic. Why, Caro would quite like to elope from a masked ball herself.

It was too vexing of the chit to have accepted Gervase at all, but since it plainly was no love match for either party, Caro felt the engagement would be little handicap to her plans. It would, of course, be a great pity to lose Mr. Upshaw just as she had found him—such an attractive man, and such an excellent dancer!—but Caroline was willing to make any sacrifice policy demanded.

Gervase watched Caro's gaudy carriage draw away from the curb and then closed the door on the sight. He was more irritated than he had let her suspect. A masquerade ball! They had not been the fashion in London in years; the *bal masques* at Vauxhall Gardens, where the demi-mondaines prospected for new protectors, had made the very notion of a masked ball revolting to the *ton*. What was worse, she would almost certainly invite Celia, Augustus, Lady Mulford, and quite a number of other people he would not like to see at such an entertainment.

Thoughts of the Honorable Augustus Templeton in mask and domino recalled Gervase to the task before him. Pausing before Augustus's door, Gervase knocked, then opened it gently.

From the inner chamber he could hear Augustus berating his Russian valet, Sasha, both in English and a language Gervase didn't recognize. He intruded himself into this inner sanctum, passing the valet as he left bearing an armful of discarded neckclothes.

"And don't think because we're not in Petersburg that I can't have you flogged, you bloody fool, because I can—and I *will*!" Augustus called after him, and then caught sight of Gervase. "Oh, hullo, Coldmeece. I didn't hear you come in."

"You were otherwise occupied," said the earl, settling himself into an armchair.

Augustus gazed into the mirror, giving one final admonitory twitch to his spotless cravat. Pale yellow trousers adorned his lower limbs, and a waistcoat that seemed almost designed to harmonize with the walls further embellished his person. He regarded his reflection critically, seemed satisfied with the cravat's perfection, and took up a pair of silver-mounted tortoise-shell brushes and began arranging his hair.

"Sasha don't mind a bit of talk," Augustus said offhandedly. "He's heard worse."

He was likely to hear worse today, Gervase felt, considering that the matter of a coat had not yet been embarked on.

"Besides," Augustus went on cheerfully, as an afterthought, "he don't understand English—not above half, anyway."

Gervase was sure that Augustus suspected a scold was in the offing, and was choosing this method of averting it. The first coat—a rather surprising creation in peacock—was rejected, and Augustus seemed disposed to go into the reasons for this at some length.

"Charmed as I would ordinarily be to hear more on this fascinating topic," Gervase said, "I begged the favor of an interview with you to discuss quite another matter—but first you may offer me your condolences." He folded his arms and waited.

"Condolences?" said Augustus quickly. "Did Celia—?" He brought himself up short, and assumed an air of unconcern. "Very well, Cousin, I condole with you most particularly—only, pray, why?"

"Caroline is giving a masked ball in this very house," Gervase said. "In one month's time. She assures me I shall hardly notice."

Augustus stared at him in astonishment; then his naturally volatile nature won out. He laughed, and, turning to straddle a chair, he leaned on the back of it and regarded his cousin.

"The woman's mad," he said comprehensively. He considered a moment, then added, "And for that matter, why the devil did you say yes, Coldmeece? If you denied her the ballroom, she could hardly hold it in the street."

"You don't know the Countess as well as you think, if you think that, Augustus. But in addition to all other considerations, it was borne in upon me by Caroline that due to the unfortunate behavior of a number of Darwens at the ball I held last night, I can hardly fail to hold another—at least, if I wish Caro's talent for gossip used to quell rumors, rather than start them."

Augustus regarded his cousin with an expression of disapproval. "Why you ever let that woman gammon you into having her for your hostess I'm sure I never—" He broke off, and a sudden shock seemed to galvanize him. "I say, Gervase—*what have you done to your coat?*"

The earl looked down and realized, to his dismay, that Lady Charlotte's small handprints were entirely visible. "Jam," he said shortly.

"Jam?" said Augustus in affront. *"Jam?"* he said again in outrage.

The earl meekly admitted that Lady Charlotte had been responsible for the jam marks, but that Augustus should absolve him from all charges of having mauled the coat. He was wondering how to steer the conversation back to betrothals and marriages, but Augustus was far from ready to abandon the vital matter of Gervase's coat.

"Weston!" Augustus fulminated. "Where's the good in wasting Weston on a fellow like you? Scott. *Hoby!* They'd do as well. If I were Weston, Gervase, I should refuse to cut your coats. Shocking way you carry on!"

Gervase agreed that it was, indeed, shocking the way he carried on, and then wished cautiously to know if he was to wish Augustus very happy, considering his announcement at the ball. But again Mr. Templeton eluded him.

"In fact," he said broodingly, "I shouldn't wonder if he *hadn't* refused. Sleeve. Very unlike him. Still, you know, I wonder what she can possibly mean by doing it? Shockingly high-handed."

"Weston?" the earl asked, floundering.

"Weston?" demanded Augustus in surprise. "I was talking about *Caro*! I do wish you'd keep to the point, y'know, Cousin, bargin' in on a man in the dead of night to tell him about a masked ball and then nattering off about coats. You really ought to send her back down to Coldmere."

"Caroline? She wouldn't go."

"*Charlotte*, of course! Stands to reason Caro wouldn't be pawing you all over with jammy hands. Not but what she wouldn't like to, but—well! But if she's going to give a masquerade, it would be nice to know what the theme is. Very important. She'll invite me, no doubt?"

"Oh, undoubtedly," said the earl, who had come to the conclusion that if there were anything more peripatetic than Augustus's conversation in the morning he had yet to meet it. "Perhaps Caroline will invite Lady Louisa as well," said the earl boldly, determined to introduce the subject by main force if necessary. "Caroline seemed much struck by her at the ball last night."

Augustus grinned at him. "Thought she was shockin', did she, and expensive? Caro'd say the same about any female that dressed well. Not that it ain't true, of course, but Caro'll catch cold trying to come the gracious hostess over Louisa. Louisa's been condescended to by experts. She told you she'd met Princess Lieven?"

"She said the Princess had given her permission to waltz, in Vienna." The conversation finally seemed to be heading in the right direction, albeit tangentially.

Augustus spread his hands wide, as though to indicate no more need be said. "Well then! But I do hope Caro's not going all over Greeks. Nasty fellows, the Greeks, always turning into olive trees or something. Make damn drafty costumes, too.''

''I fancy Caroline intends to go as a shepherdess,'' the earl said repressively, ''not that it matters. Augustus, I had hoped to talk to you—''

''But you *are* talking to me,'' protested his cousin, an expression of limpid idiocy writ large upon his features. ''Why else would you be here? Take my advice, Gervase— no good will come of letting Caro dress herself up as a shepherdess in your ballroom. She's sure to want to bring in sheep. Nasty beasts, sheep,'' he added ruminatively.

''But, Augustus,'' said the earl, ''did you not say last night that you intended to marry?''

''Well, of course, but not at a masquerade ball! And I ain't marryin' Caro, no matter what she's dressed as, so you can set your mind at rest on that head. It's my belief the woman took a brain fever in Italy, what with Byron and all.''

''I can see, Cousin, that you are in great distress and now is not the moment to discuss either your approaching nuptials or Lady Louisa's income settlement.''

''Settlement?'' Augustus came to some degree of attention. ''Aunt Josie can't settle anything on Louisa. Her money's booked.''

''True, but mine is not, and I can. Augustus, if you are marrying—''

At this inopportune moment a footman intruded to announce apologetically that there was a person wishing to see Mr. Templeton. This person, it appeared, had a horse with him.

''A horse?'' Augustus said, then, ''Of course! In the Park! Anyone could see she was a prime goer, a bang-up piece of blood-and-bone, wasted on that gudgeon. Told him to bring her around. I thought she'd be perfect for Celia. Wait till you see her, Gervase. I shall be down directly.'' Grabbing the coat Sasha offered him, he shrugged into it without looking at it, gave his hair a last hasty swipe with the brushes, and dashed out. Moments later, his voice floated up the stair. "Hi! You! Don't jab at her mouth like that! Come here, now—"

Rant and wriggle and chase off after masked balls as he might, Augustus could not evade the methodical workings of Gervase's mind. He knew Augustus intended to marry Lady Louisa Darwen. He knew, too, that nothing could be more disastrous—why, at the very least, the boy was in love with Lady Celia.

The last unfortunate reflection reminded the earl that, while Augustus might be in love with Lady Celia, it was the earl who had pledged to marry her. One meeting with Celia had convinced him that *they* would not suit, while one glance at Celia and Augustus, so young, so glowing, so obviously in the throes of love, was enough to make even the most hard-hearted wish to wish them very happy.

But now Caro, devil take the meddlesome woman, had managed to drive Celia into the earl's arms in spite of all— and there, it seemed, the child was determined to stay, though it made three people miserable. With this unhappy thought foremost in his mind, Gervase turned to the business of the day.

The morning was not much farther advanced when it burst in upon Lady Louisa in her rose-gold Georgian bed-chamber. Louisa's routine the day after major balls was as fixed as it was inviolable. She slept until late afternoon, then had chocolate and muffins.

Today, however, Louisa had not completed the first phase of this comfortable schedule when the second was rudely thrust upon her.

Lady Mulford bustled into the room, banging the door open loudly. She was followed by Campbell, wheeling a tray which held pots of chocolate, preserves, and bread. Lady Mulford shut the door vigorously behind them and then proceeded to throw open the heavy curtains. There was a muffled shriek from the bed.

"Louisa!" Lady Mulford said in great agitation. "Louisa! Oh, do wake up, silly girl, it's nearly ten, and something dreadful has happened. Louisa! Oh, *do* wake up!"

Louisa groaned, and raised herself from the depths of a mass of blankets like Leviathan rising from the deep. "Aunt Josephine," she announced, in tones of discovery. Her aunt had a wine and amber cashmere shawl about her shoulders, a snowy lace cap upon her silver curls, and a stiff cream-colored card in her hand. She waved the card at Louisa.

"Louisa!" Lady Mulford said fiercely. "Coldmeece is marrying Celia, and Caro Darwen is holding a masked ball in a month!"

Louisa groped behind her for a pillow and slowly sat up.

"Four weeks!" Lady Mulford went on. "The end of May—and That Woman holding a *masquerade ball* at Coldmeece House! I do not know how she could ever have persuaded Gervase to agree to such an infamous undertaking. He *swore* to me that he would be *firm* with her this Season, because of Celia and *how* could he do such a thing? And the wedding! Of all the *unsuitable* places to offer for Celia—Lady Jersey says he proposed right in the middle of the dance floor!—and now what *are* we to do? Oh dear! Perhaps *Aunt Serena* will wish to come up to Town. Oh *dear*! And it is very nearly a whirlwind courtship, you know, which always look so precipitous and not a *peep* out of Gervase as to when the wedding's to be—"

"It is my belief that the wedding's to be put off as long as possible; Coldmeece wants to marry Celia as much as she does him," Louisa said flatly, stirring herself to collect a cup of chocolate from the tray.

This announcement had the effect of halting Lady Mulford's peroration in midsentence. "Louisa!" she exclaimed in shocked tones. "You could not possibly be implying—oh, I know you do not care for Gervase, even though he has been all that is amiable—"

"Excessively," put in Louisa.

"—and even invited dear Mrs. Edgeworth to visit us, which I am sure we all particularly enjoyed, but—oh, where was I? Yes! You cannot think that Gervase forced Celia to accept his suit against her wishes?" Lady Mulford looked horrified.

"Coldmeece *couldn't* make Celia do anything she didn't wish to. As for the rest—oh, Aunt, my head's in a dreadful muddle, and I really think I ought to talk to Celia before offering my humble opinions. Where is she, poor little thing? She was so dreadfully knocked up last night."

"Louisa! I do wish you wouldn't allow Gussie to teach you that *horrid* slang. Celia's still asleep; I sent Rigsby in to see before I came to wake you."

"Then, Aunt, you and I can have a comfortable coze before I totter off to quiz my unregenerate cousin," Louisa said obligingly, wishing Aunt Josephine had let all of her sleeping nieces lie. "Really," she went on, "it *was* a stupid idea to make Celia's come-out ball such a mad crush. Anyone who had ever spent five minutes alone with Celia—which, I suppose, does leave out Coldmeece—would have seen that the *last* course of action to recommend itself would be a fete like that. What *can* the man have been thinking of?"

"My dear, it was *you* he was thinking of!" Lady Mulford burst out. Though she immediately regretted it, she at least had the felicity of seeing her niece's eyes fully open for the first time that morning.

"My dear cousin the Earl of Coldmeece was thinking of me?" said Louisa. "How very kind of him!"

"Oh, dear," said Lady Mulford nervously, beginning to pleat the edge of her shawl. Her niece was not diverted.

"Aunt Josephine," she said warningly.

"Really, Louisa, it was only that he thought a—a *busy* Season, such as would naturally attend upon Celia's come-out—and the ball, of course—would serve to—to 'fire you off with a flare.'"

"And am I supposed to stand in need of, er, 'firing off with flare' by my good cousin?" Louisa asked dulcetly, more enraged by the thought of the earl's managing ways with each passing moment. Now Louisa wished she *had* let Augustus have his way and announce their betrothal at the outset. She could have had a quiet Season, dear Aunt Josephine need never have been so horridly vexed, and Celia—

Louisa was forced to admit that there would still have

remained the problem of Celia. There was one good thing in all of this; she was in a position to see that Celia, at least, did not suffer from the earl's passion for order.

How could she have been so deceived in the man? Louisa thought, with an unhappiness that surprised her. She had become far too fond of her earlish cousin; it had been so easy to assume that he would act as she would wish in any circumstance. But *how* could he have offered for Celia? It passed understanding. First, Louisa decided, she would talk to Celia and discover her feelings. Then she must see Augustus—

" . . . and Gussie's preposterous announcement at the ball last night!'' Lady Mulford's words cut across Louisa's thoughts.

"Beg pardon, Aunt?'' said Louisa innocently. "I was not attending.''

"I *said*,'' Lady Mulford told her, "that you should be *glad* Gervase takes an interest in your future. *He*, at least, understands that you are quite old enough to marry—and that you could not expect to meet an eligible *parti* if you stood in bed all day!''

"Coldmeece said that?'' Louisa asked, diverted.

"Louisa! He said no such thing!'' Lady Mulford gasped, and Louisa went off into peals of laughter at her aunt's confused attempts to explain precisely what the earl *had* said, and to retrieve his good name.

"Oh, never mind, Aunt, I'm sure your immaculate godson is a very paragon of all the virtues, but you were talking about Gussie, I am sure.''

"Oh, well, dearest, I was simply saying that you should thank your stars that Gervase is standing by you as a representative of the family, what with Augustus giving himself over to such mad starts as that preposterous announcement of his.''

"Oh?'' said Louisa. "What announcement, Aunt?''

"Why, Louisa, I was sure you knew! When Gervase announced that he and Celia were to wed—though *not* in the middle of the dance floor as Sally says; Lady Vane was right there, and she said they had just that moment come in from the terrace, the one overlooking the garden—and

Augustus told him—Gervase—that *he* might wish *him* very happy as well, because he—that is, Gussie, darling—was to be married as well. Well! Everyone was positively *gasping*, and—''

''Did he say who it was that he intended to marry?''

''No, not a word, darling, and it is so *peculiar*! Why, for all he was home two years ago for the Little Season, no one had thought he'd formed any *tendres*—Perhaps it is a Russian lady, but I am sure his dear papa would never approve, or Aunt Serena. Oh, Louisa! *You* must talk to Augustus, and explain to him that on no account must he displease Aunt Serena!''

''I am sure it is all a hum, and Gussie isn't marrying anyone.'' Yes, that was the ticket! Surely the incident could be fobbed off as one of Gussie's larks.

''Oh, no,'' said Lady Mulford firmly, dashing Louisa's hopes. ''He could not possibly have been teasing Gervase. Lady Vane says— Well, there's no need to go into that now, but the boy is serious, and everyone is wondering *who* the girl can be! I will write to Euphemia at once and tell her *all*—news like this is much better received of a *sister*, and really, one can *not* place the least reliance on Gussie's doing so—and perhaps she will know—''

''I wonder what I shall wear to Caro Darwen's masquerade?'' Louisa said hurriedly, twitching the gilt-edged card of invitation from her aunt's grasp and quickly scanning it. ''Something calculated to set the *ton* on its ear, I think. She says we are all to come costumed as Fantastic Personages—that should be simple enough to arrange.''

Lady Mulford primmed up her mouth. ''I had thought that perhaps I would tell Lady Coldmeece that we were engaged that evening. I cannot think that any party of That Woman's would be the sort of entertainment Celia would find enjoyable.''

''Oh, my, no,'' said Louisa in amusement. ''But think, Aunt, by keeping Celia from attending this masque, you are depriving untold *scores* of persons sadly in need of her edifying lectures and her uplifting presence.'' Since coming to London Louisa had heard a great deal about Caro's fast set and its pleasures, mostly in the form of admonitory lectures from Aunt Josephine on the perils of London Society, and the thought of the methodistical little Celia swimming among Caro's "loose fish" was irresistible, if alarming.

"I shall certainly be unable to 'deprive' them, as you put it, if you present this affair to Celia in such an enticing light!" she said tartly. "Caro Darwen is up to some mischief—that much seems clear—and I had rather not allow her to embroil Celia, or, indeed, any of us, in her schemes. I am depending on you, Louisa, to keep the news of this masque from Celia."

Louisa snorted. "And shall I also swear all London to silence? However, you are right, Aunt; we ought virtuously to deny ourselves the opportunity to watch Caro make a fool of herself yet again, for the sake of the child. Oh, and speaking of children, did you know Caro has brought Lady Charlotte up to Town? It is very odd, as women of her sort generally do not boast about being mamas."

"In my experience, women of Caro's sort generally want anything they cannot have," Lady Mulford said. "And Gervase, as little Charlotte's guardian, took her to live at Coldmeece more than a year ago."

"Little Charlotte has my sympathy," said Louisa, stifling a yawn. She rubbed her forehead wearily. "This is *not* a civilized hour of the day to be about, Aunt, I do assure you."

Lady Mulford inspected her niece critically, and suggested she would feel the better for a little breakfast. "And then perhaps you would look in on Celia, for the natural vitality of youth should have restored her to herself by noon, certainly."

Louisa agreed that this was very likely so, as she gingerly prepared to venture out from under the bedcovers. She devoutly wished there were such a thing as the natural vitality of extreme decrepitude, for she was certain she would require it to survive the day ahead.

Louisa was not far wrong in this gloomy assumption. An hour later she tapped at Celia's door and then opened it gently, only to find Celia wide awake, staring at the ceiling. When she saw Louisa, she gave a guilty start, then sat up. Louisa handed her a robe of aquamarine watered silk, and Celia obediently put it on, swinging her feet over the edge of the bed as she did so. There were dark circles beneath her eyes, and they were puffy, as though she had spent the night in tears. Louisa, seeing this, nodded wisely to herself, and decided to take matters slowly.

"And how did you find your first ball, Cousin?" Louisa asked matter-of-factly, handing Celia her silver hairbrush. "I would not have wakened you for the world, but Aunt Josephine feared you might never come down."

"Oh," said Celia. She pulled off her bed cap and began fluffing out her short silver-gilt curls distractedly. "I believe I liked it," she said slowly, "for it was wonderful to be so admired. But everything was very strange, and I do believe, Louisa, that so much unbounded admiration is bad for the character, as it gives one a false and deceitful view of one's self."

"That is not a problem I find that I share, dear Celia," Louisa said dryly. "But did you *like* it? The dancing? The music?"

"Oh, yes!" said Celia. "That is, I—well . . . Oh, Louisa! I am to *marry* Coldmeece!" she finished tragically.

"Yes," said Louisa encouragingly. "And I must admit we did not know what to think when we heard, and why you could not have told us on the way home last night— but that is neither here nor there. Perhaps now you will tell me what happened?"

Celia turned her face away, and her cheeks turned a becoming pink as she stared at her toes. "You must think me a shocking fribble, and after I told you I could not love the man, and that this marriage could only be a vain and frivolous institution. But at the ball I discovered that which convinced me it was my duty to accept him—and so I did."

Louisa tactfully forebore from asking the question uppermost in her mind: Had the earl actually offered for Celia? She said only, "But, Cousin, you know I could not think anything you do shocking—don't look so Friday-faced at me, you ninny, I still love you! I do wonder, though, how you conceive it your duty to embrace frivolity. But perhaps you could explain it to me?''

"Well, you see, Louisa, I . . . I had had no notion, I promise you, of . . . of shattering a man's life beyond repair, when I said I wished to cry off.''

"What?" said Louisa, not unnaturally taken aback by this statement. "Celia, darling,'' she said, after seating herself on the rumpled bed in preparation for further shocks, "would you mind *very* much explaining the entire story to me *very* clearly? I fear my understanding is not so good as I had thought.''

"Why,'' said Celia, looking surprised, "Lady Coldmeece came to me and explained all!''

"All what, darling?'' Louisa prompted after a moment.

"But I have just told you, Louisa. It was when Lady Coldmeece came to me and explained that Coldmeece still loved her, and was marrying me just to spite her for marrying his brother Edmund, you understand, and that if I should marry him, not only would I find him a Cold and Distant Spouse whose heart was Ever Pledged To Another, but that he was in addition shockingly clutch-fisted, and persecuted Lady Coldmeece constantly by withholding from her the Society of her Only Child, so I should find him a disagreeable man all around. So naturally I *had* to accept his suit!''

"Did you?'' said Louisa, a desire to murder Caro Darwen taking strong possession of her.

Celia frowned. "Well, of course. And he came to me on the balcony and said I was intending to throw him over! Everyone knows that Lady Coldmeece jilted him for a title, and now is chasing him only because he is the earl, and when I saw to what lengths she was willing to go, and how dreadful it would be for him if *two* women were to throw him over because of his title, even though I would not have refused him precisely because he *was* the earl, as Lady Coldmeece did—only she refused him because he wasn't an earl, I think—and what a lowering opinion he must have conceived of the entire race of women, which

144

my dereliction could only foster—and after all, the poor man is over thirty years of age; he *must* marry, or the earldom will go a-begging soon! That must be what dear Papa meant.''

''And so you are marrying the earl just to give him a better opinion of women?'' Louisa asked carefully, wishing to be certain she understood the matter entirely.

''Yes,'' said Celia, ''and because I had not perfectly understood before how *many* people knew all about the secret agreement between dear Papa and the earl.''

''But, Celia!'' Louisa protested helplessly, and then dropped her hands to her lap. She knew it was no use telling her martyr-minded cousin that no one would have taken such an agreement seriously even had all England known, and would only have thought the better of the earl for not holding a child of Celia's age to it. She sighed, and instead asked, ''Will you like to be the countess of Coldmeece?''

Celia looked suddenly stricken. ''It—oh, Louisa! I *must* marry him now! I have promised! What can I do?''

''I think,'' said Louisa, rising to her feet and putting a comforting arm around Celia's shoulders, ''that you can come and make a good breakfast, before matters go any further.''

''Perhaps,'' Celia said a few hours later, ''my papa was correct about dissipation and such things, for now I see how little in the way of fulfilling work may be accomplished by persons going constantly to balls if it is true that a few country dances may render one unable to leave his bed for *days*!''

Louisa looked up from the copy of *The Bride of Abydos* that she was idly perusing. The two young ladies were occupying the back drawing room, neither having any real taste for other activity. Lady Mulford had gone out; it was Louisa's opinion she was going to ring a peal over the abominable earl, and Louisa approved. Even though the matter of settlements and agreements and bequests in Celia and Coldmeece's marriage had been settled by their parents about the time Celia was born, if Coldmeece *were* to marry her there were a thousand pressing matters to attend to. At the very least, out of common politeness, he should have been here today to pay a morning call on his betrothed. Of course if he had, Celia would very likely have shrieked and fled from the room, but at least the gesture would have been made.

Louisa wondered if *all* Frankish persons were quite, quite mad.

She had just returned to the poem, and was mentally composing a letter of gushing (and spurious) devotion to *dear* Lord Byron, when the door burst open. Augustus Templeton, resplendent in yellow pantaloons and a deep blue coat, strode into the room.

"Louisa!" he said strongly. "I *must* talk to you! It's the very devil of a mess, and—"

Celia, who had been sitting in a high-backed chair by the window, leapt to her feet with the prophesied squeak. Augustus turned and saw her.

"Ah," he said lamely. "Lady Celia. Ah." He bowed.

"Oh," said Celia, blushing fierily. "Mr. Templeton. How do you do?"

"Excuse me," said Louisa, gamely stifling a grin, "I must see to the housemaids." She rather felt the young lovers ought to be alone.

The drawing room door closed behind the tactful Louisa, but Celia was unable to raise her eyes from their intent study of the tips of her shoes. It had not until this awful moment occurred to Celia that she must have mortally offended Augustus. Indeed, he must despise her utterly!

At these melancholy considerations Celia sniffled dolefully.

"I beg your pardon, Cousin Celia?" Augustus said glacially. At this point Celia hiccupped audibly, and Augustus turned to face her; so far from castigating her, he seized her by the shoulders and scanned her tear-damp face with anxious eyes.

"I say," he said helplessly. "I say, Celia! Oh, dash it all, don't *cry*, Cousin!"

This was all that was needed to break down the last of Celia's reserves. "Oh, Gussie!" she sobbed. "It is the most dreadful thing! I don't know *what* I've done!" she wailed, and threw herself on his chest.

Augustus put his arms around his cousin's slender shoulders. He stroked her bright curls and tried to rally her spirits. "Please," he begged, "don't take on so, Coz. Whatever it is, we can soon put it right." He coaxed Celia to sit down upon the sopha, sat down beside her, and provided her with his handkerchief.

Celia assayed a watery sniff and tried to look brave. "Oh, no," she assured him mournfully. "No one can help me. I am going to marry Lord Coldmeece—and I thought I wouldn't mind—but I *do*!"

As Celia was looking straight into Augustus's eyes, the declaration affected him so strongly that he took her hand and pressed it to his lips. This devotion accomplished, his mind turned on practical matters.

"Well," he said bracingly, "that's all right! I don't mind telling you, Cecy, if you *didn't* mind marrying Gervase, I should be—that is to say, everythin' amiable and all that. But I thought you and Louisa'd worked it out between you. You were going to have your Season, and you weren't going to marry him at all."

"Oh, but I am," Celia informed him lugubriously. "He asked me."

"Asked you?" repeated Augustus. "You can't marry everyone that asks you, Cousin. It isn't done. You had best," he said, with a gallant attempt at lightness, "tell all."

So once again Celia explained that Caroline Darwen had made it known to her that all London already knew she was destined to marry Lord Coldmeece, and that Celia had not had the heart to deal the earl's faith in womankind yet another crushing blow and shatter his secret heart forever. She then sat quietly, regarding the stunned Augustus with round, tragic eyes.

"But damn—I mean, dash—it all, Celia, you wouldn't shatter Coldmeece's secret heart forever if you refused him! Man hasn't *got* any! There's only one thing to do,

147

Cousin. You must go and tell Coldmeece you've changed your mind. And forget all that rot about shattered hearts! He won't mind a bit, I promise you.''

''Oh, but I can't, Gussie,'' Celia gasped. ''Don't you see? I should feel such a fool, and—and *cowardly*! I do not love him, but—but perhaps I can *grow* to love him. And—and—I am persuaded that—that no person of character could ever countenance such—such *scaley* behavior as jilting him.''

The slang expression from Celia's lips made Augustus laugh; he gathered her into his arms again and gazed down into her sky blue eyes. ''Adorable widgeon!'' he teased, voice husky with emotion. Celia colored delicately and Augustus came to his senses with a start. ''Lord!'' he exclaimed, releasing her abruptly. ''I must be out of my mind! Dreadfully sorry, Cousin; frightfully rag-mannered of me.''

Celia, suddenly held at arm's length, looked baffled. Augustus attempted to explain, a tinge of color coming to his high cheekbones. ''I must wish you very happy, Celia, if you are set on this crack-brained notion of yours, but what I must *not* do is—well, I'm as bad as Louisa!''

''What has Louisa done?'' Celia asked, intrigued in spite of herself.

At this cue Louisa opened the door with a firm hand. She had been very wicked to leave Love's Young Dream unchaperoned for so long, but they were so *very* much in love. It was just like Gussie to have lost his heart at last to his cousin's affianced bride, just as he had betrothed himself to Louisa. ''Nothing that you are ever likely to do, Cousin, or think of doing, so I'm told. Did you still want to talk to me, Augustus?'' she asked, putting a brave front on the uncertainty she felt.

''To you, my dearest cousin, always,'' he began grandiloquently, but Louisa, catching sight of movement through the curtains, had advanced on the window.

''Augustus,'' she said in a peculiar voice, ''there's a horse in the back garden.''

''A horse?'' asked Celia eagerly.

''Yes!'' said Augustus sounding relieved at the interruption. "I swore I'd see you decently mounted, didn't I? She's the sweetest little thing, almost a match for Prometheus."

"She's eating Aunt Josephine's rosebushes," Louisa commented.

"Blast it!" said Augustus roundly. "I *told* the man to tether her around the side—I wanted to surprise you."

"You'll certainly surprise Aunt Josephine," muttered Louisa.

"Oh, Augustus!" Celia breathed in awe. "She's beautiful! What is her name? And her breeding? Oh, you must tell me all about her!" Celia scampered back from the window to seize Augustus's hand and drag him out of the drawing room.

Louisa followed them out into the garden.

The groom, as it turned out, *had* tethered the mare around the side and had gone to report this fact to the head groom, whereupon the mare had untied herself and gone foraging. Augustus, moving quickly, soon had the dangling lead in hand, and held the prize for her new mistress's inspection.

"Well, Celia, what do you think?" he asked in offhand tones.

Celia's eyes were now round with delight. Under Augustus's indulgent gaze, she came forward to stroke the velvety shoulder. The mare nuzzled Celia's golden curls and tried delicately to remove the ribbon from her hair.

"*Oh*! She is perfect! I will love her, I know! You—you will still ride with me, Augustus? Oh—but you haven't told me her name."

"Her name," Augustus informed Celia, as the mare was led away to the stables by the abashed groom, "is Wollstonecraft."

"*Wollstonecraft?*" Celia demanded in disbelief. "Oh, Gussie, what sort of a name for a horse is that?"

"She is a vindication of the rights of women," Augustus explained gravely. "So it seemed the proper sort of name."

Celia laughed merrily, her silver-gilt curls gleaming in

149

the sunlight as she tossed her head. "Oh, Gussie, how silly! As if Mrs. Shelley had anything to say to the naming of this horse! I shall call her . . . Folly—for that is what your name for her certainly is!"

Louisa, who knew, as apparently Celia did not, that the vindicator of the rights of women was Mrs. Shelley's celebrated mama, said nothing. Though her sins were legion, no one had ever accused Louisa Darwen of stupidity. It was perfectly plain that Augustus and Celia were madly in love. And it was equally obvious, Louisa thought with an inward sigh, that nothing was going to come of it without her help. She understood English customs well enough to know that under no circumstances would Coldmeece repudiate the betrothal. And from certain unhallowed listening at doors she was wide awake to the fact that the very last thing her stubborn cousin Celia would do was cry off from this disastrous marriage.

Therefore, something must be done. Augustus wished to marry Celia, Louisa was not cruel enough to stand in his way—and she dared swear that Coldmeece would thank her for a little judicious meddling in the matter. That left only Celia to deal with.

"Oh, I wish to ride at once! Louisa—mayn't I?"

Louisa shook her head. "No, my angel, the path of duty is thine. We must be here to receive callers, for I am certain that all the *ton* will be here this afternoon to help you celebrate last night's triumph."

At this not too subtle reminder, Celia looked stricken, and Augustus grim.

"Tomorrow, then," said Augustus gallantly. "I'll call for you at ten. And Louisa, will you ride with us?"

"Oh, yes!" said Celia.

"Ten?" said Louisa mockingly. "How likely is that, I ask you? Come along, Celia, Aunt Josephine will have strong hysterics if she sees you standing out here without bonnet or shawl like this."

Louisa shepherded Celia back into the confines of Mulford House, thinking resentfully that a Season that was to have been all frivolous pleasure was turning into a great deal of work.

Chapter
NINE

At noon that same day the Dowager Countess of Cold-meece rode with Mr. Kennard Upshaw in the Park. After the early interview with her brother-in-law, she had spent the remainder of the morning enscribing the last of the invitations to her masquerade; the first batch, as Gervase had so unkindly surmised, having been sent with the dawn. Now her plans were well in train, and only the cooperation of the man she had cast in the role of romantic hero necessary for Lady Celia Darwen-Neville's elopement to become a reality.

And once Lady Celia had eloped—and with an *American*, too!—and had ruined herself socially for Seasons to come, then Caro could make Gervase see what any man of proper feeling would have known without prompting. She, Caro Darwen, was the queen of his heart, just as she had been before she had married his brother Edmund.

The Park was comparatively deserted at this unfashionable hour, and Caro was sorry there were not more people about to appreciate the splendid sight she and Mr. Upshaw presented. After some desultory small talk in which Kennard took amused and curious part, Caro finally brought the conversation around to the matter she wished most earnestly to discuss.

"I come to you, Mr. Upshaw, because, foolish though it seems, there is no one else in the family to whom I can turn—and I am so desperately in need of help! I pray that you will be able to oblige me."

"Indeed," drawled Kennard in his lazy way. "Then

perhaps you will be able to oblige me, Lady Coldmeece, by calling me Kennard—if we are to stand upon such intimate terms, you see.''

Caro favored him with one of her most dazzling smiles. ''Kennard,'' she said caressingly. ''Yes, indeed I shall. But it is the most vexing circumstance which forces me to call upon you.''

Caro leaned across her sidesaddle confidingly, and soon Kennard was in possession of the whole: Caro, while the merest *child*, had been in love with Gervase, but had been forced by her tyrannical and unscrupulous family to accept Edmund when he fell heir to the titles and dignities of Coldmeece. Now that Edmund was dead (and Gervase was the earl) and she was free again, she had been horrified to find that Gervase, having been cut to the quick by her marriage to his brother, had gone so far as to offer for his young cousin, Celia Darwen-Neville.

''It is only, I am sure, foolish pride and injured sensibilities that have forced dear Gervase to this drastic step. I am even persuaded that he feels a renewed tenderness for me. But Mr. Upshaw—Kennard—he has offered for the poor dear child in the most ill-considered fashion possible! I know I can make him see where his heart lies, but *not* if he is to marry that girl within the Season. He feels that he knows his own mind, but I assure you, this is not at all the case.''

''Is it not?'' asked Kennard, enchanted. He was amused and diverted by the transparency of the motives behind her every action, and by her magnificent disregard for consistency.

''No, it is not!'' declared Caroline with some vehemence, causing her flashy gray to toss his head excitedly. ''And this is where you can be most particularly helpful.''

Kennard wondered idly if the beauteous Caro even suspected that her plan to supplant Lady Celia in Coldmeece's affections and marry him herself was not only underhanded, but very probably illegal, as she had been his brother's wife.

''Command me, radiant one,'' drawled Kennard mockingly, earning himself a burning look from Caro.

"Lady Celia," Caroline explained, "is the innocent victim of poor Gervase's wicked machinations. She is a very great heiress, and only seventeen. I am convinced that a handsome and romantic foreigner, such as yourself, but still her cousin for all that—"

"Countess, you flatter me," murmured Kennard.

"—surely such a man could bring her to see that it is not at all in her interest to marry a man such as Cold-meece . . ." She let her sentence trail off suggestively.

Kennard sat up straighter in his saddle. "You mean marry the chit myself?" he demanded.

Caro shrugged. "It doesn't matter to me, so long as she cries off from Coldmeece—I mean, if you were to find that your feelings were in accord, then, naturally—"

Kennard cut off the end of her sentence with a roar of laughter. "No, your ladyship, pray don't try to make amends. I fancy I know where your true sentiments lie. But even if I could turn Lady Celia up sweet—now, I'm not saying I will, mind you, but if I *could*—what makes you think that Coldmeece or the rest of the family would consent to it?"

"Well, I confess that I had thought about it," Caro admitted coyly. "And the matter much exercised my mind, until I came up with the perfect solution. You must elope with Lady Celia."

This took even Kennard aback. After a moment, he said lightly, "Eloping with heiresses isn't exactly in my line, Lady Coldmeece."

Caro eyed him in mocking surprise. "But is that not in very truth what you came to England to do? The life of an overseer on an island plantation can hardly be to your taste, and I see no reason you should not further both our ends—and bring happiness to a great many people—by doing so. If you were to gain control of Lady Celia's fortune, you would never again be troubled by . . . gaming debts." She smiled at him archly.

Kennard was struck dumb by this more or less accurate and totally unflattering summation. "You seem to be remarkably well informed," he said slowly. He had indeed come to England to marry, and richly, and he was appalled to find that Caro Coldmeece knew this; he could not imagine how she had divined it. Let him once be labeled fortune hunter, and he well knew how many doors would abruptly slam in his face. "I wonder that Coldmeece has not already called me out, such a desperate character as you paint me."

"Oh," said Caro airily, quite innocently delighted with Kennard's confirmation of her clever guesses, "I saw no reason to mention it—yet. All gentlemen have gambling debts; it doesn't signify. But you see, this match would be much to your advantage, and I assure you, you will find it so very much easier to attach *this* heiress with my contrivance. You see, in a month I am holding a masked ball at Coldmeece House."

"Are you indeed?" said Kennard, who was not as innocent in the ways of London Society as he chose to pretend. "I wonder that Lord Coldmeece allows it."

Caro flirted her lashes at him. "I have my little ways, Mr. Upshaw. But do you not agree that if one were to wish to elope, very romantically, from a masked ball, he would find it convenient to have the hostess's assistance—and a carriage with all the necessities for a flight North ready to hand?"

Once more Kennard stared with amazement at his companion, and then burst into laughter. "Very well, radiant one. If you wish, I shall pay court to the fair Celia, and do what I may to detach her from her cousin. But as for detaching her from one cousin only to marry her to another—there, my dear cousin-in-law, I shall have to keep you in suspense a while longer."

It did not seem, however, that Kennard was at all in doubt about his own intentions. As April passed into May, he was a frequent visitor at Mulford House—more frequent, in fact, than the earl, which caused Louisa no end of malicious amusement, even as she regretted the absence of the one truly entertaining man in all of London.

It was all very awkward. She had intended a marriage of convenience, to be sure, but not one in which her husband was idiotishly in love with someone else and making a cake of himself over the matter. There were times when Louisa wished nothing more than to give all of her various cousins the shaking of their lives.

She had the opportunity, if not the courage, to fulfill part of that desire this morning, for no less a person than the Earl of Coldmeece graced the Mulford House drawing room. Louisa's heart had leapt most impractically upon beholding him, and she imagined that, bowing over her hand, he held it a moment longer than necessary. The conspiratorial gleam of wry amusement in his expression seemed to enfold the two of them alone, and Louisa, absurdly heartened by the fact, felt she had been forgiven all the duplicities of the Coldmeece ball.

He had come to pay an impeccably correct morning call and to apologize to Lady Celia for his dereliction of the past few days; business matters at Coldmeece had urgently required his attention.

"Oh, Gervase," chirped Lady Mulford, well content; her drawing room was satisfying full of visitors that morning. "My dear boy, you must have a thousand things to put in hand before the wedding—but you must not punish yourself by doing them all! You must allow me to be of help, since the Dowager's poor health prevents her. Why, I vow you have been so run off your legs with work that you have forgotten to set the date!"

It was plain that Lady Mulford could see no cause for tears other than those of joy at Celia's betrothal to the earl. It was equally obvious that Lady Celia, and perhaps the earl, could see cause for a great many. There was a short, appalled silence before Gervase answered.

"Dearest Godmama, since the matter has been settled for such a very long time, I hardly see any reason to hurry matters. Time enough for a wedding when the Season is over."

Celia sat with her eyes downcast and said nothing.

Louisa thought longingly of the book of poems tucked safely behind the sopha pillow, but reluctantly abandoned the idea of attempting to read in this crush. Aunt Josephine had been right; for Celia's sake, she must be very careful of the reputation she had been so careless of at the ball.

Still, if the invitations that had been pouring in all week and the company in the drawing room today were any indication, she had nothing to fear. Lady Vane was here, and Mrs. Harrington, and Mr. and Miss D'Urberville . . . yes, quite a pretty selection.

The earl was dutifully making conversation with Celia; his tone caught Louisa's attention, and she glanced curiously in their direction.

" . . . Indeed, Lady Celia, your presence is more than adequate recompense for any amount of inconvenience, I am persuaded," the earl was saying.

Celia darted a frightened glance at him and then resumed staring at her hands. The earl's features settled into a thunderous frown.

Really, thought Louisa in despair, if this was how they taught Frankish maidens to dissemble, it was a wonder there was a secret unbetrayed in all England!

"I am sure," Celia said finally, in a small but determined voice, "that you are all that is kind, Lord Coldmeece, but my dear papa always said that such praise, insincere as it must be, can only indicate a dislike for the person addressed. Do you not agree?"

"Ah—" said Lord Coldmeece.

Louisa most virtuously refrained from giggling. "*I* am sure," she interjected helpfully, "that our noble cousin did not mean to be insincere, dearest Celia, and that he expressed himself just as he ought to feel." She averted her eyes demurely, trying to keep her expression sober in the face of th earl's sudden look of mocking amusement.

"I fear, Cousin Louisa, that I owe you, as well as Lady Celia, an apology," he said.

Louisa looked back at the earl. Celia, apparently considering herself relieved of the necessity of making polite conversation with her betrothed, gratefully turned to Miss D'Urberville. The earl, taking this hint, drew his chair a trifle nearer Louisa.

"Do you, my lord?" said Louisa, raising her brows.

"Definitely." He looked amused, as if by some private joke, but continued soberly, "I feel I have been neglecting you, as well as Lady Celia, and that such behavior could only be called—churlish, shall we say?''

"You, my lord Earl?" said Louisa ingenuously, widening her eyes. Then she smiled graciously. "I wouldn't say *churlish*, precisely."

"You are too kind. I will refrain from asking how you would have described me. No, I was churlish," said the earl firmly, "and that when I most particularly wished to compliment you on the way you led me on."

"I?" said Louisa innocently.

"Yes," said the earl. "You led me to believe you a shy and sheltered miss, untouched by the East and unused to Society. Your behavior at the ball, Cousin, gave the lie to that particular Banbury tale."

Louisa wrinkled her nose pertly, taking this as a compliment, but the mention of the East caused her to purse her lips and glance warningly at Celia. Still, there was much that could be said without mentioning the *hareem* at all, and so Louisa painted for Coldmeece a glowing picture of life in the fashionable capitals of Europe now that Napoleon was gone. She found that Celia had turned from Miss D'Urberville and was listening avidly; occasionally she would interject a breathless question, so absorbed in Louisa's tales she seemed not to mind the earl's presence.

"Oh, yes," Louisa told her, in response to an eager query, "Gussie is terribly brave! I know that dueling is not-at-all the thing here in England, but he fought a duel once, in Italy. It was with a fellow with a most peculiar name; we called him Mr. Pollydolly, and one day Gussie told me he had shot him—all in the best form, and only in the shoulder, never fear."

"But why would Augustus do that?" asked Celia, wide-eyed.

"Oh," said Louisa airily, "I wasn't supposed to know the reason, but—"

At this interesting moment the butler announced Mr. Upshaw, who appeared, handed his cane, gloves, and hat to a footman, and embarked upon an impartial round of broad flowery compliments to all the ladies. Then, after some indecision, he took up a post between Celia and

Lady Mulford, and engaged the former in a discussion of Folly's paces. Gervase returned to Louisa.

"And did you know the cause of the duel?" he inquired.

"Oh, yes, of course, and I thought it was the silliest thing! I am afraid I lack the proper temperament to appreciate such excitements."

"Lack the proper temperament?" he said skeptically. "A lady of your romantic sensibilities? Surely not."

Louisa shook her head, smiling warmly at the earl. "No, I fear I have sadly misled you, my lord. Among the many virtues I lack are a romantic soul and maidenly sensibility." She glanced over at Celia, who was smiling up into Kennard's face and prattling away merrily in a fashion that made Louisa think Gussie had better return to defend his conquest. "However, Celia possesses not only youth, beauty, and fortune, but a most romantic soul, little though you might guess it. I'm not prepared to swear to the maidenly sensibilities, mind," she added frankly.

"I can attest that the future countess of Coldmeece has more than enough sensibility," the earl said bleakly. "But you, Lady Louisa, what do *you* hope for from this Season? Lady Celia's future is determined, and it is rumored that Augustus too is to be married. Do you never wish for the same security?"

Louisa felt a sudden irrational certainty that Gussie had told Coldmeece everything, and that the earl was baiting her. "I daresay I long for a home and the security of marriage as much as you do, my lord Earl." Louisa smiled sweetly at him as the barb flew home. "But I have no plans beyond seeing Celia happily married."

The earl looked at her with a strange glint in his eyes. "Very wise, Cousin Louisa. A precipitous marriage makes for great unhappiness."

"As your lordship would be the first to point out," said Louisa demurely.

After a moment, he smiled. "And *are* you fond of Byron?" he asked, indicating her book of poems, which had somehow worked its way from behind the cushion.

It was a ruthless change of topic that Louisa quite admired. She decided she did not trust this particular smile of his, an expression designed to wreak emotional havoc in the bosoms of impressionable females. He could never have turned its charm upon Celia, or the child wouldn't have the least objection to marrying him. Fortunately, Louisa thought, *she* could admire the man without pining away for something she could never possess. Smiling back, she picked up her wayward book and said, rapturously and truthfully, "Oh, yes, I *adore* Byron! Why, *The Bride of Abydos* had me in absolute *whoops*!"

As *The Bridge of Abydos* was luridly—and, Gervase suspected from Louisa's expression, inaccurately—set in a Turkish seraglio, he could see that it might. "I see you are something unique in the line of poetry lovers," he commented.

Following this lead, they carried on a light discussion of some of Byron's more notable literary effusions, until the earl felt he must take his leave. He said he must do himself the pleasure sometime soon of showing both her and Celia some of the sights of Town. He was sure, he added, that Louisa's flair for artistic appreciation would carry them over any spots of dullness they might happen to encounter.

Louisa's eyes narrowed thoughtfully as she watched Coldmeece bow over Celia's hand. No one could guess from his demeanor that he found his betrothal unwelcome; Louisa would hardly have credited it had she not surprised that look in the earl's eyes as he spoke of Celia's sensibilities. Now, if only Gussie would come to his senses, *he* could marry Celia, with Louisa's gracious help and assistance, and, she dared swear, the earl's eternal gratitude.

Louisa couldn't begin to imagine why Augustus had taken such a maggot of propriety into his brain at this late date. England had driven him mad—it was the only explanation. Surely money, family, and earlish gratitude could combine to quell any scandal attached to a sudden alteration in Darwen marital plans—and if Gussie would only act sensibly, he and his bride would be in Russia and could ignore the entire matter. However, Gussie had lost his brains when they landed on Dover Beach, and Louisa could at present do nothing to aid her dear friend.

Her thoughts were once more interrupted, this time by Kennard Upshaw, who had taken advantage of the earl's departure to seat himself next to Louisa.

"Do I pass inspection, Lady Louisa?" he asked with a grin.

"Oh, quite, Mr. Upshaw," said Louisa dulcetly. "In fact, at a distance, in a poor light, any number of people might take you for Augustus Templeton."

Kennard raised an eyebrow, undismayed. "Why, Cousin, how especially charmin' you are this morning! You must be quite missing your *cicisbeo*— though perhaps that's understandable, in the circumstances."

"Those being?" said Louisa. She was not particularly irritated by Kennard's attempts to discommode her, but while this verbal fencing was mildly amusing, it was not as enjoyable as it had been with Lord Coldmeece, and didn't seem nearly as witty.

Kennard threw up his hands in a gesture of conciliation. "Peace, Lady Louisa!" he said laughingly. "Let's cry friends. I only meant, of course, that we both share the peculiar condition of being strangers in our ancestral homeland, and that you would be missing familiar companions as much as I."

He smiled so disarmingly that Louisa was moved to forgive him. "I am sure you miss Augustus at least quite as much as I, Mr. Upshaw—for were he here, he would be able to lesson you in the proper way to tie a cravat." Honor satisfied, their talk turned on Kennard's experience of London, which Louisa found somewhat similar to hers.

"All this fuss over a little bit of mud!" Kennard said. He lowered his voice confidingly. "I swear, it doesn't seem worth it, somehow. Does it, Lady Louisa?"

Louisa chuckled appreciatively. "No, I certainly think it doesn't! And mud is indeed the word for London, Mr. Upshaw. I don't think a day has passed since I've been here that it hasn't rained."

"And it can hardly be what you're used to, raised as

you were in Turkey. Do you ever find yourself missing the Sultan's palace, Cousin?" he asked innocently.

Louisa hoped she didn't look as stunned as she felt. She was saved from having to make a suitably innocuous reply by the arrival of Augustus, who burst precipitously into the room in a whirl of shoulder capes.

"Dearest Aunt Josephine!" he announced, bending over her hand in proper style.

Lady Mulford beamed upon him fondly. "Oh, Augustus, is it not wonderful? Gervase and Celia are marrying at the end of the Season! It was just this morning decided. Now we shall have a ball to close the Season, as well as one to open it!"

Augustus straightened slowly, and Louisa was alarmed to see that all the color had gone out of his face. Why had her normally tactful aunt chosen this manner to make the announcement, and for that matter, when this morning had the earl made any such proclamation?

"I had thought he was being a bit behindhand," Lady Mulford went on happily, "but when I asked him about it, he said the end of the Season was time enough for the matter. I do hope you will be here to see it, Augustus."

Augustus had been looking fixedly at Celia; now he tore his gaze away and addressed Lady Mulford with every assumption of ease. "I shall be sorry not to see Cousin Celia married, Aunt. If she had consulted me, I would have advised an earlier marriage. I sail for Russia in six weeks. Excuse me, ma'am. I believe I did not give proper instruction to the coachman." With an abrupt nod to the mystified Lady Mulford, he turned and stalked from the room.

Louisa rose quickly to her feet. "Do excuse me, Mr. Upshaw, but I fear I have left my embroidery upstairs, and I hardly know what to do if I have not something in my hands." With that feeble excuse, she hurried out after Augustus.

She found him in the withdrawing room just off the front hall, staring out at the street. "The end of the Season!" he said, when Louisa put her hand on his shoulder. "I had hoped . . . But she set the date—" He turned and seized Louisa's hands, causing her to utter a startled squeak. "But that doesn't matter! Marry me at once, Cousin, and honeymoon with me in Petersburg! We, at least, shall have everything according to plan."

"Oh, Gussie, don't," begged Louisa in real agitation. "Coldmeece was asking me who you were going to marry, just this morning. I think he suspects."

"How could he?" Augustus demanded magnificently. "He asked *me* about it the day after the ball, but I put him right off it. Now, where shall we go? You can honeymoon in Paris if you like; no more of London for us!"

Louisa tried unsuccesfully to remove her hands from his grasp. "Oh, Gussie, you can't be serious! Marry *me*? You don't want to do that!"

"Haven't we had this discussion before, sweetest Coz?" Augustus said with suspicious lightness. "You proposed, I disposed. Nothing's happened that will change that."

"What about Celia? And while we're considering Celia, whatever happened to your brains, Gussie? What possessed you to enact that Cheltenham tragedy over the wedding announcement just now? Depend on it, it's only that Aunt Josephine's got some maggot in her head about propriety, and it will turn out she's mistaken Coldmeece's meaning, or something of the sort. Now *do* let go of me!"

Augustus, fretting under the lash of these multilayered accusations, finally chose one at random and defended himself. "I don't give a fig for Celia!" he declared roundly. "And I'm sure it's no bread and butter of mine whom she marries, or when. And what's that Upshaw person doing here, anyway?"

Louisa uttered a faint groan. "Quizzing me about the *hareem*. Gussie, *who* could have told him? And in front of everyone, too."

"Goose! When he's been living in Caro Darwen's pocket since he came to Town? Depend on it, she has told him all. But don't worry, once we two are wed, *her* barb will be drawn. Only give me leave, and I'll go break the news to Mama at once!"

"But Gussie!" she protested in distress. "You know

you cannot wish to marry me. You are in love with Ce—''

Augustus released one of her hands and placed a finger on her lips. ''Hush-a-bye, Lady Lou. Talking pays no toll, as you know full well.'' He smiled sadly down at her, all affectation vanished. ''Celia is to marry Gervase, and has made up her mind to it, it seems. Now you must marry me, sweet cousin, stunning the family inexpressibly, and we will away to Russia, where I shall be a blinding light of diplomatism. Mama will be happy, at least.''

It was Louisa's opinion that Celia had made up her mind not to disappoint by word or deed the expectations of the champion of propriety she believed Augustus to be. Louisa also thought that ''stunning the family inexpressibly'' would prove to be a pallidly inadequate description of the feelings her marriage to Augustus would evoke. She sighed.

''Well, my angel,'' she said rallyingly, ''if you are going to do anything cork-brained—mind, I'm not saying I agree!—you will have to procure a Special License at once.''

''A special license?'' Augustus demanded. ''What the devil for, Louisa? Six weeks is plenty of time to call banns.''

''Well, perhaps it is,'' said Louisa vaguely. ''But one never knows, and I'm sure it would be useful.'' Very useful for stalling Gussie while she figured out what to do. As long as their betrothal was secret, anything might yet be arranged. Once banns had been called, and their contract made public . . .

''True,'' agreed Augustus, pulling her close to drop a chaste kiss on her forehead. ''Very well, if it will make you happy, a Special License I shall procure on the instant. But do promise me you'll give me at least half an hour's notice before the ceremony, will you, Amber Pearl?''

Touched by the use of her name, and feeling unaccountably treacherous, Louisa nodded. ''And now *you* had better think of what you will say to Aunt Josephine when you go back in there. Instructions to the coachman! Augustus, you *walked* here this morning!''

"Good God!" said her cousin, electrified. "Louisa—does it show?"

Laughing, she led him back to the parlor, where he played his part with such consummate skill that Celia was quite convinced he did not love her at all.

Chapter
TEN

A fine spring morning found Lady Celia driving in the Park with Kennard Upshaw, and handling the reins in fine style. Mr. Upshaw had handsomely offered to teach her to drive his match-bays, and although Augustus had glared, Aunt Josephine saw nothing wrong in Celia's driving with her cousin, be he never so American.

Lady Celia had a great deal on her mind, and even the joy of tooling such a pair of sweet-goers could not distract her from her woes. Try as she might, the Earl of Coldmeece was no more desirable to her than he had ever been. In addition, she was more and more possessed of the mortifying suspicion that Augustus, deny it though he would, was unhappy with her. She signed despondently. Papa *had* been right—all females were a snare and a delusion. And had she more resolve, she would put Augustus firmly from her mind and direct her attention to the task of uplifting the earl. She sighed again. It would be a noble undertaking, and to be a countess was a great thing.

But she had no desire to be Countess of Coldmeece. She was sure that the earl disapproved of her, that she was not what he looked for in a wife. Celia was by far too young to realize that even a small difference in years yawns like a chasm when one is young, or that the earl's supposed dislike and aloofness were little more than the nervous impressions of an uncertain and self-conscious young girl.

"Sweet Celia, can it be that my company is repugnant to you?" Mr. Upshaw's soft American drawl cut through her unhappy introspection. She turned wide blue eyes on her companion.

"Oh, *no*, Mr. Upshaw! I was only thinking what deceitful creatures we females be—even when we do not particularly wish it."

Kennard threw back his head and roared with laughter. "Sweet Celia! I am bound *you* could not be deceitful, even if you *did* wish to be!"

"Oh, no, sir, there you are wrong. I am the most abominable creature alive, I promise you."

"Tell me, how can you say so? You will have to offer me proof, fair one, or I won't believe you, I promise." So saying, he took the reins back into his own hands, collected the bays to a slow walk, and set himself to the task of coaxing out Celia's tale of woe.

This was not a difficult feat. Shy outside the family circle, with the unfortunate habit of prosing on in a manner ill suited to her years, Celia had difficulty forming friendships with young ladies of her own age, and her engagement effectively warned off the young bucks who would have flocked to her side. Others might not have noticed Celia's isolation, but Mr. Upshaw, in the course of a rather chequered career, had made it his business to notice such things, and had been quick to exploit it. He was now reaping the reward of his industry; his little cousin Celia regarded him as a trusted advisor, and had no hesitation in confiding in him.

"You see," she began, studying her clasped hands in their fine kid gloves, "Papa always said that females were by nature vain and deceitful, and so I have always done what I might to—to be forthright in all my dealings with others, whatever their rank or station in life might be. But now, Mr. Upshaw, I find that I have played someone false—and when I had no notion of it, either!"

Not unnaturally intrigued, Kennard gently pressed to hear more. Under his practiced coaxing, Celia gradually revealed that, though the earl was a murderous, dissipated old *roué*, he was also a broken-hearted rejected suitor. Therefore, though she was in love with another, her respect for this unnamed beloved's high moral principles, her duty to her papa, and her pity for the earl's shattered heart had compelled her to accept Coldmeece.

Urged to reveal the name of her mysterious moral arbiter, Celia shook her head sharply, and said only, "Oh, I *could* not—he has not the least notion—and he does not care for me at all!"

Mr. Upshaw privately doubted this very much. It took no great mental power to deduce the identity of Celia's love, although the thought of Augustus Templeton as a moral preceptor was almost too much for Kennard's bland control of his features.

He contented himself for the moment with suggesting that perhaps Celia's cavalier did not expect her to take the undeniably extreme step of marrying the earl; that perhaps, if she were free, this anonymous Galahad might declare himself?

At this Celia flushed, then turned quite pale. "Di-dissolve the betrothal?" she gasped. "Oh, I couldn't! Papa would never approve—and only think how distressing to the earl!"

"One can see that you would be reluctant to present Coldmeece with a repetition of his previous unhappy experience," he said sympathetically. "But have you considered, my dear cousin, how distressing a man of his lordship's undoubted sensibilities might find it to be married to a woman who married him for reasons having little to do with love?"

"Oh, but he knows I do not love him," said Celia with devastating simplicity. "It was all arranged by our fathers, you see. And I am sure Lord Coldmeece is too old to look for *romance* in his marriage."

"Oh, of a certainty," Kennard agreed soberly, wondering a little at his own ability to keep a straight face. Nothing more clearly betrayed Celia's own extreme youth than her innocent certainty that a man of Coldmeece's age was in his dotage. "Far too old to hope for love, but it is common enough for an affection to grow between the partners in a marriage. Are you certain, my dear, that you could offer him such affection with your feelings otherwise engaged?"

167

Celia looked down at her hands again, and the corners of her mouth trembled. "I . . . I must be, I suppose. It will not be so very hard?" she asked hopefully, turning a beseeching gaze upon Kennard.

"I fancy you would be the best judge of that, Celia," said Kennard austerely. He pulled the horses to a halt for added emphasis, and continued impressively. "But if you will allow me to presume upon both our connection and our acquaintance, my dear cousin, and upon my own wider experience, I would say that it would be far, far better to cry off even at the church door, than to let Coldmeece marry you under the illusion that you will come to care for him."

"Oh!" said Celia in stricken accents, and Kennard with difficulty kept his face set in judgmental lines. "Mr. Upshaw, you—you will not speak of this to anyone, will you?" She clasped her hands together and stared up at him with round, trusting blue eyes.

Kennard possessed himself of one of her hands and squeezed it reassuringly. He wondered why he was throwing away such a cuddlesome matrimonial prize on such a gudgeon as Augustus Templeton.

"You may trust me, sweetest Celia—I shall be perfectly discreet."

Celia sighed with relief, and Kennard squeezed her hand again and then urged his willing horses into a brisk trot. "And now you may tell me, Cousin, all about your costume for Lady Coldmeece's masked ball. What?" He lifted his brows as if in disbelief. "Never tell me you haven't heard? And when I know for a fact your invitation was among the first sent out, too!"

Now that the earl had actually sent an announcement of the engagement to the *Gazette*, and the date of the wedding was fixed, Lady Mulford was deeply embroiled in wedding plans. Louisa dutifully was keeping her aunt company in the library.

"Louisa?" said Lady Mulford from behind a great many bits and pieces of paper. "Do you know if Celia mislikes yachting?"

"Yachting?" Louisa looked up in surprise; inspired by her conversation with the earl, she was re-reading *The Bride of Abydos*, and finding it oddly flat. "I suppose so, for Celia likes anything new, but why do you ask?"

"Oh, it had slipped my mind until just now. Gervase called yesterday and wished to know, for he thought he would take Celia on a cruise on the *Day-Dream*—that's his yacht, you know—for their honeymoon, if the dear child did not take it amiss."

"Perhaps he will ask her, Aunt," said Louisa, with suspicious mildness. The thought of the earl's upcoming nuptials was unaccountably irritating. She supposed the boat was fitted out in the first style of elegance, too, and kept bright and trim with paint and polish, and just the sort of vessel on which one might comfortably take an extended cruise—to Turkey, say. She pulled a wry face at her aunt as Lady Mulford's secretary re-entered the room with an urgently required list. "Pray do not regard me, Aunt, I am only out of sorts this morning."

Lady Mulford clucked sympathetically. "You ought to have gone with Kennard and Celia, Louisa."

"I, Aunt? I had rather go with dear Lord Byron than in any curricle driven by a novice, thank you!" With that she returned to her book. Discussions of trims, guest-lists, principal residences, and the like jumbled along in the background, but did not interfere with Louisa's thoughts. The young lovers of Abydos also failed to hold her attention, and it was a great relief when the sound of carriage wheels heralded Celia's return.

That young lady burst unceremoniously into the library, Kennard Upshaw in tow. "Oh, Lady Mulford!" Celia exclaimed. "Why did you not tell me the Countess of Coldmeece had invited me to her ball?"

Swiftly and accurately assigning blame; Louisa glared past Celia at Kennard; he gave her a sweetly mocking smile in return and bowed slightly.

"But, Celia, darling," protested Lady Mulford, flustered, "we did not suppose you would wish to attend. It is likely to be a sad crush—and a masquerade. Well, it is not at all the thing, dearest, and with so many other calls upon our time . . .''

Celia's brow wrinkled in pretty confusion. "But I do not wish to be backward in any attention to Lord Coldmeece's family, and—is not his lordship to attend? The ball is being held at Coldmeece House—surely he will be there?''

After a moment, it was reluctantly allowed by Lady Mulford that the earl would in all probability attend the masked ball.

"Then it is my duty to attend too,'' said Celia with decision. "I must support him, even if I very much dislike it. And I have never seen a masked ball,'' she went on, looking more cheerful, "and perhaps I shall find it diverting.''

"I am sure Lord Coldmeece would excuse you, Celia,'' Louisa put in hastily, after a glance at her stricken aunt. "Indeed, I am sure he does not wish you to trouble yourself, or he would have sent round earlier to remind you of your obligation.'' The thought of innocent Celia actually attending this entertainment of Caro's, which was certain to turn into the lowest sort of brawl, was enough to make a hardier soul than Louisa blench.

"No,'' said Celia, her expression indicating a determination adamantine and inarguable. "I must go to this ball. It will look excessively odd if I am not there. Even Lord Coldmeece said so.''

"The earl said so?'' said Louisa in surprise, and was rewarded by seeing Kennard's lazy smile widen.

"None other,'' he affirmed. "His lordship rode by in the Park while I was explainin' about the ball to Lady Celia, and he thought it perfectly proper for her to attend. I offer my humble services as her escort if you two ladies are otherwise engaged that evening.''

Louisa looked at her aunt. Lady Mulford looked quite as stunned as Louisa felt, and Louisa's heart sank. It was in anticipation of just such a mistaken sense of duty on Celia's part that they had kept the invitations to Caro's masked ball a secret from her. Now the cat was among the pigeons, deliberately set there by the smiling Kennard

Upshaw. Celia was determined; persuasion was plainly useless. The only course was for Aunt Josephine to forbid Celia to attend, and Louisa knew only too well how inadequate Aunt Josephine would prove to the task of standing up to a Celia in the throes of a Righteous Cause.

"His lordship was very nice," Celia told them, sounding surprised, "and he invited us, Louisa, to go riding with him and Augustus Friday at ten. I said that we would, of course."

"But Celia," Lady Mulford objected feebly, "you couldn't have a costume made up in time—why, it's in less than two weeks!"

"Ten o'clock!" Louisa gasped. "Celia—in the *morning*?"

"I shall contrive something," Celia told Lady Mulford serenely, ignoring her cousin's plaintive cry; for the first time, Louisa considered a quicker end for Celia's troubles than marriage.

Louisa had the opportunity to pour out her heart to Augustus later that same day, when she chanced upon him in the garden at dusk. He had come by, he told her in response to her surprised query, to see if Folly might actually be throwing out a splint as she had seemed to be the other morning. Augustus had straitly enjoined the groom to foment the area, but the man was not-at-all what Augustus could like in the way of an ostler, and so he had come himself to check on the mare's progress.

"Well, at least you do not have designs on the poor remains of our roses!" said Louisa in mock relief. "Hardly a bud on any of them, and that wretched beast has eaten every one."

"Celia?" said Augustus absently, plainly not attending.

"Gussie," said Louisa in a minatory tone, "the *horse*, my angel. What has come over you? You seem quite distracted."

"The pangs of love," offered Augustus, in tones that robbed the words both of their sting and any resemblance to the truth.

Louisa was not fooled. "Gussie . . . ?" she said ten-

171

tatively. "My dear, you know I'll release you from our betrothal—indeed, I could hardly hold you to it. You may go off to Petersburg footloose and fancy-free if you chose."

"Not quite fancy-free, Cousin." Augustus reached out and tugged on a lock of Louisa's fox red hair, threatening the entire mass with imminent disarray. He heaved a sigh, and said more strongly, "It don't signify—and you know Aunt Josie'll be the happier for seeing you spliced. Oh, I applied for that Special License you wanted—we can be married as soon as I have it in hand."

"That's as may be, Gussie-my-love! You know I'll not stir a step toward the parson before you've spoken to your mother and father."

Augustus pulled a wry face. "Such delicacy of mind, Amber Pearl! What would they say about you back in the *hareem*, neglecting your opportunities so?" He gave her hair another playful tug and the whole thick curling mass cascaded down over her neck and shoulders.

Augustus uttered a muffled but very sincere oath and caught at Louisa's wayward tresses with both hands. He then stood looking at her in some confusion, his hands clutching her hair and resting lightly on her shoulders.

"Now here's a fine to-do," Louisa said matter-of-factly. "If you can't do it up again, I shall be forced to creep up the back stairs to my room, or I don't know *what* Aunt Josephine will say." She shook her head slightly, lips pursed in mock reproof.

A dangerous glint of mischief appeared in Augustus's eyes; before Louisa could take heed and slither out of reach, he pulled her closer and kissed her with expert thoroughness.

It was pleasant enough, Louisa decided analytically. But her cousin's advances, scandalous and improper and unexpected though they were, were oddly unexciting, and she had no particular desire to prolong the experience.

"Really, Gussie," she said sternly, pulling free, "if Aunt Josephine saw us, she'd have a spasm!"

Augustus cocked his head and looked at her, and the corner of his mouth quirked. "How now, sweetest Coz—

no raptures? Not even an attempt at maidenly sensibilities?"

"Why?" asked Louisa. "When you know I have none and I still need you to put up my hair?"

"Someday, my girl, you will be carried away in the grip of a grand passion," Augustus prophesied darkly, leading her to sit on an ornamental stone bench, "and then let all and sundry beware."

"Grand passions are very boring and very tiring," said Louisa calmly, arranging her skirts and submitting her hair to Augustus's ministrations, "and I have already had one today, and so do not wish another, thank you."

"Your morning chocolate was cold," Augustus guessed.

"No, worse. Your vile and abominable cousin, the odious earl of Coldmeece, tricked poor innocent Celia into riding with him on Friday."

"Then Gervase will hear about the Corn Laws," responded Augustus, pulling Louisa's hair back and beginning to braid it. "Poor lamb—he does make her so dreadfully nervous."

"Then how will she feel when she is married to him?" Louisa snapped, and felt Augustus tense. With an effort, she took a lighter tone. "But you haven't heard the worst yet. They are not the only ones who are to suffer—he says that you and I, my dear Gussie, are to accompany them, if you please! And they mean to ride at *ten*!"

"That will get you out before noon, thou lazy slug-a-bed," said Augustus unsympathetically, giving her hair a particularly sharp twist and sliding some pins into the braids. "There you are—it should pass muster."

"What a great goodness you have had so much experience doing up ladies' hair, Gussie-my-pet," said Louisa archly, turning to look at him.

He grinned broadly. "Ah, but most of them weren't ladies, my dear Cousin. And now that we have quite shattered the conventions, it is high time that you were inside, and I am off to tax my much maligned relation with his high-handedness at promising me to a party all unasked."

"If he'd asked you, would you have refused?" Louisa asked, brushing off her skirts as she rose.

"No," said Augustus cheerfully. "But it never hurts to have a few wounded sensibilities to bruit about." With a wave of the hand to her, he strolled off.

Louisa watched him go consideringly and wondered, much against her will, whether kissing her cousin Coldmeece would be as unexciting as kissing her cousin Gussie.

By the following morning Louisa had made up her mind that she must take matters into her own hands. She would go to Coldmeece and explain matters to him and persuade him that Celia must marry Augustus. It would be quite simple to arrange, really; Augustus and Celia could elope to Russia, and by the time they came home again, they would have been married for ages and the scandal would have been quite forgotten.

The earl would naturally leap at the chance to get out of an unwanted marriage; Celia would be sensible and Augustus would be reasonable, and everything would be marvelous.

She was interrupted from this fantasy by a knock on the door. It was Teale, to see if Louisa required her services. The tone of the dresser's voice implied that Lady Louisa needed more help than even Teale could give. Louisa waved her away. "No, no. Campbell can do for me later. Is Lady Celia awake?"

"Awake and dressed this hour and more," said Teale austerely.

Louisa, who had felt that *she* had been up with the dawn, refused to rise to this leading remark. "Thank you, Teale," she said graciously. "I believe I will look in on her. She is still in her bedroom?"

Teale grudgingly admitted it, and Louisa wrapped her magnificent velvet dressing gown around her and swept regally from the room.

Lady Celia Elizabeth Darwen-Neville, heiress, toast, and acknowledged beauty, stood gazing disconsolately out of her window into the busy street below. She envied the people passing beneath her; surely they did not have so many unpleasant things they had to do, and surely they did not find their lives so hollow.

"A penny for your thoughts, Cousin?"

Celia gasped and started, but it was only Louisa, hair tucked untidily up into her nightcap and wrapped in one of the most extravagant of her many peculiar dressing gowns.

"Oh, how you startled me, Louisa!" said Celia in relief. "I was just . . . I was just wondering, I—Have you ever been in love, Louisa?" she finished abruptly. It was not at all what she had meant to say, and she stood staring at Louisa, appalled.

Louisa did not make the flippant response Celia half dreaded. Instead, she said, "I am not perfectly sure; if I ever was, it was a long time ago. Do you think *you* are in love, Celia?"

"I . . ." Celia was torn between truth and duty. She sat down on her boudoir chair and looked at her cousin miserably. "Oh, Louisa. It is so very difficult—and everything is happening so fast! And I am already late for my fitting with Madame Francine."

"Well, then, Celia," said Louisa equitably, "be just a little more late, and I will accompany you."

Rather less than half an hour later, Louisa was to be found showing off one of her new walking dresses in Celia's company. She had thus far been unable to induce Celia to confide in her on the topic of love, and while she very much wished to give her cousin some good advice, Louisa could not feel that reading the unhappy Celia a rousing scold on the advisability of doing as one really wished would have any good effect.

They turned up Curzon Street, with Celia pointing out more sights of interest than Louisa had thought could be found on a London street.

"—and that one there, Louisa, as you know, is Coldmeece House." Celia stopped to regard the edifice with awe. "Augustus told me that Coldmeece had it entirely refurnished, with green silk wallpaper and gilt furniture—and I will wager the roof does *not* leak!"

Louisa was startled into laughter by this sudden descent into practicality. "Very likely you are right, my love, for I find that, in general, country houses may be depended on to leak, while town houses nearly never do."

As Louisa spoke, she noticed out of the corner of her eye the determined approach of a small sturdy child. As Louisa turned curiously, the small child threw himself down on the ground at Louisa's feet.

"No, no, Lady Charlotte, you're to come right along now and don't go running off like that!" A stout woman, clearly the child's nurse, came trotting up, slightly out of breath, and bobbed a small curtsy to Louisa and Celia.

"Beg pardon, miss," she said to Louisa, "but I only took my eyes off her for a minute, his lordship being wishful that she should have an airing, the weather being so fine, and myself having just brought her back from the Park this very instant. Come along, now, lamb," she added to the child.

"Won't!" said Lady Charlotte. Her nurse reached for her, but the child drew back with an expression of such horror that the woman was momentarily dismayed.

"I collect, then, that we have the pleasure of making the acquaintance of the niece of the Earl of Coldmeece?" said Louisa, leaning over to examine this marvel. So this was Caro's daughter, the child the earl's brother had not lived to see. A pair of button-brown eyes in a very dirty face gazed speculatively back.

"Oh, yes, miss, and a more pretty-behaved child you won't find anywhere—when she's as wants to be, if you'll take my meaning! Come along then, Miss Charlotte, *do*!" At this blandishment, Charlotte shrank back against Louisa's ankles and clutched at Louisa's skirts. The nurse wrung her hands. "Oh, whatever am I to do, when his lordship is after coming home, and the little one sitting in the street?" she wailed. She then scooped Charlotte up by main force, but her little ladyship yelled alarmingly and struggled so that she slipped from her nurse's arms and landed on the sidewalk, which only caused her to cry harder.

Celia gazed at this apparition in horror. Louisa, who

had grown up in a household filled with children of assorted ages, crouched down on her heels and said cheerfully, "Dreadfully spoilt, aren't you, poppet?" She rummaged in her indispensable for a moment and extracted a peppermint, which she popped into the child's mouth when Charlotte stopped to draw breath.

"There, now," Louisa said with satisfaction into the sudden silence. "You mustn't carry on so, Charlotte—at least, not to us. I am your cousin Louisa, and this is your cousin Celia. Being a Darwen, you have a great many cousins, as you will soon discover." So saying, Louisa sat down on the stoop of Coldmeece House and scooped Charlotte onto her lap.

At that moment Lord Coldmeece's carriage pulled up before the house, and the earl stepped down from the vehicle. He cast a glance over the little group and said, without apparent surprise, "Good morning, Lady Louisa, Lady Celia. How charming to see you both again."

He smiled invitingly, and Louisa found herself smiling in return. She rose to her feet and shifted Lady Charlotte to her hip. The earl's raised eyebrow was gratifying, and she ignored the strangled sound from Celia. Beaming upon the earl, she extended her hand. "How do you do, Lord Coldmeece. I have just had the felicity of making the acquaintance of your niece, and I find her to be a most singular child."

"Fortunate indeed," returned the earl gravely, "as I fear my household woefully inadequate to cope with additional children. But perhaps you would care to stop in for refreshment?" he continued, gesturing them to precede him up the steps. "I perceive my young niece has rendered you sorely in need of some."

Louisa, looking down at her dust-draggled gown, could only agree. The earl then turned to Celia. "It is always, my dear, a pleasure to see you—but might I ask what brings you to my door on such a lovely morning?"

"I am going to the modiste's—it is for a fitting of my dress," said Celia uncomfortably. "It is not that I approve of so much time and effort being expended on useless display, sir, but—"

"Yes, of course, I quite understand," said the earl hastily, firmly shepherding them through the front door. He turned to collect Charlotte from Louisa's arms. Louisa obediently handed Lady Charlotte over to her harassed uncle and tried desperately to keep a sober face. Celia and the earl really did bring out the worst in each other.

The housekeeper appeared as if summoned by sorcery, to await the ladies' pleasure. The earl, still holding Charlotte as if the child were a protective talisman, said that he would await them in the library, and added that Celia must make free of his carriage for her trip to the dressmaker.

"Oh no, sir," said Celia faintly. "It is not any distance at all. If I could just have a message sent 'round . . ." This matter disposed of, the ladies followed Mrs. Leadbury up the stairs.

The earl, after patiently listening to a recital of the incident from the nurse, delivered Charlotte back into her care. Bracken then approached to inform his lordship that Augustus Templeton had been awaiting his lordship's pleasure in his lordship's library for over half an hour. The earl was tempted to bid Gussie to go to the devil, but he instead advised Bracken to have sherry sent in. He had hopes that the boy was regretting his impulsive betrothal and would welcome help in getting out of it. A few judicious words and a little effort should send Augustus to the Court of the Tsar without the encumbrance of a wife. Now familiar with Louisa, Gervase was certain that she could be easily persuaded to prefer other arrangements. Gervase was prepared to be generous, too—providing only that the woman promise to give up Augustus. And if Augustus chose to think he was being jilted—well, that was his affair; in any event, he would know nothing about it until far too late. And as for Louisa—

Gervase suddenly thought of Louisa's wide, moon-silver eyes staring at him over Charlotte's curls, and remembered the supple movement of her body as she settled the child comfortably on her hip. And the way she had of looking up at him through those long darkened lashes . . . Yes, definitely other arrangements must be made for Louisa.

With an almost physical jolt, Gervase realized that he was thinking about his cousin in the most ineligible possible fashion. Whatever else she might be, she was still a Darwen, and a lady of Quality, and not to be treated as a Cyprian, however admirably she might fill that role.

Extremely vexed with himself, Gervase entered the library and noted that Augustus's mental state was all that could be hoped. He leapt to his feet in great agitation upon beholding the earl, then sat down again as suddenly as he'd risen. "Ah," he said. "Coldmeece."

"I am sorry to have kept you waiting, Augustus. You should have had my staff send for me. I was occupied with Lady Coldmeece, who demanded that I call upon her first thing this morning about some more of her nonsense for this masquerade of hers. For an entertainment that will be no trouble to me, it seems to be an infinite amount of fuss."

Augustus laughed sharply. "Everything that woman does is an infinite amount of fuss, Gervase. I think you'd be well advised to marry her—to someone else, of course!—and let her run *his* affairs, not yours."

"Excellent advice," said the earl dryly, "but where do you suppose I am to find an eligible duke, preferably a royal one? They are not so common as the novelists would have one believe, and I am sure Caro would settle for nothing less."

"Aye, very true," said Augustus with a grin. "But tell me, Gervase, you aren't thinking of letting *Celia* attend that blasted ball, are you? Aunt Josie and Louisa both say she oughtn't, and I must say, I don't think it would do, myself."

"But what harm can it possibly do?" he protested mildly. "Caro will know better than to do anything rash in my house, and you and I will both be there to see Celia comes to no harm."

"I still don't like it, Gervase. This kind of turnout is far more Louisa's style than Celia's." Augustus stopped abruptly and looked unhappy.

The earl, pouring out sherry, affected not to notice. He offered a glass to Augustus, and placed the decanter at his elbow. He hoped there would be enough time for Augustus to disclose his feelings before the ladies arrived. "I know you did not seek me out at this early hour to discuss Caro's foibles," he prompted after a moment.

"Well," said Augustus unhappily, "no." He stood up and began to pace about the room. "It's a devil of a mess, Gervase, and it's my own fault—though I don't see how I could have done anything different, you understand. It all seemed perfectly sensible—and it still does, I suppose. But you see that Lady Mulford wouldn't be the least help."

"Naturally," said the earl calmly, wondering what curse had been laid on him that all of his relatives should suddenly have run mad. "But perhaps, once I am in possession of the facts, I will be able to assist you."

With the help of an efficient housemaid, Louisa's dress was soon restored to a presentable condition. Celia, whose toilette needed far less repair, sat beside her hat and pelisse on the large tester bed and watched Louisa tidy her hair.

Louisa had had an idea, and thought this was the perfect time to put it into execution. She would manage to distract Celia somehow, and see the earl alone. Once she had Coldmeece's ear, it would be a simple matter to explain to him why Celia must marry Augustus and not himself, and enlist his aid. Accordingly, she looked sideways at Celia, and said, as if in idle reflection, "You must admit, Celia my love, that in spite of everything, Lord Coldmeece is really the most amusing man."

"I think he is *hateful*!" said Celia half hysterically. "He is so *old* and—and ugly, and he is forever laughing at one, or making nasty remarks a person can't understand and that don't make any sense. And he is so *tall*!"

Angered by this unflattering assessment of the earl, Louisa turned to face Celia and said rather sharply, "In that case, Cousin, I am surprised you ever accepted his suit—or *does* the earldom carry all?"

Celia looked both shocked and sulky. "That is an entirely different matter," she said stiffly, "though you, I realize, would not know what it is to do one's duty!"

Louisa drew herself majestically up to her full height. "Perhaps I do not, but neither will I ever marry a man I despise and cannot love, to make him miserable for the rest of his life!" With an outrage only half feigned, Louisa seized the opportunity to make a grand exit. She swept out of the room, feeling that she was just in time to keep Coldmeece from making the most disastrous mistake of his life.

When she reached the door to the library, which stood slightly ajar, she heard voices and realized the earl had company. Recognizing Augustus's voice, she put her hand on the knob to enter, when her mind registered the subject of the discussion and she froze where she was.

"There's nothing wrong with Louisa," Augustus was saying defensively.

"My dear man, no one is saying anything to disparage the lady," the earl responded in a deadly drawl. "Her breeding, at least, is unexceptionable. But her upbringing—well, the less said about that, the better, as we both know. And after *that* having been dragged up all no-how everywhere on earth by my flutterbye godmother . . . You'll surely admit her manners are not at all first rate. By your own account, she is lazy, bad-tempered, woefully extravagant—conduct hardly likely to bring credit to any establishment, let alone that of a young diplomat in a consular post. It's no fault of hers, and I'm certain she means well, of course—"

Augustus laughed harshly. "Too kind, Gervase! The only thing Amber Pearl means to do is—What I mean is, it don't much signify, do it?"

Louisa pressed trembling hands to her temples. Once she had thought that Gussie would take her part against any outsider, but all he had done since they had come to London was to insist that she must mind her manners! And that, when it had always been *Augustus* who approved of all she did, and told Lady Mulford he didn't see anything wrong with Louisa's unladylike cleverness.

As for the earl—she'd thought they got on so well, that she'd found in him a kindred spirit with whom to laugh, and he—had only been showing her off to Augustus, like a—like a *horse*, or a prize sheep, trying to prove that she would not make a suitable wife. And all the time he had despised her utterly!

Louisa had not known that anything could hurt so much and still leave one whole in body. Oh, how *could* Gervase . . . In sudden furious despair, Louisa realized that she'd fallen in love with her noble cousin weeks ago, which was doubtless just what the vile man had been scheming for, with his smiles and his coaxing ways.

Oh, if only she were a man, she'd shoot both of them! No, she would go in there right now and tell them both exactly what she thought of them, and she would tell Augustus she would rather *die* than marry him! She moved forward, heart hammering and color high, but the earl was speaking again and she stopped to listen once more.

"But really, Augustus, what else can you expect of her? She hasn't a penny, for all that she's so free with her aunt's money, and I fancy she knows well enough how little hope she has of catching any husband, let alone a rich one. Why shouldn't she wish to marry you and secure her future, especially as you've never done anything to discourage her?" The earl sounded completely disinterested in the whole affair, and that was somehow the final insult. Louisa had lost the heart she hadn't known she possessed, and the object of her affections was wholly indifferent.

So the earl thought she was a fortune-hunting adventuress, did he? And that, not content with bankrupting her aunt, she had entrapped her cousin into offering for her? She took a deep breath, forcing herself to be calm. Very well. Let him think that a while longer. So Gussie didn't like her manners? Well, she would show him and the odious earl just how outrageous she could be—and she would start pressing Gussie for an immediate marriage at the same time. *That* would show the pair of them! She would make Coldmeece sorry he had ever laid eyes on her! Reckless, was she? Extravagant?

With an effort, she turned her mind from these channels and summoned up all of her training. One of her first lessons in the *hareem* had been the art of smiling when one felt least like doing so.

She turned at a step behind her, and saw Celia coming down the stairs. At the sight of her woebegone face, Louisa recollected the quarrel she had forced on her little cousin and was instantly penitent.

"You left your bonnet upstairs, Louisa," Celia said hesitantly, holding it out.

Louisa instantly went over to her, took the proffered headgear, and hugged her hard. "Thank you, Celia," she said in what she hoped were normal tones. "I should have hated to have to return for it. And I am sorry for quarreling with you, for now that I come to consider the earl more fully, I am certain you are right about him." With that, she led Celia to the library door and knocked firmly.

Chapter ELEVEN

Gervase had hoped that if Louisa were provided for, Augustus would be willing to break their engagement. Now, however, he could see that Augustus would never be sensible; he was insisting he would marry Louisa come hell or high water, whether he wanted to or not. And two people more likely to make each other miserable Gervase had never seen. Not the most charitable could deny that Louisa was quite unconventional, and Augustus had an odd streak of propriety that would only widen with age.

And though Gervase, who had been somewhat shocked to discover his own improper interest in the matter, had spoken with more venom than he'd intended to Augustus in the library, he had spoken the truth. Louisa, however, enticing, was no fit match for Augustus—as Augustus would, to all their sorrow, be the last to admit.

That left Louisa. She was a practical woman, and would be easier to deal with than Augustus. Gervase frowned. Augustus had undoubtedly been right; a mere competence would not be sufficient recompense for her giving up Augustus and his money. Well, Gervase would raise the amount—within reason. After this morning, he was all the more determined that Louisa should not marry Augustus, and he was willing to pay.

He glanced at the pages of legal vellum, each elegantly inscribed in the law clerk's sloping hand. He had half a mind to take the papers around to Mulford House now, and see what Lady Louisa's reaction would be. . . .

"It seems most satisfactory. All that remains is to settle

the amount, and obtain my cousin Louisa's signature, and the matter is done," he said to Salvington. He folded and tied the document and set it on the corner of his desk under the piece of marble Lord Elgin had brought him from Greece. He'd decide how best to approach Lady Louisa on the matter later.

The next item to be dealt with was Augustus's rapidly approaching departure for Russia. He cast his eye over the letter of recommendation Augustus would carry with him. "When does he sail?" he asked idly.

"Mr. Templeton has passage out on the *Atropos*. She sails in three weeks—just after her ladyship's ball, in fact."

"Yes, thank you, Salvington. I had forgotten the ship." So Augustus must bring Louisa to the altar within the fortnight if they were to marry before he left for Russia. Well, Gervase thought smugly, with a glance at the settlement papers, he would forestall that!

Discussion then turned on his lordship's coming marriage, and led, inescapably, to the plans for renovating the countess's suite at Coldmere. From there it would have been but a short step to consideration of the state of the whole of his lordship's estates, had not Bracken chosen that moment to discreetly announce a caller.

"Who is it?" Gervase demanded, relieved at this interruption to tedious business and inclined to be sociable.

"I was instructed to inform your lordship, when your lordship inquired, that it was your lordship's cousin as desired to speak with you."

"Thus narrowing it down to half the population of England," drawled Gervase. He was somewhat surprised to find that the caller ushered into the library was his American cousin, Kennard Upshaw. He had seen little of Upshaw since the ill-fated ball at Coldmeece House; Augustus had told him, in great indignation and at great length, of Mr. Upshaw's particular attentions to Lady Celia, but Gervase had paid little heed.

"I hope I am not disturbin' you, sir," he said in his soft American accent, removing his high-crowned beaver and tucking it under one arm, "but I had hoped to find you at home. I have a matter of interest to your lordship to discuss."

"Please sit down, Mr. Upshaw, Gervase invited. Salvington gathered up his legal folders and left quietly. The earl, wondering in a bemused sort of way how many more Darwen cousins he'd have to put up with today, offered his guest suitable refreshment. Kennard decided in favor of a glass of Canary, and Gervase waited patiently for him to broach the matter which had brought him here.

"You'll forgive the bluntness of an ignorant provincial, m'lord," began Kennard with his charming smile, "but, knowin' you're a busy man, I think it best to come directly to the point. New as I am to the company of all my charmin' English cousins, it hasn't escaped my notice that the Darwen family is encumbered with the embarrassin' presence of a certain female relative."

Coldmeece stared at Mr. Upshaw in surprise. So his feelings about Lady Louisa were so obvious that even an American could see, were they? "Go on, sir," he said stiffly.

Mr. Upshaw did not seem particularly affected by the earl's coldness. "Of course, out of the gratitude I bear the Darwen family for makin' my welcome to London so particularly warm, I was eager to render your lordship, as head of the family, any small service that might be within my power to perform. And so I was castin' about for a suitable recompense for your lordship's kindness, when it occurred to me that your lordship might be very well pleased to be done with the lady in question."

"I trust you are not suggesting murder, Mr. Upshaw," Gervase said at last.

Kennard's dark eyebrows flew up, then he laughed with real amusement. "Murder! Lord Coldmeece, I was suggesting marriage—mine and the lady's."

The earl glared at Mr. Upshaw in a decidedly unfriendly fashion. So Lady Louisa had more than one string to her bow, did she? It would almost serve her right to be married to a man like Upshaw!

"Perhaps, Mr. Upshaw, you are ignorant of the fact that the—lady—has other commitments?"

Upshaw raised a quizzical eyebrow at the earl. "Commitments? Oh, nothing to signify, I'm sure, my lord—and if things fall out right, I'm sure I could induce her to cry off them fast enough. It's too bad for our wedded bliss—and your peace of mind, my lord Earl—that there are a few small snags in the path of true love." Kennard leaned gracefully back in his chair and sipped delicately at his wine.

Coldmeece regarded the man before him with distaste. He had a strong urge to send Upshaw packing, but a vision of Lady Louisa tearing up the settlement agreement and daring him to do his worst decided him against it.

"And what might these few snags be?" the earl inquired acidly.

"Oh, merely the small matter of bein' able to support my bride in the style she fancies. Very expensive tastes, y'know. I've a few ventures in hand, of course, but a wife's expensive, and—well, I should hate to think the lady would have any case to regret her choice of husband, don'tcha see?"

"I see," said Gervase slowly. "So it comes down to a matter of dowry, does it?"

Upshaw slanted a glance at the earl. "As head of the family, m'lord, and the person responsible for all such things, you, at least, should be aware that the dowry is the *bride's* portion. Now, it's a very charmin' custom, I'm sure, but it would look just a bit behindhand for me to be spendin' my beloved's settlement on her upkeep, wouldn't it?"

Gervase was struck almost speechless by this effrontery. He had little doubt now that Upshaw and Lady Louisa had worked this out between them, waiting only until Augustus had declared himself to spring the trap. It would be worse than futile to offer Louisa that pension; she was plainly after much bigger game. She must be an unprincipled adventuress, and Upshaw an unmitigated scoundrel, and galling though it was, he would have to acquiesce to their extortionate demands or see Augustus entrapped into an unhappy marriage.

"For that amount of money, " Gervase said in cold

fury, "the two of you had better be prepared to provide me a great deal of recompense."

"Oh, we are, your lordship," Kennard assured him, with a look of injured innocence. "I plan, if all goes well, to remove my dearest bride instantly—and permanently—to America." He regarded the earl with the smug look of a tomcat well pleased with a night's work.

"I see," said the earl icily. "In that case, it appears congratulations are in order, Mr. Upshaw. I wish you and your blushing bride all the happiness you can expect, and you may be sure you will hear from my man of business as soon as the notice of your engagement appears in the *Gazette*. Far be it from me to deny two people so perfectly suited to each other the felicities of matrimony." He stood, and Kennard uncrossed one perfectly clad limb from the other and rose as well. He held out his hand to the earl. Gervase ignored it.

"Good day, Mr. Upshaw. It is unfortunate that pressing business will deny me the opportunity of seeing you again before you leave England."

Upshaw favored him with an irrepressible grin. "That's as may be, my lord, and may I say that the misfortune is all yours? I shall look forward to making the acquaintance of your man of business in the very near future. Oh, don't trouble yourself—I'm sure I can find my own way out." With a cheery salute Kennard left the library, and Coldmeece could hear him whistling cockily to himself before the front door closed behind him.

As Prometheus had been none too happy with the hurly-burly attendant upon Gervase's ball, and as Caro's promised to be far worse, it had been decided—by Gervase—that the mettlesome stallion should be stabled elsewhere that night. As Lady Mulford's stables stood nearly empty, it had also been decided—again by Gervase—that Augustus should cozen his aunt into allowing him stall space for the beast the night of the masquerade.

It was late afternoon by the time the Honorable Augustus Leslie Templeton had quite made up his mind to go to Mulford House to discuss the matter. Nonetheless, he was at last prepared for the ordeal, and as the May sunlight sent slanting rays across the square, he mounted the front steps and rapped smartly on the door.

He was admitted by Royton, who said that Lady Mulford would be with him shortly, and was left to cool his heels in Lady Mulford's charming front parlor.

Mr. Templeton had been feeling guilty ever since his unpleasant conversation with Gervase. Why, Coldmeece had made it sound as if Louisa had tricked him into offering for her, when in reality, as Augustus had tried to explain, they had both felt it would suit.

However, Gervase had been all too right about one thing: Louisa's rigs and rows, which had seemed perfectly acceptable and amusing on the Continent, were all wrong here in England. Augustus was forced to admit that this problem could be laid at his door; when she'd been extracted from that blasted Turkish palace, Louisa hadn't had the least notion how to go on, and had looked to him for instruction. But Gervase had opened his eyes for him, Augustus thought grimly, and that light-hearted tutelage had pretty well ruined Louisa. If he didn't marry her, Augustus knew, no one would, and that would break Aunt Josephine's heart and leave Louisa in desperate straits in later life.

Well, he would marry Louisa; it was his clear obligation. Furthermore, he was starting to wonder uneasily if she might have overheard this morning's disastrous conversation with Gervase—if she had, she'd be playing off every prank she could think of out of sheer bad temper and to pay back the earl. Augustus had no desire to see what other outrageous rigs Louisa would run; he'd taught her too well and she was too inventive—Lord alone knew what she'd be up to next! No, the best—the *only*—course was to marry her out of hand and take her away from England at once.

Somehow, though, Augustus no longer had any taste for his convenient marriage. He flopped inelegantly onto a sopha, long legs sprawling, and drummed his fist on the arm. If only everything had been different. He had never thought to fall in love at all—but had he not been betrothed to Louisa—if Celia had not accepted the earl at the ball . . . But he had, and she had, and now everything was ruined forever. He only wished he could stop comparing Louisa to Celia, to the former's detriment. Louisa wasn't Celia, and never would be.

Oh, Amber Pearl, Augustus thought ruefully, if you knew what I was thinking, how you'd laugh!

As if his thought had summoned her up, Louisa appeared in the doorway. Augustus struggled to his feet. "Ah, Louisa."

His cousin peered at him closely. "Has Prometheus dropped you on your head, Gussie? Whatever is the matter?" Without waiting for an answer, she extended her hand and allowed Augustus to usher her to a chair. "Royton told Aunt Josephine you were waiting to see her, so I thought, of course, that he had muddled the message and meant me instead."

"No," he said at last. "That is to say, Louisa, it's not that I *mind* seeing you—"

"Charmed, I'm sure," interjected Louisa.

"—but I really *must* see Aunt Josie. It's only that she's the head of the family—oh, not the Head of the *Family*, that is to say, but the head of—well, it wouldn't do any good my talking to Royton or Rigsby or—what *is* the name of your cook?"

"Um," said Louisa, who hadn't the slightest idea. "Yes, Augustus, now that you have explained matters to me in this pellucid fashion, I can see very clearly that you must not talk to the cook." She fixed Augustus with a wise eye. "But you have not told me just what it *is*!"

"Oh, it's Prometheus," said Augustus offhandedly. "You see, he—"

Lady Mulford chose this moment to make her appearance. Augustus bolted to his feet. Giving one of Louisa's hands a fierce squeeze, he begged the favor of a private word with her later, and set himself to the task of winning Lady Mulford's consent to the temporary housing of Prometheus in her quiet stables.

"Which is not a 'small matter,' Augustus," Louisa merrily quoted some time later, "as Prometheus is not a small horse!'' Uttering a squeak as Augustus lunged for her, Louisa swayed lithely out of his reach and danced away across the flagstones of the stableyard.

"Still," said Augustus cheerily, "she did say yes."

"On the condition he should not be here above one night, and be securely tied, remember," Louisa reminded him firmly.

"Prometheus is gentle as a lamb!" Augustus said in wounded tones. "Still, it's a weight off my mind to know he'll be here the night of the masked ball."

"Or so you hope," Louisa finished.

Augustus grinned at her and swung wide the stable door to usher her in ahead of him. Nodding to the head groom, he paced up and down the aisle, studying the accommodations available for housing his prize.

"Down here, I think," said Louisa, walking toward the untenanted stalls at the far end. "As far from the mares as possible. You never know."

"Tsk-tsk-tsk," said Augustus, wandering over to inspect the stalls. "Such indelicacy. Louisa, you shock me. You really do."

"Never," she said. "But really, Gussie, I did wish to have a word alone with you." She looked back over her shoulder at the groom and stableboy, then nodded at the end stall.

"No, I wanted to talk to *you*," countered Augustus soberly. He followed Louisa into the empty loose box and closed the stall door to give them a modicum of privacy. "I wished to apologize, my love, for being so very disagreeable a companion to you these last few weeks, and since I know that to be true, there's no need for you to try and turn me up sweet."

"I would never try to turn you up sweet," Louisa told him. "And very likely you were entirely justified in being on your high ropes, for London is such a provincial little place that it's quite true I haven't the least idea how to go on in it."

Augustus smiled, a bit crookedly, and possessed himself of her hands. "Wretch!" he said cheerfully. "It is as much my fault as yours, as you'll kindly have the courtesy to admit. After all, I, who have stood to you as your preceptor in all things—''

Louisa struggled to remove her hands from his firm clasp in order to box his ears, without success. ''If I took *you* as my preceptor, Gussie, I should have to be queer in the attic! Oh, do let me go, you abominable creature, and I shall agree that you have been as dreadful as you please!''

''Always accommodating,'' he said, releasing her.

Louisa moved over to the loose-box door, looking back at him over her shoulder. Now that the time had come to set her plans in motion by reminding Augustus of their agreement, she was strangely reluctant to begin. His next words, however, drove all compunction from her.

''But I did not drag you out here to apologize, but to commiserate,'' he told her gently. ''Listening at keyholes can be dreadfully fatiguing, can it not?''

Louisa whirled around, small spots of color flaming in her cheeks. For once, she was completely dumbfounded. ''But,'' she gasped, in what she knew to be a most hackneyed fashion, ''how did you know?''

''Don't forget, I know you. So I started wondering if you might have been outside the library door. Louisa, Gervase had no right to say any of those things—''

Then why did you agree with him? Louisa longed to ask, but she managed to keep silent.

''—but even so, don't start one of your rigs over it. You can't put Gervase out of countenance—''

''Oh, can't I?'' snapped Louisa.

Augustus held out a hand as if to quiet her. ''No. And if you try, it will only hurt Celia.''

With extreme difficulty, Louisa kept a lid on her temper. It was one thing to know you weren't entering on a love match, but it was quite another thing to have your groom constantly throwing the name of his true love in your face.

''I would never, never wish to injure my dear little cousin,'' Louisa said through clenched teeth. ''And I am fully sensible of the noble feelings that cause you to make this outcry on her behalf. However,'' she added briskly, ''I suspect I owe you an apology as well. Ever since the

Coldmeece ball you have been pressing me to stop shilly-shallying and marry you immediately. With your departure to Petersburg almost upon us, I have come to see that you are right, in this as in all things, O my lord protector and the delight of my eyes.''

''Louisa!'' Augustus seemed torn between laughter and exasperation.

Not trusting her self-control any further, Louisa turned and fled the scene before he could say anything else.

Well, Louisa thought to herself late that evening, you have gotten what you wanted. Poor Augustus! She smiled reminiscently at the stricken looks her professed intention to wed him immediately had caused, gallantly though the poor lamb had tried to hide it. If she had had the least intention of holding Augustus to their agreement, she would have felt very guilty indeed; as it was, she could at least be tolerably certain Gussie would remember he was to marry her. That should keep him from carrying off Celia before Louisa had everything properly arranged.

She pursed her lips, calculating. Yes, a fortnight to Lady Coldmeece's masked ball. It would be easy for a couple to elope from there—particularly when their path would be smoothed for them.

However, if this worthy scheme were to come to fruition, she had best stir herself. The first thing to do was sit down and make a list—in Turkish, of course, for discretion's sake—of everything that need be done by the ball. Humming tunelessly to herself, Louisa rummaged through her dainty escritoire but found to her indignation that she had no writing paper, no ink, and no quills. Hardly surprising, when she'd forbidden the Mulford House servants the run of her rooms. Still, it was most vexing.

Knowing that her aunt would have a completely stocked desk, Louisa decided to ransack it for supplies, rather than summon her maid. Accordingly, she made her way downstairs to the small room Lady Mulford used as a study. As her aunt was absent, having taken Celia to some humdrum drum or other, Louisa felt justified in making free of her writing desk.

This indispensable and elegant little item was crammed with billets and cards of invitation. Louisa picked through them without interest. Balls and parties and routs and picnics and *al fresco* luncheons and musical evenings and no writing paper in sight. She turned over one card, and stopped, frowning curiously. A yellowish slip of paper lay beneath. After a moment, Louisa pulled it out and examined it.

It was a bill, from Hoby, for some coats and waistcoats. Louis wrinkled her nose in puzzlement. It must be one of Gussie's bills, but whatever was it doing here? All of Lady Mulford's bills went directly to her secretary.

Louisa's burrowings seemed to have dislodged a veritable nest of the things. She leafed hurriedly through the bundle. Weston, Scott—dear heavens, it was a bill from Tattersall's Horse Repository for a pair of carriage horses! These weren't Gussie's bills; they were *Kennard Upshaw's*!

At that moment, the door opened. Louisa started guiltily, and Lady Mulford, splendid in mauve tabby silk and feathers, sailed into the room and instantly threw herself onto the settee.

"Louisa! *There* you are, darling—how perfectly splendid! I thought you might have gone to bed and there'd be no one to console me. Rigsby is a dear soul, but just the tiniest bit methodistical, and she would have *no* patience. Lady Weatherby—*such* a madcap, and quite a high flyer in the nineties, far before your time, dearest—but she will invite everyone who is anyone to her parties, and of course they *will* come, and I vow my feet are positively *aching*! A sad crush, and, I am bound, a raging success, but I am not as young as I used to be, so I crept out. Dear Kennard will bring Celia home later, all quite convenable, as he's her cousin, and I—Louisa? Darling, are you feeling quite the thing?"

Lady Mulford bustled to her feet and reached out to feel Louisa's cheek. When she caught sight of the disordered mass of cards and invitations under Louisa's fingers, her brow cleared "Oh, is *that* what has you in the mopes? Now, darling, there's nothing to fuss at in a few morning calls. We have already discussed Lady Deauville, and decided you need not go to her breakfast after all. Really, no one will remark it—''

''Aunt Josephine,'' said Louisa, ''I have to talk to you.''

Lady Mulford looked at her niece strangely. ''But of course, darling,'' she said. She settled herself back on the settee, folded her plump hands in her lap, and waited expectantly.

Louisa was keenly uncomfortable. She knew she had no business poking about in her aunt's desk, whatever her motives, but having done so and found those bills, she could not just ignore the matter. But how to begin?

After a moment she started, haltingly. ''You know, Aunt, when I was first out, you and Gussie took especial care to warn me of men who might seek to romance me for my money, if they thought I had any.''

''Yes, of course. Although I own you never seemed to pay any particular heed—not that you came to any harm.'' Lady Mulford looked puzzled.

''Oh, no. The fortune hunters were generally the most charming of companions, Aunt, and really very entertaining, so long as one was a penniless young female with no prospects. But I recall you telling me the ways in which they could impose upon a person, and, well, you see, Aunt—oh! This is the most *confounded* muddle!'' Louisa cried in exasperation, throwing herself down on the settee beside her aunt.

Lady Mulford, thoroughly bewildered, frowned. ''Louisa, I do hope you are not saying that . . . But how *could* you have, when I or Gussie have been with you nearly every moment? Or dear Gervase—but he is as rich as the Golden Ball, so that cannot have anything to say to the matter,'' she concluded decisively.

Louisa gave a sardonic whoop at this tangled expostulation, unraveling it with the ease of long practice. ''I wish I *may* say to his lordship that his godmama has taken him for a fortune hunter! No, dearest and darlingest of aunts, it is not *I* who fear to be enmeshed in the loathly toils, as Gussie would say. But—you see, my love, I must confess; I have been snooping in your desk.''

Lady Mulford regarded her dubiously. "But I have told you, Louisa, that Lady Deauville's breakfast—"

"Not Lady Deauville's breakfast," Louisa declared, "but Kennard Upshaw's bills!'" She threw her arms around her aunt's neck. "Dearest Aunt, I did not mean to pry, but now that I have, I confess I do not know what to think!" She drew back and regarded Lady Mulford with serious pale gray eyes.

Lady Mulford's brow cleared as if by magic. "Oh, is *that* all that has been troubling you?" She got to her feet and went to the front of the little desk, scrabbling around in its disorder and emerging at last with the offending bills clutched firmly in her hand.

"I could not think where they had gotten to. I was certain I had them in my jewel case, but Rigsby must have brought them down here. Admirable woman, a treasure, but so *organized*. And I know dear Kennard will want me to keep a close account of them." Beaming brightly upon the stunned Louisa, Lady Mulford, grasped the bell rope and pulled it smartly. "Now, dearest, we shall have sherry and biscuits, and I shall tell you all about Lady Weatherby's drum. That dreadful Caro Darwen was there, and what must she do but gloat—yes, positively!—over Celia's attending her masquerade! Do you know, dearest, I do believe that Caro would not scruple to do Celia a mischief. Yes, truly I do! But most fortunately, that will soon be beyond her power," she finished in relief. She peered at her niece. "Oh, Louisa, you still look a bit peaked. How, dreadful for you that you should have worried yourself to pieces over the merest *trifle*. You know, darling, I had hoped I was wrong, but it is plain to see that England does not agree with you at all."

With a sigh Lady Mulford dismissed unmentioned the topic of Louisa's potential marriage into London's *haut ton*. "Perhaps, after dear Celia's wedding, we might go to France, or Italy. It will be a shame that Augustus will not be with us, but you know he is going to have a career in St. Petersburg. How very odd it seems, to be sure, but I am certain a diplomatic post will be the best thing for him—dear boy, he has so much *energy!*"

"Oh, yes, I think St. Petersburg will suit admirably, Aunt Josephine," Louisa said dispiritedly. Despite her aunt's airy dismissal of Mr. Upshaw's bills, Louisa was not comforted.

"Louisa! You have not been attending to a word I've said!"

"Oh, Aunt, you know I hang upon your lightest syllable," said Louisa. She summoned up a smile, aware that Aunt Josephine had just offered her what would have been her heart's desire a month ago. It would be blackest ingratitude to continue sulking, but somehow she knew that leaving England would not lift her blue mood.

"I must confess, Aunt," she began, as they sat over the sherry and biscuits, "that it did give me a turn. And I cannot think why Mr. Upshaw would keep his duns here, rather than in his own desk. After all, he must know how likely you are to misplace things."

"Why, Louisa, you know I am always *most* careful!" said her aunt indignantly. "It is my opinion that bills cannot be any more important than tickets and travel permits, and you must admit I have never mislaid any of those. Besides, it is only until his funds clear from his American bank," she went. "Traveling is *so* expensive, as you know, and since he lost most of his luggage in that dreadful accident, he needed to make a number of purchases immediately, so we agreed it was the simplest thing. And after all, he is my dear sister Sophronia's son, you know."

Louisa realized that the situation was far worse than she'd thought. "Do you mean that *all* Mr. Upshaw's bills come directly to you? But what about when they come due?"

"Why, I pay them, of course. Louisa, dear, I am not quite such a pea-goose as you seem to think! It would hardly do for dear Kennard to be thought behindhand in his accounts, would it? It is really very simple, and since Gervase positively *insisted* on paying all the expenses of Celia's come-out, I needn't even think of applying to that disobliging Mr. Dumbarton for an advance."

"Oh," said Louisa numbly, and sipped her sherry.

There didn't seem to be a great deal she could say, after that.

Since her discovery of Kennard Upshaw's bills in Lady Mulford's desk, Louisa had considered a number of plans, from confronting Mr. Upshaw herself, to informing Lady Mulford's trustee, to closing her eyes to the entire matter. Unfortunately, the obvious course of action was also one she positively loathed the thought of, and it had been some time before she could force herself even to consider it.

She must go and lay the entire affair before her contemptible cousin, the Most Noble the Earl of Coldmeece. He was the head of the Darwen family, and this *was* his responsibility. At least when she had told him, she could stop worrying about it herself. Let Coldmeece shoot Mr. Upshaw, or whatever the English did with brigands, and Louisa would own herself obliged to him.

Not, however, obliged enough to alter one with her plans for the night of Caro's masked ball, now but three days hence.

These schemes were proceeding apace, and Louisa was quite pleased with them. Augustus had been browbeaten and cozened into agreeing to elope with Louisa from the masked ball, and to hold this plan in strictest secrecy, much against his better judgment. The few times Louisa had seen him since, he had looked positively grim; that was at least an improvement on Celia's company, as Celia had taken to reading improving works and saying zealous, militant things about serving the masses. Lady Mulford had dosed poor Celia with every nasty nostrum in Rigsby's formidable arsenal, but she still looked red-eyed and lachrymose.

Welladay, thought Louisa contentedly over her breakfast toast, all will soon be set right. Meanwhile, she would go and cut up the abominable earl's peace, and then come home and take a nice, long nap.

Her easy assurance lasted until she was actually rapping at the door of the Coldmeece town house. She was admitted by Coldmeece's butler, a great Frankish lout with a face like a tomb, and conducted to the library to await his lordship. His lordship appeared within a very few minutes; if he was surprised to see her at this early hour, and without an attendant maid, he showed no sign of it.

"Lady Louisa," he said. "To what do I owe the unexpected honor of this . . . visitation?"

Despite her good resolutions, Louisa felt a flash of anger. She could tell instantly he thought he knew exactly what she had to say and didn't think it worth the hearing. Well, she would show him! She took a deep breath, and began.

"I felt, Lord Coldmeece, that as head of the family you had best be consulted. It is a matter concerning my aunt and Mr. Upshaw."

The earl's mouth tightened to a grim slash. "Yes," he drawled in a blighting tone. "I fancy you would find yourself concerned, as it's a matter of money."

Louisa looked at him in surprise. "Do you mean that you already know?"

"It wasn't that difficult to guess." The earl looked positively disgusted. "You may recall, madam, that I am closely acquaintanced with all parties concerned."

"Oh," said Louisa blankly. This was not going at all as she had expected. If the earl *knew* Kennard Upshaw was fleecing her dear aunt, why had he not put a stop to it? And furthermore, she thought, anger kindling, he had no reason to stare at *her* as if—as if she were a toad! For Aunt Josephine's sake, however, she would grit her teeth and persevere. "But, Lord Coldmeece—"

He held up a hand. "You need have no fear for your financial well-being, madam," he cut in. "I have the entire matter well in hand, I assure you. Indeed, it was a waste of both our time for you to come here on this errand at all." There was a note of finality that seemed to indicate he felt the interview was at an end.

"*My* financial well-being!" said Louisa in outrage, rising to her feet. Did Coldmeece think her only concern was that Aunt Josephine might no longer be able to support her? "I thank you very kindly, Lord Coldmeece, but you need not concern yourself with *me*! I am quite able to manage for myself!"

"Yes, you've proved that admirably," he said bitterly.

"And since I have seen no evidence of your 'having the matter in hand,' as you so magnanimously call it," she went on ruthlessly, "I am forced to conclude—"

"You'll see your 'evidence,' as *you* call it, at the proper time. You need have no fear of being forced to moderate your habits one iota on anyone's account." The earl rose to his feet and regarded her scornfully. "May I have a footman escort you home?"

"No, thank you, my lord," snapped Louisa, clenching her fists. She smiled viciously at him. "Only permit me to say that your condescension and understanding so far exceed anything I had expected to find in my family that I am rendered quite speechless."

"You are never that!" he snapped back, but Louisa was already stalking out the door.

How *dared* she? How dared that woman come here, unchaperoned and dressed to the nines and flaunting her eyes at him, and try to extort more money out of him? Gervase glared at the library door in impotent rage. He could only suppose that, not content with his agreement with Upshaw, she had had the audacity to come herself to wring new concessions from him. That—that Turkish adventuress! How could he ever have cared about her, have worried about her happiness if she were married to Augustus? It was plain to see that Lady Louisa had no more heart nor morals than a cat, and anyone who loved her was doomed to a lifetime of pain.

Denied any target for his anger, Gervase occupied himself by searching out the settlement agreement for Lady Louisa Darwen and tearing the papers into very tiny pieces. That Augustus was now saved from marrying that virago was not comfort enough, somehow; Gervase dwelt lovingly on the hope that that cad Upshaw would have the good sense to drop Louisa over the side once they were well out to sea. He wished he'd never set eyes on her, the damned meddlesome, managing, interfering harpy! Better for everyone if she *had* stayed in that god-lost seraglio— or if he had dropped her in a sack into the Bosphorus, as she'd claimed he intended. How dare she come waltzing into London, bear leading Augustus and worming her way into Celia's innocent confidence, planning all the while to throw the lot of them over for an unprincipled American scoundrel!

Had Gervase not been a Darwen and a gentleman, he would have expressed himself even more strongly, conscious of the raging hurt that burned within him. When Caro had thrown him over for the title, he had sworn he was done with love, and would soberly marry only the most suitable female for the good of the family. And now his peace was shattered by a most *un*suitable female—and furthermore, one he despised!

Gervase threw the scraps of the settlement into the fireplace. He couldn't just wash his hands of the matter; they were his cousins, and he was responsible for the family. In fact, they were all his cousins: Augustus, Celia, Kennard, Louisa—damn his grandfather for a profligate fool! What business did the old man have to sire such a monstrous lot of Darwens? Had any man ever been cursed with so many appalling relatives?

And he wasn't done with them yet. There was still Caro's blasted ball. Well, at least his brother Edmund hadn't married a Darwen, much good it had done him! He could only hope to God that when Louisa jilted Augustus, the boy would have the sense to elope with Celia and take her far, far away, although this was probably too much to hope for. After this Season, Gervase only hoped never to set eyes on any of his exasperating relations again.

His sentiments were at that very moment being wholeheartedly echoed by Lady Louisa Darwen as she stormed back to Mulford House in a fine fury. In her case, however, the animadversions were less restrictive: she never wanted to see anyone English—or, in fact, anyone at all!— ever again.

Caro Darwen, exquisitely clad in a trailing lace gown that was quite unsuitable for a simple morning at home, sat up very straight and glared at her caller. "Really, sir,

I hardly see how you can have the effrontery to face me! I *trusted* you, and only see how you have repaid me: Celia is still to marry Coldmeece!"

Kennard Upshaw grinned at her and strolled across the room to the fireplace. He took the time to lean decoratively on the mantelpiece before he answered. "Well, my dear Dowager Countess," he said, not one whit discommoded, "I thought it was high time to keep you from spoilin' all my plans for your ball."

"*Your* plans?" Caro said. "But you have done nothing! All these weeks, when I had counted on you to detach Celia from Gervase—and all you have done is ride with her in the Park as they plan their honeymoon!"

"And all this while I've been workin' to achieve your amiable aims. I've come up with the perfect plan, but if you don't mind your pretty manners, Countess, Coldmeece'll forbid Celia to attend your ball."

All Caro's irritation instantly vanished. She clapped her hands together. "A plan? Oh, Kennard, you must tell me at once!"

Kennard undraped his lazy length from the mantelpiece and seated himself beside Caro on the sopha. "You see, your ladyship, it's all very simple. I intend to elope with Lady Celia from your little party just as you originally planned. I must admit, it was the idea of marryin' her afterward that stalled me, but then I realized that I needn't marry her at all."

"Oh!" said Caro, looking radiantly pleased. She had come to quite regret the necessity of wasting Kennard on Lady Celia; the man was so charming, and so obliging—and so very, *very* handsome! Then she looked alarmed. "Not marry her?" she echoed, shocked and intrigued. "But Coldmeece will call you out, you know. She's still his ward and his cousin, even if he won't marry her after that."

Kennard's sardonic smile widened. "What a complete cad you think me, darlin' Countess—and stupid, too, it seems."

Caro bit her lip in silent vexation. He smiled at her and poured himself a cup of tea. "Have I ever mentioned, my dear lady, how very lovely you look when you have been crossed?" he continued calmly.

"No!" she snapped. "And if you do not tell me what you intend this *instant*, I shall—"

He held up a hand for silence. "You may not have been enmeshed enough in the family circles to know," he said with a maddening air of superiority, "but I fancy it will soon be common knowledge that little Lady Celia has formed an attachment of the heart—to her cousin Augustus."

"Augustus?"

"There's no accountin' for taste," Kennard told her piously. "At any rate, Cousin Celia's preference is quite marked. Yet, due to an admirable delicacy, generally so lacking in a female"—here he grinned at Caro—"the child is loath to cry off her engagement to the earl, believing him to have been disappointed in love as a youth. And so," he concluded, spreading his hands wide, *"Voilà. C'est tout."*

Caroline stared at him for a moment in silence. "But . . . but . . . but you have told me *nothing*! How do you know all this? What does Celia's stupid romance have to say to anything? And how does it have anything to do with your not marrying her?"

"I am a prudent man," said Kennard, grinning at her, "and I have here in my pocket a Special License. After I have conveyed the fair Celia to a safe house I have arranged not far from town, I shall simply inform the excellent but impulsive Mr. Templeton that his lady fair has jilted his noble cousin and thrown herself on my mercy. I shall then send Mr. Templeton, with Special License, off to his *inamorata*, hinting heavily that they must marry immediately to save her from ruin. After that, it remains only to tell the earl that the two of them have eloped. He'll find that easy enough to believe, and even should he wish to pursue the matter, they'll be married when he finds them—a circumstance it will be difficult for even such a man as Coldmeece to overlook." Kennard sat back and sipped his tea, watching Caro closely.

"You sound as if you don't care for Gervase," said

Caro, flirting a glance at him from beneath her lashes. Suddenly a new thought struck her. "But Kennard—you were to have married Celia for her fortune. And what if Augustus does not believe you? You will be ruined, and possibly shot, and you may have to marry the chit after all."

Kennard studied her over his teacup, then he set it down firmly. "I find the latter consequence far more distressin' to contemplate than the former, Countess," he told her. "I've been ruined before, you see. As for Mr. Templeton, I have always found that not only is love blind, it is also extremely stupid. And as for Lady Celia's fortune"—he looked steadily at Caro until she blushed and dropped her eyes—"I have other resources."

Chapter
TWELVE

The day of the masked ball, Louisa crept into Coldmeece House through the service entrance. After calming the cook with a medley of threats, cozenings, and bribes, she was allowed to see Mr. Templeton's highly temperamental Russian valet for the purpose of a private word.

But even Lord Coldmeece's very superior male cook, who had righteously insisted on being present during this most irregular interview, was unable to follow their conversation, as it was held entirely in French.

Sasha's cooperation was solicited and assured, and Louisa breathed a sigh of relief. Now all was properly in train, and the fact that neither of the principals had an inkling of their roles in tonight's entertainment was a trifling matter; nor was she in the least discommoded by the certain knowledge that her visit would be reported to the earl at the earliest possible moment. These minor matters would interfere not one whit with her plans, and therefore did not concern her. With a light heart she bid Sasha farewell and beat a hasty retreat from Coldmeece House.

She was still congratulating herself when she was hailed by a familiar voice.

"Hi! Louisa! What are you doing here?" Augustus Templeton, immaculate as usual, vaulted down from Prometheus's back and strode toward her, leading the horse. The great bay stallion, ears flicking as if he shared his master's indignation, minced after him. "You haven't been to see Coldmeece again, have you?" Augustus demanded suspiciously.

Louisa ground her teeth against a sudden flash of irritation. "I'd willingly never set eyes on the man again! No, I have merely been suborning his servants, in the pious hope that they'll poison his breakfast hemlock, or something of the sort."

"Gervase don't drink hemlock for breakfast," Augustus told her. "In fact, sweet Coz, I've never seen him indulge in it at all. Don't tell me you two have been brawling again! The last time he wasn't fit to speak to for days."

"I'm sure I don't think he is *ever* fit to speak to!" snapped Louisa, and was infuriated by Augustus's knowledgeable chuckle.

He took her arm. "I'll walk you home, Amber Pearl, and you can explain to me why it's his fault you were eavesdropping at the door."

On the homeward walk Louisa, to divert Augustus's attention from more dangerous topics, tried once more to convince him of Coldmeece's utter perfidy. But by the time they reached Mulford House, Louisa had the uncomfortable feeling that she'd been arguing a losing proposition. Surely Augustus must see how vile, deceitful, and cozening Coldmeece was! Before bidding him farewell, she mendaciously promised faithfully to await him at the stables at ten o'clock that night. She then went off to her room, still seething.

Men! Kennard Upshaw was a rogue and a scoundrel, Augustus was no help at all, and as for Coldmeece—Louisa had never been so angered by any man in her entire life; she had never liked him, no, not from the first, and his vicious criticisms of her to Gussie had been the final straw.

But if her great and noble cousin thought he had seen willfulness and extravagance from her already, she would go him one better. He still thought she was marrying Augustus; tonight she would really give him something to fear for, and then, *then* she would tell him that she had no intention of marrying Augustus, and furthermore, she never had.

Louisa smiled triumphantly. One word from Celia and Gussie would marry her over the anvil if necessary—which it wouldn't be, as he now had a Special License in his pocket. And Celia would say that word. In the harem, Louisa had learned to be a shrewd judge of character; she rather thought that Celia was almost ready to decide that anything would be better than marriage to the earl, even eloping with the man she loved. And *that*, thought Louisa, rather incoherently, would show the great and powerful Earl of Coldmeece!

Once safely in her room, Campbell helped her out of her walking costume and into a dressing gown in silence, then prudently disappeared. Louisa sat cross-legged on her bed and began to take down her hair, scattering pins everywhere. A slow, sly smile curved her mouth. Yes, she would dance at his ball tonight, and tell the high and mighty earl that his heir had eloped with his bride, with *her* connivance, and that would serve him well.

Once her hair was unpinned and falling about her shoulders, Louisa stood up and stretched languidly. Tonight she would show Lord Coldmeece Lady Louisa Darwen at her most formidable—and let him reflect upon that!

Some hours later, Louisa sat combing her hair dry before the fire in her bedroom. She glowed with the contentment of one who has chanced all on a single throw of the dice and expects the results to be exceedingly amusing. Setting down the comb, she held up her ornate silver hand mirror to admire once more the results of her labors. This morning the glass had reflected only an undistinguished face surrounded by an even more undistinguished mop of sandy-mouse curls. Now, however, that same face was framed by a sleek, glossy mane of flaming chestnut opulence.

Who cared if respectable women didn't dye their hair? Louisa stuck out her tongue at the mirror. She wasn't respectable—wasn't that what everyone was saying anyway? And surely even Aunt Josephine must admit that she looked ever so much better with her hair a rich, luscious red, rather than a washed-out straw color. She was not such a superstitious ninny as to think red hair unlucky—and henna was not so much more than a hair wash such as she had seen advertised in the *Gazette*. And who used those, if not the Frankish ladies?

Having disposed of European proprieties to her satisfaction, Louisa returned to the task of drying her hair. When this was at last accomplished, she twisted the waist-length mane up into a knot at the base of her neck and secured it with ivory hair skewers.

Just then came a knock at the door, and Aunt Josephine's worried voice could be heard through its panels. Catching up a towel and hastily wrapping it around her head, Louisa dulcetly bade her aunt enter.

Lady Mulford bustled in and paused, staring at Louisa's towel-wrapped head.

"Oh . . . it is just an herbal treatment, Aunt. I hoped it would take my mind off this sick headache I have had all day."

"Well, it isn't any wonder, with your sleeping till noon one week and gadding about to dawn the next!" Lady Mulford scolded. "Regular habits are conducive to a feeling of well-being, and—oh! But I won't trouble you, dearest, if you're feeling poorly."

"Not at all, Aunt," Louisa said, patting the bed beside her invitingly. "It is only the headache. If it keeps on, I may cry off from the ball tonight. Will Celia be too disappointed if I do not go?"

Lady Mulford wrung her hands in vexation. "That is the very thing I wished to speak to you about; Celia has said she will not go to the ball!"

"Not go to the ball?" said Louisa in bewilderment. "But why? She was mad to go only a few days ago. Have she and Coldmeece quarreled?"

"Oh, no! That is, I do not *think* so. She has been very retiring, this past week, and even Augustus has absented himself—and you know he used to run tame in this house even more than Gervase!"

"Well, I think it would be the height of foolishness to try and persuade her to go to the masquerade, when we have been racking our brains this past month to find a way to prevent her," said Louisa decidedly. "Perhaps you could dispatch our regrets to the Countess—unless you,

Aunt, still wish to go? I shall try if I may to find what has blue-deviled poor Celia, without, of course, allowing her to change her mind about the ball. Then, dearest Aunt, *I* shall bespeak a tray in my room and spend the evening in virtuous indolence.''

Lady Mulford inspected her niece critically. ''Do you know, Louisa, I do not think you have the headache at all! But that is quite all right—if it means we need not socialize with That Woman tonight, such duplicity seems rather mild, really.'' Patting Louisa forgivingly on her cheek, Lady Mulford hastened off to pen her regrets to the Dowager Countess of Coldmeece, and Louisa wrapped herself in a paisley silk dressing gown and went off to see her unhappy cousin.

She found Celia's room in a state of utter chaos. The formidable Teale stood in the middle of the room ineffectually remonstrating with her charge, while Celia hurried back and forth between wardrobe and dressers, flinging armloads of her London finery willy-nilly into her old trunks.

''Good heavens!'' said Louisa inadequately. ''Celia, what are you doing?''

Celia stopped her packing and turned to face Louisa. She squared her shoulders, and her chin rose up with the obstinacy of a martyr under fire. ''I am not going to the ball,'' she announced. ''In fact, Cousin Louisa, I cannot deceive you—I am leaving Mulford House forever!''

With a sinking feeling in the pit of her stomach, Louisa knew that here was trouble indeed. ''You may leave us, Teale,'' she said with an assumption of briskness she did not feel. ''I am perfectly competent to assist Lady Celia with such packing as she may be presumed to require. And there is no need to bother Lady Mulford with any of this, as she is quite busy, and trusts me to deal with matters of this sort. Is this quite clear?''

''Perfectly, my lady,'' said Teale, her expression sour. ''But Lady Celia,'' she added beseechingly, ''surely you can't want to run off like this—not in the middle of the Season?''

Celia drew breath for further explanation of her position, but Louisa forestalled her. "That will be *all*, Teale," she said firmly, and, defeated, the dresser withdrew.

As soon as the door had closed behind her, Celia's shoulders slumped, and the armful of dresses she had been clutching slipped to the floor. "Oh, Louisa!" she said piteously. "I did not wish you to know. I don't know what to do, but I do not know what *else* to do, either!"

"Perhaps you will tell me what you are doing, before you do anything else," said Louisa gently, drawing Celia over to sit on the bed. "Good heavens, Celia, you can hardly expect to simply tell Aunt Josephine that you aren't going to the Countess's ball and then tiptoe home to wherever with all your trunks! And what about the earl?"

"I am not going to marry the earl," said Celia quietly. "I meant to tell both of you, only I thought it would be easier after my trunks were packed. I thought then Lady Mulford would see that my intentions are serious."

"Oh, Celia!" Louisa cried with real relief, throwing her arms around her surprised cousin. "You are *not* set upon marrying Coldmeece—oh, how wonderful!"

Celia emitted a muffled squeak. "But *Louisa!*"

Louisa laughed aloud. "Silly cousin! I have been racking my brains for weeks hoping to make you see what a dreadful man he is! Your refusal can have nothing but a much needed salutary effect on his character. You must believe me, he is hardly deserving of you. But you cannot leave *now!*"

"Oh, but I must!" Celia protested. "How can I stay? I had hoped I could grow to . . . That is, in time . . . But I—I—Oh, Papa would not approve! So I could not marry Lord Coldmeece, knowing as I do that I am a vile creature who can never reciprocate his feelings," wailed Celia, with a lightning change of heart.

Louisa rightly interpreted this to mean that Celia had been attempting virtuously to fall in love with the earl since her come-out ball, been woefully unsuccessful in this endeavor, and had finally realized that she could not endure a loveless marriage. Now it only remained for Louisa to point out to Celia that Augustus awaited with open arms and a Special License.

Wondering what on earth would have become of the lot of them if she, Louisa, had not been able to keep her head during the emotional alarms and excursions of the past weeks, Louisa patted Celia's hand and said briskly, 'Well, you are *not* a vile creature, and he *has* no feelings, and you cannot leave now, dearest cousin, because now that you are free, there is someone who will have a number of things to say to you. That is, if he isn't a right clunch,'' she added.

''Augustus,'' Celia gasped, all color leaving her cheeks. ''Oh, Louisa, I cannot! He will despise me utterly! It was that which kept me from crying off from the earl after my come-out ball. I could not bear him to think so of me. But I cannot possibly!''

''Ho!'' said Louisa,, bouncing up and down on the bed with unladylike glee. ''Gussie has been head over heels from the first moment he clapped eyes on you. Do you really think he'd rather see you marry his cousin or bury yourself in wasteful spinsterhood? As he would say himself, that cock won't fight, Coz!''

Celia stared at her with a stunned expression. ''Oh, Louisa, I had never thought . . . do you really think it possible that—that Augustus might care for me?''

''I am quite certain of it,'' said Louisa with admirable gravity. ''Have you told Lord Coldmeece of your decision yet?'' Celia shook her head. ''Then let me suggest you lay all before Augustus, and let him assist you.''

''Oh, but I am not going to the ball tonight, and I had hoped Lady Mulford would lend me her carriage tomorrow to take me home to Yorkshire. So I shan't see him at all. Unless . . . that is—no! I must go!'' Celia gasped and began to weep from sheer nerves.

Louisa put her arms around her cousin and drew her head onto her shoulder. ''There, Cousin, don't cry. I'm sure you must do exactly as your conscience bids you. Of course Aunt Josephine will send you home, if that is what you really wish. *I* shall go to the ball, and say all that is necessary. You may send a note to the earl, and I promise most faithfully to deliver it, and you need never be fussed

211

again, poor darling. You will be safe and nevermore need deal with the dreadful Darwen family.''

"Oh, Louisa, I am so very tired," Celia whispered. Then she sat up and heaved a tremulous sigh.

"Well, and so you should be," said Louisa. "I shall send Teale to you with a soothing *tisane*, and then you must take to your bed and rest, for traveling is so very fatiguing. Oh, and let Teale see to your trunks."

Celia nodded docily, like a tired child. "Oh, if I must, Louisa. But I do not wish to delay."

"Of course not," said Louisa firmly. "But do not forget to write that note." With that, she went off in search of Teale, and then to explain to her aunt that everything was perfectly under control.

At eight of the clock on the evening of the ball, Louisa Darwen sat in solitary splendor in front of her dressing table mirror. Lady Mulford had retired early to her bed, Celia was asleep under Teale's watchful eye, and Louisa had put the alarms and excursions of the day behind her to dress for the masquerade.

Louisa picked up the tiara, admiring its delicate foil streamers, and tried to recall what the diaphanous gold tissue costume had been supposed to represent. Oh, yes; Aurora, goddess of the dawn. She regarded the spangle-sewn bodice—what there was of it—with trepidation. She would just have to keep the scarf well about her shoulders, although its gold-tissue folds would hardly be much concealment. However, even if she walked into the ballroom stark naked, Coldmeece could hardly hold a lower opinion of her than he did now. She held the gauzy dress up against herself and giggled. How fortunate that she had the red domino and mask from her original costume for Caro's masquerade, for otherwise she would never get a step beyond her room.

If the very fabric of London Society—and more important, the Earl of Coldmeece's composure!—did not crack stem to stern this evening, it would not be through the want of any effort of Lady Louisa Darwen's.

* * *

The evening was going as well as might be expected, in Coldmeece's opinion; more plainly, he found it a dead bore. He was nothing but grateful that Lady Mulford's party had sent their regrets at the last minute. This was not at all the sort of evening he would wish for an innocent young girl like Celia. It was all Caro's set: half flash and half foolish, with more than a few rakes and fortune hunters among them—including, of course, Mr. Kennard Upshaw, more distinctive in plain evening dress than many of those in their elaborate costumes. Upshaw had smiled formally at the earl when presented, and Caroline had seated him on her right hand at dinner, but the American had been intelligent enough not to press his company on the earl.

Caro had not been in the best of humors since she had been informed, late in the day, of the defection of the Mulford House ladies. At the least, it had given her something else to pout about besides his refusal to don any sort of costume for this charade.

Gervase regarded the costumed crowd without interest, until Mr. Templeton, standing beside him, stiffened and gave vent to a muttered oath. Curiously, Gervase looked in the direction of his young cousin's gaze, but could see nothing to excite such a passion, although the young woman slowly descending the staircase was certainly worth staring at, with a mass of flaming hair only half-up and sleek curves inadequately shielded by a Grecian dress of gold tissue. Gervase was surprised; it was quite unlike Caro to have invited such an out-and-outer to take the shine out of her like this.

He raised an inquiring brow to the stricken Augustus. "Do you know her?"

"No!" said Augustus hoarsely, and promptly excused himself to dash in the direction of the fair unknown.

The earl took another, keener look; a malicious smile twitched at his lips, and he strolled casually after Augustus.

Louisa had barely gained the ballroom floor when she was accosted by an unmistakable figure in the clothes of a gallant Cavalier.

"Louisa!" the masked figure hissed. "What the devil are you doing here? And what have you done to your hair?"

"Good evening, Gussie," said Louisa lazily. "Henna, and a desire to waltz, though not precisely in that order. I have some good news for you, my angel, and then you must present me to Coldmeece. I am simply perishing to renew our acquaintance."

"I don't doubt it!" snarled Augustus, taking Louisa by the arm and attempting to steer her off the floor. "How *dare* you paint yourself up like a Covent Garden nun and come here in that indecent dress! Come along, my girl, we're going home this instant, and when Aunt Josie sees you, well—"

"Celia has abandoned Coldmeece, and is going home to Yorkshire tomorrow, if no one prevents her. I have her note to the earl right here," said Louisa, languidly bestowing that billet on Augustus. "As for myself, dear Cousin, I have no desire, nor any intention, of marrying you, so you may consider yourself fancy-free to do as your heart leads you. *I* have come to dance, and —"

"And so you shall, Cousin Louisa," came the familiar and half expected voice from behind her. "How kind of you to come. Do, please, give me the felicity of this waltz," the earl of Coldmeece continued smoothly, holding out his arm.

With an arch smirk at Augustus, Louisa walked off with Coldmeece, leaving Augustus clutching the letter from Celia. Without the least compunction, he tore it open and began to read.

"How pleasant that you contrive to continually surprise me," said Gervase. He held Louisa rather closer than the waltz demanded or the Patronesses would have approved, and there was something about the pressure of his arm that made the diaphanous tissue of her gown seem even thinner. The predatory gleam in his gray eyes should have put Louisa on her guard, but she was too high-flown with the success of all her plans to note the warning.

"Surprise you, my most noble cousin?" she said mockingly. "And how might I have done that?" She leaned back against his arm as he swept her around in the graceful figures of the waltz and looked up at him through heavily darkened lashes.

"By appearing here at all—and in such a costume—after our last conversation, of course."

With difficulty, Louisa refrained from stepping on the earl's foot. Only the knowledge that her gilded kid sandals would have little effect prevented her. "But Lord Coldmeece," she protested, affecting a small, puzzled frown, "how *else* would a lazy, bad-tempered, extravagant, fortune-hunting adventuress behave?" She slanted a glance at her partner and was pleased to see an expression of consternation on his face. "You see, my lord, after tonight it will no longer be any concern of mine *what* opinion you hold of me. And I have been most extremely displeased by your meddling."

"Meddling!" said the earl, a tinge of color staining his cheeks. "If you had been anything other than a—" He bit back the rest of the sentence as the music ended, and Louisa slithered out of his embrace and out of reach.

It was really too delightful to see Coldmeece flustered, but she had a number of other reasons for being here tonight and must not spend all her time indulging herself. To start with, she strongly felt she should make sure that Augustus had done what she'd intended.

Augustus was nowhere to be found, and Louisa had half rejected her plan to confront Kennard Upshaw in favor of one last dance with Coldmeece and a dramatic early exit. This flash crowd wasn't really to her taste, and the looks her daring costume was earning her were making her more than a trifle uneasy. Well, she'd had her fun, she thought, a smile tugging at her mouth, and now she would go home and watch the fireworks that were sure to follow.

"Lady . . . *Louisa*?"

Louisa turned at the sound of her name to confront Caro Darwen. The dowager countess was fetchingly clad as a shepherdess from the court of Louis XVI, and was goggling at Louisa with fascinated dismay. Louisa swept her an overly deep curtsy. "Countess! How perfectly charming to see you again."

"Yes! Well!" Caroline was obviously distracted. She beckoned to Louisa to come closer. "I *must* have a private word with you, Lady Louisa. Come with me."

Caro's choice of a private spot proved to be Coldmeece's library; recalling her last visit to this room, Louisa could not suppress a twinge of disquiet. Caroline lit several candelabras from a taper and then sat down on the love seat, radiant in the wash of golden light. "I . . . I hardly recognized you, in that—well! A most *singular* costume, Lady Louisa. I am sorry now I did not think of awarding prizes this evening, for you would certainly win one."

"Oh, your ladyship," Louisa said, making Caro a graceful salaam, "if my humble *hareem* frock finds favor in your eyes, it is through no virtue of mine. Allow me to have one made up for you, Lady Coldmeece; I am certain it would suit you admirably."

Caroline stared at Louisa with doe-eyed incomprehension, plainly at a loss.

"Perhaps I might know what you wished to say to me, Lady Coldmeece?" said Louisa helpfully.

Caro's wits had not entirely deserted her, it seemed. "Oh, you must forgive me, my dear, but I was so surprised to see you here, especially as Lady Mulford had written that you were not coming. Has Lady Celia come also?" she added hopefully.

"I'm afraid Lady Celia was forced to deny herself your society this evening, Lady Coldmeece," said Louisa sweetly. "She had a pressing elopement."

"*Elopement?*" gasped Caro, stricken. "But she can't be eloping!"

"Why not?" said Louisa.

"Because I, dear Cousin, am *here*," Kennard Upshaw, elegant in formal evening dress, strolled into the library and shut the door firmly behind him. His gaze traveled up and down Louisa's semi-exposed limbs in a way that made her feel quite peculiar.

"Kennard!" squeaked Caroline. Kennard smiled at her and leaned back against the mahogany desk.

"I don't know what it is about closed doors that always makes me wish to open them," he said pensively. "It's been this way ever since I was a child. Most distressin' to m'mother, but there it is. When I saw you spirit off Lady Louisa, dear Caroline, I thought it only proper to toddle along and tell you that your sweet cousin-in-law Augustus Templeton has quit your charmin' party and is at this very moment roaming the streets of London in the guise of a cavalier—in search of his horse, no doubt." Kennard beamed upon both ladies.

Louisa carefully wiped all trace of alarm from her face. "I daresay Coldmeece will be delighted to hear that you were planning to elope with his bride," she said.

"Oh, one cousin's the same as another, in the matter of elopement," said Kennard airily, "and it seems sweet Celia is destined to elope with someone tonight. I hardly think, Lady Louisa, that after your appearance here tonight I need stand in dread of anything you might say to Coldmeece. He'll hardly take you seriously, now, will he, your ladyship?"

Again, Louisa was conscious of Kennard's experienced gaze on her body; she'd been a fool to wear this dress. "Perhaps not. But Aunt Josephine certainly will," she said, glaring at him. "And I don't think you'll find her quite so willing to hold your vowels, after tonight."

The easy smile faded from Kennard's face, and Louisa knew she'd made a grave mistake. Then he smiled again and turned to Caro.

"Darling Countess," he said, taking her elbow and raising her to her feet, "perhaps you would like to go and make merry with the happy revelers. I'm certain Coldmeece doesn't yet know of his bereavement, but he'll need to be comforted, all the same."

To Louisa's dismay, Caroline did not blink at this outrageous proposition, but dutifully expressed her desolation

217

at being called away on such an important errand and slipped from the room before Louisa could stop her.

"Now," said Kennard silkily, coming over to stand in front of Louisa, "I'd be most interested to hear what you mean by that peculiar statement—and who else you've favored with a similar tale."

Louisa refused to step back, clinging to the certainty that nothing could happen to her in the middle of a London ball. "It's perfectly simple," she said. "I found your bills in Aunt Josephine's desk, and it doesn't take a genius to see that you have no intention of ever paying them. As soon as I knew, I told Lord Coldmeece, and you may be certain he will take appropriate action. And now," she said regally, drawing herself up, "if you are through taking leave of your senses, pray oblige me by collecting them again and allowing me to rejoin the dancers. It is just barely possible that I may be able to salvage something of amusement from this evening."

Unfortunately for her hopes of carrying off the prize in the encounter, Kennard did not seem the least discomfitted by this speech. So far from allowing her to pass, he went over to the library door and leaned against it, his arms crossed and a look of sharp speculation on his face. And when Louisa swept indignantly up to the door, he did not move aside.

"Permit me to pass, sir!" she demanded.

"Not so fast, your high and mighty ladyship," Kennard drawled. "There's a couple of things that bother me about this, and they're all you. And you'll oblige *me* by sitting down so that we can have a nice, civilized little discussion about them." With a wave of one hand, he indicated the love seat; with a turn of the other, he locked the library door.

"I'll scream," said Louisa instantly.

"Scream away," Kennard said amiably. "Everybody's in the ballroom or the card room, including most of the servants. Who'll hear you?" Grinning at her knowingly, he slipped the key into his pocket.

Louisa's eyes widened, but short of wresting the key

away from him by brute force, which didn't seem very feasible, there was nothing for it but to obey.

Once she was seated, Kennard made free of the earl's decanters. He poured canary into two glasses and handed one to Louisa. Feeling in need of a restorative, she condescended to take the glass and sip cautiously. Kennard said nothing for a few minutes; he tossed down the first glass of wine, then poured himself a second and drank that more slowly, his green eyes narrowed and fixed on Louisa.

"Well, sir," she said, placing her wineglass on the nearest table with a decided click. "Surely you cannot intend keeping me here all night. For one thing, I'm not at all the young lady you were looking for."

"I'm not so sure about that," he said, eyeing her keenly. "You think you've put quite a spoke in my wheel, don't you, your ladyship?"

"As a matter of fact, yes, I do think it!" said Louisa valiantly. "And you had just better take the next ship back to wherever you came from—it is too much to hope that you will compensate Lady Mulford for her losses."

"Is it?" Kennard asked silkily. "Do you add omniscience to your many other irritating qualities? I have reason to know you have said nothing to Coldmeece—and should you refrain from disturbing your aunt as well, I see no reason things should not continue as pleasantly as they have."

"Pleasantly!" cried Louisa, leaping to her feet. "So I'm to keep silent while you ruin my aunt, and do who knows what else? You can't think me that biddable—unless you're as stupid as you are heartless!"

Kennard raised his eyebrows. "Actually, I'm neither, and I doubt very much that any of my poor bills could possibly put a dent in the Mulford fortune. You've been living off your aunt for years, Lady Lou, and quite handsomely, too. Why not allow me the same privilege? Besides, our aunt will have such reason to be grateful to me, she'll undoubtedly not hear of any repayment of my debt."

"Grateful?" said Louisa, tensing.

"Why, for my heroic attempts to save your reputation,

219

and my silence upon the subject. Yes, the more I think on it, it really is too bad of Cousin Augustus to cheat me out of my elopement—and when it's all arranged, too.''

Louisa stared at him, real fear cutting through anger for the first time. However, she controlled both voice and expression, saying composedly enough, "I collect, then, that you mean to turn this farce into a real abduction, and try to spirit me off somewhere out of petty revenge.''

"Not so petty," said Kennard with a smile. "It would pretty well ruin you. I'd like to see you waltz through the sacred portals of that dull little social club those high-nosed Patronesses run if word got out. If the thought of having every door closed to you doesn't terrify you, it will Lady Mulford. So perhaps you'll reconsider, Lady Louisa?'' He regarded her complacently.

Goaded far beyond the limits of her control, Louisa's temper finally got the better of her. With a fervent Turkish oath, she grabbed up the first thing that came to hand and flung it at Kennard, then ran to the door.

Kennard made the tactical error of ducking, thereby moving directly into the trajectory of the wineglass. It broke against his chin, leaving a nasty-looking cut.

"Damn you," he snarled in Louisa's ear, grabbing her as she pounded vainly on the door. "You're going to regret that, Lady Louisa!''

Mulford House was quiet and dark as Augustus approached it, but as he came up the front steps the door was opened by an unsurprised Royton. Stepping into the hall, Augustus was surprised to see his valet waiting patiently.

"Sasha! What the devil are you doing here?'' Without waiting for a reply, Augustus turned back to Royton. "I must see Lady Celia immediately. It is absolutely vital.'' Augustus was prepared for a brisk argument, but instead Royton simply said that if Mr. Templeton would be so good as to step into the parlor, he would see if Lady Celia was at home. Augustus, hopeful, prepared to wait patiently—all night, if need be.

It was not much above half an hour later that Celia,

hastily roused, and dressed by the vigilant Teale, came into the room. Her eyes widened wonderingly as she saw Augustus.

"Gussie!" she gasped. "But—have you seen Louisa?"

Augustus laughed. "I've seen a great deal of Louisa tonight, and I'll be—dashed—if I don't think she *planned* all this! It would be just like her. Tell me, sweetheart, how did she arrange for you to come to your senses tonight?"

Celia colored at the endearment. "Come to my senses? But, Augustus, I have been dreadfully wicked! I feel quite abandoned and dead to shame. I simply could not bear to go to that ball, or—or anything else! But Louisa promised she would not tell you," she finished tragically.

"I would forgive Louisa for anything but that," said Augustus firmly. "In fact, I already have. Tell me, dear heart," he continued, advancing on Celia, "could you bear to be the least bit more wicked? I feel that matters have all been arranged, and it would be cruel to disappoint Louisa after all her work."

Celia looked up at Augustus, face radiant. "I—I shall try to be wicked, Augustus, if you particularly wish it," she whispered shyly.

"Then marry me," he said. "Marry me now—tonight—immediately! I can't offer you a title, but—"

"Oh, Augustus, I will!" cried Celia, throwing her arms around his neck. "I shall be wicked!" she vowed determinedly.

The dancers had just gone down to early supper. Gervase had searched for Lady Louisa in vain, and had then given his arm to his sister-in-law. Caro looked very well pleased with herself, an expression Gervase mistrusted. But he had no intention of quizzing her.

He had just left her seated in a circle of adoring gallants and gone to fill his own plate when a footman brought him Celia's letter. He took the crumpled and unsealed missive, glanced at the signature, and asked the footman who had given it to him. Upon hearing that it had been Mr. Templeton, he dismissed the man and took the note over into a quiet corner to read it carefully.

Stripped of its lugubrious rodomontade, the essence was simple and cheering. Lady Celia had discovered herself shatteringly unworthy of him, and trusted him to publish this information in the proper quarters.

Since Augustus had obviously possessed himself of the contents of this interesting communication, a liberty Gervase was more than willing to forgive under the circumstances, it was hardly surprising that he was nowhere to be seen. Doubtless he had gone with all haste to lay his hand and heart before Celia before the child changed her mind again.

Gervase smiled. And that meant that *he* could tell Lady Louisa that all her Byzantine scheming had been in vain, and she might whistle for her extortionate and extorted dowry. He doubted she'd find Kennard Upshaw willing to marry her without being well paid for it—and that left Lady Louisa Darwen once more penniless and without resources. The thought of Lady Louisa Darwen forced at last to listen to reason was such a beguiling one that it put the earl of Coldmeece into a very good humor indeed.

Returning to Caro's side, he adroitly removed her from her covey of gallants. "Tell me, my dear sister-in-law, have you seen Lady Louisa this evening?" he asked once they were private.

Caroline looked oddly guilty. "Oh! But I have not seen her since she was in the library with Kennard earlier."

"I see," said Gervase, disappointed. "Then I perceive it is too late to prevent the elopement?"

"Oh, much," Caro agreed happily. "But Gervase, I do not precisely see what that has to do with Lady Louisa, when it is Lady Celia who is eloping," she finished, looking vaguely indignant.

"Does the entire town know?" demanded Gervase.

Caro dimpled prettily. "No, but when I saw Louisa I wished to know where Celia was, and it was she who told me that Celia was eloping and could not attend."

"Good God!" said Gervase, torn between irritation and laughter. "You make it sound the merest commonplace!"

"Well, I confess I found it quite puzzling, as Kennard

222

had been by my side all evening, but then he assured me that it was *Augustus*—''

"What has Upshaw to do with any of this?" Gervase demanded sharply.

Caro, regarding him warily, decided she had said too much and did not answer. Gervase lost patience and shook her until the combs fell from her carefully disordered hair and she uttered muffled squeaks of protest.

"Gervase! You are hurting me, and I do not like it!" she said pettishly.

He brought his face close to hers. "You know how much I care for your likes, dear sister, and after tonight I care even less. Be open with me—or this is the last social function you will grace for many a Season to come."

"I don't *know* anything!" said Caro defensively. "I left them together in the library an hour ago, and I have not seen Kennard since, even though he was supposed to take me in to supper. But it doesn't signify. He said he would not marry Celia if he eloped with her, so I don't suppose he will marry Louisa either. And now, you ungrateful wretch, let me be! I don't know *why* I ever thought I was fond of you! You are rude, coarse, ungrateful—''

"Rich, and titled," Gervase supplied automatically, his mind working rapidly. Ignoring her protests, he dragged Caro off to inspect the library. It was ominously vacant. As he paced the room, his foot grated on some shards of broken glass, which, examined, turned out to be the remains of a wineglass. Gervase dropped the pieces back to the floor and added up the evidence. Kennard and Louisa were gone, probably together, and he was no longer as certain as he would like to be that Louisa had gone willingly.

"*Damn* the woman!" he snarled, abandoning Caro and striding urgently from the library.

Chapter
THIRTEEN

After an interminable and uncomfortable time, the coach lurched to a halt. Louisa crouched on the floor of the carriage, where she had early been flung, and regarded the door warily. A few moments later it was opened by Kennard Upshaw, muffled in a driving coat and carrying a lantern.

"Alight, fair damsel," he intoned. He beckoned, and Louisa gingerly unbent her cramped limbs and rose to her feet.

"Take me back to Coldmeece House at once!" she demanded, her voice shaking with anger.

Kennard smiled at her. "No. Now, is it your ladyship's pleasure to walk or be carried?"

Mustering the shreds of her dignity, Louisa permitted him to assist her from the carriage. He ushered her up the walk to the small two-story house, walking close behind her so she couldn't bolt. He escorted her up the stairs to a small, snug parlor on the second floor, where a fire was already burning cheerfully. Louisa moved toward it, hoping to drive out some of the chill of what had seemed an endless journey.

"You'll excuse me," said Kennard from the doorway. "But the horses must be seen to." He closed the door behind him, and she distinctly heard the lock click.

Louisa paced furiously back and forth in front of the fire. She was sorrier than ever that she had chosen this revealing gown to wear to the masquerade.

Some minutes later Kennard returned, to be greeted by

Lady Louisa at her most imperious. "Perhaps now you will be so good as to tell me what you intend to do?" she asked icily.

"Do?" said Kennard in surprise. "Why, I think I have already done it, Lady Louisa. Your reputation is in ruins, and you know full well you haven't enough allies in the *ton* to let you brazen it out. The only question that remains is, what is to be done about *that*?"

"Do go on, Mr. Upshaw," said Louisa evenly. "So far, being ruined doesn't sound so bad after all. I shall be able to do as I please, since I'll have nothing to lose."

"True enough. But Coldmeece will have a great deal to lose. His heir's run off with his bride, and his sister-in-law . . . well, everyone isn't as fond of dear Caro's mad starts as I am. I don't think the family can stand another scandal. Coldmeece will pay, and pay well, to keep this night's work quiet. Enough to pay the bills, you might say." He moved toward the door and unlocked it, then turned back to Louisa, his body carefully blocking the exit. "Whether the almighty Darwens will pay to get you *back* or not, of course, I can't presume to say. I wouldn't, but then, my taste has never run to sharp-tongued shrews with little beauty and—"

"And no money!" snapped Louisa.

Kennard gave her a mocking bow. "As you say, Lady Lou. And I do trust you'll spend a damnably uncomfortable night, your interfering ladyship!" He turned on his heel and stalked out of the room, slamming the door behind him.

The key sounded in the lock as a final grace note. Louisa sank into the nearest chair and put her head in her hands.

Though Caro had unfolded all she knew of Kennard's original plan to kidnap Lady Celia, no amount of encouragement would induce her to disclose the location of the house Kennard had rented, and Gervase was forced to conclude that she did not know it. As soon as Champion had been saddled, Gervase set out in search of his missing cousins. He turned the great chestnut down the nearest road that led out of the city, trusting that Kennard had taken the easiest and most obvious route. As he rode, he contemplated the evening's events thus far.

By now Celia and Augustus might already be married; it was no difficult task to find a clergyman in London during the Season, and Augustus must have made some plans when he intended to marry Lady Louisa. That at least was a great relief; now Augustus would be a dazzling, if useless, junior member of the diplomatic corps, and Celia would make him a charming wife. And while it was true that an elopement was a scandal, much was pardoned to those with youth, beauty, and fortune—and they would be absent from England long enough for those only interested in the business of others to have discovered new scandal broth to brew. Gervase supposed that in due time Augustus would be a ponderous elder statesman, gray and full of gout, his sweet-natured light-mindedness construed as great Christian forbearance and deep insight. Celia would have a house in Town, a number of beautiful offspring, and no doubt devote herself to every program for social reform that crossed her path. Augustus would therefore be knighted eventually for service to the Crown, and no one would care then that their marriage had not been celebrated in fashionable style.

Two of his too-numerous Darwen cousins disposed of to his satisfaction, Gervase turned his attention to the troublesome remainder.

Kennard Upshaw must leave the country at once. Gervase's yacht, the *Day-Dream*, was anchored at Dover; Upshaw could be got aboard and conveyed into France before anyone was the wiser. As for Lady Louisa—

Gervase's gloved hand tightened on the reins as a vivid image came to him of Louisa as she had appeared at the ball, her hair an unnatural hellfire copper and that scandalous gold tissue gown clinging to every curve. She had had the audacity to taunt him with her unsuitability—and he suspected she had come to Caro's ball solely to tease him.

On the outskirts of Town, he stopped a detachment of the Watch, and learned that a carriage had passed by this route about an hour before. Encouraged by this news, he urged Champion to quicken his pace to a trot.

The fire had burned down to embers by the time Louisa could rouse herself to take stock of the situation. She had no doubt that it was bad. Kennard had her at his mercy; he would force Coldmeece to pay over vast sums of money for his complaisant silence. She raised her head from her hands. The thought of Kennard Upshaw holding Coldmeece to ransom for her reputation was intolerable. She would rather be ruined than endure that.

She rose to her feet and cautiously tiptoed to the door, her ear pressed to the wood. The house was silent. Had Upshaw returned to Caro's ball, to cloak his absence? He must have an alibi, because blackmail would not work unless he had the power to conceal, as well as reveal, Louisa's shame. If she were Upshaw, she would wish to be obviously attending Caro's ball at this moment. But whether her reasoning were sound or not, she must assume Upshaw gone.

The window shutters were open, thank the Prophet, and as Caro had chosen a full-moon night for her ball, Louisa could see clearly. The room was at the back of the house, and below the window the roof sloped away. The window slid open grudgingly, and by the time Louisa could lean out to survey her escape route she was breathing heavily. It must be after midnight; the sky was beginning to cloud over and soon the moon would set. The thought of traversing dark unfamiliar country roads in her skimpy costume nearly made her decide to remain where she was; before she could change her mind, she swung one leg over the sill and set her foot on the slate roof. Her foot slid alarmingly, and she stopped to remove her gilded kid sandals and stuff them into her exiguous bodice before chancing the roof. To her great relief, there was a trellis running up the side of the house, and her departure was, all in all, less eventful than her arrival had been.

Once on the ground, she could see that the house was still dark. Emboldened, she padded around to the carriage house. She could see the bulk of the carriage, and at least

227

one horse, inside, but the building was securely locked, and the window too small for her to climb through. The ground floor windows of the house were all shuttered and barred, and it was, in any event, unlikely that Upshaw had left the stable keys there. There was nothing for it but to walk.

Squaring her shoulders, Louisa set off in what she devoutly hoped to be the direction of Town.

Outlandishly masked and garbed figures still whirled about the black and white marble dance floor, and clusters of candles still burned brightly in the rose-garlanded chandeliers as Kennard Upshaw reentered the ballroom at Coldmeece House. He might have acted too impulsively this evening, but what was done was done, and he trusted a night alone in the country would improve Lady Louisa's temper. In a few hours he would ride out and fetch her back, and restore her to Lady Mulford with few people the wiser.

It had only been on his ride back to Town that it occurred to Kennard that he might not find the redoubtable Lady Louisa Darwen waiting for him as tamely as Celia, in Louisa's place, would have waited. That too was little concern of his—if the jade preferred a walk on the lonely country roads at night to the comfort of her imprisonment, well—doubtless she deserved whatever might befall her.

As he circled the dancers, searching for Caroline, he remarked the absence of the earl. It was unlikely that Coldmeece would leave his wayward sister-in-law in sole command of the house during a ball like this, but he supposed it was possible. He eventually found Caro standing alone by a window that commanded a view of the street. She looked uncommonly subdued.

"Keeping yourself for me, Lady Coldmeece? Now that is an unaccustomed kindness." He took her hand and kissed it.

Caro withdrew it, wrinkling her nose. "Pah. You smell of the stables, Kennard, and—Kennard! You've hurt yourself!"

Kennard dabbed gingerly at the dried blood on his chin.

"I'm afraid it's going to leave a scar—that minx Louisa threw a glass at me. Will you still adore me in my disfigurement, Cruel Fair?"

Caro chose to ignore this. "Coldmeece has gone off in search of Lady Louisa—and I cannot imagine what possessed you to take her anywhere! He rode out of here using such language, and swearing he would strangle both of you. I should be very much surprised if he did not shoot you when he returned."

"And would you like him to shoot me, Sweet Caroline?" asked Kennard softly.

Caro unconsciously reached out a hand, which Kennard took. "N-no," she admitted, blushing. "But I do not see how I can stop him. He has grown quite strange of late, and I do not believe he is as fond of me as he once was."

Kennard chuckled, a mocking gleam in his green eyes. "I imagine I am safe here for a while. I left Lady Louisa in an old house ten miles from Town, and Coldmeece may search till doomsday before he finds her."

"But, Kennard, what if she should escape? You took her where you intended to take Celia, did you not?"

"It is true that an accommodation that would serve for little Lady Celia can hardly be as secure for the formidable Lady Louisa, but whatever happens, Countess, you need have no worries."

She regarded him with a hint of uncertainty. "But, Kennard—" she began.

Kennard Upshaw's smile broadened. "Sweetheart, you need not have a care in the world. And now, if you can stand my stable reek, I beg of you the felicity of a stroll in the garden. It's a lovely evening."

Louisa had no idea how far she had come, and she had a horrid suspicion she was walking in the wrong direction. Her gauzy dress offered no protection from the night chill, and her feet, protected only by the thin kid of her sandals, were dreadfully sore. Just as she felt matters could be no worse, the traitorous moon ducked behind a cloud bank and it began to rain. Within moments the first fat drops turned into a soaking downpour, and Louisa choked on a sob of utter dismay, hurriedly looking about for shelter.

The earl urged Champion to a faster trot. He would stop at the first inn he passed and ask after the coach. If he were lucky, the fugitives would have stopped there for the night and he need go no further. If not—well, if Upshaw were adhering to what Caro said had been his plan, his hideout must be a simple enough place to find. He'd intended Augustus to find it, after all.

Champion was the first to spot the huddled figure on the stile; he whickered and sidled, ears flicking forward. Coldmeece reined in and patted the gelding's neck soothingly. He peered over the horse's ears at the shivering, bedraggled figure.

"I suppose you are going to sit there all night and stare at me, you abominable man?" asked an acid-edged voice from the gloom.

Gervase was surprised by the intensity of the relief he felt. He smiled and dismounted, leading his horse forward. "Why, Cousin Louisa," he said in blandly pleasant tones, "fancy meeting you here."

The evening's excursions had not been kind to Lady Louisa Darwen. Her dashing gold tissue gown was disintegrating from the effects of the weather and her adventures, and her legs were covered with scratches from thorns and brambles. Her hair, done *en déshabillé* for the masquerade, was now tousled in earnest, minus its fanciful gold ribbon tiara and falling down her back in a dreadful tangle. As the final shattering *coup de grace*, the antimony, malachite, and kohl she had painstakingly applied to her face was streaking down it in sooty smudges.

"Oh, help me down from here!" she demanded, conscious of Coldmeece's askance look. Angrily, she mopped at her face with the edge of her shawl, but only succeeded in making matters worse. "I might have known it would be you," she went on in spite of herself. "Why couldn't you have gotten here sooner?"

"Be thankful, madam, that I am here at all. There was some doubt that you were in need of rescuing," Gervase pointed out. "Am I to take it that you found Mr. Upshaw's attentions unwelcome?"

"How—how *dare* you—" Louisa sputtered indignantly for a moment. "Lord Coldmeece, perhaps being assaulted and kidnapped is *your* idea of a welcome attention, but it is hardly mine!"

Considering the way Louisa had looked at the masquerade, Gervase could hardly blame Upshaw for such impetuosity. Well, he was a reasonable man; he would admit as much to the American after he'd soundly thrashed him for having dared lay hands on Lady Louisa Darwen.

"Isn't it? After your choice of costume this evening, I would have said abduction was exactly to your taste."

"You dreadful man!" she burst out. "Did you ride all the way out here to *insult* me?"

Despite his anger at everyone involved in this evening's escapades, Gervase could not repress a smile at Louisa's bedraggled dignity. "Perhaps not," he said with suspicious mildness. "Allow me to offer you the assistance of an escort home. I take it you have no idea where Upshaw is now?"

"I wish he were at the devil, and you with him!" Louisa said roundly.

"But how unhandsome, madam," Gervase said, extending his hand to her, "when I am doing my uttermost to preserve the shred of your reputation—a hopeless task, I fear."

Louisa slapped the helping hand away and squelched over to Champion's side in furious silence. He tossed her up, and mounted behind her, causing the horse to sidle nervously at the unaccustomed double burden. He then turned the gelding's head toward home, holding him to a walking pace. After a few moments' silence, he attempted to resume the conversation.

"Assuage my curiosity, fair cousin," he said. "Tell me why Upshaw carried you off. Caro told me he had planned to elope with Celia."

Louisa craned violently around and nearly lost her seat. "Yes, I can imagine. Well, she is safe from him—and from you, too!"

"Having eloped with Augustus—and in the nick of time," Gervase commented, steadying her. Her body was warm, and could be clearly felt through the thin tissue of her dress. "So finding your girlish hopes dashed in that quarter, you decided on second best?" he went on. "Well, Upshaw isn't rich, but he is resourceful."

"Let me down this instant!" Louisa gasped. Cold-meece tightened his grip on her waist and showed no sign of acquiescing to this demand. "How many times must I tell you that I wish Mr. Upshaw at the devil?" she went on hotly. "I had rather marry *you* than Kennard Upshaw, even if he weren't robbing my featherpated aunt blind—something *you* didn't seem to mind at all!"

"Robbing Lady Mulford? Kennard Upshaw?"

"*Yes!* I *told* you that—and you said I need have no fear for *my* comfort. As if I cared about that! And when I told him what I knew, at the ball, he decided to hold my reputation to ransom."

"Which ransom I was to pay, I take it?" he said dryly. "And so you escaped—a matter far more dangerous than the loss of a reputation, I would have thought."

"I had rather be dead than beholden to you!" Louisa snarled. With that, she turned her head away and stared fixedly at Champion's ears.

Gervase frowned. Apparently Louisa had never been in collusion with Upshaw at all. Who, then, was the woman Upshaw was prepared to marry, if sufficiently recompensed? Then something else she'd said struck him.

"Do you mean to say that you knew Augustus and Celia were going to elope?" he said incredulously.

"I have been trying to make them do so for weeks," said Louisa, and began muttering in Turkish.

He shook her slightly. "Stop that. I want to talk to you."

Louisa twisted round again, her kohl-streaked face scant inches from his own. "Well, I do not wish to talk to you! You seem to think this entire evening's madness is *my* fault, when *you* were too intolerably conceited to listen to me. Now I *am* ruined, and though I do not care for myself, it will certainly make Aunt Josephine very unhappy, and it is entirely *your* fault. And what are you going to do about it?'' she demanded.

Gervase kissed her. Her mouth was cool, and tasted of roses—and then she elbowed him hard in the ribs. Champion shied violently sideways in protest, and Louisa and Gervase toppled off into the mud.

"Stay away!" Louisa cried, scrabbling backward from where she had fallen. Gold tissue and English mud appeared evenly mixed on her person.

Champion tiptoed delicately back to inspect the disturbance, and whuffled inquiringly at the back of Gervase's neck.

Gervase, thoroughly appalled at what he had just done, though it seemed to him that he had· wished to do it for weeks, got stiffly to his feet and took the reins in his hand.

"If you will have the courtesy to remount, Lady Louisa, perhaps we may return to Town before there is any further occasion for scandal."

Louisa slowly rose to her feet and cast a speaking glare at the earl. The rest of the journey passed in an awful silence.

Dawn was just making its appearance as they rode up Curzon Street and stopped before Lady Mulford's door.

Gervase had had a great deal of time for reflection on the ride back. Now that he knew they had been working at cross-purposes to the same ends, Louisa's apparently eccentric actions seemed quite reasonable, and his own reactions correspondingly unhandsome.

As he dismounted before Mulford House, he tried to make amends. "Lady Louisa, I realize that my conduct these past weeks has been the product of a gross misapprehension on my part, and I hope I will be given the opportunity to repair those errors."

"Are you going to keep me standing in the street all day?" asked Louisa icily.

Without another word Gervase bowed, and raised such a din with the brass knocker that he attracted to the door not only the under butler, but Lady Mulford as well. Despite the early hour, she was dressed in a fashionable morning robe.

"Why, Gervase!" she said in surprise. "How did you know?" Then her gaze traveled past him to the bedraggled figure on horseback, and her eyes opened wide. *"Louisa!"* she shrieked. "What are you doing on that horse? And— *Louisa*! Your *hair*!"

With scant regard for her modesty, Louisa scrabbled down from Champion's back and ran to her aunt. "Oh, Aunt Josephine, I had the most dreadful night!" she wailed. She glared at Gervase so fixedly that Lady Mulford looked at him in wonder. "It was horrible!" Louisa added defiantly.

Lady Mulford placed an arm around her niece's shoulder and began urging her toward the door, making soothing promises of hot baths and tea. The earl bowed to Lady Mulford. As the door closed, he told Louisa that he would do himself the honor of calling upon her later that morning.

"Don't!" snapped Louisa, turning back to slam the door in his face.

Coldmeece House was deserted when Gervase arrived there, the last of the revelers having departed, and even Caroline nowhere to be seen. As he started up the main stairs, Bracken approached him.

"These were left for you, my lord," he said deferentially, proffering two folded and sealed letters.

Gervase jammed them into his pocket without looking at them. "Have some hot water set up to my room immediately," he said shortly. "And a bottle of brandy."

Later, wrapped in his dressing gown and stretched out before the fire with a glass in his hand, he found the time to read his messages. The first was from Augustus, announcing that he had removed to his parents' house in Town and would be sending for his things at Gervase's convenience. The fact that he had taken Lady Celia to wife was glossed over in a hasty postscript.

Gervase grinned and skimmed the letter at the fire. He must remember to draft an announcement to the *Gazette* in Celia's name, repudiating the first engagement notice. Lord and Lady Templeton could shoulder the burden of welcoming their wealthy new daughter-in-law into the family without any help from him.

He turned to the second letter, scanned it incredulously, and began to laugh.

Kennard Upshaw had married the Countess of Coldmeece early this morning, and hoped to have the felicity of an early meeting with Lord Coldmeece's man of business. He trusted in his lordship's generous nature, and remained his very obedient servant and cousin, Kennard Darwen Upshaw.

His lordship sent the second letter after the first. It seemed matters had been taken out of his hands; whatever punishment Kennard merited for his treatment of Louisa, Caro would be sure to provide.

Gervase poured himself another celebratory drink. His problems with his multitudinous relatives were very nearly over; there remained only Louisa—and at some unmarked point during the night's adventures he had finally realized what he wished to do about Louisa.

Chapter FOURTEEN

At four in the afternoon, Josephine Mulford tapped nervously on her niece's door. The bed was empty when she entered, and Lady Mulford cast about for a moment until she discovered her niece curled up in a chair facing the window, clad in a dressing gown *à la russe*, of royal blue velvet lined with chinchilla and embroidered in gold. Louisa was staring at the window with every appearance of deep interest, her performance marred only slightly by the fact that the heavy velvet curtains were still drawn. Her silver hairbrush lay in her lap. Lady Mulford had never seen her niece looking so drawn. Even the rich artificial red of her hair was not enough to distract Lady Mulford from Louisa's doleful expression.

"Louisa?" said Lady Mulford. "Are you all right? I thought you must still be asleep. Celia—she is Mrs. Templeton now, you know, and how odd it seems!—came to call and wished to see you, but I told her you were still abed. I did not tell her that you had been out . . . riding with Gervase, but I suppose she will hear that anyway. Everyone will," she added gloomily. "But I do not mean to scold you, darling."

"It is the most famous thing," said Louisa heavily. "I had never suspected Celia of such sense as to actually marry Gussie. I only hope she will not find Petersburg too shocking."

Josephine peered at her niece. "I do not think she will; Celia has a remarkably resilient mind, you know. *I* only hope she does not tease herself too much over Gervase. They would never have made a good match."

Louisa opened her mouth for a vitriolic animadversion on Coldmeece's character, and found she hadn't the heart for it. "Aunt Josephine, I have behaved dreadfully, haven't I?"

"Louisa! If Gervase has been saying such things to you, I shall—I shall box his ears! You have never given me the least cause to regret bringing you to London," said Aunt Josephine stoutly.

"Dear Aunt, that is very kind of you, but the truth is, I have done my very best to raise a scandal, and it is only thanks to Gussie—and the earl—that I didn't. Yet," Louisa added gloomily.

"Louisa?" said her aunt. "You are not sorry that Celia has married Gussie, are you?"

Louisa shook her head. "No. I just wish . . . Oh, I wish everything had been different!" she cried passionately.

Lady Mulford patted her hand reassuringly. "You will feel better when we get to Paris," she said. "We will leave at once. I am certain that London does not agree with you at all."

Feeling perilously near tears, Louisa could only agree. Lady Mulford patted her once more and tiptoed out of the room, leaving Louisa alone with her unhappy thoughts.

If only she and Coldmeece had not misunderstood each other at every turn, perhaps—

Louisa buried her face in her arms and wept.

Some time later, Louisa heard the click of the latch. Assuming that her aunt had sent Rigsby with tea, she gestured vaguely with her hairbrush. "Just leave it, please."

"And what am I to leave?" The sardonic tones mocked her, and Louisa jumped up and spun around to behold the earl of Coldmeece lounging in her doorway.

Though he too had been up all last night, he showed no sign of it. His curly brown hair was brushed neatly back, his cravat was impeccably tied, and the gray eyes glinted with amusement as he stepped into the room and shut the door firmly behind him.

"It may interest you to know," he said, "that Caroline has married Kennard Upshaw, so you are amply recompensed for last night."

"You get out of here at once!" said Louisa, bereft of originality.

The earl bowed. "Ever gracious. Am I to understand that you are awake to impropriety at last, and tremble to entertain a gentleman in your boudoir?"

"You are no gentleman, sir—and I object to being crept up on!" Her earlier listlessness gone, Louisa militantly faced her foe.

"Do you?" said Gervase with interest. "Then behold me penitent. But as I told you earlier, I intended to call upon you today, and it is well after noon." He crossed the room and seated himself upon a hassock, seeming to dare Louisa to rebuke him for his presumption. "Kennard and Caro are married, I shall settle his bills, and your aunt need never know she was deceived. I understand Mr. Upshaw will be sailing for America soon—with his charming bride, but without my niece—and since Mr. and Mrs. Templeton will be leaving for Russia in a few days, matters have fallen out quite neatly. That only leaves you, Lady Louisa. Even without Kennard to carry tales, you are quite ruined, you know," he added chattily.

"Yes," said Louisa, "and thank you very much!" She tugged her dressing gown tighter about her. Had the earl only come to mock her? How he must hate her, Louisa thought miserably.

The earl smiled easily. "We always seem to be at daggers drawn, Louisa, and I cannot think why. True, I have said you are lazy, extravagant, and bad-tempered. You are. I did not wish to see you married to Augustus, and nothing I have seen has caused me to change my mind on that head, but I am far from being your enemy."

"Oh, are you not?" said Louisa hotly. "I could have been quite happy with Gussie, but nothing would serve but that you should meddle, out of a high-handed sense of your own consequence!"

"You would never have been happy with Augustus," said the earl firmly. "As for him, he needs an asset, not an ornament—and not an amazon to ride roughshod over him, either. Great-aunt Serena would have disinherited him, and the two of you would have been miserable within a twelvemonth.''

''Money!'' said Louisa. ''It is all you Franks ever think about!''

''It's far better to think about it than not, especially when you haven't got it,'' he said inarguably. ''And since I did not make Augustus fall in love with Celia, I refuse to take all of the blame for, er, wrefting him from your side. Since you cannot now marry him, hadn't you better consider what you're going to do? You have no reputation, no prospects, and no reasonable hope of marriage.''

''The first thing I shall do is throw you out of here, since I need consider no one's opinions if I am ruined,'' said Louisa hotly.

''True. But I do hope you will consider mine, if only a little, when we are married.''

''*Married!*'' said Louisa, stunned. ''I'm not going to marry you!''

''Why not?'' Gervase asked equitably. ''I'm indulgent—I can afford to be. I am also tolerant, as well as generous—again, I can afford to be. In short, Lady Louisa, I can afford you—as Augustus never could.''

''I am damnably expensive, and my behavior is outrageous!'' snapped Louisa.

''I hope so,'' said the earl. ''I would hate to expend the sacred Darwen consequence on anything undeserving. Lady Celia, you must agree, would hardly have been worthy of it. Well, Louisa?''

Louisa felt oddly breathless. ''I have never *heard* anything so ridiculous! And—and I would want a very large dress allowance, and closed-stove heating. And I would *not* live at Coldmere!''

''What? Not even with closed-stove heating? I hope you will change your mind, for it is truly beautiful now that it's in good repair, and I feel that I owe it to the nation to restrict your appearances upon the Town.'' He paused. ''You haven't said yes.''

"I—I . . . This is some sort of trick! You could not possibly wish to marry me!"

The earl rose to his feet. "Why not? Your family is excellent, your lack of fortune is irrelevant, and you are a most delightful and entertaining companion—when you wish to be. For my own peace of mind, as well as the security of the realm, I feel that we ought to be married. Think of how delighted Lady Mulford will be."

"Of all the crack-brained reasons . . ." Louisa hesitated. "What if I don't wish to marry you?"

"Then I should take myself immediately away—if you truly don't wish to marry me."

Louisa stared at him, her eyes very wide and pale.

"I flatter myself that you are not indifferent to me," he added. "You see, you took such very great pains to impress me at Caro's ball."

"I didn't!"

He raised his eyebrows and smiled. "Didn't you?"

Louisa did not answer, and Gervase held out his hand to her. "Come here, Louisa." Hesitantly, she put her hand in his, and he drew her close. He took her gently by the arms, looking down at her knowingly.

"I paint!" said Louisa desperately. "And I dye my hair!"

"And I hope you will continue to do so," said the earl, and fitted his mouth to hers.

His lips tenderly explored hers until Louisa swayed dizzily against him and clutched at his shoulders for support. His arms closed around her, and his hands tangled in her long, hennaed hair.

"If you don't marry me, my darling Turkish Delight," Gervase whispered in her ear, "I *will* have you sewn in a sack and dropped in the Bosphorus. Marry me, Amber Pearl. You will not be bored . . . and neither will I."

"Yes, my lord," Louisa said demurely. She sighed contentedly and rested her head on his shoulder, secure in the knowledge that she was home at last.

EPILOGUE

The *Fortunate Venture* had left Savannah six months before with a cargo of cotton and sugar for Bristol Harbor. After some weeks anchored at the London docks below Wapping Old Stairs, she was ready to make her return voyage, laden with spices, tin goods, Wedgwood, calico, and some hardy souls making the eight-week to three-month voyage to the Americas.

July was good sailing weather, and for those lucky adventurers provident enough to have acquired a cabin of their own, the voyage might be as pleasant and uneventful as a trip across the Channel.

Caroline Amantha Everhill Darwen Upshaw, new-made wife of Kennard Upshaw, sat before a too-small cheval mirror, swathed in a pegnoir of lace and embroidered silk, a silver and tinted-ivory hairbrush in her hand. The *Fortunate Venture* would leave with the midnight tide; the captain had insisted on his passengers boarding hours before.

The tiny cabin was crowded with Caro's possessions; many more lay crated in the hold below. Her packing for her exile from England (for it was little less, as she had confided to a few *very* close and discreet acquaintances; Coldmeece would stop at nothing to have his own way and had all but torn little Charlotte from her Mama's arms!) had been accomplished with a lack of drama that was disappointingly anticlimatic. Gervase had made no objections no matter what family heirloom her fancy lighted upon, merely stating flatly that Caro might take anything she liked, save her daughter. Really, he *was* the most disobliging man! How fortunate that she had realized that in time!

And, after all, thought Caro, carefully brushing the hair that lay like golden silk about her shoulders, it was only her right to take some small consolations with her to compensate her for losing the delights of London. Why, she was even to miss the wedding of the Season, which was a great pity. In typical fashion, Gervase had paid little attention to her honeymoon plans, being obsessed with his own. All London, it seemed, must be drawn into Coldmeece's wedding arrangements, and on September 1, 1819, in St. James's Church in Piccadilly, the tenth earl of Coldmeece would marry a woman who had been raised in a Turkish harem.

Caro set down her brush and began smoothing the Lotion of the Ladies of Denmark into her flawless skin. If all the town was tattling with that *on-dit*, it was not she who had revealed the secret, she thought virtuously. Kennard had been most adamant on that point, although, really, it would be only what Gervase and Louisa both deserved, after their behavior. But Kennard had said . . .

Kennard. Even now the thought of her husband of less than a month could bring a tinge of rose to Caro's ivory cheek. How besotted with him she was, she thought admiringly. Only Kennard Upshaw could make the journey to the wild Americas bearable.

As if her thoughts had summoned him up, Kennard scratched softly at the door, then opened it. He stooped to enter the small cabin, the gesture threatening the seams of his handsome coat of bottle green superfine. The draft from outside made the candle flames flicker and dance wildly, and Kennard quickly shut the door behind him. He crossed to the small table beside the bed, and poured brandy into a neat silver cup.

"Phah!" he said. "Even at this time of year, the wind from the river cuts like the very devil. I am here to tell you, little wife, that the captain, the pilot, and the harbormaster all agree; we shall be on the outbound tide not an hour hence.'' He regarded her quizzically. ''What? No tears? And here I thought you'd be on deck for a last glimpse of Merrie England.''

''I do not see what there is of interest on deck, and in any event, I have already seen it.''

Kennard's appreciative gaze took in the diaphanous peach silk and lace pegnoir comprehensively, and Caro dimpled roguishly.

''I agree,'' he said, and set down the silver cup. ''There's a great deal more of interest here.''

The shift in wind as the *Fortunate Venture* reached the open sea woke Caroline. Disoriented by the unfamiliar rocking motion, she groped about her until she clutched Kennard's nightshirt. Awakened, he sat up and cradled her protectively against his chest.

''Frightened?'' he asked softly.

''I . . . no. But it does go up and down so!'' Caro protested.

''I trust, darlin', that you are not one of those females afflicted with seasickness. Do you know, I never thought to ask you. Improvident of me.''

''We Everhills have always been extremely delicate,'' Caro announced proudly. ''But I do not think I shall be seasick. Do tell me about the Carolinas, Kennard.''

''Again? You must be worn out with hearin' about them.''

''Oh, well, I most particularly wish to know how to go on when I arrive. I do not wish your American ladies to think me at all rag-mannered or behindhand.''

''My American ladies, as you call them, sweet Caroline, will fall all over themselves to curtsy to you, and call you Countess Caro, likely as not. And only think, not fifty years ago we fought bad old King George to stop doin' that very thing.''

''I do wish you would talk of important things, Kennard, and not about the poor king. He is quite mad, you know. But tell me—oh, you have said that bonnets are all the crack in Charleston, and that the ladies go about with little pages to fan them and carry their packages, and—

will you buy me one, darling? I have had to leave all my servants behind. Why, you know, even my maid would not come with me. She is the most ungrateful creature!''

''I should think so, not wishin' to cross the ocean to live among strangers the rest of her life,'' Kennard commented dryly.

''Oh, but Kennard! You are not a stranger, and neither am I, and—Oh, Kennard, how shall I go on among all those people? They don't know who I am!''

''Then, darlin' Countess, we shall just have to teach them, shan't we?''

CELIA:

In June of 1819, His Majesty's warship *Atropos* left Calais for Russia. Aboard her were the newest diplomatic ornament to grace Tsar Alexander's court and his wife of less than two months, the Honorable Augustus Leslie Templeton and Lady Celia Darwen-Neville Templeton.

There is not so much space for passengers on a British ship of the line as is popularly believed; the Templetons' trunks were stowed anywhere space could be found for them, to the great inconvenience of their owners. Celia and her abigail Teale shared one of the two tiny cabins made available to them, while the other was occupied by Augustus, Sasha, and diplomatic gifts for the tsar.

Augustus stood on the deck in an out-of-the-way place and let the early morning wind disorder his careful coiffure in a fashion he would have shuddered to contemplate not two months earlier. Now he had graver concerns on his mind. It was still a number of weeks until they reached St. Petersburg and could leave this cursed instrument of torture they called a ship.

Augustus was himself an excellent sailor, and had never had any reason to suspect that anyone else might be otherwise. And so, two weeks after the masquerade ball at Coldmeece House, with the stunning news of the earl's rebetrothal still the prime article of gossip among the upper ten thousand, Augustus had taken his new bride to the embarkation port of Dover, there to cross the Channel to Calais and the waiting *Atropos*.

Celia had been seasick for the entire crossing. If Teale had not been with them . . . Even at this remove, Augustus shuddered at the thought. Teale had risen admirably to the occasion of crisis, and earned Augustus's undying gratitude on the spot. It was most unfortunate that they had only had a few days' respite in Calais before the *Atropos* sailed, since once aboard Celia's misery began afresh.

Celia had not uttered one word of reproach, but her rosy cheeks had paled to alabaster and Teale had forbidden her to try to leave her bed in the cramped, stifling cabin below. Even ministrations of brandy and tincture of opium had not enabled Celia to keep down more than a few teaspoons of a watery gruel, and it was the thought of Celia's suffering for the rest of the long voyage that had driven Augustus on deck at this early hour. The freshening wind tugged and worried at the capes of his cloak, and his elegant hat remained prudently tucked beneath his arm.

The ship's surgeon had declared wisely that all bouts passed in time and no one had ever died of it. Augustus had damned the man for a heartless fool, and only the fact that swords and dueling were both out of fashion had kept the matter from becoming even worse. Sasha had helpfully offered to poison the surgeon, but this had done little to lift Augustus's spirits. His Celia lay ill, and he was helpless.

"Augustus?"

The dear, familiar voice came from behind him, and he turned, stepping forward. Celia, pale but determined, came toward him, swathed in shawls and leaning heavily upon Teale for support. Teale's expression was disapproving in the extreme, but apparently this had been one of those rare occasions when the whim of the usually biddable Celia was not to be questioned.

"Celia!" Augustus was caught between delight at her presence and fear for her safety.

"Oh, Gussie, I was feeling so much better, really I was, and Sasha told me you were upstairs."

Augustus caught up her cold hands in his own, without even trying to explain to her that aboard the *Atropos* he was "on deck" and not "upstairs." Celia looked commandingly at Teale, who bobbed and withdrew, although not without a basilisk gaze at Augustus.

"Darling!" said that oblivious aristocrat. "Are you certain you should not be in bed? You're cold as ice—and where's your pelisse?"

"Oh, Louisa always said that it took shawls to keep one really warm, and so I thought—but I did not know it would be so cold here! It is so very stuffy in my room."

Augustus could not disagree with this, but the fact remained that in a very few moments it would be blue roses that bloomed in Celia's cheeks. "I have a better cure for the cold than shawls," he said invitingly, and wrapped Celia warmly against him under the folds of his cloak.

"Oh, that is ever so much better," Celia agreed, snuggling close. She looked questioningly out at the sea around them. "I cannot see the land anywhere," she said doubtfully.

"It's there, though, all right and tight," Augustus reassured her. "And we'll be to Petersburg before you know it," he added optimistically.

Celia looked less than sanguine about this pronouncement, but loyally said that she supposed Gussie was right. "And you have been to Russia before, so you can tell me how to go on there," she went on, determined to be cheerful.

"Lord, yes," said Augustus. "I've told you about their horses—well, just you wait till winter. I'll buy you a troika and a match trio to pull it. You'll like that, sweetheart."

"Oh, yes," said Celia faintly.

"And there'll be balls, and races, and wolf hunts, and—"

"Wolves?"

"Absolutely," Augustus went on blithely. "Monstrous gray brutes, and they chase after sleighs and—"

Celia gave a little gasp. "In—in St. Petersburg?" she asked in a quavering voice that instantly recalled Augustus to himself.

246

"Idiot!" he said roundly, looking down at her expression of wide-eyed consternation. "Not you, angel, myself. Of course not in Petersburg. I'm dashed if I know how I could be such a fool as to frighten you so. Miles out in the country. The wolves, I mean. Nothing to concern yourself with."

He gave Celia's shoulders an encouraging squeeze, and Celia leaned her head on his chest. "Well, if there *are* wolves, I am quite certain you shall know precisely how to deal with them, Gussie," she said firmly. "I am not afraid, and I shall like Russia extremely!"

This touching proof of his wife's devotion so made Mr. Templeton forget himself that when the *Atropos*'s midshipman came to bid them to breakfast, that worthy young man had to cough quite loudly indeed to make his presence known.

LOUISA:

The September wind was brisk and businesslike this evening, ruffling waves into whitecaps and biting into any person foolhardy enough to be on the *Day-Dream*'s deck, but the countess of Coldmeece did not care. She merely wrapped her sables more securely about her, regarding the receding shore gleefully. "Good-bye, England!" she called, and even pulled one warmly gloved hand out of her enormous sable muff to wave at the heedless cliffs of Dover.

"Don't sound so brokenhearted, my love. We are coming back, you know," said the earl dryly.

Louisa tucked her hand back into the muff and turned to look at her husband of less than twenty-four hours. "Oh, but not for . . . oh, months and months," she said. "And—"

"And I have promised to have closed-stove heating installed at Coldmere," the earl finished for her. "Well, it's to be hoped the damn—deuced contraptions work," he added darkly, and Louisa smiled.

"You'll like it," she prophesied. She tilted her head and

247

slanted a languorous glance at him through her darkened lashes. ''You'll see, O my lord husband and the delight of my eyes, it will be ever so much . . . warmer.''

Gervase uttered a muffled oath and grabbed her shoulders. ''For heaven's sake, Louisa—''

Words apparently failed him, as he caught her up close in his arms in an impetuous fashion that gratified Louisa considerably.

Ever since their rather abrupt betrothal, Gervase had been friendly, even—most annoyingly—cousinly, but he had treated Louisa with a certain formal reserve that she had found rather disconcerting, all things considered. It had seemed a very long time indeed from betrothal to wedding day, although everyone had assured Louisa that indeed, three months was the veriest nothing, and implied almost unseemly haste upon Gervase's part. However, the wedding day had dawned at last, and very early this morning she had been a demurely blushing bride and become the Countess of Coldmeece, to Aunt Josephine's great delight—the extent of which, Louisa supposed, could be judged from the vast number of lace-trimmed handkerchiefs she had dampened during the ceremony. The earl and new countess had not stayed for a wedding breakfast or reception; outside the church door Gervase had handed Louisa into his racing phaeton and driven them at a breathtaking pace to the coast and his waiting yacht.

It had been, to Louisa's way of thinking, a most exciting day, and in the proper fashion. She had never had the least anxiety that Gervase's driving, however fast, might land them in the ditch, nor that the *Day-Dream* would miss the evening's tide. Certainly her husband knew to a nicety how to arrange things; no fear that his wife would not find her creature comforts well attended to.

At the moment, however, Louisa's comfort did not seem to be uppermost in Gervase's mind, if the vigor of his embrace was any indication. Oddly enough, she made no protest at this rough treatment, contenting herself with meekly tipping her head back for his kiss. Gervase's reserve, she discovered with interest and delight, had apparently vanished with the English coastline.

Eventually Gervase pushed her back, looking somewhat shaken. "For heaven's sake, Louisa," he began again.

"Yes, my lord?" said Louisa, calmly rearranging her rumpled sables while casting a speculative glance at the earl.

"Someone might see us," he said inadequately, running a hand through his wind-tousled hair. Then he frowned, looking puzzled. "What happened to my hat?"

"It blew overboard a few minutes ago," Louisa told him, with the it's-nothing-to-do-with-me air of a complacent cat.

The earl lunged, the countess squeaked, and the earl administered what he considered suitable chastisement for such provoking behavior. "For heaven's sake, Gervase!" Louisa mimicked some minutes later. "Someone might see us."

"Let them," said the earl. "It's my yacht. It's almost pitch dark anyway."

"Turkish treatment," said Louisa, looking inordinately pleased.

"I intend," the earl told her grandly, "to be master in my own house."

Louisa slid agilely out of his grasp. "Then with my master's permission, his humble slave will retire to await his pleasure." She made a low, graceful bow. "And I promise *you* some Turkish treatment tonight, my lord!" she added, smiling wickedly.

"Louisa—!"

But she had already vanished into the darkness, leaving Gervase holding only her sable muff.

An hour later the earl paused before the carved door to the owner's cabin. Now that he had the right to enter Louisa's bedroom any time he chose, he felt oddly diffident about the matter. Still, they were married now, and surely she'd had plenty of time to prepare for bed. Squaring his shoulders, Gervase tapped firmly on the door and then opened it and strode in.

He stopped dead. The room, far from being in decent darkness, was still illuminated by the lamps mounted on gimbals in the cabin walls. His bride reclined, *à la oda-lisque*, upon the bed, clad in a brilliant array of peculiar garments. Voluminous pantaloons of rose brocade; a tightly-fitted long coat of violet, heavily embroidered in a rainbow of colors, its long tails caught up by the wide sashes tied around her hips; a small, round, pearl-embroidered hat . . .

A roll of the ship obligingly slammed the door shut behind him. Louisa, most regrettably, giggled, then rose from the bed in a shimmer of vividly-hued silks. Her hennaed hair was a river of flame past her waist. She moved towards Gervase with a swaying, flat-footed walk he'd never seen her use before.

"Louisa?" The earl's voice was husky, and he tried again. "What . . . ?"

"I promised you Turkish treatment," said Louisa. Her cheeks looked exceptionally pink, although innocent of rouge, and she did not meet Gervase's eyes. "Well, this is what I wore in the *hareem*. I had Madame Francine make it up when she did my trousseau. I told her it was for a masquerade."

"Well," said Gervase inadequately, staring. This was no Byronic *houri* in spangles and gauze, but the total effect was seductive in the extreme.

Louisa lifted her head and shook back her hair. It sparked in the candlelight. "I wanted," she said with great dignity, "a proper wedding night."

Gervase smiled and reached out for her. "Don't you mean an improper one, madam wife?"

Without obviously dodging, Louisa managed to be out of his reach. "I have been *very* well taught," she went on, moving as if to slow music, and beginning to untie one of the tasseled scarves around her hips. "So if my lord husband will be graciously pleased to be seated . . ."

"Frankish persons," said Amber Pearl severely, some time later, "have no patience. Really, Gervase, I told you I could dance—a little!"